I0788391

JUST DESERTS

BY

JIM GATH

<u>ALSO BY JIM GATH</u>

I Hear You, Horse.

Diary Of a Horseman

264 West 40th Street

Custerfluck

COWBOY

Luna Sonora

<u>SERIES</u>

The Legend of Eighmyville Hollow

JUST DESERTS

"In the dark shadow of the grove, on the margin of the brook, he beheld something huge, misshapen, and towering. It stirred not but seemed gathered up in the gloom like some gigantic monster ready to spring upon the traveler."

~ The Legend of Sleepy Hollow

CHAPTER 1

Rhinebeck Mayor Barbara Green was standing at the center of the big red ribbon, holding it up with her left hand while holding an oversized pair of scissors in her right.

Hal Wood stood to her left, Councilman Mike Wiechowski to her right and each of those men was flanked by several folks that were on the board of the Women's Center.

"Ladies and gentlemen," Mayor Green addressed the small crowd loudly enough to be heard, "it is my extreme pleasure to be here with you to open the new wing of this wonderful building. And, with its opening, this building shall heretofore be known as The Harold Wood People's Center."

Her comment was met with enthusiastic, but polite, applause from the crowd of forty to fifty people.

"Hal", she said, "would you kindly do the honors?"

She handed the scissors to a smiling Hal.

"Folks", he said, "never in my wildest dreams could I ever have imagined a place like this coming to fruition. But obviously, it has." And he chuckled somewhat nervously. "I - and the board (he waved with each hand in the direction of those standing behind the red ribbon) – would like to thank each and every one of you who have contributed to this effort. And, especially, the anonymous donor whose generosity has made the construction of this new wing possible. Thank you – whoever you are."

More applause.

"Thank you", he said. "And, before I cut this ribbon, I'd like to thank – in particular – our great friend, Bill Parker, for the incredible piece of artwork that you'll see displayed on the wall of the new wing. It's called 'Clouds', isn't it Bill?" And he looked over in our direction and Parker nodded.

More applause.

"So, without further ado……" and Hal fiddled with the scissors and cut the ribbon as several phone cameras flashed. "Come on in!"

And people moved toward and into the new, large room. Inside, white-shirted waiters and waitresses carried trays of hors d'oeuvres. There was another small bar set up along one wall, too.

"Cool that Hal gave you a shout-out", I said to Parker as we ambled along with the crowd. Parker just shrugged. "I guess", he said, though I knew he was proud.

And, there, along one wall, was Parker's 'Clouds'. It was fashioned from brass and several different kinds and colors of polished steel and aluminum. It was about six feet long, three to four feet high and, and because of the way he'd attached the metals together, it was somewhat three-dimensional. It had taken him several weeks to create in the large garage back at my farm.

Bill Parker was a fixture at my place. My late step-father and my late Mom had hired him to, basically, run the farm, which he'd done for several years. Once my folks had passed and I'd inherited the place, I kept Parker on to keep doing what he'd been doing.

For years, before moving up to this part of the Hudson Valley, Parker had been on the Englewood, New Jersey, police force, spending his last few years there as a detective. He'd retired after having received a bullet to the spleen in a botched drug bust. Although he'd fully recovered, he'd been able to retire on almost full disability.

Not only did Parker work at the farm, earning what little money I paid him, but he'd become my best friend. And, with me being an only child, he had become the brother I never had. And nobody was more surprised at that little turn of events than I. I'm not a guy who likes to get too close to most people. Oh, yeah – I'm friendly and all but, well, you know. Not a lot of real close friends. Not like Parker, anyway.

Anyway, before I'd inherited the place and moved here from LA, Parker had had a modest little metal-working craft thing going on. In his spare time, he made little doodads and geegaws and such and sold them at various fairs and craft shows around the Hudson Valley.

He was good at it, too. As a matter of fact, before crafting 'Clouds', he'd made a real nice piece that's now hanging in an exalted spot in The Coffee Spot, a local diner where a bunch of us have breakfast every morning.

Mike Wiechowski walked up to us as we were scarfing a few of the canapes. Mike was not only a town councilman, he was one of our best friends and a fixture at our every-morning breakfast.

"Nice turnout", he said.

"Mmph", Parker and I muttered, our mouths full of shrimp and tuna tartare.

Swallowing, I said, "Yeah - and Hal's pretty psyched, too. This is a really big moment for the guy. I mean, think what he's accomplished here."

Oh, I should mention that Hal is also one of our breakfast cronies. Actually, there are six of us who meet every morning. Seven, if you include our friend, Gordon, who shows up, like, once a week or so.

We call ourselves 'The Geezers', primarily because we're a little long in the tooth. Come to think of it, maybe a better word would be 'weathered' or 'mature'. Well, except for moi, that is. I'm probably about twenty years younger than most of the guys. But, yeah – I still consider myself a 'Geezer' and they do, too.

We all sit at a big round table near the rear of the joint, discuss things of vast import and solve most of the world's problems over coffee and some of the best breakfasts to be found this side of the Pecos. And it happens every day, without fail, rain or shine.

There's Bob – Bob Marquardt – who's a big bear of a guy who owns a large farm not too far from mine. Marquardt's more or less the de facto leader of the Geezers - maybe because he's so big, I don't know. But, Bob's a smart, practical, very level-headed guy, too, so there's that.

Joe Mariani's a retired insurance adjuster or something. Skinny as a rail with what appears to be a lifelong brush-cut, Joe's never subtle and, more often than not, pretty cantankerous. He's got a good heart, Joe does, but sometimes you wouldn't know it by his running commentary and snide remarks.

Hal is also a retired something-or-other and he's not very tall and is what you'd probably call 'chubby'. But, in his retirement, he's almost personally responsible for conceiving and building the Women's Center – now to be called the 'Harold Wood People's Center'. He put together a small, but effective, board, raised all the necessary funding, got the town to donate the land and contracted for and oversaw the construction of the building. It was a huge feat.

Hal also drives an old, white Crown Victoria – an ex-unmarked cop car – that he'd gotten from the New Paltz Police Department when they'd upgraded their rides. It even has the driver's side spotlight still attached. Hal loves his Crown Vic, although it's often fodder for Geezers' humor.

Parker and I are pretty close to our resident town councilman, Mike Wiechowski. Mike's as solid as the day is long and, together, we've been through a couple of very intense situations where we've seen to it that some pretty bad people have gotten their well-deserved comeuppance. Mike also keeps the group informed about all the behind-the-scenes goings-on within the council and the Town of Rhinebeck.

Gordon Myers is the newest Geezer and, like I said, he joins us about once a week. His loving and longtime wife, Shirley, keeps an eagle eye on his weight, which is always right around the tipping point, as far as she's concerned. And, with The Coffee Spot's oversized breakfasts, Gordon is able to escape Shirley's good-natured clutches only every few days. Gordon retired from the New York Central system a few years back and he and Shirley live in a lovely condominium community on the north end of town.

Several people came up to Parker and oohed and aahed about his artwork, shaking his hand and asking him how long it took him, how he did it – all that. And, he was downright informative, too. Well, for Parker, that is, who usually tends to keep his mouth shut and observe his surroundings. Must be the detective in him.

Mike took me aside and said, quietly, "You know, Hal's been pumping me a bit about where that money came from. He didn't say anything about it for the first few weeks or so but, now, I think he suspects that I know. I keep telling him that I've got no idea."

"Keep the secret, Mike – that's all I can tell you", I said. "If he ever really finds out, we're going to have to explain a whole lot of shit about where it came from and that's a whole lot of explaining that I don't wanna do."

"I know, I know. I'm just telling you, is all. Fear not, though – my lips are forever sealed."

"I know they are, Mike. Just giving voice to the obvious, is all." And I smiled.

"Okay, look", he said, "I'm gonna sneak out in a minute or so. Last night's council meeting went on 'til almost eleven and I told Linda that I'd be home early, tonight. Which", he said, looking at his watch, "isn't really going to happen, but if I stay any later, I might have to sleep on the couch."

"You get outta here", I said. "See you in the morning."

And I noticed that it took him a good five minutes to get to the door, what with various people stopping him along the way.

Oh, yeah – the money. The money for the addition to the Center.

Long story, but it was all legal and above board. Without going into details, now, it involved a Russian oligarch who had ventured into town and a guy I used to work for in LA – who'd somehow found his way to this berg, too. That guy – his name was

Farrell, Thom Farrell – had defrauded the firm that bought out our old company and a number of people had gotten hurt as a result.

It's complicated.

But, the fifty-k that had found its way to the Center's bank account had been the oligarch's ill-gotten gains – he was involved in illegal arms shipments - and he, through Farrell, had tried to bribe Mike to fast-walk a project with the town.

Mike freaked when that happened, but Parker and I told him to take the cash and that we'd deal with the oligarch and the other guy. Which we did.

The oligarch's real name was – or is – Evgeny Volkov, but he anglicized it to Gene Wolfe. Through a quite complicated – though, again, very legal – scheme, Parker and I had delivered our very own special form of justice to him. He ended up leaving the country and leaving behind some very expensive real estate that had become…..

Well, like I said, it's complicated.

But, yeah – go figure – a real honest-to-goodness Russian oligarch, right here in little ol' Rhinebeck.

I looked over to see Parker trying to separate himself from a couple of dowagers who were obviously more interested in talking about his artwork than he was. I figured I had to save his sorry ass and went over to the little group.

Parker seized the opportunity and introduced me. "Ladies", he said, "meet J.D. Spencer. J.D. – this is um…."

One of the women said, "Claire, Claire Andrews", and she put out her hand and I shook it. "And this is Ruth Montgomery." And I shook Ruth's hand, too.

"It's a pleasure, Claire…Ruth", I said. "But, if you'll excuse us, I need to steal Bill for a moment."

"Oh, why, surely", said Claire. "It was so nice meeting you, Bill. And you, too, J.D. And, Bill – again – your artwork is just superb. Thank you for creating it and thank you for donating it." And Ruth concurred, saying something, but I didn't really pay attention to it.

We extracted ourselves and Parker said, "Let's get outta here".

"I've been ready for ten minutes, but you were over there making googly eyes at those two", I said, nodding in the direction of the dowagers.

"You're just jealous, asshole. Come on."

On the way out, we caught Hal's eye and both of us waved at him and gave him a thumbs-up. Then I pointed to the door. He got it.

Once in the parking lot, Parker and I went our separate ways – him to his pick-up and me to my aging Subaru Forrester, which I'd inherited from Mom – which she'd inherited from my step-dad, Bill. Parker and I'd see each other in the morning at The Coffee Spot for our daily Geezers' meeting before our workday began.

Speaking of trucks, I have a truck back at the farm, too – a big, honkin' Dodge dually that I'd driven from LA when I moved east, my two horses accompanying me in their trailer on the cross-country trek.

My horses – Zeus and Ceres – are full brother and sister and they're both a sight to behold, being huge Percheron/Thoroughbred crosses. Their daddy was a big black Percheron and their mommy was a good-sized dark bay Thoroughbred.

Zeus stands a shade over eighteen hands tall and Ceres is only about an inch shorter. Both of them had taken after their sire in the color department – they're jet-black. And they are gorgeous, just friggin' gorgeous.

The 'kids', as I call them, live in a pasture at the end of my lane, directly adjacent to my big, red barn. Actually, Parker and I had fashioned an enclosure inside the barn that they can access by walking through a doorway, in case they want to get in out of the elements.

I work them in the pasture every couple of days, just to make sure they get enough exercise and I – or Parker and I – try to ride them once a week or so. Usually, that takes place right there in the pasture, having them each go through a walk/trot/canter routine for a good half-hour. But, sometimes, we've been known to take them out and wander around the farm.

I'm particularly proud of a trick that I'd taught them both. As a kid, my grandfather had shown me how to train a horse to do it and I'd worked with the kids and they'd learned it, too. While sitting on their back – one at a time, of course - I can get each of them to rise up on their hind legs – like Roy Rogers used to do with Trigger - and they can hover there for a good four or five seconds.

And, when an eighteen-hand horse rises up like that, his or her head is a good twelve feet off the ground. It is *very* impressive.

When I got back from the Women's Center – er, the People's Center, as it was now called – I pulled down the lane past the house and parked in front of the two-vehicle garage on my right. Dismounting from the Subaru, I walked a hundred feet or so down to the pasture.

Both of the horses must've been in the back of the pasture because, at first, I couldn't see them in the darkness. But, as I got closer, I heard a snort, andand from out of the gloom, I could make them out, coming toward me. It looked like two massive shadows coming my way.

"Hey, kids", I said, as they came up to the gate. "Wassup?" I reached up and rubbed both of their faces. "Everything copacetic? Oh, I see…..you guys think I have something, don't you? Well, I do. Hang on."

And I reached into a small aluminum garbage can that sits near the gate. And, from it, I pulled several horse treats. I doled out a few to each kid, alternating back and forth between them.

"Okay, that's it, for now", I said. "I gotta get to bed. It's later than usual. Y'all have a good night and I'll see you in the morning. Love you guys." And, after one last rub on each of their foreheads, I turned and walked up toward the house.

The house is, indeed, an old farmhouse, but it had been lovingly cared for by my mom and Bill. Bill had had it - and the farm – for something like twenty years before he and Mom got married and she moved in.

When I came east and walked in, it was like being home. Instantly. Oh, I'd been there to visit a few times, but the feeling I had when I first walked into it, after arriving late one night from the last leg of our cross-country drive, was amazing. It was like I was meant to be here. And I guess I am.

There's a pretty big kitchen, a large living room with a fireplace, a small dining alcove (which I never use) and three bedrooms and a bathroom upstairs. I'd made a rudimentary office out of one of the bedrooms and had taken the small bedroom in the back of the house for my room. The master bedroom – at least in my mind – still belonged to Mom and Bill and it would always remain that way.

A good-sized, raised porch runs along most of the back of the house, with a door into the kitchen. That porch is just about my favorite spot in the house and I spend an inordinate amount of time there.

Right off the porch, down the three steps to terra firma, sits a large garden. Mom always had that garden and, more or less in her honor, I decided to carry on with it. Some years, she'd grow flowers and, some years – usually alternating years – she'd grow vegetables.

Thanks to a lot of work by Parker and a little by moi, this year features flowers. A lot of flowers, of all kinds. It really looks nice and, every couple of days, I cut a big bouquet to take with me to The Coffee Spot. Gretchen, our favorite-waitress-recently-turned-owner of The Coffee Spot places them in a big vase (pronounced 'voz' because it was kind of expensive) that sits along one wall, underneath another piece of artwork that Parker created and donated to the place.

A number of old, towering maple and elm trees line the driveway-slash-lane up near the house and the front yard holds several, too.

Walking up the steps to the porch, I realized that it was only a few minutes after nine.

Hmm, I thought – I think the Yanks are playing the Angels in Anaheim, tonight. Maybe I'll go in and catch an inning or two. I don't usually watch west coast games – they're a little too late – but, maybe an inning or two would be just what the doctor ordered.

I grabbed a Diet Sprite out of the fridge, headed into the living room and turned on the tube.

Yep – there it was. Bottom of the second, the Yanks were up 1-0, on a Stanton home run. Cool, I thought. And I laid down on the couch.

The next thing I knew, the post-game show was on. Shit – I must've fallen asleep. I could see that the Yanks had prevailed, 7-5. Okay, fine. Great.

Now to bed.

Ten minutes later, the sandman came to call again.

When my alarm went off at six the next morning, I realized that I was cold. Huh?

This being my first year here in the East, I was still trying to get used to the change of seasons. I'd gotten here in April and the spring had transitioned into summer and all of that was fine – I was used to the warm climate of Southern California.

But, now? Now, at the beginning of October?

Yeah, the days had really cooled off and the nights were getting downright chilly, if not cold. And I hadn't gotten used to keeping the window open only a couple of inches overnight and, by morning, it was pretty damned cold.

A thought hit me – I'd have to check out the furnace pretty soon.

Anyway, I screwed up my courage, got out of bed and got myself dressed and did my toilette. Then, I pulled on a hoodie to fight off the frigid fifty-degree temperature.

When I walked outside, there was a little fog hanging over the hay field and the kids' pasture. It was really pretty - like one of those photographs you see of farms at dawn. And I was blown away by the fact that I actually live on a farm that looks like that.

I could barely make out the kids through the fog, but I saw that their heads were down and they were grazing their breakfasts. I gave them a 'good morning' shout and a wave and headed for the car. When I started it, I had to turn the wipers on to get rid of the mist that had landed on the windshield overnight.

A few seconds later, I drove up the lane and headed to The Coffee Spot.

Time for our daily Geezers meeting.

CHAPTER 2

The Coffee Spot is on Route 9, just a mile or so south of downtown Rhinebeck.

It sits on the right-hand side of the road, heading south, right next to what was an old, fallow farm that is now in the early stages of being transformed into a town park, called Ethel Jaekle Park. It'll be a good-sized park, too, taking up almost twenty-two acres. There'll be ball fields, picnic grounds, walking trails, a tennis court or two and a fancy new playground for the kids.

As I said, it's still in the early stages of construction, with a few pieces of machinery shuttling about, moving some earth here and there and some of the old fields being turned over so nice, clean grass can be planted next spring. The plan, I guess, is to have it open to the public by Memorial Day.

I turned into the diner's gravel parking lot and saw that, as usual, I was the last Geezer to arrive. As I was pulling into my usual spot, I noticed Parker's and Bob's trucks, Mike's Grand Cherokee, Joe's ugly old Corolla and Hal's unmarked Crown Vic. No sign of Gordon's ride, though.

As I entered and walked toward the table to my left, Gretchen waved me over to the spot where her 'voz' sat in front of Parker's artwork that hung on the wall.

"Morning, m'dear", I said. "What's up?"

"Well, J.D.", she said, "you know it's getting late in the year and, if they haven't already, the flowers are gonna stop growing pretty soon."

Yeah, right. I'd kind of noticed the pretty steep fall-off in the garden's floral production, recently.

"I know, right?", I said. "What're we gonna do about this?", I asked her, motioning at the 'voz'.

"Well, that's what I wanted to mention. I think we should make our little display, here, kind of coincide with the season, don't you?"

"Well, sure", I said. "But how are we going to do that? I mean, there aren't any flowers in the wintertime."

"I have an idea", she said.

"Shoot."

"Look – Halloween's coming up in the next couple of weeks. Why don't we put a big ol' jack-o-lantern here on the table? You know, with a face carved in it and, maybe, a flashlight inside."

That's kind of a cool idea, I thought. "Okay."

"And, then, before Thanksgiving, we'll put, like, a cornucopia or something here. I'll get Artie to put some gourds and so on in it." Artie ran the kitchen.

"Yeah", I said. "And, for Christmas and Hannukah, we'll get a little tree and decorate it all up." I was warming to the idea.

"There you go", she said.

"I like it. And, then, next spring, we'll go back to the flowers."

"Uh-huh. And, when it's not a holiday, we'll get some dried flowers to put on the table. So, look – why don't you get a big pumpkin and maybe you can get Parker to carve it?"

"Okay, yeah, sure. They're selling pumpkins up at Williams' and I'll run by and get a big one. And I'm sure that Parker will be glad to be the artiste. Give me a couple of days and I'll bring it with me."

"Perfect", she said. "Now – go sit down and try to get a leash on those dogs", her head nodding toward my fellow Geezers. "I'll be right there with the coffee."

Gretchen is one of the finest people on God's green earth. She's been a waitress here at The Coffee Spot for the better part of two decades and she loves it. She's probably in her late forties or early fifties, but it's hard to say for sure. Small and rather wiry, she doesn't carry an ounce of extra flesh on her. She hasn't had the easiest life, either, having had to work since she was a teenager to help her single mom out with the family's expenses.

But she'd found a home, here. And, no matter what, her attitude is always the same.

And her attitude hasn't changed one iota, either, since she took over ownership of the place a few months back. That's right – she's not only the owner, she's still the head waitress. She refuses to give that up.

See, that oligarch who'd come into town – Wolfe - had actually bought The Coffee Spot from its founder, Irv, who'd had it since he opened the place back in the mid-to-late '90s. And, because Parker and Mike and I had found out about some of Wolfe's extra-legal shenanigans, we were able to….um, persuade him…..to turn the place over to Gretchen. Wolfe was rich – hell, he was a friggin' oligarch. And, so, the money he lost by turning over the place to Gretchen in return for not being outed to some really bad-assed dudes, was simply his cost of doing business.

Oh, yeah – the land that the new park sits on? Wolfe had bought that, too. And, with our little act of 'persuasion', we'd had him give it to Gretchen, too. And, for tax reasons and because she's such a terrific gal, she donated all of that land to the Town of Rhinebeck, with specific instructions that it be made into a park. Ethel Jaekle was Gretchen's mom's maiden name, hence, the name Ethel Jaekle Park.

It's complicated.

But, yeah, Gretchen is the owner of The Coffee Spot and, as I said, Artie – who's Irv's younger brother - runs the kitchen. The two of them are great friends and they run the place like a true partnership.

As I sat down in my usual chair at the table, the guys were laughing and talking about something that was in the day's paper. Bob almost always brought one of the daily newspapers to our 'meeting' as, usually, something in it would trigger a conversation.

Joe gave me a brief recap.

It seems that a Peekskill woman had had her bright yellow jet ski, along with her trailer, stolen right out of her driveway. When she'd looked at her home security video, she'd seen a late model red Jeep Renegade driving away with it, although she couldn't make out its plate.

She posted the video on a local social media site and received a number of responses that, yes, people had seen a red Jeep hauling a yellow jet ski. The woman had then alerted the State Police, who'd put out a BOLO on the vehicle and trailer.

Long story short, one of the cops spotted a bright yellow object parked behind some trees on the side of a road and somewhat hidden from view. Upon investigating it because of the BOLO, he found that it was the jet ski in question. And the woman got her jet ski back, unharmed. The alleged perpetrator was still at large.

Anyway, the guys were marveling at the woman's good luck and at the wherewithal she'd used in posting the video.

Gretchen had poured my coffee and had filled the other guy's mugs in the middle of Joe's little story. And, because Joe is Joe and Gretchen knows it, she'd kind of rolled her eyes and split for parts unknown during his soliloquy.

"You know, cameras are being put up all over, nowadays", said Mike. "As a matter of fact, every other electrical pole that the town's putting up, especially in the more populated neighborhoods, has a camera attached to the top of it."

"Yeah, and we've just had a couple installed at the People's Center", said Hal. "Wide-angle ones – one in the front and one in the back."

"Can't hardly pull off the road to take a leak, anymore", said Joe, "without it somehow being posted on Facebook."

"Hey – that reminds me, Joe", said Parker. "The other day I saw a video posted where some guy with an old Corolla – just like yours, as a matter of fact – was trying to write his name in the dirt on the shoulder of the road. I think it was up along Round Lake Road. You wouldn't know anything about that, wouldja?"

"Oh, bite my crank", said Joe.

Gretchen walked up to the table.

"Well, gentlemen,", she said, "I'm sorry to say that I heard a little bit of the end of that conversation and I'm glad to know that you're keeping it classy, just like always. Now, what's it gonna be?"

And we all ordered. There were variations on the types of eggs and meats, along with an order or two of waffles. Artie had recently come up with nice and spicy sausage patties and those were proving popular, today. And, naturally, we all ordered home fries, which were some of the best, anywhere. Gretchen, of course, wrote nothing down. She never did and she always got it right.

"So, how're things in the executive suite?", Bob asked, as Gretchen re-filled all of our mugs before heading into the kitchen with our orders.

"Pretty good", she said. "But, you know, I never realized how many little details and so on that go into running this place. Like calling the guys to come and wash the windows and the landscaping guys to fiddle with that little garden thing out front. And the heating and A.C. guys and the people who service the freezers and refrigerators. There's a ton of things."

"Ah, the life of a restaurant mogul", I said. "You mean it's not all sitting around and counting your money?"

"Ha! Far from it, J.D.", she said. "As a matter of fact, this morning, I have to call the guy we always use to plow the parking lot in the wintertime and make sure he's all set to go. Won't be long, now."

And, as Gretchen walked away, there were several grumbles from around the table concerning the inevitable onslaught of winter.

"That reminds me, J.D. – we'll have one more cutting of your field, this year. And we should do it in the next week or so."

I had a deal with Marquardt. I would give him whatever hay he cut, baled and took from my big alfalfa hayfield, in return for as many bales as Parker and I thought that we'd need for the kids for the winter. Bob, in turn, sold the hay to a couple of local feed stores.

Everybody made out well, too. I didn't have to pay for feed for the winter, the local stores got hay for a deeply discounted price and the ultimate consumers saved a couple of bucks on each bale they bought.

Using a rough estimate - a high estimate - of two bales a day, we'd figured that we'd need somewhere in the neighborhood of two-hundred-and-fifty bales to get us from the end of November until early next May. In the first two cuttings of this past spring and summer, we'd loaded about a hundredand and fifty bales up into my hay loft.

"Cool, Bob", I said. "Any time – you just let me know, but your guys know what to do. Oh - and I think we'll probably need another – what, Parker – eighty, ninety bales?"

"Yeah, that oughta do it", he replied, nodding.

"Okay, I'll let you know when we're coming", said Bob.

Just then, Gretchen swooped in, her arms full of plates. "Hot stuff, you guys. Back off", she said, unerringly doling out each of our meals.

Once Gretchen set the plates down, all conversation came to a screeching halt. Discussions were one thing, eating was another. And, for the next few minutes, only the occasional, "Pass the salt, will ya?" and the like were the only phrases uttered.

When we were finished and had dutifully placed our entrenching tools onto our plates (a Gretchen 'demand'), Mike asked Hal, "Hey – what movies you got coming up?"

Hal had instituted a weekly Wednesday 'Movie Night' at the People's Center a few months back and they had become quite popular, with fifty or sixty people in attendance on most nights. None of the movies were anywhere near the first-run, but that was fine. There were romantic comedies, some of the classics and a lot of films that had come out during the audience's 'heyday'. In other words, a lot of films from the fifties, sixties and seventies, though there were occasionally some newer ones thrown in for good measure.

"Well,", said Hal, "we've got 'Forest Gump' coming up next week. And there've been quite a few requests for 'The Godfather' – part one, that is – but that's about three hours long, so we'll have to plan to start an hour early when we show that. Ah, I don't know – a bunch of 'em – I'll have to look. Oh – but, in two weeks, we're showing 'The Producers'. That movie's funnier than anything."

"Mel Brooks is a genius", said Joe. "And Zero Mostel in that? With his eyes bugging out all the time? Perfect."

"You're right, Joe – I love Mostel in that", I said. "And 'Springtime for Hitler and Germany' is priceless, with those dancing chicks at the beginning? I mean, it took guts to do all that. Nobody but Brooks."

Gretchen appeared out of nowhere, motioning for us to hand her our empty plates. "Give 'em up, guys."

We all obeyed and she asked us if we wanted anything else.

Nope. We were good.

So, she bade us a fond farewell until tomorrow's meeting.

"Well, gentlemen", said Bob. "I guess it's time to call this meeting to a close. All in favor?"

And we all voted with what has come to be known as the 'Geezer Knuckle-Knock', where we all knock on the table at the same time as our means of voting. It was always unanimous.

That done, we all stood up and each of us pulled out a twenty-dollar bill and tossed it into a little pile in the middle of the table. That more than covered our breakfasts and gave Gretchen a very nice tip. That was also one of our little rituals.

We all filed out, nodding to some of the other regulars on our way, and headed to our vehicles.

Parker asked me as we walked, "What's on tap for this morning?"

I said, "I think we oughta take a run down to Crockett's. We're almost out of grain and we're really low on bran and treats."

"And pie", he said, wiggling his eyebrows.

"Well, of course, pie", I said.

Crockett's, the nearest feed store, also featured some of the best homemade pies in creation. Apple lattice, cherry, peach – when they're in season – raspberry, the occasional lemon meringue and, and our go-to choice of pies – strawberry-rhubarb. Usually, two pies would accompany whichever of us went – or both of us – on the return trip home, along with the feed for the kids.

"You wanna take my truck?", he asked.

"Nah, let's take mine. She's been sitting there for a couple of weeks and I want her to stretch her legs a bit."

"Deal", he said. "Meet you back there."

And we both headed to our vehicles, Parker to his pick-up and me to my trusty Subaru.

When we reconnoitered back at the farm and were walking toward my dually, Parker asked me, "Hey – what do you hear from Ron, lately? Anything?"

I said, "Y'know, I haven't talked to him in a couple of weeks. Wanna give him a call?"

"Sure, why not?"

Ron was a friend – a good friend. He and I had worked together at that newspaper company and, as I said, its president had ultimately defrauded an investment firm that took it over. But that's a story for another day.

Anyway, once our company had been bought, both Ron and I had lost our jobs. We'd each done okay, severance-wise, but we'd found out about the fraud and, eventually, had figured out a way for the fraudster - the guy who had run our company - to pay dearly.

Ron was a computer genius and a hacker of the first order, especially after he'd been fired and was on his own. He was so good that, once the FBI had somehow gotten wind of him and his illegal hacking, had hired him instead of having him arrested. It seems that his expertise was of significant value to the Feebs and that was now his job: hacking bad guys for the feds.

Ron had stayed in LA and spent a couple of days a week at the Federal Building in Westwood and, a lot of the time worked from home so the Feebs could claim ignorance of his work if he ever got outed.

On several occasions, Ron had been an integral part of Parker's and my little extracurricular forays into serving a certain form of justice to wrongdoers who would have probably otherwise skated. At least from the law.

Ron was a good person.

I pulled out my phone, hit him on speed dial and put it on speaker.

"Yo!", he half-shouted by way of answering. "I thought you'd fallen off the face of the earth. What is up, my man?"

"I've got Parker here with me", I said.

"Dude!", said Ron.

"Hey, Ron", Parker answered him.

"What's going on with you guys? Anything?"

"Nah", I said. "It's been pretty quiet 'round these parts. You?"

"Ah, dude – I'm still working on that far-right extremist project. The one that I told you about a few weeks ago. And I gotta tell you, it's almost enough to make your damned hair stand on end. I mean, these assholes are all over the lot, right now."

"What do you mean?"

"Well, what I mean is that they're poppin' up all over the place, lately. Like, in the last year or so, a ton of new ones have come online and the old standbys – you know, like the Proud Boys and the Oathkeepers and the like – those guys are recruiting from just about everywhere. It's a fuckin' mess, you guys."

"You having any luck with 'em?", asked Parker.

"Oh, yeah, sure. But it's like herdin' cats or playing 'Whack-A-Mole' or something. We bring down five guys and six more pop up. I dunno, man, I think it's gettin' way out of hand."

"Fu-u-uck", said Parker.

"Yeah, fuck. Our little department that's been working on it has grown from – what? – four or five guys too, maybe, close to twenty, lately. And that's just our LA office. And, from what I understand, all the offices are adding people and we're still behind the eight ball."

"Wow", I said.

"Fucking douchebags", said Parker. "We fought a goddamned war and tens of thousands of guys died to stamp out the fuckin' Nazis. And, now? Now, we've got shit-ass American citizens walking around with friggin' swastikas and shit. Something's gotta be done."

"I know, dude", said Ron. "But this is feeling a lot like the war on drugs, y'know? Like, everybody talks about it and little things get done, but it's become almost acceptable to the great unwashed of this country. Hell, man – most people don't even pay any attention to it, but it's there. Oh, yeah, boy – it's there. And it's only gonna get worse."

"That's encouraging", I said.

"Sorry to bum your high, man", said Ron. "Aren't you glad you called?" And he laughed.

"Hah, yeah", I said, unenthusiastically. "But, look – if there's anything we can do…..but I don't know – this area's pretty – um, progressive, y'know? I'd be surprised if any of those guys are around here."

"You would be surprised, m'man", said Ron. "But, because your area's in my territory for following this shit, just know that there are some of those groups not far from you. I think they're pretty much on the other side of the Hudson but, like rabies in raccoons, they just might cross the river."

"Rabies in raccoons", I said. "Nice analogy."

"I thought you'd like it. Look, guys – I hate to rush you, but I gotta get ready for our daily seven ayem. I gotta get some shit together for it."

"Okay, dude – gotcha. But, hey – let's keep in closer touch than we have, recently, okay?"

"Right on. I'd dig that."

And, a few seconds later, we disconnected.

"Fuck", said Parker, again. And, then, a few seconds later, "Alright – let's go get that feed."

"And pie", I said.

"And pie."

And we headed to my truck.

<u>CHAPTER 3</u>

We made our way to Centre Road and headed south. Centre magically becomes Clinton Hollow Road after a few miles and eventually ends up in Salt Point, which is really nothing more than an exit off the Taconic Parkway. There's a C-store, there, and Crockett's Farm Supply, with a couple of random houses thrown in for good measure.

We went into Crockett's and ordered three fifty-pound bags of red wheat bran, three fifty-pound bags of Equine Senior grain and three bags of horse treats from Julie, the woman who was almost always behind the counter.

"You know the drill – just go over to the barn and Ronnie'll load you up. Oh – we just put out a few new pies. Check 'em out – I think there's even a pumpkin."

We sauntered over to the big wooden table that sat in a fairly prominent place on the sales floor and, yes, indeedy – there were five pies sitting on it.

"Should we try the pumpkin?", I asked Parker.

"Sure, why not? We gotta get us some whipped cream, though. Wait – hey, Julie! You got any whipped cream over there in the cooler?"

"Sure do. Not sure which shelf, though."

"Okay, thanks. Now, which other one should we get?", he said, surveying the bounty before us.

"How 'bout the apple cinnamon?", I asked. "Says it's made with local apples."

"A discriminating choice", he said, picking up the pumpkin pie. "I'll go fetch the whipped cream."

A few minutes later, we were loaded up with horse supplies and pie and headed back north.

About a half-mile up the road, I said, "Shit!" and slowed down.

"What?"

I pulled into the next driveway I saw and, while turning around, said, "Gretchen wants to get a big ol' jack-o'-lantern for that table where we keep the flowers. Flower season's just about over and she wants, like, a carved pumpkin for Halloween, some kind of gourd thing for Thanksgiving and a little tree for Christmas. That kind of thing."

As I got the truck headed back toward Crockett's, I continued, "I told her that I'd bring her a pumpkin and was thinking of getting one at Topps or Williams, but I just saw a bunch of 'em back there at Crockett's. Nice, big ones, too. I'm gonna go back and get one."

We pulled back into the parking lot and walked over to the big display.

I said, "Oh, by the way – I told her that you'd carve it for her."

"Me?"

"Yeah, you're the artiste, right?"

"I ain't carved a pumpkin in twenty years", he said.

"Well, no time like the present. There – how 'bout that one?", I said, pointing to a big, round guy.

"Yeah, why not? And you want me to carve it?"

"Yep. And I think I'll pick up one of those little lights – you know, like a little candle that runs on a battery - and we'll put that inside of it."

"We've got a couple of those in your garage. They're sittin' on a shelf."

"We do? Why would we have any of those?"

"Hell, I don't know, man – but we do."

"Okay, cool. Let me go in and pay for this bad boy and you carry it to the truck, okay?"

He nodded and picked it up. "Sucker's heavier'n it looks", he said.

Our business with Julie once again transacted, and we headed back toward the farm.

A few minutes later, I noticed that Parker was kind of quiet, all of a sudden, and could see that he was somewhere else.

"What?", I asked him.

"Huh? Oh, I was just thinking about what Ron told us a little while ago. You know, that those crazy fucking right-wing groups are popping up all over. I mean, how could that happen? How can it be happening?"

"I don't know, man, but there seem to be a whole lot of white supremacists and anti-Semites and all that - hell, even fucking neo-Nazis – lately, and that, somehow, think they can get by with their shit without anybody calling 'em on it."

"That carny-barker shyster we had in the White House seemed to give 'em all the green light", he said.

"The thing that's fucked up", I said, glancing over at him, "is that those people have probably always been around and have always had those nutso beliefs, but they stayed down in the woodwork until the fat boy, there, gave 'em the high sign that they could come out. And they have. And they are."

"Yeah. It sucks. Hey, look – we're coming up on the Golden Potato, pretty quick."

"The Golden Russet", I corrected him.

"Yeah, right – whatever. Anyway, you wanna stop there and pick up some donuts?"

The Golden Russet is a small, general-store-slash-pseudo-restaurant that's owned by a nice young couple who are trying, mightily, to make a go of it. They have a small selection of canned goods and things of the sort, but it's not what you'd call a real 'destination' store. Craig – the husband – mans the grill and, recently, they'd been serving their fair share of breakfasts and lunches. There are a couple of small booths and one big table right in the middle of the floor. Jenny is in charge of the baked goods. Well, that and their three-year-old son, who is generally in attendance.

And, Jenny puts out just about the best homemade cinnamon donuts you'll find anywhere. We often stop on the way to or from Crockett's and snare a half-dozen. Mike, too, lives near there and he's always taking a bunch of 'em into the office.

"Why not?", I said. "I'll stay in the truck and you run in and get 'em."

I pulled into the little dirt strip that serves as a parking area and noticed that a couple of the tables out on the front porch were occupied. Nice to see people here at this time of day, between breakfast and lunch.

Parker came out holding a paper bag and got back into the truck.

"They only had three left", he said. "Want one?"

"Sure."

"We'll split the other one", he said, handing me one of Ms. Jenny's fried cakes.

I backed out and headed back north on Centre Road, with one hand on the wheel and one hand on my donut.

We got back to the farm about ten minutes later and unloaded and parked the truck, having put all the supplies in their proper places. Parker carried the pumpkin over to the garage and set it down.

"So, you really want me to carve this thing, huh?", he asked again.

"Yep. And, I might add, that Gretchen's expecting you to do it and it's gonna be sitting there for all to see, so you best not fuck it up."

"What should I carve? I mean, what do you want it to look like?"

"Hell, I don't know, man. Just, like, a Halloween jack-o'-lantern. Don't overthink it."

"Alright. Maybe I'll take it into the workbench and see if I can come up with something. But don't expect too much – pumpkins ain't my forte. But, first – let me carry one of the pies up to the house. I don't want you to drop one of 'em."

Once the pies were safely on the kitchen counter, Parker said, "Alright – I'll be in the garage" and off he went.

____

Right about that time, Fred 'Flint' Stone was driving up Route 9 on his way to an address in Red Hook. A homeowner had called him and asked him about repairing the walkway leading up to his house. Flint would check it out and give the guy a price.

Stone ran a one-man masonry company, sometimes hiring part-time workers if the job called for it. The name of his company was 'Flint Stone Masonry' and he proudly displayed a large and rather lousy rendition of Fred Flintstone on the side of his panel truck, with the words, 'Yabba-Dabba-Doo!' seeming to emanate from Fred's mouth. Naturally, he'd used 'Fred' without authorization. Who cares? he'd thought when he'd had it done. It's not like anybody's gonna bitch about it.

He was driving a little slower than usual because he was really into the show he was listening to on WAAN-FM. It featured a live phone interview with a Minnesota member of the Proud Boys.

WAAN – "Your Two-A Network Station" ('Two A', as in Second Amendment) – was Stone's go-to radio station. It broadcasts a number of syndicated shows from the likes of Michael Savage, Charlie Kirk and Dan Bongino. Those guys, he thought, always hit the nail right on the friggin' head. This country is going into the shitter and somebody'd better do something quickly or the aliens and the coloreds and the Jews are gonna take over.

The guy on the radio – the Proud Boy – was talking about how, after the January 6th thing, his and several other organizations were decentralizing and moving down into more local levels. For one thing, the heat was on the mother ships and the leaders couldn't make a move without the (bleep) feds looking over their shoulders.

For another thing, a lot of guys were trying to get involved with more local politics and so on. He told about a couple of them who'd recently gotten elected to school boards. If they could get more of their own into places like that – even local police forces – they could really start to make a difference.

The guy called it 'bottom-up' activism.

Interesting, thought Stone as his GPS announced his turn left turn onto Garden Street. "Your destination is on the right", it informed him.

He pulled into the driveway and headed up the walkway in question. Hmm, he thought. Not too bad. Break up and pull out a few broken sections and lay in a few new ones. Piece of cake.

He walked up onto the porch and rang the bell, clipboard in hand.

Twenty minutes later, he had an eight-hundred-dollar job.

____

My phone rang.

Gretchen's name came up on the screen.

"Hey, Gretchen – what's up? Everything okay?"

"Well, yeah, J.D., but I have to tell you something."

"Uh-oh – this doesn't sound good", I said.

She laughed and said, "Oh, no, no, no – really, it's nothing bad. It's just that you guys are probably going to see another worker around The Coffee Spot in the next few days."

"And you're telling me this – why?", I asked.

"Well, because it's my niece."

"Your niece? I didn't know you had a niece."

"Yeah – it's my sister's daughter. My sister Lauren's daughter. They live in Ohio."

"And?"

"And Suze – her name's really Susan, but everybody calls her Suze – well, Suze is going to come here for a while. I don't know how long she'll be here. Maybe only a few weeks, if that. And I figured that I'd put her to work while she's here. She was a waitress for a while at a Cracker Barrell, back home, so she can do the job."

"Well, the Cracker Barrell sure seals the deal for me", I said, with my tongue firmly planted in my cheek. "When's she getting here?"

"Actually, she's coming in this afternoon, so she'll probably be with me in the morning. Look – I called Mike, too, and told him. I just want you guys to be extra nice to her – she's having some problems, lately."

"She staying with you?"

"Yeah. Well, at least for a little while. If she decides she wants to stay around here, she'll get her own place. But, for now, she'll be staying with me."

"How's that hitting you? Having somebody else around your place?"

"Ah, I can deal with it for a little while. I've got an extra bedroom, so – you know – we'll be okay. Heck, if we find out that we can't stand being that close to each other, she can always camp out in the office at the diner. We can get her a little bed or a cot or something and we've got that small employee shower in the back. So, either way, I don't see it as being a problem."

"What's her name again?", I asked.

"Suze."

"Right. Okay – I'll tell Parker. Actually, he's down in the garage, carving your jack-o'-lantern, right now."

"Oh, good. You going to bring it in the morning?"

"That's the plan", I said. "Unless Parker completely screws it up."

"He won't. And I can't wait to see it."

And, after another couple of things, we disconnected.

I sauntered down to the garage to tell Parker about Suze and to see how he was doing on the pumpkin. When I walked in, he was bent over the workbench, seemingly putting the finishing touches on it. He had three or four different sizes and styles of knives on the bench in front of him.

"Hey", I said.

"Hey, yourself. Here,", and he flicked away a couple of errant pieces, "take a look. Wait – hold on a minute." And he put one of the little lights in the bottom of it and turned it on. "There."

Natch, I had been expecting the usual – you know, like a couple of triangle-shaped eyes, a triangle-shaped nose and a smiling mouth with a few randomly scattered teeth. A typical jack-o'-lantern.

What I saw was really something else.

He'd actually carved the profile of a witch, stirring a cauldron with a long, gnarled stick, all in front of a big crescent moon in the background. The witch looked toothless, replete with a sharp, hook-like nose, a pointy chin and long, straggly hair, all brought to life by the little light inside.

"Holy shit", I said, honestly impressed.

"Like it?", he asked.

"Dude – I had no idea."

"What – you think I'd put some piker piece in The Coffee Spot?"

"Well, no, not really. But I didn't think it would be this good."

"Ye of little faith. Alright,", he said, reaching in and turning the light off, "I'll leave this right here and you bring it with you in the morning, okay?"

"Yeah, sure. But you have to give it to Gretchen. This is a work of art, dude."

"Yeah, well, we'll figure it out. Now, I gotta clean this shit up and get outta here. I'm going down to my daughter's for dinner, tonight." His daughter and her family lived down between Hyde Park and Poughkeepsie and he generally went down there for dinner every couple of weeks.

"Okay, cool. Hey – I just got a call from Gretchen and she said that her niece – her name's Suze – is coming from Ohio to stay with her for a while."

"Yeah? I didn't know she had a niece."

"She said it's her sister's – Lauren's – daughter."

"Why's she coming here?"

"I dunno", I shrugged. "She said something about Suze having some problems, lately, but she didn't go into them. Anyway, I guess Gretchen's going to put her to work at the place while she's here."

"She staying with Gretchen?", he asked.

"Yeah, at least for the time being", I said. "Gretchen says she has an extra bedroom so it shouldn't be any trouble."

"When's she getting here?"

"Today."

"Huh. Interesting. I guess. Okay, look – I am outta here. Catch you in the ayem."

"Deal", I said.

"And don't forget the damned pumpkin."

"Well, duh", I said as we walked out and closed the big garage door.

The thought hit me and I said, "Hey – that pumpkin and Halloween remind me of 'The Headless Horseman'.

"And that reminds both of us of the ninja horseman, right?"

"You got it, Ace."

"I wonder….", he said, glancing at me.

"Yeah – I wonder, too."

We fist-bumped and he headed for his truck and split.

CHAPTER 4

Early the next morning, Eric Gallagher's phone rang. He saw that it was Flint Stone.

"Yo, Flint – what's up?"

"Yeah, hi, Eric. Look, I was wondering if you'd like to make a hundred bucks."

"Sure, man. Whaddya need?"

"Well, I got a small job up in Red Hook, tearing out a couple of sections of a sidewalk and putting new ones down. And I thought you might like a small job. The two of us can probably knock it out in a couple of hours, easy."

"A c-note for a couple hours' work? Yeah, boy – count me in. When?"

"I've gotta finish up a job, not far from there, this morning. I figured I'd do that, grab a little lunch and do the Red Hook thing early this afternoon – like, around, one. We should be done by three, a little after."

"Cool. Want me to meet you there?"

"That'd be perfect. I'll text you the address as soon as I get to where I'm going. It's right off Route 9, though. Piece of cake."

"Okay, cool. And I'll be there at one. Want me to bring anything?"

"Nah – I got what we'll need."

Good, thought Stone, after he'd hung up. Another guy would make that job a breeze and, and if he did it by himself, it'd take a couple of hours longer - and a lot more work on his part. Plus, Gallagher was a good worker. For a hundred bucks, he couldn't go wrong.

He turned on the truck's radio and there was Alex Jones, interviewing Jon Voight, talking about how our streets are now filled with criminals who are being allowed to rob innocent people and that the country must be turned around from that kind of injustice.

He pulled into a McDonald's drive-thru, ordered a couple of Egg McMuffins and a coffee and pulled into a space in the parking lot to eat. He kept the truck running so he could listen while he ate.

A few miles away, I was pulling into the parking lot at The Coffee Spot, the jack-o'-lantern on the passenger's seat next to me. I thought that my idea of securing it on the seat was rather brilliant. I put the seat belt around it and, yep – it had been held firmly in place all during my rather short journey.

When I got out and opened the passenger's door, I actually took a picture of it, all strapped in, with my camera. Not that I was going to show it around, but if it came up, I'd have visual proof of my pumpkin-safety genius.

I walked a foot or two into the diner and caught Parker's eye. I waved him over, pointing to the outside. As in, "Hey – come and get the pumpkin". He shook his head. I gave him 'the look' and waved again. This time, he got up and came over.

"Dude,", I said, "you gotta be the one to give that to Gretchen. It's your work."

"Yeah, but you bought it", he said. Parker wasn't one to show off in any way, even though we all knew that he was always proud of his work.

"Fuck that", I said. "Come on – you go get it and I'll find Gretchen."

So, he went one way and I went the other. I spotted Gretchen coming out of the kitchen with a couple of plates on a tray. I gave her a little wave and she gave me a head nod in acknowledgment. "One sec", she mouthed.

She put the plates down in front of a couple sitting at a nearby booth and, holding the tray, walked over, just as Parker appeared at the door. I opened it for him.

"Got your jack-o'-lantern, darlin'", he said to Gretchen.

"Ooh – I can't wait to see it. Here – let me set that 'voz' down on the floor and you put it on the table." And she led the way over to the table next to the wall.

"Okay, Gretchen – turn around", I said. "Let Parker get it all set up and the little light turned on, then you'll get the full effect."

She smiled and did that, while Parker put the pumpkin down on the table, reached inside and turned the light on.

"Okay", he said.

When Gretchen turned back around to look at it, she looked as surprised as I had been when I first saw it.

"Oh, my lord, Bill! Are you kidding me? A witch?!?" And she bent down to look closer.

"And, look – she's stirring a cauldron. And that moon! I've never seen a pumpkin carved like this. It's like….like…a little 'tableau' – isn't that what you'd call it?"

"Well, I don't know if I'd go so far as to say that, but – "

"Oh, stop, Bill", she said, interrupting him. "Yeah. Yeah, that's what it is. It almost tells a little story. Isn't that what a tableau is?"

"It is, indeed, Gretchen", I said. "Good one."

She reached up and gave Parker a big hug, then turned around and said in a loud voice, "Excuse me! Excuse me, everyone!" And various sets of eyes focused on her from around the place.

"Look what our friend, Bill Parker, just brought us. One of the best-carved jack-o'-lanterns you ever did see. Come on over and check it out when you get a chance. And", and she turned to Parker, "thank you, Bill."

There was a smattering of polite applause, but not much – mainly because most people weren't overly excited about a friggin' pumpkin. But Gretchen was and that's what really mattered.

Dutifully, all the Geezers got up and walked over.

"Nice", was the general reaction but, Joe, as our resident turd in the punchbowl, said, "Lotta freakin' works for a pumpkin." But he redeemed himself, slightly, by saying, "Good job, though."

Once we all sat back down, Hal said to Parker, "Hey, Bill – do you suppose you could do a couple of those for the Center? Maybe one for each of the large rooms?"

"Well, probably", Parker shrugged. "I guess."

"Excellent! Tell you what – I'll pick up a couple of nice ones, today, and bring them in the morning – so you don't have to go out of your way, okay?"

"Sure", said Parker. He thought for a few seconds. "And I guess I could have 'em ready for you in a couple of days. Would that work?"

"Oh, absolutely. They'll be perfect for our little Halloween film fest. On two Wednesdays in a row – well, next Wednesday and the week after – we'll be showing two Halloween-themed films. The first one is 'Hocus Pocus', which is pretty funny, and the next week – on Halloween – we've got 'Sleepy Hollow'. You know, the headless horseman flick with Johnny Depp."

Parker and Mike and I exchanged glances.

"Great idea about those movies, Hal", said Bob. "You're turning into quite the impresario."

Hal chuckled and said, "Yeah, I'm having fun coming up with those movies."

Just then, Gretchen walked up to the table, accompanied by a young woman dressed in Coffee Spot waitress garb.

"Hey, you guys", said Gretchen. "I'd like to introduce you to my niece, Suze. She's from Ohio. Suze – these are the Geezers." And she went around the table, introducing each of us.

I kind of gave her a quick once-over as the guys welcomed her and made small talk. She looked to be in her early twenties, slim and a little over average height. Red hair may have its origins in some form of red but had obviously been enhanced by something that came out of a bottle. It was straight, fell to just about her shoulders and her long bangs partially hid her eyebrows.

No doubt, Suze was an attractive young woman, albeit in a Midwesterner-goes-hip sort of way, as proven by the tattoo sleeve that ran up her left arm.

"Where in Ohio are you from?", asked Joe.

"Chillicothe. Ever heard of it?", asked Suze with an easy smile.

"Sure, I've heard of it. South of Columbus, right? I've got some cousins that live in Columbus. One of 'em works at Ohio State."

"THE Ohio State", said Suze, laughing.

"Oh, that's right – they've gone with that, haven't they? Did you go there?"

"Nah – didn't go to college. Went right to work after I graduated. Well, after a little traveling around, first."

"Ever been to Rhinebeck, before?", asked Bob.

"Nope. First time. Seems like a nice place. Kinda quiet, though."

"Well, you want excitement, you're only a couple of hours out of the city", he said.

"I know. I can't wait to go down there."

"Gotta be careful, though. The city can be pretty tough on out-of-towners", said Mike.

"Oh, I can take care of myself", said Suze, with a smile.

"And, she can, too", said Gretchen. "What's that thing you do, again?"

Suze gave Gretchen an 'Aw, jeez' look as if she really didn't want to talk about it.

"Krav Maga", she said.

"Wait - what the hell is – what did you say, again? Krav something?", asked Joe.

"Krav Maga" said Suze. "It's, like, a way of fighting and self-defense – but it's not a martial art like karate or Jiu-jitsu or Taekwondo. It's different than those things. But, you know, it's like them, in a way, too. Kinda." And she shrugged.

"You any good at it?", Joe pressed her.

"Ah – not really. I mean, I can probably take decent care of myself if I have to, but I've only been doing it for a little less than a year. Takes a long time to be good."

"Oh, stop", Gretchen said to her. And, then, looking at us, she said, "Suze was the Central Ohio Champion in her weight class."

"Wow", was the general consensus.

"Yeah", said Suze, "but it was a really small competition. Can we talk about something else?", she asked, obviously a little uncomfortable talking about herself.

"How long are you going to be here?", asked Mike.

"Well, um – I don't know, exactly. I think I'll wait and see", she said, glancing at Gretchen.

"She's staying with me, for the time being", said Gretchen. "If she decides to stay for a while, we'll work it out. Alright, you guys – enough of this. What are you gonna have?"

"I'd better get back to my station", said Suze. "I don't want to screw up on my first day. Nice meeting you all."

And we all said, basically, the same thing back to her.

"She seems nice", said Hal, after Suze had left.

"Oh, she's a doll", said Gretchen. "She's got a couple of issues, but I'm going to help her take care of them. Now – order, will ya?"

We gave her our orders and off she went to the kitchen.

And, for the next few minutes, we kibbitzed about Suze and her staying with Gretchen and all that like a bunch of old biddies.

The food came. We ate. Bob called the meeting to a close, the twenties fluttered to the table and we all got up and headed out, with Hal reiterating to Parker that he'd bring a couple of big pumpkins in the morning.

As we were filing out, Gretchen caught my eye and tilted her head in the direction of the side door – the employees' door. I knew that she wanted to talk to me. I pointed at Parker's back and raised my eyebrows to her. She nodded.

I nudged him on the arm and said, quietly, "Gretchen wants to talk to us, outside." He nodded.

We kind of hung around in the parking lot for a minute while the other Geezers mounted their steeds and split. Then, we walked around the corner of the building, just as Gretchen was coming down the few steps from the door.

"What's up?", I asked her.

"Okay, you guys", she said. "I hate to do this, but I think I've got to ask you for your help. Again."

"Anything, kid – you know that", said Parker and I nodded.

"Alright, look – I'll just come right out and say it. Suze is pregnant. But it's early – she's only, like, less than eight weeks along and she does not want to have a baby. No how, no way. She said that it was a mistake – some kind of one-time thing and she doesn't really even know the guy and she's just too young to be a mother and - well, no matter what you or I or anybody else thinks, she wants to terminate it. And that's entirely up to her."

Neither one of us knew quite what to say. Or were supposed to say. So, we didn't say anything. We just nodded in agreement with her last sentence.

"Here's the deal", said Gretchen, continuing, "The state of Ohio recently passed a six-week law. That means that it is illegal to terminate a pregnancy in the state if the woman is more than six weeks along. This is utterly ridiculous because, really, most women don't know they're pregnant by six weeks. I mean, they miss their period after four weeks – which happens quite frequently, by the way – so most women don't even think about it 'til almost week six."

We were listening pretty intently because, quite honestly, this was all kinda news to us.

"Then, say it is week six, week six-and-a-half, and they take a pregnancy test and find out they're pregnant. In Ohio, now, that means that the woman is out of luck, termination-wise."

"Do you mean that it's already too late to get an abortion as soon as they've found out they're pregnant?", I asked.

"That's exactly what I mean. And that's exactly what the state of Ohio recently passed into law. From what I gather, Ohio's become one of the worst states in the nation for that."

"Ah, Jesus", said Parker. "This country's going backward so goddamned fast it makes your head spin."

"I'll say", said Gretchen, shaking her head. "It's a shame, too."

"So,", I said, "that's why Suze is here – in New York State, right? Because here, she can legally terminate the pregnancy - am I correct?"

"Yep. Here, it's up to twenty-four weeks", she said.

Parker and I both nodded and he asked, "When's she gonna do it? And, where?"

"Well, we looked into it and there's a Planned Parenthood down in Poughkeepsie. And Suze called them and they said that she could make an appointment to go in and have herself thoroughly checked out. I guess they'll give her a complete physical or something. And, then, if she really *is* pregnant - and there's no reason to think she isn't – I mean, that's what the test showed. Then, if she really is, they'll give her some counseling and then, if she still wants to do it, they'll schedule a time for her to go in and have it done."

'Wow", I said.

"Yeah, wow", said Parker.

Gretchen just nodded.

"Okay – what do you need from us?", I asked.

"Well, when she has the procedure done, I want to be there with her, for sure. And I will be. But, for this first appointment, I'm sure she can get by without me. And, honestly, it might be hard for me to get away from here for the better part of two days – which, I'd imagine, will be pretty close together. You know – right in the middle of the busiest time of the day."

"You want us to drive her down and back", I said.

"Well…."

Parker and I glanced at each other and he said, "Of course, we'll do that, Gretchen."

"Hell, yeah", I chimed in, almost immediately.

"Oh – you guys are the best! Simply the best!", she said, hugging both of us.

"When's the appointment?", Parker asked her.

"I don't know yet. Suze is going to call them, this morning. She should know then. But it should be in the next day or so, I'd imagine."

"Well, just let us know when you know", said Parker.

"I will."

"Hey", I said, thinking. "You know that this will mean that Suze knows that we know, right?"

"About the pregnancy? Yeah. And, really, she's cool about it. I already told her that I was going to ask you guys to give her a ride down and back." She paused, then said, "Suze is a pretty free spirit. To her, this is really no big deal. Just something that has to be done. It's just that it can't be done in Ohio."

"Well, just by looking at her, you can tell about that free spirit thing. I mean, that sleeve tattoo and all is kind of a dead giveaway", I said.

"Oh – you didn't see it" Gretchen laughed. "When she got here, she had a ring in her nose, too. I told her that that would have to go if she's going to be working at The Coffee Spot. I might even ask her to wear a long-sleeved shirt, too. I don't know. The customers might not think it's right."

"Forget about it", said Parker. "People around here are pretty cool about things like that."

"Well, some of them are and some of them aren't", she said. "I don't know – that's on page two. Listen, guys – I've gotta get back in there. And, again, I can't thank you enough for doing this. It means a lot. To me and to Suze."

"Then, we'll wait to hear from you later", I said.

"I'll call you as soon as I hear", she said. And she headed back up the steps to the door.

"Jeez", I said, once she'd gone inside.

"Life can be pretty complicated", said Parker, "can't it?"

"I'll say. Alright – let's head out."

"Meet you back there", he said.

CHAPTER 5

Mark Fisher was still thinking about last night's school board meeting.

Although his position on a number of issues diverged rather vividly from a number of the other board members' and a good swath of the parents in attendance, there had also been a larger-than-expected turnout from those who agreed with him.

He'd made a motion to exclude a book from the middle school and high school libraries due to what he felt were inappropriate subjects for young minds. That book was *Gender Queer*, a rather graphic novel and memoir by Maia Kobabe that recounts his/her journey of coming out as a bisexual in high school. He wasn't alone in wanting to ban that book, either. School systems around the country had also banned it, encouraged, in part, by the Moms for Liberty group.

There were a number of comments from parents at the meeting and, and because it was evident that the subject was taking up far too much time during the meeting, the board president had shelved it for the time being.

Fine, Fisher had thought at the time. He had a more important issue to discuss, though he had no particular motion to make.

And that was Critical Race Theory, or CRT.

He had taken the position as the one board member who spoke on behalf of a number of the district's parents who were concerned about that subject.

And, last night, he had spoken about how CRT seeks to divide people, rather than bring them together, based on their skin color. And he had seen a Black Lives Matter poster in the high school and had spoken out about it. That it was political in nature and should not be allowed in a school. And he suggested strongly that the board oversee and, yes, even demand, that any form of CRT be banned from the classroom.

He wasn't at all surprised when the board president and several other members spoke up and said that CRT is *not* taught in schools – that it is a legal framework that had been developed years ago at Harvard Law School. It doesn't exist in schools' curricula.

But the whole idea of teachers spending time talking about issues like slavery and all that it entailed only seems to paint white people in a bad light. Plus, many slaves loved their lives and were happy with them. But that's not the way it's portrayed in American schools. And he thought that was just wrong.

And, yeah, maybe it wasn't really CRT, but people understood that the phrase stood for something that he felt was being taught to our children in a very biased and corrupt way.

And, hoo, boy – that had ignited a firestorm.

Again, because he was in the minority – actually, he was alone on the board – most of the parents went nuts trying to silence him and a lot of them spoke out against his views during the public comment portion of the meeting.

Fortunately, again because of the organizing prowess of the Dutchess County Moms for Liberty group, they had turned out a couple dozen parents who agreed with him. And, yes, they had their time at the microphone, too. And, because of that, he had estimated that the pros and cons on the subject came out about fifty-fifty – a lot better than he thought it might.

Anyway, it was a start.

But he'd left it at that, last night, not wanting to get into the 'Pledge of Allegiance', which he thought should be said every day, by every student in the district – even in the high school. So many schools had jettisoned that practice in recent years and he thought that that was almost un-American. He'd bring that up another time.

For now, he had to get back to work. He had a couple of his technicians out on the road and several more working here at the shop. Four years ago, he'd started Fisher Computer Repair ("Let Fisher Fix it") and it had grown substantially since then. Nowadays, he finds it more and more difficult to keep up with all the business coming his way. He might even have to add a few more people.

"Mark", he heard his assistant say, "that Intel guy's on line one."

Okay, he thought – back to business.

When Parker and I had gotten back to the farm, we talked about the Gretchen/Suze situation. Honestly, both of us were a little floored by the whole thing. I mean, we didn't even know that Gretchen had a sister, let alone a niece. Nor had we known about that whole Ohio abortion thing. I guess we didn't pay enough attention to the news.

But, shit – how crazy was that? That new law in Ohio?

"The fuckers insist that women have babies, then pull the rug out from under them as soon as the kids are born – especially those in poverty. Plus, they're cutting money out of education as fast as they can. What do they think's gonna happen to all those kids?", Parker spouted. "That ain't pro-life, son. I don't know what it is, but it ain't pro-life."

"I know", I said, pretty dejectedly. "But, if we can help Suze, at least that'll be helping one person. One at a time, I guess."

"Best we can do", he said.

A little while later, Gretchen called and said that Suze's appointment at Planned Parenthood was scheduled for nine-thirty tomorrow morning. And, would we still be okay with that?

I told her that it'd be fine. I knew Parker'd be cool with it.

"As a matter of fact, Gretchen, maybe we'll just leave The Coffee Spot after breakfast". I asked her. "Would that be okay?"

"Well, yeah – sure. That way, Suze'll already be there – she can put in a couple of hours ahead of that and you guys can just leave when you need to."

"Cool. I'll tell Parker. And, Gretchen – don't worry, we got this."

"I know. And I appreciate it – really. It's just that I never saw this coming and it's….well, it's all a little unsettling."

"I totally understand", I said. "But, like all things, this, too, shall pass."

"Yeah, I hope so", she said. "Okay, I've gotta go. And, thanks, again, J.D."

I walked down the lane, found Parker emptying the horse poop cart and told him about the call I'd just gotten from Gretchen.

"Yeah, fine", he said. "Look – we gotta take your car, right? I mean, the three of us in my truck just won't work. So, I'll come by here a little early, tomorrow, drop the truck off and ride with you to breakfast. That way, I won't have to leave it in the parking lot for a couple, or three hours. We can just drop Suze off and head back here."

"Deal."

"Hey", he said. "Let me ask you – what do you think of Suze?"

"What do I think of her? Hell, man, I don't know. I just met her and she seemed okay – why?"

"Well, I'm just thinkin' that she has a little bad-ass in her", he said.

"Why? Because of the tattoo and the nose ring?"

"Ah, yeah, sure – maybe. There's that, but also that she's doing that whole Krav Maga thing. Done right, that is a lethal thing to know. We had a couple of guys on the force who knew it and used it a few times with some knuckleheads who didn't wanna come along peacefully and tried to fight their way out. Whupped their asses, bad. And, in no time, too. Like, in a flash, it was over."

"I don't think I'd ever heard of it before."

"Yeah, I guess it was started by the Israeli Defense Forces or their security forces. And, it's some sort of combination of offensive and defensive moves. I dunno – whatever. I just know what I've seen and it can be rough. The fact that Suze is even half-decent at it - well, that makes her kind of a badass."

"I suppose", I said. "Look – I gotta run to Topps. My cupboard is bare and my larder is empty. Want me to bring you anything?"

"Nah, I'm good. I brought some leftovers home from my daughter's house, last night. That'll get me through 'til my next run. Oh, wait – you might get a package of ham so we can whip up some sammiches if we want to."

"Got it." Parker and I often eat a sandwich in his office in the barn at lunchtime. He's got one of those little refrigerators in there.

A few minutes later, I was on my way to the grocery.

At exactly one o'clock, Flint Stone pulled into the driveway of the house in Red Hook. Gallagher's truck was already parked out front and he was standing next to the sidewalk. He seemed to be assessing what needed to be done.

Stone was listening to Alex Jones on the radio as he pulled in and Jones was saying how unfair the January 6th Committee's hearings have been. That they had no rebuttal witnesses and that half of what they said was bullshit. Stone wanted to catch the end of Jones' little rant, so he sat there for a minute.

"Hold on", he said to Gallagher, out his window. "Be right there. I wanna hear this."

Gallagher sauntered over and heard what was on the radio. Both men listened for another minute or so.

When the show broke for commercial, Stone turned off the engine and got out of the truck.

"I gotta say, Flint – I'm one-hundred percent in agreement with Jones. Fuck, man – you know this whole thing is bogus. It's a goddamned political hit job, is what it is."

"You watched any of it?", Stone asked him.

"Hell, no. Wouldn't waste my time."

"Yeah, me, either."

"They're all just trying to cover up the fact that the election was fucked six ways from Friday, man. This is just chaff that they're throwing up so people will buy their bullshit – that the election wasn't stolen. And it was, man. It really fucking was."

"Yeah, I know", said Stone. "Hook, line and sinker."

"I dunno - we gotta take this country back, man - that's all there is to it", said Gallagher, as they walked toward the back of Stone's van. "Goin' downhill fast. We gotta do something."

"I know", said Stone, "but what can we do? I mean, we're just a couple'a of hard-workin' shlubs. Us and everybody else. We got no power."

"Well, I met some guys, recently, and I like the way they're thinkin'."

"Yeah? Who?"

"Ah, just some guys, man. They have little get-togethers pretty regularly and talk about this shit. And, maybe, what can be done about it? Nothing big. Nah – nothing crazy, man. Just some shit they might be able to do around here."

"You mean like the Proud Boys?"

"Well, they ain't the Proud Boys or the Oathkeepers or anything like that – though some of the guys know some of those dudes. They're friendly with 'em and all. But, no – this is just a group of local guys. I don't even think they have a name but, if they do, I don't know what it is."

"You been to any of their meetings? Or get-togethers or whatever you call it?"

"Yeah, I have been to a couple. They were pretty cool."

"Where are they? When are they?", asked Stone.

"Um, well, dude. I'd have to let 'em know that you might be interested 'fore I can tell you. They're trying to keep it all on the DL."

"Well, maybe I would be", said Stone. "Interested."

"Want me to mention it to 'em?"

"Hell, yeah. Why not? You'd do that for me?"

"Sure, man. We've known each other quite a while and you're an okay guy, so – yeah. Yeah, I'll mention it to 'em. See what they say."

"Cool. Thanks, man. Just let me know."

"You got it."

And, a beat later, "Okay, look – those are the sections that hafta go", said Stone, pointing at three cracked sections of the sidewalk. "I figure we'll break 'em up and put the pieces in the back of the van. The guy said he doesn't want 'em lying around."

Gallagher nodded.

"Then, we'll mix up some shit – I got four or five bags of Sakrete back there, along with my wheelbarrow. Lay out a form with some two-by-fours and pour the shit in there. Then, we'll scrape out some of the mix so it looks like three sections and not just one big one. Sound about right?"

"Yep. Piece of cake. Let's do it."

And they began pulling tools out of the van.

While I was at the grocery store, I ran into Vic Leder.

Parker and Mike and Ron and I had helped Leder and a bunch of other parents, a few months back.

Their early-teenaged kids were on a local traveling baseball team and Leder and a few other parents were convinced that the manager – the guy who, basically, ran the team – had been screwing them out of a bunch of money.

We'd done a little investigating and found that yep, this guy – his name was Vinal – had, indeed, skimmed money off the top of some of the team's travel costs and had pocketed over twenty-thousand dollars.

And, through our somewhat unconventional method of doing things, had not only gotten the parents their money back, but we'd made sure that Vinal was confronted with his own little form of justice.

"So, how'd the team do this season?", I asked Leder after we'd exchanged pleasantries in the middle of the bread aisle.

"Pretty well, actually – considering that I took over the team after Vinal left. I mean, I didn't really know anything about managing a baseball team. I'd never done it before. It took me a while to get my feet under me, but we almost made the playoffs, so we did better than I'd expected we would."

"Well, good for you guys", I said, meaning it. "You going to run the team, next year?"

Leder nodded and said, "Yeah, I think I might. I really had a lot of fun. And the kids seemed to listen to me, which is a big plus. Even my kid." And he laughed.

"Well, I'll have to catch a game or two."

"You do that, J.D. Hell, you guys certainly pulled our butts out of the fire. We'd love to see you come around."

"Can't wait", I said, trying to get away as smoothly as possible. "Well, good to see you, Vic", and I held out my hand and we shook.

Nice guy, I thought, pushing my cart down the aisle. I was glad we were able to help him.

Ten minutes later and eighty dollars lighter, I headed back to the farm.

When I got there, I put the groceries away and carried the package of ham down to Parker's office. I'd also picked up a jar of pickles and a couple of bags of chips. Why not? I thought. Live a little.

Once I'd put that stuff away, I went over to the kids' gate to see them for a minute. I noticed that they were putting on their winter coats and were beginning to look a mite shaggy. Oh, well – it's that time of year, I thought.

When I was a kid, my grandfather told me that horses putting on their winter coats had nothing to do with the weather. That, in late fall, winter and early spring, you can have cold days and warmer days.

It all has to do with the length of daylight.

The horses' bodies know that the days are getting shorter in the fall and that's when their winter coats come on. When the days begin to get longer in the spring, they start to shed them.

And, yeah, the days were most definitely getting shorter, now. It was dark by right around six o'clock and, and once daylight savings time ends, it'll be dark by five.

"Look at you guys", I said to them, while we were all standing at the gate. "Gettin' a little hairy around the edges. And that poop on your side looks exceedingly attractive, m'boy." Zeus had obviously rolled on the ground and his left rear flank had found its way into one of their piles of manure. When their hair is short, that stuff'll usually fall right off but, now, with their longer coats, it has a tendency to stick. No matter – I usually just curry it off or, on warmer days, hit it with the hose.

We fooled around for another few minutes and then, after a couple of treats to each of them, I bid them adieu and headed back to the house.

The World Series wouldn't start 'til Friday and, yep, the Yanks were in it. With the Mets, no less! A Subway Series! I thought that was pretty cool, though I had been hoping for the Dodgers. After all, they were my old hometown team. But the Mets had whipped 'em in six.

Anyway, that meant no game on TV tonight.

Shit.

I might have to break down and order Netflix or something.

As I was walking up the porch stairs, my phone rang.

Ron.

"Wassup, dude?"

"Hey", he said. "Quick question."

"Shoot."

"You ever hear of a group called the 'Ministers of Defense'?"

"What – like a music group? No, I don't think so."

"Negative, my liege", he said with a chuckle. "I'm talking about a right-wing group called the Ministers of Defense."

"Oh. Oops. Well, no, obviously not. Why?"

"Well, you know, with our sniffing around at all those groups, recently, and with me assigned to your area, I've heard a few things about some rag-tag goofballs who may or may not be going by that name. At this point, they're really nothing, but a few of them might have ties to some of the larger groups."

"Like the Proud Boys and that?"

"Yeah, like that. Anyway, I don't really think they're anything to worry about, but they're just something that's floating around the periphery of our radar and I thought I'd just check with you to see if you've heard of anything."

"Nope. Sorry."

"Not a problem, dude. But if you do hear of anything, give me a holler, 'k?"

"Ministers of Defense, huh?", I said. "Cool name, though."

"Yeah, right? But, as I said, if they even exist at all, they're probably a small bunch of fat boy knuckleheads who'll prance around in camo thinking they're special ops guys when, in reality, Meal Team Six is more like it."

I laughed and said, "Like, 'C'mon, guys – we gotta go do a revolution but, first, let's hit the drive-thru at Mickey D's."

"Precisely, m'man. That's what most of these groups are like, but a few of them are starting to cause some righteous trouble. It's kinda our job to nip those things in the bud if we can."

"Y'all don't arrest them or anything, do you? I mean, what can you do?"

"Nah – nothing like that. But we can make some of the leaders know that we're snooping around 'em. You know, toss little hints at 'em and such. Scare 'em into thinking they've got targets on their backs. Then, we hope they give it up and go back to being regular plumbers or delivery drivers or whatnot."

"Does that work?"

“Sometimes.”

“Okay, dude. I’ll keep my eyes and ears open and I’ll mention it to Parker, too. And, if anything pops up, you’ll be the first to know.”

“Sweet”, said Ron.

And that was that – we disconnected.

I went into the house, thinking about how screwed up things were getting.

<u>CHAPTER 6</u>

As promised, Parker was at the farm bright and early the next morning.

We got into my car and headed for The Coffee Spot.

"You know how to get to that Planned Parenthood place?", he asked me.

"Yeah, I looked it up. We go down 9 into town and then we make a left on Church Street. Church becomes East-West Arterial and it's only a couple of blocks from there, on the right. Piece of cake. A little less than a half-hour."

"My daughter and her family live off East-West, probably a little farther east, though. I usually take the back roads from my place."

"Yeah, I saw that, too, but from The Coffee Spot, it's a straight shot down 9."

"Funny,", Parker said, "but I've probably driven past that Planned Parenthood dozens of times, but I never knew it was there."

"No need for you to, I guess."

"Yeah."

When we walked into the place, Parker walked over to the guys, but I spotted Suze taking an order from a nearby booth. I hung for a sec 'til she had written it down and came over to me.

"Morning, J.D.", she said with a smile.

"Suze", I said, nodding. "Hey, listen – the ride down to the place'll take about half an hour. But, finding a parking place and all, maybe we should give it forty-five minutes. What time's your appointment, again? Nine-thirty?"

"Yeah."

"Okay, then we should leave here around eight forty-five. That work for you?"

"Sure, whatever. And, thanks, man. I really appreciate it."

"Parker'll be going with us. He'll ride shotgun."

"We might need that, considering all the things that are going on with those places, lately", and she winked.

"Yeah, well, he's an ex-cop, so there's that."

"Good to know. Alright, I gotta get this order in. See ya." And off she went to the kitchen.

As I walked over to our table, it hit me that I hadn't thought about some of the problems that Planned Parenthood had been having. Yeah, but this was New York and everything's cool, here.

"Gentlemen", I said as I took my unassigned assigned seat. "Que paso?"

Well, it seemed the conversation was centered around a little thing that had happened a couple of nights ago. According to Hal, he'd seen a tweet from a reporter from the New York Times that said that Charlie Kushner, Jared Kushner's father, had been in a restaurant in Rhinebeck, earlier that night. And, that the father put his son on the phone to say hello to the wait staff.

Oh.

"Oh", I said.

"Yeah, well,", said Joe, "we were wondering if it was this place." And he laughed.

"Had to be Terrapin", said Marquardt. "Guy like that probably doesn't come into greasy spoons like this. Terrapin's more his style."

Terrapin is a fancy, expensive restaurant, right in the middle of downtown Rhinebeck. The kind with twenty-dollar appetizers and forty-and-up entrees. None of us Geezers had ever been there.

Just then, Gretchen walked up.

"Hey, Gretchen", said Joe. "Any truth to the rumor that Jared Kushner's father was in here the other night?"

"Who?"

"You know", said Joe, "Jared Kushner – Ivanka's husband."

"Oh, for the love of God", she said. "I hope not. Why?"

And, again, the little tale was told. Once it was and Gretchen had rolled her eyes a couple of times, Joe said, "The old man might make quite a catch for you, Gretchen. Got money out the wazoo, from what I hear."

"There's not enough money in the world for that, Mister Joe. You oughta know that by now."

"Yeah, I do. I was just shittin' ya."

She looked over at me and raised her eyebrows, as in, "We okay for this morning?"

I nodded and smiled.

"Okay, then. Now that we all know that I will never be Missus Kushner – or Ivanka's mother-in-law - what're y'all gonna have? Oh – by the way, Bill – I've had several people compliment us on the jack-o'-lantern."

Parker smiled and nodded and Hal said, "Oh, that reminds me, Parker – I have two big pumpkins out in the car for you."

"I'm ridin' with this guy, this morning", said Parker, indicating me with his chin. "When we're done here, we'll put 'em in the back of his car."

"Good, thanks", said Hal. "Don't let us forget."

"I won't."

"Ahem", said Gretchen. "Gentlemen?"

And we all ordered, as ordered.

While we were waiting, Mike asked Hal, "So – what's the movie tonight?" It was movie night at the People's Center.

"Well, we're going a little off the beaten path, tonight, Mike. You know, we usually show funny movies or romantic comedies and, well, most of them are pretty light fare. But, tonight, we're showing 'Yentl' – the Barbra Streisand film. It has a lot of good music in it and it was pretty popular with our (finger quotes) target audience when it first came out. So, I think they'll like it."

"She won some awards for that, didn't she? Streisand?", asked Mike.

"Yeah, like an Oscar or something", said Bob. "And nobody's got a voice like hers."

We were all in the process of agreeing with him when Gretchen came at us with her tray. "Back off, you guys – hot stuff."

And, just like always, silence ensued while our individual feed bags were in the process of being emptied.

Once I laid my fork down, I looked at the clock on the wall. Eight-twenty-five. Cool. We had time enough to finish up here, move the pumpkins into the car and get ready to split with Suze. But I didn't want to dawdle.

Plus, we wanted the other guys to leave before us so they didn't see Suze getting into the car with us. That would require some kind of explanation and, well, that wouldn't work.

I needn't have worried. Bob said he was in a hurry, Mike had an early meeting and Joe just went along with the crowd. So, as soon as Gretchen cleared the table, we all stood up, rained our twenties onto it and made for the door.

Parker and I walked with Hal to his Crown Vic, grabbed two monster pumpkins and headed for the back of my Subaru.

"Jesus, Hal – these are big enough", said Parker. "They're like friggin' beach balls."

"Well, it's a big place", said Hal. "I figured the pumpkins have to be big, too."

We got them situated in the back and put a couple of old rags that I had lying in there around their bases so they might not roll around. They were pretty secure. Good enough for gummint work, anyway.

"Okay", said Parker. "I oughta have these done for you by this weekend or the first of the week. That okay?"

"Oh, absolutely", said Hal.

"And, tell you what – either I'll bring 'em to the place or J.D. and I'll bring 'em over – probably one morning after breakfast, soon as they're done."

"Works for me", said Hal. "Okay – I'd better get going. I'm going over there, now, to make sure we get all the chairs and tables set up for the movie, tonight. See you guys in the morning."

We said our sayonaras and Hal fired up the ol' Crown Vic and pulled out like an old lady. Because that was Hal.

"I told Suze we'd leave about a quarter-to-nine", I said. "It's almost that, now."

And, like clockwork, the employee door opened and here came Suze and Gretchen.

"I saw you guys all leaving", said Suze, "so I came right out."

Gretchen asked her, "You sure you're going to be alright, now?"

"Oh, hell, yeah, Aunt Gretchen – it's just a check-up."

Gretchen playfully back-handed Suze's arm and said, smiling, "I told you not to call me that – makes me feel old."

"Right – Gretchen", said Suze, returning the smile.

"We've got this, kid", I said to Gretchen. "Quick trip down, a little check-up and a quick trip back. Depending on how long Suze's thing lasts, I'd say we ought to be back here by late morning."

"You'll call me when you're finished", Gretchen said to Suze.

"Promise."

"Okay", said Parker. "Let's saddle up."

The two women gave each other a little hug and Parker opened the front passenger's door. "Madame", he said, with a little bow.

"I thought J.D. said you were riding shotgun", she said to him.

"I shoot better from the back seat. Now, hop in."

We headed out and went south on Route 9.

After a couple of minutes, Suze said, "I don't know how I got myself into this mess. Well, hell, yeah – I do know. But I just fucked up and didn't take my pills for quite a while. I went for the more *natural* means of birth control. Meaning I didn't do anything. Idiot."

Parker: "Didn't you -?"

"Use protection?", she interrupted him. "Yeah, well…..no. I guess it was the heat of the moment or something. Again, complete idiocy."

"Live and learn, I guess", I said.

"Fu-u-uck", she said. "I seem to have a habit of learning things the hard way." She paused, then said, "Anyway, I gotta get this behind me and just move on from there, I guess. One step in front of the other."

We drove in silence for a couple of minutes.

"Hey", Parker said from the back seat, "tell me a little bit about this Krav Maga thing. Really – you any good?"

"I can kick your ass, old man", she said, laughing.

"Ooh – that's low", he shot back as I glanced over at her to see the grin on her kisser.

"Nah, I was just kidding, Parker. But, yeah – I'm pretty good at it. See, you learn to use all of your body parts, like the hands, the knees, your feet, your elbows – everything. And you use them almost all at once, all at the same time. And you learn the most vulnerable parts of your opponent and you attack those parts."

"Okay", he said.

"See, the idea is to strike as hard as you can as fast as you can. You just go for broke, right away – no fucking around. You go in for the kill – or, well, you know – right from the get-go. And you take no prisoners, you just try to immediately devastate your opponent. Never give 'em a chance."

"Yeah", he said. "I saw a few guys back on the force use that against some bad guys. The – um, confrontations – were over almost before they began. Pretty rough shit."

"That's the idea", she said. "Hey – is that the Hudson over there?" She was looking through the trees to her right.

"Yep. That's Henry Hudson's river", I said, realizing that I'd just sounded like an old fart. Inward cringe.

"Looks wider and bigger than I'd imagined it", she said.

"It's one of the largest rivers in the country", said Parker. "Starts up around Albany, somewhere, and ends up in the Atlantic."

"I'd like to go see it up close, sometime", she said.

"Well, that's easy enough", I said.

A few minutes later, we made our left turn onto Church Street. "This turns into East-West Arterial in a couple of blocks", I said. "Then, the Planned Parenthood'll be on our right side."

As we slowed down, looking for it, we saw something we hadn't expected to see. At least, I hadn't expected to see it and I'm sure Parker hadn't either. I didn't know about Suze.

There were probably twenty to thirty people milling about in front of the building, some with placards and some without.

"Fuck", said Suze.

"Ah, Jesus", said Parker.

I saw that there was a circular drive running in front of the building and I turned in. Slowly.

When the crowd saw us, they kind of surged toward us, yelling and shouting. I noticed that none of them looked particularly dangerous – there were a number of middle-aged women, a few younger women and only a handful of men, probably the younger women's husbands or something.

"KILLER!", they shouted. "BABY KILLER!" And shit like that. How they knew we were here for an appointment was beyond me – maybe they screamed at every vehicle that drove in.

"Oh, fuck", I said.

"Pull right up in front", said Parker, leaning over the front seat. "I'll get out, open Suze's door and put my arm around her and walk her in. You just sit here with the doors locked 'til I get back. Won't take but a minute."

I looked over at Suze and she didn't look the least bit flustered. As a matter of fact, she held her head proudly and stared right back at the protestors.

"Alright, Parker – let's do this", she said.

And Parker got out, opened her door and put his arm around her shoulders. And the two of them, in tandem, walked through a gauntlet of shouts, screams and placards being waved in their faces.

I was relieved to see that violence didn't seem to be a part of the mix. It was pretty much just intimidation – or attempted intimidation. Which, I could also see, wasn't working at all with my two friends. They both walked into the front door like they owned the place.

I was extremely proud of them.

Once they'd gone inside, the crowd turned and came my way. Oh, great, I thought.

They surrounded the car and kept up their yelling and screaming. One middle-aged maven even hawked a loogie on my windshield. That was an attractive move, I thought. Basically, I just sat there and smiled and gave them a little wave if they got too close to a window.

Less than a minute later, I saw Parker coming through the front door. And, then, the crowd bailed on me and headed for him. He just walked toward the car like they weren't even there. Actually, he'd adopted his detective persona and looked like he meant business. Which was kind of funny, because they gave him plenty of room coming down the sidewalk.

He opened the door and the noise from the crowd got a lot louder. He sat down and closed the door and it got a lot quieter, again.

"Alright", he said, "let's blow this pop stand."

And I put the car in gear and slowly made my way out of the driveway. A couple of the protestors half-heartedly walked in front of me and another glob of spit hit the windshield but, other than that, we had pretty clear sailing.

"She said she'll call you as soon as she's finished. The lady at the front desk said it should take about an hour, maybe a little less. They took her right in."

"Okay. What'll we do 'til then?", I asked, having not thought about it ahead of time.

"Shit, I dunno. Maybe go grab a cup of coffee?"

"And a piece of pie?", I asked.

"Now, you're talkin'. Go right, here. There's gotta be someplace on this road – it's, like, a main road."

About a quarter mile up, on the left-hand side, we spied a Denny's.

"Pull in there", said Parker, pointing at it. "Y'know, Denny's has some pretty good pecan pie. They're kinda famous for it."

"Well, let's go relieve 'em of some of their inventory", I said, hitting my turn signal.

Twenty minutes later, we were on our second mug of coffee and our plates were clean in front of us.

"I could go for another piece o' that pecan", said Parker. "It was good – almost as good as Crockett's. Which, by the way, they haven't had, lately. Have to ask 'em about that."

The waitress gladly brought us each another piece.

We talked about this and that, but nothing earth-shattering. Actually, we were just wasting time 'til my phone rang.

Which it did, in another few minutes.

"Suze", I said, answering.

"Done. Come get me", she said.

"On our way. Five or six minutes. And you wait inside 'til Parker comes and gets you."

"Nah, fuck that. Just pull up out front – I'll come out on my own. I'll just ignore the fuckers."

"You sure?"

"Hell, yeah, I'm sure. Now, just get over here, will ya?"

On the way back to the place, I said to Parker, after telling him the plan, "That Suze is one tough cookie. She takes zero shit."

Parker said, "Y'know, I'll bet that Gretchen was that way when she was younger, too. I mean, she's probably mellowed a bit, but, still, she takes shit from nobody."

"Maybe it runs in the family", I said.

He nodded.

And, just like before, the same crowd of protestors did the same thing they'd done before. By now, we knew they were harmless, though – just a bunch of people protesting something they didn't believe in. Which was fine – First Amendment and all.

"Y'know, in some parts of this country, these pro-life people are a helluva lot more violent than these fools", said Parker. "These people, basically, look like they ain't got anything better to do and this is a social thing for 'em. Probably come out here every day to hang with their buddies."

As Suze saw me pull into the driveway, she came out and down the sidewalk, getting to the curb before we did. She was surrounded by people yelling, "BABY KILLER!" and all that, again, but she simply paid them no mind.

As I pulled up, she opened the back door and slid in. "My knights in shining armor", she said.

"How'd it go?", I asked her.

"How do you think it went? I'm pregnant, goddammit. But I made an appointment for an abortion for the day after tomorrow. Same time – nine-thirty. They said it'd take just about as long as this appointment took – like, less than an hour, start to finish."

We headed west and, and as we came to the turn onto Route 9, she said, "They were awfully nice. I mean, really. They gave me some counseling and all that, which I didn't really want but, because they seemed to care so much, I went along with it. And, really, I'm glad I did. It was nice."

I didn't quite know how to respond to that, so I just said, "I've heard real good things about Planned Parenthood. Like, they really do care and all."

"Well,", said Suze, "if this place is any indication, that's pretty true, I guess."

"Hey", said Parker, half-turning to her. "You'd better call Gretchen."

"Oh, right."

"Tell her we'll be there in about half an hour", I said.

"Got it."

CHAPTER 7

We rolled back into the parking lot just before eleven.

Suze said, "Good – got back before the lunch crowd."

"By the way - how do you like being a waitress?", I asked her.

"How would you like it?", she retorted, her smile softening the comment. "Sucks. I mean, it's fine and all, but it's not really what I envision doing for very long. Might be great for Gretchen, but not for me, y'know?"

"Gotcha", I said. "Okay – you wanna just jump out and we'll keep going?"

"Sure", she said as I stopped the car. "Okay, you guys – thanks. Really. You guys are great."

"Tell Gretchen we'd like to stop and chat, but we've got some chores to do up at the farm", said Parker.

"Will do. See y'all in the morning." And she got out and walked toward the employees' door.

"Well, there you have it", I said, pulling out onto the road. "Suze."

"I like the kid", said Parker.

"Yeah, me, too."

We drove for a minute, and then Parker said, "Hey, that pie was good, wasn't it?"

"Sure was."

"We'll get some more on Friday morning."

"Yep."

Right about then, Mark Fisher walked back into his shop, having come from making a 'house call' to repair a customer's desktop computer. He, along with a couple of his employees, made house calls fairly often because that kind of personal touch seemed to bring him a lot more business. Plus, laptops are one thing – they're easy to carry and bring into the shop – but desktops were a lot more work for the average Joe. Not to mention, he charged a hefty fee for each house call.

"Mark, a woman called a few minutes ago, asking for you", said Krista, the secretary-receptionist-office manager. "She said it's kind of important."

"What – did she forget her password or something?", he asked.

"Har-dee-har-har-har", said Krista. "You haven't used that one since yesterday. No, I asked her what the problem was with her computer and she said it wasn't about computers. That it was personal. What – you got a side chick I don't know about or something?"

"No, I'm not suicidal", he chuckled. "Did she leave her name and number?"

"Yeah, I've got it right here, someplace.....okay, here it is." And she handed him a piece of paper.

"Alright", he said, looking at it, "I guess I'll call her." And he walked into his office and sat down at his desk.

Sheila Branson, huh? he thought. Never heard of her. Oh, well.....

And he picked up the phone and dialed.

After the second ring, he heard, "Sheila Branson."

"Oh, hi, Ms. Branson. This is Mark Fisher at Fisher Computer Repair. You called?"

"Why, yes, Mark - and thanks for getting back to me so quickly. Have you got a minute?"

"Well, I, uh – "

"It's rather important, Mark. And, really, it's about how our group might be able to help you with the school board."

"Your group?", he asked.

"Yes, Moms for Liberty."

He thought for a couple of seconds. "Ah, yes. There were a few of those women at the school board meeting the other night if I'm not mistaken."

"Correct", she said. "And I was the one who saw to that."

"You were?"

"Yes. See, Mark, I'm the de facto head of our local – uh, chapter, if you will – of the Moms for Liberty organization. Have you heard of us?"

"Well, maybe. I don't know, though, really. But, haven't you folks been involved in what's been happening down in Florida?"

"Yes, Mark, that's us. And we've been fortunate enough to have gained some real traction down there, too. I'm sure you've heard the governor's stance on many school issues, like the masking mandates and his drive to remove a lot of offensive literature from schools and from the textbooks they use. He's a very big supporter of ours."

"Well, Florida's certainly at the forefront of getting involved in our children's education", he said. "Actually, some of the things that I'd like to see happen here in Rhinebeck are based on Florida's actions."

"And that's exactly why I would like to meet with you, Mark. We feel that we can be of some very valuable assistance to you."

"I see", he said. "Well, you know, of course, that I've only recently gotten onto the board and I'm but a single voice against several others who rather vehemently disagree with me. As do most of the district's parents."

"Oh, I understand that, Mark. And that's why we think we might be able to help you. As you saw from the turnout the other night, we are very good at organizing and turning out the right kind of people, the right kind of parents. And, I might add, the group we put together the other night was done on very short notice."

He gave a little chuckle and said, "Well, I have to say that I was pretty surprised that I heard from *anybody* that agreed with me, let alone several people."

"We can do better than that, too, Mark."

"How?"

"Like I said, we know how to organize. And it isn't just at school board meetings, either. We are often at things like town council meetings and public gatherings and the like."

She continued, "And it's not solely about education, either. We delve into other issues that we feel are important. Conservative issues, Mark. For example, in some areas of the country, we're helping to put pressure on state legislatures to tighten down their states' laws on abortion, given the recent Supreme Court decision."

"Okay", he said, coming to a decision. "I guess I'm sold. At least on having a meeting with you."

"Great, Mark. When and where would be convenient for you?"

"Well, I'm pretty busy all day long, what with running this business. And I don't usually finish up 'til late. At that point, I go home and help my wife with the kids. I have two – one's in kindergarten and the other's three. So, you see, my wife's pretty much shot by that time of day and I head home to spell her. But I could probably do an early breakfast if that'd work for you."

Branson said, "I'm an early riser and breakfast would work, just fine. Where would you like to meet?"

"Well, I live just south of town and I drive up Route 9 to the store every morning. And, there's a place on the left-hand side – kind of a diner, really. It's called The Coffee Spot. It's right next to that new park they're putting in. Do you know it?"

"Oh, sure. I drive by it all the time, but I've never been in there. Want to meet there?"

"Sure", said Fisher. "But it has to be early. I open up around eight-thirty."

"Just tell me what time and I'll be there", said Branson.

"How's seven? Does seven work for you?"

"Certainly", she said. "And how's tomorrow?"

"Tomorrow's fine, Sheila. I'll meet you there at seven."

And, after another nicety or two, they disconnected.

Hm, thought Fisher – if these people really can help me.....

"Mark – you finished?", he heard Krista yell to him. "Bobby's waiting on the line. He needs to ask you a question about a job he's on, right now."

"Yep, I'm good", he said, picking up the phone and punching the blinking light. "Hey, Bobby – what's up?"

About fifteen miles south and a little east of there, Flint Stone and his crew of two others were working on demolishing the old brick steps that led up to the Annandale Arms Apartments. Stone had gotten the job to replace the brick flooring on the front porch of the building, along with the steps.

It was most definitely a three-man job and it'd probably take them two full days to pull out all of the old bricks and another three days to lay in and cement grout all the new ones. It was a pretty big job – at least for Stone.

He'd hoped to get Gallagher to crew for him, but Gallagher'd gotten another gig that would last for a couple of days so he'd gotten ahold of a couple of other guys that he often used. And they were good, too. Hard workers and they knew what they were doing.

For one thing, they were careful with the old bricks. They chipped away the grout and pulled the old bricks up, separating the ones that weren't broken or chipped from the ones that had damage.

Stone had brought his dump trailer with him and the guys stacked the good used ones in the back of it. Stone knew a place that would pay good money for old red, unbroken bricks. He figured he'd get about five hundred bucks for what they'd save and he'd split that little side bit of profit with the two workers so it was in their best interest to do that part of the job right.

The other, broken, bricks were put into a small dumpster that Stone had delivered and sat out in the street in front of the building.

As they were breaking for lunch, Stone's phone rang. It was Gallagher.

"Hey, Eric. What's up?"

"Ah, I'm working a gig that's a real pain in the ass. Gotta carry a ton of shit from a backyard out to a dumpster. We can't get our Bobcat through the opening in the fence. Shoulda taken your job, but this one came in first."

"Sorry to hear that, man – but you didn't call me to complain about that, didja?"

"Um, no. Look, dude – I talked to a couple of those guys last night. You know – the ones we talked about."

"Yeah?"

"Yeah", said Gallagher. "And a couple of 'em would like to meet you."

Nice, thought Stone. "Cool", he said. "How do we go about doing that?"

"Well, most nights, after work, they stop in for a few brews at Maude's, out on 199, about a mile this side of the bridge. You know the place?"

"Yeah – I have been there a couple of times. The right-hand side of the road going west, right?"

"Yep, that's the one. Anyway, they suggested you meet 'em there."

"When?", asked Stone.

"Oh, the next couple'a of nights – doesn't really matter. But somewhere between, like, five-thirty and seven."

"That'll work. Probably won't be tonight, but I'll be there tomorrow night, for sure. You'll tell 'em?"

"Nah", said Gallagher. "But if you're gonna be there tomorrow night, I'll make a point of being there, too. You know, like to introduce you guys and so on."

"Good", said Stone.

"Hey – how's the job going?"

"Going good, m'man. We'll probably get about half a stack for the decent old bricks we're pulling outta here. Gonna split it with the guys."

"Fuck", said Gallagher. "And here I am, carrying shit like some old pack mule. Ah, well – such is life. See you tomorrow."

"Yep."

Good, thought Stone. It was high time that he tried to make a little bit of a difference – whatever that meant. But, from what he'd been hearing on the radio and what little he'd seen on social media, guys were sorta mounting up all over the country. He guessed that he should, too.

As he grabbed his lunchbox out of the truck and walked back toward the house to eat with the other guys, he noticed that there were some scudding clouds overhead and there was a definite chill in the air. Well, that's October, he thought. He was glad he'd remembered to wear his hoodie, this morning.

____

Back at the farm, with the chores done, Parker had taken Hal's pumpkins into the garage and was thinking about what he'd do with them.

I went in to join him because it had begun to drizzle and, though I'd been out with Zeus and Ceres, they decided that standing inside the barn was a better idea than standing there, getting wet. So, following their lead, I'd ducked into the garage.

"What're you gonna do with 'em?", I asked Parker, obviously meaning the pumpkins that were sitting there on the workbench.

Staring at them, he said, "Y'know what I was thinking? I was thinking of carving 'em like the two faces of the theater. You know, one with a big smile and the other with a sad face. Look." And he showed me what he was talking about in a picture on his phone.

"I was thinking about that", he continued, "because Hal wants to put 'em in the big room where they show the movies, right?"

"Oh, yeah. Hey – good idea."

"Yeah – I figure he can put one on one side of the screen or the stage and one on the other. Sort of like bracketing the screen. And, when he shows those two Halloween-type flicks, it oughta look pretty cool in that dark room with the jack-o'-lanterns all lit up inside."

"Y'know", I said, "you just may have missed your calling, being a cop. You could've been an artiste or something. You're good at this shit."

He chuckled and said, "Yeah – a starving artist? I don't think so, amigo."

He turned one slowly on the bench, looking for the right spot to do the carving. "Yeah – here", he said. A few seconds later: "Hey, listen – I don't wanna pry – but you doing anything with that Spencer Sales Associates thing?" He was still eyeballing the pumpkin.

Oh, yeah – that.

See, once I'd left LA and the career I'd had back there, I figured that I needed something to do once I got here. So, I'd put together a two-day seminar that I call the 'Spencer Sales Circle', run by a company called Spencer Sales Associates – which was moi. Without going into a lot of detail, it's designed to maximize salespeople's effectiveness by identifying and polishing up all of their efforts during the sales process, from the original contact with a potential client all the way through to closing the sale.

At first, I thought I'd market it to small and mid-sized companies but, in reality, it had been a few graduate business classes at colleges and universities that had shown the most interest and, actually, had been the sum total of my business.

The thing is, I'm not sure I like doing that. Not anymore, anyway. I'd gotten some money from Mom's estate – along with the farm - and I had some socked away from what I'd earned in the newspaper business, which was not inconsequential.

I really just like living on the farm, doing whatever it is I do around here. And, honestly, living here is dirt cheap, at least compared to LA. So, I really don't need the extra dough. Not really, but the five grand – plus expenses - that I take in from each seminar certainly doesn't hurt. Plus, I kind of like doing it – the act of actually giving the seminar, that is. It's like I'm onstage or something and people – well, most people, anyway – seem to pay attention. I just really don't like having to go through the process of looking for business, though. Plus, I don't really want to travel. So, yeah – it's kind of a quandary.

Ergo, Parker's question was one that I really didn't have an answer for.

Maybe I should send out another round of emails to the 'prospect list' I keep in my small upstairs office. It seems that the few times I've done that, I've gotten a job. I don't know.

"Fuck, man – I don't know", I said. "Maybe I should send out a few emails, but my heart isn't really in it. You know that." I didn't say anything for a few seconds, then, "Whadda you think I should do?"

"Totally up to you, dude", he shrugged. "Whatever you want. Life is short – do what you want to do."

So, with that piece of useless advice ringing in my ears, I decided to do what I usually do: ignore it. Probably.

"Look", said Parker, "I'm gonna start on this, now. And, yeah – I think I'll go with the theater faces. But though I love you like a brother, I don't want you breathing down my neck while I'm working. So, you go do your email thing or go watch TV or go play with yourself, I don't care. Just get the hell outta here and let me work."

"Fucking artiste", I said. "Alright, you put on your beret and do your little art shit. I'll be up in the house."

"Bite me."

It was raining a little harder when I left the garage, so I hot-footed it up to the house.

Shit, I thought when I got up onto the porch, it was getting cold. And I don't think I've got a warm jacket. Hell, back in LA, we didn't even think about stuff like this. And, damn – I'd probably need two – a jacket to wear in weather like this and a winter thing for when it really gets cold.

Wait – what's the name of that place I've passed in town? Shit, I couldn't remember, so I looked it up on my phone. Oh, right – Cabin Fever Outfitters and it's right on Montgomery Street.

So, I hustled back down to the garage and told Parker that I was going to run down into town and buy a couple of jackets.

"You're gonna need 'em", he said, over his shoulder. "This ain't like La-La Land in the late fall and winter."

So, twenty minutes later, I'd been lucky enough to find a parking place on Montgomery Street, just up the block from the store. The rain had let up to just a sprinkle and I was kind of looking around as I walked.

I noticed a flyer on a streetlight pole – which wasn't all that unusual. People were always putting up things like that. But this one caught my eye – and not in a good way. I stopped to look at it.

And I didn't like what I saw.

There, on an eight-and-a-half-by-eleven flyer was the big, black, bold headline, 'NO CRT IN SCHOOLS' and, below it and dominating the flyer, were the letters 'CRT' – in even bigger and bolder letters - with one of those red circles with a diagonal line attached, printed over the three letters. But that was it. Nothing that identified a group or individual who may have put it up.

I looked down the street and saw a couple of other ones on a couple of other lamp posts, but some of them must've been torn down because they weren't on every one of them.

Now, I was adroit enough and well-read enough to know that this was a bogus issue, as far as it is taught in schools, but that, for some reason, it had gained traction in some parts of the country.

But, Jesus, I thought. Rhinebeck? Really – Rhinebeck?

This just doesn't seem like the kind of place where this stuff would pop up.

Maybe I was wrong.

CHAPTER 8

I removed the flyer from the lamp post and folded it and stuck it into my pocket. I figured that I'd show it to Parker. Maybe even Mike, too, because, maybe, the issue had come up in the council. Plus, I didn't want any more of those things floating around town, though I didn't go so far as to walk down the street, tearing them down.

I walked into the store and, twenty minutes later, walked out with a fleece-lined vest, a lightweight, but sturdy-looking, Patagonia jacket, a lined heavy-duty jacket with a hood and a wallet that was lighter by a whole lot.

Okay, fine, I thought. I'd probably have these for years and, and if I amortized the cost over that time period, my yearly outlay wouldn't be so bad. At least that's what I told myself.

I wore the vest and carried the other two jackets out to the car, the skies only offering up a fine mist at that point.

As I headed out of town, I kept my eye on the lamp posts, but noticed that I didn't see any more of those flyers – they seemed to be only along Montgomery Street, one of the two main drags in Rhinebeck. I didn't know what that meant, but I did notice it.

Back at the farm, when I pulled up in front of the garage, I could see Parker still working on his pumpkins.

"Dude", I said, getting out of the car and grabbing my new purchases. "Look."

"Wow", he said. "Fancy duds. Patagonia, huh? Good shit, but expensive. Hey - and you got a vest, too. I love mine – keeps your body warm enough but your arms are free. Nice winter thing, too. Good job, m'man."

"Yeah – expensive as shit, too."

"What isn't?", he asked.

"Oh, hey", I said, pulling the flyer out of my pocket. "Look what I found on a bunch of light poles along Montgomery Street."

Looking at it, he shook his head and said, "Fuck. This shit is pure lunacy. Like, this CRT doesn't even really exist, but a bunch of goofy-assed fools think it's for real. And these were posted along Montgomery Street?"

"Yeah."

"Ah, maybe it's just some right-wing goofball who has too much free time on his hands. This whole area's pretty progressive, for the most part. Not so, across the river but, on this side of it…..Ah, hell – but you never know, these days."

"I thought I might show it to Mike in the morning – see if anybody's mentioned 'em to the council."

He shrugged. "Sure", he said. "Hey, look – I'm 'bout outta here for the day. Do you need anything before I split?"

"Nope. I'm good. Oh – by the way, I laid in some ham and mustard and a jar of pickles into your fridge, yesterday."

"Cool."

"Oh, yeah - and while I was at Topps, I ran into Vic Leder. Remember him? The guy who led us to Vinal."

"Yeah? How's he doin'?"

"He said he's doing well. And he thinks he'll coach the team again, next year. Says he had a lot of fun with it after Vinal left."

"Cool. Maybe we'll catch a game or two."

I nodded.

"Hey – how're those things coming?", I asked, pointing at the pumpkins on the workbench. "Can I take a look?"

"Nope. Not 'til they're done. It's going quicker than I thought it would, though. I should have 'em done by tomorrow – early. Maybe we can take 'em over to the place tomorrow afternoon."

I nodded again. "Cool. Just let me know. Alright, get outta here. I'll catch you in the ayem."

And I headed to the house and he headed to his truck. He gave me a couple of short toots as he drove out.

I took the tags off of my two new jackets and hung them on wooden hooks that were on the kitchen wall. Huh, I thought. I've been past that coat rack hundreds of times in the past few months and never gave it a thought. And, now, for the next few months, it'd be a part of my daily life. Not an earth-shattering thought, by any means, but, well, you know.

I half-thought of going upstairs and doing something with the Spencer Sales Associates thing but talked myself out of it in about three seconds. Maybe tomorrow.

I screwed around doing this and that for a while. Tossed some dirty clothes into the washing machine and swept the kitchen floor and I don't know what else. Then, as it started to get dark, I heated up a can of Grandma Brown's Bean Soup and made a grilled cheese and tomato sandwich.

I took my early dinner into the living room and turned on ESPN. They had Wednesday night college football games, usually smaller schools, though. And, tonight, it would be Western Michigan and the University of Toledo. Kick-off was only a couple of minutes away.

I ate and I watched the first couple of quarters. At the half, it was WM up by ten. In the rain. With a crowd of no more than fifteen hundred.

Ah, screw it, I thought, and hit the hay early. Don Winslow's 'City On Fire' was waiting on my nightstand.

The next morning, when the alarm went off, it wasn't even really light, yet. And it was six-fifteen.

I did my morning ritual and headed out to The Coffee Spot, noticing that Mom's garden, which had been so abundant only a couple of weeks ago, was now well past its prime. Only a few lonely hearty flowers were left and a lot of the plants had turned yellow and were wilting. And that made me kind of sad.

And, when I got to the diner, I was – naturally – the last Geezer to arrive. I waved to Gretchen when she spotted me and nodded to Suze, who was taking an order from a table near the door.

As I walked to our table, I could see that the guys seemed to be pretty intense. I mean, they were all bent over their mugs and talking quietly, but there were a couple of evident frowns.

"What's up, you guys? Gretchen raise the prices or something?", I asked, sitting down.

"Nah, nothing like that, kid", said Joe. "Something happened at the People's Center last night."

"What? What happened?" I was concerned, wondering if there'd been a health problem or something.

"Well,", said Hal, "I was just telling the guys that – as you know – I drive past the Center every morning on my way here. And, this morning, there was graffiti painted on the side of the building. I could see it from the road."

"Graffiti?", I asked.

"Yeah – it was in red paint. And it said", he leaned forward to say it softly, "'Fuck Jews'."

"What?!?"

I looked around at the guys and saw nothing but steel-eyed looks.

"Yeah. And it's still there, too."

"What on earth -?", I said.

"Look", said Parker to me, "the only thing we can think of is that, last night, they showed the movie, 'Yentl', right?"

"Oh, that's right", I said, turning to Hal. "You said you were going to show that, this week."

"Well, we did. And, I must say, everybody enjoyed it immensely. And we had a big crowd, too. Probably close to a hundred people."

"Then maybe some dickhead found out about it and did that thing to the building", I said, as Gretchen walked up and filled my mug.

"That's the only thing we can figure out", said Bob. "Oh, J.D. – Gretchen knows about it. We told her a few minutes ago."

Gretchen was also pretty stone-faced. "Let me ask you, Hal", she said, "did you have flyers or something printed up? I mean, how do you promote your movies?"

"Well, yes – I design some perfunctory flyers on my computer and have a bunch of them copied at the UPS store. Then, we divvy them up to some of our patrons and they hand them out as they see fit. Oh - and we also put a bunch of them up around the Center, like around some of the walls. And we also put a flyer on each of the doors to the outside, so people can see it when they come in."

"You don't think any of your patrons did it, do you?", asked Mike.

"Oh, dear me, no", said Hal. "I mean, they're all pretty up there in years and I've never even heard a whisper of antisemitism around there. I suppose it's possible, but I'd be floored if that were the case."

"Then somebody saw one of the flyers", said Mike. "Had to be."

"Do any workmen or delivery guys come in there?", asked Bob.

"Oh, sure – but not many. Here – we get one food delivery a week and it's the same guy every time. Same with the beverage guy. They've been our delivery men almost since we opened. And they're nice guys, too – I can't imagine that either one of them would do something like this."

"How about any workmen?", asked Parker.

"Nope, not recently", he answered. "The only other service we have is our garbage removal. We have that small dumpster out back and it's emptied every week."

"Do you know the guy who drives that truck?", asked Parker.

"Oh, hell, no", said Hal. "I don't even know if it's the same guy every time. I've never even been there when the truck comes. It just drives in, empties the dumpster, and leaves."

"What are you going to do about the graffiti?", I asked.

"I don't know", said Hal, "but we have to do something pretty quick – like, today. This morning. We simply can't have that on our wall. It has to be cleaned off - and maybe painted – as soon as I can call somebody to have it done. Which should be in a little while", he said, looking at the clock on the wall. "I don't think any of those places open 'til eight - and, quite frankly – I don't even know who to call."

Parker and I looked at each other.

I said, "We'll do it. Parker and me. As soon as we're done here."

"Oh, I can't ask you fellows to do it", said Hal, shaking his head. "I'll call somebody – don't you worry."

"Nope", said Parker. "We got this. We'll run by as soon as we leave here and see what we'll need. And we'll have it back to normal before noon."

There was silence around the table for a few seconds, then Bob smiled and gave the Geezer knuckle-knock, which was joined by all of us, almost immediately. Gretchen even reached in and joined us.

"Breakfast is on the house, today, gentlemen", said Gretchen. "Order whatever you want."

We ordered our usual, not wanting to take advantage of Gretchen's generosity. And, of course, our twenties would end up in the middle of the table when our daily 'meeting' was over.

"Y'know", I said, after Gretchen headed to the kitchen, "I wonder if something's going on around here. Look what I found on a lamp post on Montgomery Street yesterday." And I pulled the flyer out of my pocket and laid it on the table.

"Aw, Jesus", said Joe. "This shit? Around here? Really?"

And there was general verbal mayhem – although in hushed tones – about the ridiculousness of this issue ever even seeing the light of day. About how it was a buzzphrase for the extreme right wing in trying to ignore or erase part of the nation's history. They thought it put white people in a bad light. Which is exactly where so many of our ancestors belonged.

"This ever come up in your council meetings, Mike?", I asked him.

"What – the issue or the fact that these flyers are on the street?", he asked.

"Well, both."

"Not that I know of. I mean, the subject has never come up in any of our meetings and I don't know if we've had any complaints about the flyers. I don't think they've been up for very long, have they?"

I shrugged. "I have no idea."

Just then, Suze walked up to greet us. And, after some small talk, she pointed at the flyer, lying on the table.

"Hey – see that? I just saw one of those over there", she said, surreptitiously pointing with her thumb.

"Where?", Mike asked.

"At that booth", she indicated with a tilt of her head. "The second one in from the door.

See? There's a guy and a woman sitting there. As I walked up to refill their mugs, she had one of those in her hand. She slipped it under the table when I walked up, but I couldn't help but see it. I mean, that red color kinda stood out."

We all kind of looked over at them, but not all at once.

"Who are they?", Joe asked.

Suze shrugged, but Mike said, "I can't really get a good look at them, but the guy might be that fellow who recently got elected to the school board. I'm not sure, though."

"Want me to ask him?", asked Suze. "I don't care – I'll just say something like, 'Hey – aren't you on the school board or something?' You know, play kinda dumb."

"No", said Bob. "I don't think so – right, guys? I mean, maybe they're just like us – wondering what the hell this is all about." We more or less concurred because Bob could be right.

"Well, whatever", said Suze, who was wearing a long-sleeved top, this morning, to hide her tats. "But that's the type of shit we see all the time in Ohio. The whole state's going nuts, as far as I'm concerned. Alright, you guys – I gotta split. Duty calls." And she gave the table a little finger wiggle wave and went off toward the kitchen.

Over at the booth in question, Sheila Branson had been explaining the Moms of Liberty organization to Mark Fisher – its origin and its philosophy and so on. From where Fisher sat, his philosophy was pretty much aligned with theirs. That the country had been under the thumb of left-wing radicals for decades and that it was sliding rapidly into a form of socialism. There were too many people of different races and different colors flooding onto our shores and that was diluting the America that the founders had envisioned. Plus, what was being taught in America's public schools seemed to blame the white race for so many of its problems.

"So,", he said, after hearing her out, "let's say we agree on most of the issues you've mentioned. I'll cut to the chase: How can your organization help me in my position on the school board? Y'know, I'm but a single voice on it. The others are almost diametrically opposed to what I believe."

"Yes, Mark, true. But, as I said, one of our strengths – one of my strengths – is organizing. Hold on….."

Suze had walked up to their table and asked if everything was okay. "You haven't touched much of your eggs, there, mister. Something wrong with them?"

"Oh….oh, no. No, they're fine, thank you", said Fisher. "It's just that we've been talking and, well, I'm afraid they've gotten cold."

"Want me to bring you some hot ones? I'll be more than glad to", said Suze.

"Oh, no, that won't be necessary", he said. "But that's very kind of you. We'll just be a few more minutes, so if you'll bring me the check, that'd be great."

"Sure, will do. More coffee?", she asked, holding up her pot.

"I'll take a little more", said Branson. Suze topped off the mug and raised her eyebrows to Fisher, who nodded in acceptance.

"Be right back with your check", said Suze, spying on the flyer that was on Branson's lap.

She went for it.

"Oh", she said, pointing at Branson's lap, "I hope you'll pardon me, but I couldn't help seeing that flyer. That CRT stuff is just plain crazy, in my opinion."

"Oh. Oh, that", said Branson, quite taken aback. "We were just discussing it. It does seem a bit – well, I don't know – a bit wrong, if you ask me. The CRT."

Fisher nodded in agreement.

"Yeah, it is. I'm glad I'm out of school", replied Suze, with a little chuckle. "Okay, I'll be right back with your check."

"See?", Branson said after Suze had left. "What we've been talking about isn't as unpopular an opinion as some of those left-wingers would have you believe, Mark. We think it's a lot more prevalent than the mainstream media makes it out to be."

Fisher nodded again, still kind of surprised by what he'd heard from the waitress.

"Okay, Mark. Here's what I propose to do", said Branson. "We'll prepare more flyers, something like this one, and will post a lot more of them than we did on what we called our 'test run'. Then, at next month's board meeting, we'll turn out a couple dozen people to demonstrate in front of the building – with signs and all. And we'll alert the media, too."

"Okay", he said. "But do you really think the media would show up?"

"I can almost guarantee it, Mark. This is pure fodder for them. The media loves this kind of stuff – especially TV news. Anyway, we'll do that plus have a larger number of people in attendance at the meeting than we did the last time. All supporting you and your proposals."

"Well, at least that'll make people sit up and take notice", he said.

"Yes, it most certainly will - and it'll also provide cover for people who feel the same way we do, but have been reticent to come forward. You'll see – it'll make a difference, a big difference."

Suze walked up and laid the check in front of Fisher, but Branson grabbed it and said, "This is on me, Mark."

"They're leaving", said Joe, quietly, a few minutes later. "Walking out the door." We all kind of nodded.

Suze came over.

"Well, you guys – those jamokes aren't on your side, that's for sure", she said. "The lady said something about CRT being 'a bit wrong', I think were her actual words. And the guy nodded in agreement. And they were very hush-hush when I dropped off their check – but they both seemed really into whatever they were talking about."

"You'd make a good spy", said Joe.

"I'd make a good lot of things, pal", she said, with a grin and a wink. "Alright, that's it. Customers await." And off she went.

"I like her", said Joe. "She takes zero shit."

We hung around for a few more minutes, then all of us got up to leave. Hal and Parker and I hung back to coordinate our mission.

Hal said, "Alright – you guys want to meet me over at the Center?"

"Yep – we'll be right behind you", said Parker.

And we headed out of the place and mounted up – Hal to his Crown Vic, Parker to his truck and me to my Sube.

And off we went.

<u>CHAPTER 9</u>

When the three of us met up in the People's Center parking lot, Hal led us around the corner of the building – to the west-facing side.

And there, a couple of feet in from the corner were the words, 'FUCK JEWS' in red spray paint, each of the letters being about a foot tall. The paint had dripped a bit, making the whole thing almost look like blood running down from the letters, though I know that wasn't the asshole's intention when he did it. Or she did it.

"Fuck", said Parker, shaking his head. He moved closer and inspected it, scratching one of the red letters with a fingernail. "Looks like you've got enamel paint on the walls. That's good because the spray paint probably didn't soak in – it's probably just on the surface."

"You don't think it'll need repainting?", Hal asked.

"I don't think so, Hal, but let's see."

"How're we gonna get it off of there?", I asked.

"I've got a little trick up my sleeve, mon ami. And it just might work. Hal – you got any baking soda, there in the kitchen?"

"Baking soda? Well, I don't know, but probably", he said.

"Let's go look."

And the three of us went in and walked back toward the kitchen. While we did, Parker said, "This would be the simplest way – if it works. If it doesn't, there are a couple of other ways to do it. But the good thing is, I don't think it'll need re-painting."

We got into the kitchen and all of us went to various cupboards. "Found some", said Hal, taking a large can of it off a shelf and setting it on the counter.

"Good", said Parker. "Now, we'll need a good-sized mixing bowl and some real hot water."

"That's it?", I asked, bewildered as to how simple baking soda and water would do the trick.

"That's it", said Parker. "Now, like I said, I'm not sure if it'll work, but I've done this before on enamel paint and it has."

Hal found a mixing bowl and we all walked over to the sink. Parker poured a bunch of the powder into the bowl and got some hot water running. Once he was satisfied with the temperature, he put some into the bowl, mixing it all into a kind of paste.

"Okay, let's go while this is hot. Oh – I'll need that sponge", he said, and I grabbed it from the counter.

Once outside, he covered the spray-painted surface with the paste. Natch, some of it fell onto the ground, but most of it stuck to the wall. When he'd covered all of the offending areas, he said, "Okay. Now, we wait for about fifteen minutes. At that point, the paint should just more or less peel right off."

"Really", I said.

"Yeah, really", said Parker.

"Oh, that would be just great, Bill. Maybe this isn't the disaster I thought it was", said Hal.

"It's still a disaster, Hal. Some antisemitic asshole defaced your building. In almost the most offensive way, too. I wanna make the motherfucker pay, whoever he – or she – is."

"How are we gonna find out who did it?", I asked. "I mean, it could've been almost anybody."

Parker shrugged and said, "Detective work, son. Like Sherlock Holmes said, 'Once you eliminate the impossible, whatever remains, no matter how improbable, must be the truth'. We've already eliminated this place's patrons. Well, probably. But somebody saw that flyer."

"Sherlock Holmes?", I asked. "You're quoting Sherlock Holmes?"

"Yes, my dear Watson, I am. Now, Hal – did your flyers have the name of this place on 'em?"

"You mean the People's Center?", asked Hal. "Yes – yes, they did."

"Okay, so people would know the movie was being shown here, in this building."

Hal nodded.

"Okay. That opens up our list of potential suspects quite a bit. I was kind of hoping that, maybe, the flyer didn't have the location on it and, therefore, somebody would've had to actually be here to have known where it was being shown. Okay, fine."

Parker led us on a walk around that area of the parking lot, looking to see – I guess – if he could spot any clues. Nope. Guess not, because he started looking up.

"Aw, Jesus", he said. "I shoulda thought of that."

"What?", I asked.

He pointed up at the corner of the building and said, "That."

"Oh, for the love of God, yes!", said Hal. "The camera!"

"It's on all night, right?", Parker asked him.

"It's on all the time. One of the fellows on our board comes over once a week and deletes the week's footage and it starts recording from the beginning, again."

"He wouldn't have done that, this morning, would he?"

"Oh, no. He usually comes over on Sunday morning and does it. No, last night's footage is still in the machine."

"Excellent", said Parker. "As soon as we get this shit off the wall – about another ten minutes – we'll go in and look at it, okay?"

"Absolutely", said Hal.

We wandered around for another few minutes, then Parker looked at his phone. "Okay – that should be ready."

And, once we got back to the wall, he carefully picked at a corner of one of the letters and, as if by magic, the corner peeled back. He gently pulled it back until the entire letter came right off the wall.

"Holy shit!", I said. "It worked!"

"Oh, ye of little faith", he said. "Come on – you guys give me a hand, here. We'll have this shit off in no time."

And, with the three of us standing shoulder-to-shoulder, we peeled off all the letters.

Standing a few feet back from the wall, we couldn't even see where the paint had been.

"I can't believe it", said Hal. "Oh, Bill – this is fantastic! Thank you."

Parker looked at me and winked, "Tricks of the trade", he said. "Okay, Hal – lead us to your machine."

"It's in the office", said Hal.

Parker sat down in a chair in front of the screen and looked down to figure out how the machine worked: play, fast forward, stop, rewind – that sort of thing.

"Okay, see?", he said. "It has the date and time down in the lower right-hand corner. Let me rewind it to last night. What time was the last person out of here, Hal?"

"Oh, probably ten-fifteen, ten-thirty. A couple of people always stay around for a few minutes to clean up."

Parker looked at him.

"Oh. Oh, no. It wouldn't be one of those folks. It's usually Marjorie and Estelle – they seem to think it's their job."

"Okay", said Parker, looking back down and hitting the rewind button.

"There", he said. "Ten-fifteen. We'll speed it up. Hold on – wait. Oh – those are your two ladies, right?" And we could see two women walking across the parking lot.

"Yep. That's Estelle and that one's Marjorie", said Hal, pointing at each woman.

"Okay, then. I'm gonna run this fast until we see anybody else in the parking lot – if we see somebody else in the parking lot."

And, the black and white images – showing a whole lot of nothing – flew by on the screen.

Suddenly, we saw something. A person. A person who walked quickly toward the building but disappeared as he or she approached.

"The camera's not focused directly downward", said Parker. "But that person's right up next to the building. This is our guy."

And, several seconds later, the person came into view again, this time walking quickly away from the building.

"Yep – that's your perpetrator", said Parker. "Let me go back and slow it way down.

Let's see if we can come up with any identifiers."

What we saw was a person – we couldn't tell if it was a man or a woman – who was wearing a light-colored hooded sweatshirt with the hood up and cinched tightly around the face. And, the rest of the face was hidden by big sunglasses. Also, the person was wearing what looked like jeans and white sneakers.

"Well, shit", said Parker. "That doesn't tell us very much. But let me go back again and see if there's anything remarkable about the way he walked – like a limp or something, though I didn't see one the first or second time."

"Looks like kind of a youngish person", I said. "I mean, he really whipped in and outta there pretty quickly. You know, like a young person would do. Not an old fart like you."

"Eat shit", said Parker, still looking at the screen.

"Judging by this person's stride", he continued, "I'd say he's around six feet tall. So, it's probably – probably – a guy. Not that women aren't that tall, but it's more unusual than it is with men. And, he's white – we can see that. And, he's not fat. We can't say he's slim or skinny by what we can see on this video, but we can see that he's not fat. Sort of normal weight for a person that size."

He rewound and we watched it again but, this time, he stopped it when the person was in the best view.

"Well, there he is. Or she is. There's our asshole", said Parker. "J.D. – can you get a decent shot of that with your phone?"

I pulled out my phone, bent down and got the image on the screen to fill my camera lens. I took three or four shots. "Got it."

"Okay, good. Now, let's run this thing forward again – past the part where we see the guy - and see if anything else pops up." So, he ran it quickly again for only a couple of seconds.

"There", he said. "There's the corner of a vehicle – see the headlight?" Hal and I both nodded.

"He must've been turning around to head out and the camera just caught the corner of the….the…look – it's truck, isn't it?" He'd stopped the video at a spot where we could see the headlights – which weren't on, by the way - and the blurry corner of a vehicle.

"Yeah, it is", I said. "It looks too big and bulky for it to be a car. Looks like some kind of a pick-up. A fairly newish one, too. Too bad this tape isn't in color."

"Take a screenshot of this, too", said Parker. And I took a few more pics.

"Looks like a light-colored truck", said Hal.

"J.D.,", said Parker, "when we get back to the farm, let's look up some late-model pick-ups on your computer. I don't wanna fuck around doing it on a phone, right now. The images in your box will be bigger. Maybe we can compare that headlight" – he pointed at the screen – "to a particular make, model and year."

"Right", I said. "Good idea."

"Hold on", said Parker, running the tape quickly from that spot forward and seeing nothing more for at least another hour. "I think we have everything we can get, right now. He or she wouldn't have come back. So, I think that's it."

He stood up and said, "Look, Hal – I don't really know if we can find the guy who did this, but the cop in me says we gotta try."

"Oh, hey", said Hal. "Do you think I should tell the police?"

Parker chuckled and said, "Now that we've destroyed the evidence?" He waited a beat, then said, "But, yeah – you should. Even after we removed the shit from the wall. Yeah – I think it'd be a good idea. Tell 'em exactly what happened and that you and two of your buddies cleaned the shit off the wall."

"I have a couple of friends on the force", Hal said.

"Even better", said Parker. "Tell them. And tell 'em that you've got this video. You can even tell 'em that you and your friends who cleaned the wall looked at it, but I wouldn't say too much more than that. I don't want 'em to think we're playing amateur detective."

"Yeah, but you are", said Hal. "Sort of."

"You know that and we know that but they don't have to know that. That'd probably just piss 'em off. Nah, just tell 'em about the whole thing the way it went down."

"I agree", I said. "And, that way, maybe they can keep an eye on the place at night. You know, send a cruiser by every once in a while."

"Yep", said Parker.

"Y'know,", said Hal, "the town's involved with this place, too. Has been since the beginning. So, the PD has a vested interest in it."

"There you go", I said.

"Okay, I think I'll head over there, now. I mean, there is a sense of urgency. And we certainly don't want anything like this happening again." And he grew quiet for a few seconds, then said, "I don't think I'll tell any of the patrons about it, though. It would just scare them and I don't want that."

"Probably a real good idea", said Parker. "Honestly, I think it was just a one-time deal – because you showed that film."

"I sure hope so", said Hal. "Okay – I should just leave this here, as is, right?" And he indicated the CCTV rig. "In case the cops want to come over and look at it."

"Yeah, I would", said Parker. "But I'd also start recording again late this afternoon, just in case anything happens tonight, which I don't believe will. But you never know."

"Okay, good. Got it."

"Alright, we're gonna split", I said.

"Aw, thanks, you guys. I'm so glad we got that stuff off the wall. That was horrible. And, honestly, I can't believe there are people like that in the area. I've never heard of anything like this happening around here."

Parker raised his eyebrows and shrugged. But thankfully, he didn't go into one of his mini-rants.

"Alright, we're outta here", I said. "We'll let you know if we can identify the truck. Otherwise, I guess we'll just see you in the morning."

And, a couple of minutes later, we were headed back to the farm.

When we got there and met in the barnyard after parking our vehicles, Parker said,

"Hey, gaucho – we haven't even touched those pies we got the other day. I'm thinkin' that we just earned some pecan with whipped cream."

"Oh, yeah. Shit, I'd almost forgotten them. Why haven't we torn into them before?"

"No idea, son, but we haven't. Let's go up and do that - and I'll tell you what hit me on the way driving back here."

All late spring and summer long and into the early fall, we'd had our mini-meetings and hang-out time on my back porch. It was a real tradition. But, now, it was getting too cold for that, so I said, "I think we have to move our base of operations to the kitchen table."

"Ya think? It's, like, fifty degrees out here. I ain't sittin' outside in fifty degrees. We'd freeze our asses off."

So, we went into the kitchen and Parker grabbed the pie off the counter, and the whipped cream out of the fridge and I fetched two forks from a drawer. I reheated a couple of mugs of the coffee I'd made but hadn't touched this morning and set them on the table, too.

"I guess this is the maiden voyage of this table", I said, sitting down at one of the six chairs around it. "Guess we'd better get used to it."

"They don't make porcelain tables like this anymore", said Parker. "Nice."

After we'd scarfed directly from the tin for a couple of minutes, I asked, "Okay – what hit you on the way back?"

"Alright. I got to thinking about that guy last night. And he was all disguised – the shades and the hoodie all drawn tight around his face."

"Yeah – so?"

"So, it makes sense that he knew there was a camera on the building. Like, ahead of time."

"Don't most buildings have cameras, nowadays?"

"Some do, a lot of 'em don't", he said. "Plus, he parked his truck away from the building – so it wouldn't get caught on camera. I mean, he didn't drive right up to the wall, jump out and paint the shit. Hell, he could've even used the truck to block the view from anybody driving past – so he wouldn't be seen doing it. But he didn't. He parked away from the building."

I thought about that for a minute. "Yeah – yeah, I can kind of see that. But what's your point?"

"My point is that there's a good chance that guy's been there before. Think about it – the disguise, which looks like it had been planned - might mean that he didn't want to be recognized. Like, maybe, somebody would know his face if they looked at the video. Some jamoke coming from across the river or something wouldn't have gone to all that trouble. At least, I don't think he would. He'd just run up and paint the damned thing. Maybe wear a ball cap or something, but the shades are what's ringing a bell with me. That, and pulling the hood tight around his face."

"You may have a point", I said. A few seconds later: "Shit, this pie's as good as advertised."

"I'll say. Hit it with more whipped cream."

"So", I said. "Who's been there? I mean, there were a lot of guys, last spring, when they were putting it up, but that was – what? - six months ago."

"Yeah, but remember – the new addition was only finished in August. That's not that long ago. Couple'a months, really. Anyway – let's just keep that in mind, because there were a number of contractors and so on coming through all the time."

"Okay."

"And, like Hal said, they got a garbage guy that comes every week. And they have no idea if it's the same guy every time or not. So, that's another opportunity to case the place, right? A real one, actually."

"Right. And Hal's already ruled out the food delivery and beverage guys."

I ate another bite, then said, "Y'know – maybe we should just let the cops deal with this. I mean, it's like, their job, no?"

"Yeah, but they won't. They're not gonna send detectives or even patrolmen out hunting some guy who spraypainted some graffiti on a building. They've got bigger fish to fry. Oh – they'll keep an eye out and, probably, even have a little meeting about it, but it'll be more like discouraging anything further, rather than tryin' to track down some fool."

"So, that's what we're gonna do? Play detectives?", I asked.

"Why not? You got anything better to do? Or is that Spencer Sales Associates stuff taking up too much of your time?"

"Ooh, that's cold", I said, but I laughed.

"Alright, run upstairs and grab your laptop. Let's see if we can identify that truck. I'll guard the pie."

CHAPTER 10

After a few minutes of exploring photos of fairly new pickups, Parker and I came to the conclusion that the vehicle in question was probably a late-model Chevy Silverado – like 2020. Probably, though it was hard to say for sure.

The truck in the photo had two vertical headlights on each side and, in looking through a lot of pics on the internet, that was somewhat unique. Not entirely unique, but pretty unique, at least among recent offerings. Plus, Silverados were fairly ubiquitous – they sold 'em by the – well, the truckload.

It wasn't the greatest piece of detective work ever attempted, but we had eliminated a lot of makes and models and like Holmes had said, if you eliminate the impossible blah, blah, blah.

Oh, and because it was light-colored on the black and white CCTV tape, we figured that it was light grey, or 'Silver Ice Metallic', in Chevy speak. It was real light, but not quite white, from what we could see.

"So, let's go with the 2020 Silverado 1500 in Silver Ice Metallic, okay?", said Parker. "What we don't know is if it's a two-door, four-door, or a crew cab, though two-doors are pretty rare, these days."

"Yep", I said. "Now, what are we gonna do with this information?"

"I don't rightly know", said Parker. "But if you – or we – happen to run into a slim, six-foot guy who's driving a '20 light grey Silverado……"

"Well, that narrows it down", I said, with my tongue firmly planted on my cheek. "There are probably only a few hundred of those guys cruising around the area at any one time."

"I know, I know", he said. "But at least it's a start. And that's what detective work is – putting little pieces of the puzzle together and hoping you get a hit."

I thought for a minute, then said, "Look – if we ever do find out who did it, the cops wouldn't do anything about it, anyway, right? I mean, like you said, it's really small potatoes. Plus, we really don't have any evidence. I mean, unless the guy does it again or gets caught in the act or something, nothing'll be done."

"True."

"I know what could be done."

He looked at me, then said, "Me, too. And we could absolutely fucking ensure that he'd never do it again."

"Bingo. Alright, let's see where all this takes us. Hey – you done with the pie, for now?", I asked.

"Yeah, guess so. It's really outstanding, though, isn't it? Especially with that homemade whipped cream. And, look," – he pointed over to the counter – "we haven't even touched that apple, yet."

"We oughta pick up some vanilla ice cream", I said.

"A la mode, my man – yes!"

———————————————

A little later, at five minutes after six, Flint Stone pulled into the parking lot of Maude's. There were several pickups and several cars in the lot – Maude's did a pretty good business for being just a small joint. One thing that it was known for was the neon sign in the front window that read, 'Cold Food – Warm Beer'.

Stone found a spot and, a minute later, opened the front door. Country music was coming from somewhere, most of the tables were filled, all the barstools were taken and a bunch of guys were standing there, leaning on the old rosewood.

He looked around and finally spotted Gallagher, who was seated at a table toward the back, along with three other guys. There was a mostly empty pitcher in the middle of the table and Gallagher, who was facing the door, saw him and waved him over.

As he approached the table, Gallagher reached behind him and pulled over another chair. The guys scootched their chairs over a little to make room.

"Flint", said Gallagher. "Glad you could make it. Sit down, and have a beer. Look – we even got your mug ready for you." And he poured some beer into it and slid it over in front of Stone.

"Thanks, Eric", he said, taking a swallow.

"Let me introduce you to these guys", said Gallagher. He started from Stone's left and went clockwise around the table. "This is Frank." Frank nodded. "Al...Mark...and this here's Lou. Guys, this is Eric."

No last names thought Stone. Interesting.

For the next several minutes, by way of introducing themselves, the guys talked about their jobs and all that. They were all in some form of contracting businesses: Frank was a carpenter, Al, was an electrician, and Lou had recently closed his little house painting business and had taken a job driving a truck for a local disposal carting company.

Finally, the conversation came around to what these guys were doing in their spare time, which was organizing other like-minded guys into a close-knit group of – well, not a militia, really, Frank pointed out – but a kind of unit.

"Um, Frank – what does the unit do?", Stone asked.

"Well, actually, we ain't done nothin', yet. Not really. But we're working on it. Our plan – if you call it a plan – is to show up at various rallies and parades and such that are kind of political in nature and show the colors."

"Show the colors?"

"Yeah, you know – support the movement to get rid of those fuckin' socialists and Jews in the government. And don't even get me started on the slime they're letting in from Mexico and shit. They're ruinin' the goddamned country."

"Well, yeah, they are", said Stone. "It's on the news every night of the week." By 'the news', Stone meant Fox News. "And I can't believe it's happening. Good for you guys – at least you're trying." He raised his mug in a toast.

Frank eyed him as he raised the mug and made what he considered to be an executive decision.

"Gallagher, here, said that you guys have talked about all of this and that you're a pretty good guy. He seems to trust you. And, for some ungodly reason, I trust Gallagher." And he chuckled. "You wanna join us?", he asked.

"Join you guys? Like, in joining your unit?" The other three guys looked at him.

"Yeah. Yeah, Flint – that's exactly what I mean?", said Frank.

"Well, what do I have to do?", Stone asked.

"Do? You don't have to do nothin'. Well, we've had a couple meetings with the group and will probably have some more. But they're pretty informal – we just get together at one of our houses or something and have a little meeting. Maybe strategize about what we wanna do. You'd have to come to them. And, of course, if we do anything in public or whatever, you gotta be there, too."

Stone nodded and said, "Let me ask you - how many guys are in the unit?"

"Well, since we're just more or less gettin' it off the ground, there's these guys and - what? – six others. So, with you, it'd make an even dozen. But, like I said, we wanna grow it to at least double the size it is, now."

Stone nodded again and thought for a couple of seconds, then said, "Yeah – yeah, sure, I'd like to join. Maybe it's guys like us that can make things happen. Somethin's gotta be done."

"Good", said Frank. "You're in."

"Attaboy, Stone", said Gallagher and the rest of the guys joined in with their informal welcomes.

"This calls for another pitcher!", said Al. "I'll go get one." And he grabbed the nearly-empty one and headed toward the bar.

When he'd gotten back and all the guys had refilled their mugs, Lou said, "You guys wanna hear something?" Lou was the most recent addition to the unit, before Stone.

They all nodded.

He leaned forward over the table and said, in a conspiratorial tone, "I did something, last night." And he smiled, though it was more of a reptilian smile.

"What d'you do?", asks Frank.

Lou leaned even farther over the table and kind of waved the guys forward.

"I hit a place with graffiti", he said quietly.

"Details", said Frank.

"Yeah, see, this place over on Rhinecliff Road – it's called the People's Center – shows movies every Wednesday night for a bunch of old farts. You know, like real movies. And, last night, they showed that Jew movie, 'Yenta'."

"You mean 'Yentl', don'tcha?", asked Al. "I mean, there ain't no movie named 'Yenta'. It's 'Yentl' – got that Streisand babe in it, right?"

"Yeah, yeah – that's the one. Whatever", said Lou. "Anyway, pretty late – like, after eleven – I went over and spray painted 'Fuck Jews' on one of the outside walls. In red paint."

"You did?", asked Frank, raising his eyebrows. "You did that?"

"Yep, I did", said Lou. "Got in and out in, like, thirty seconds, too. Unseen by human eyes, I might add." And he sat up straight, pulled his shoulders back and, this time, took a long swallow of his beer.

"Whoa", said Al. "Dude."

Gallagher said, "That took nads, man. Good for you."

Frank smiled and looked at Stone. "See? See? We even use guerilla tactics every once in a while. That took initiative, Lou. But you're sure nobody saw you."

"Nah. They got a camera up on the corner of the wall, but I wore a hoodie tight around my face and a pair of big shades. Unrecognizable, man. And I parked my truck outta camera range, too. Look, here's how I knew about the movie and all that."

He took another long swallow of his beer and continued, "This job I got, now – driving a truck that unloads garbage dumpsters – sends me over there once a week. It's on my route. So, I saw their damned movie flyer on the door while I was there the other day. It said they were showing it, last night. Plus, I scoped out the place and spied the camera. Fuck, I don't even know if it's a real camera or a fake. The rest, as they say, gentlemen, is history." And he smiled again.

Frank laughed out loud and said, "' Fuck Jews' – good one, boy! Kinda right to the point, I'd say." And he laughed again, with all the guys raising their mugs again.

For the next fifteen or so minutes, they talked about this and that, then, finally, Al said, "Hey – did you guys hear about that school board meeting over in Rhinebeck, the other night?"

Heads shook.

"Yeah, I heard about it from my wife. One of her friends was there. It seems that there's a new guy on the board and he sent everybody over the top by saying that he wants to ban CRT from the schools. He said something about a lot of the shit in textbooks painting white people in a bad light."

"Well, it's true, in my opinion", said Frank, really knowing nothing about it, except what he'd heard on Fox and a couple of radio shows. "And you say some guy on the board talked about it? In Rhinebeck? Socialist, left-wing capital of Dutchess County? Whoo! Bet that raised some hackles."

"I guess it did", said Al, "but, according to my wife's buddy, a bunch of parents were on his side, too - and were pretty damned vocal about it."

"No shit", said Frank. "Wow. Y'know, maybe there are more of us around than people think. Maybe – like we've been talking about – maybe we're onto something, here. That changes really can be made. And, maybe, we're putting this little group together at just the right time."

The guys nodded their agreement.

"Wait", said Stone, a few seconds later. "I know I'm the new guy here and all, but what you just said rang a little bell in my head."

"What'd I say?", asked Frank.

"You said 'this little group'. And that got me to thinkin'.....you told me that you – we – don't have a name, that we're just a group of guys. A group. I was just thinkin' – maybe that'd make a good name for us – The Group. It's kinda mysterious, no? Doesn't say anything, really, that might raise some eyebrows – it's just The Group."

"The Group", said Frank, and the other guys looked around at each other.

"I kinda like it", said Lou.

"Me, too", said Gallagher. "I think it's pretty cool. The Group."

Again, Frank made an executive decision.

"Well, my friend, Flint Stone – it looks like you added something pretty good in your very first meet-up. Yep, that's it – we're The Group. Guys?", he said, raising his mug toward Stone.

And they all toasted him.

Stone tilted his head in recognition and raised his mug, too.

The bullshit went on until the pitcher was gone, then all the guys – The Group – headed out. But, not before Frank said that he'd get in touch with everybody to tell them when and where the whole 'Group' would meet again. But it'd probably be within the next week or so.

"Again, man - welcome to The Group", said Frank, clapping Stone on the shoulder as they walked through the door and headed to their vehicles.

As Lou drove out of the parking lot and made a left on 199, he reached under the seat and pulled out his special phone.

____

As he did so, over at the American Legion Post 429 on Mill Street in downtown Rhinebeck, a meeting was taking place to discuss the logistics of the town's upcoming annual Halloween Spooktacular, featuring the Halloween Parade through town.

There was a fairly large group – probably twenty-five or thirty people – comprised of the owners of some of the downtown shops and stores, representatives of the Rhinebeck Chamber of Commerce, the police and fire departments, the coordinators of the Farmer's Market, the Legion, Boy Scout Troop 128 and several other volunteer citizens. And Mike, who was representing the town council.

As usual, the event was scheduled to last most of the day, beginning at 10 AM and ending around four in the afternoon or thereabouts. The highlight of the day would be the parade, which would step off at two, from in front of the firehouse on Mill Street. Kids in their costumes, along with their parents, would walk up Mill Street and make a left onto and down East Market Street.

All along Mill and Market, the stores and shops would be doling out Halloween trick-or-treat goodies along the sidewalk, with Samuel's Sweet Shop - owned by partners Paul Rudd and Jeffrey Dean Morgan – actually hosting a 'Spooktacular'. There was a costume contest being held at Mega Brain Comics, a haunted house, a Halloween-themed photo booth at the Farmer's Market and more.

It was one of the highlights of the year for kids, parents and the town's merchants.

Naturally, the meeting was lasting longer than it should be lasting, thought Mike, because, just like all meetings of this sort, too many people thought that they had to say something.

But, Police Chief Marty Eddings, who was running the meeting, was doing his level best to move it along.

Bottom line….

The Chamber would coordinate with the business owners – even those who were not located on Mill and East Market – to ensure that their sidewalk displays were set up and taken down on time and wouldn't block too much of the sidewalks.

The Farmer's Market folks would oversee all activities in their particular parking lots, just as they did every Sunday when the market was open. They'd also be adding a couple of food trucks to their area.

The Legionnaires would coordinate the parade with a couple dozen of their members walking along with the marchers. Scout Troop 128 would join them in the march.

The fire department, in front of which the parade would begin, would also offer grilled hamburgers, hot dogs, sodas and water.

The police, said Chief Eddings, would have patrols at the ends of East Market and Mill to re-direct traffic around the downtown area. Plus, the department would have a couple of cruisers in front of their headquarters on East Market that the kids could explore. Plus, they would be handing out Halloween candy, too. Officers on foot patrol would be stationed at strategic spots along the parade route.

Once most of the details had been ironed out, Chief Eddings asked Mike if the council had anything to add and Mike said that he was basically there as an observer, but added, "I think you all have a great plan, here. And if you need anything from us, just let me know and we'll jump on it right away. Oh, yes – we'll have a nice set-up in front of our building, too, though it's a block or two away from the official parade route. Plus, we're planning to set up a number of chairs and a dozen or so tables for anyone who wants to sit down and take a load off."

Actually, Mike was surprised when the meeting broke up around eight o'clock. Although it had begun looking like it would go on forever, he did see people begin to look at the time and they undoubtedly figured that they'd better move it along, so a lot of the extraneous conversation had died out.

As he was leaving, Chief Eddings asked Mike to hang around for a minute – that he wanted to discuss something with him. "Sure, but can you walk with me toward my car?", asked Mike. "I just called my wife and told her that I'd be home in twenty minutes. And you know how that is."

"Sure do", Chief Eddings, chuckling. "Come on."

As they walked through the parking lot, the chief said, "Mike, we got a report, this afternoon, about some vandalism that took place at the People's Center, last night. Have you heard about it?"

"Well, yeah, I have, Marty. Hal Wood's one of our breakfast-mates and he told us about it this morning. What a horrible thing."

"Yeah, Hal's a good friend and he called me and told me about it, this afternoon. It's antisemitism, plain and simple. And vandalism. He said that they'd shown 'Yentl' at the center, last evening, and that the graffiti appeared overnight. Obviously, somebody heard about it and thought he was making a statement. A terrible statement. Plus, it's illegal."

"Can you do anything about it?", asked Mike. "Any idea who it might've been?"

"Well, that's the thing, Mike. I had one of our cruisers stop by there to pick up the CCTV tape from last night and, in watching it, you can see somebody run up to the building, but you can't see the painting being done – the camera didn't catch it because it wasn't pointed straight down. So, there's no proof, which is what we'd need to make an arrest. Plus, whoever did it was pretty well disguised. I mean, really, we have very little to go on and there's very little we can do."

"Then whoever did it got away with it", said Mike.

"Well, yeah, I'm afraid so. And I really feel terrible about it, too, Mike. I mean, this stuff shouldn't happen – anywhere – but I never thought I'd see it here in Rhinebeck. At the People's Center, no less."

"It's happening in a lot of places, Marty – not just here", said Mike.

"I know. And, it's a damned shame, too."

Both men stopped when they got to Mike's car.

"Oh – one good thing, I guess", said the Chief. "Hal said a couple of your buddies went over there and cleaned it all off the wall. There's no sign of it, anymore."

"Yeah, that would be J.D. and Parker. They said that they were going to do that. Oh, hey – Parker's an ex-cop. Guess he spent a number of years on the force down in Englewood, New Jersey. You should meet him, sometime. You know, trade war stories and all."

"That's funny", said Chief Eddings, "I came from Jersey, too. Newark PD. Which was not really a fun place to be a cop. Heckuva lot better up here."

As Mike opened the door, Eddings said, "Anyway, Mike – I've ordered a car to drive past the Center every hour during the nighttime hours. And the whole force has been put on alert to watch out for anything that looks suspicious around any building, especially the synagogue and the churches." He shrugged. "Maybe we'll get lucky."

"Hope so, Marty. We sure as hell don't want that around here."

"Amen", said Eddings. "Now, you go on and get out of here. Otherwise, your missus might bring me up on charges." And they both laughed.

"Catch you later, Marty. And thanks for the update."

"You got it, Mike. Have yourself a good night, now."

CHAPTER 11

Before heading out to The Coffee Spot the next morning, I stepped into the garden and picked four or five of the remaining decent-looking flowers. I knew that this would be kind of a difficult day for Suze and I wanted her to know that we felt that. Somehow, I'd found a couple of little rubber bands in the kitchen's everything drawer and I used them to fashion a little bouquet.

When I walked into the restaurant, I hung by the door for a minute, spying Suze taking an order a few booths away. When she left, she headed toward me on her way to the kitchen.

"Good morning, kid", I said, holding out the flimsy bouquet.

"Dude", she said quietly, taking it and looking at it, rather askance, but smiling. "What the fuck? You givin' me flowers?"

"Well, yeah", I said, a little embarrassed. "I just know that today's, well – your thing and I wanted you to know we're thinking about you."

"Aw, that's sweet of you, thanks. But I'm just looking to get it done and over with. What a hassle, right?"

"Well,", I said, probably sounding like a dork, "I'm sure it'll go just fine. And, listen – we'll leave at the same time we did on Wednesday, okay? It'll be like an instant replay."

"Cool", she said. "Okay, look – let me go give these to Gretchen and let her figure out what to do with 'em. I gotta go get this order in."

I nodded and headed to the table and she went off to the kitchen.

As I sat down, the guys were talking about the graffiti thing at the People's Center.

"I was just telling these guys that I ran into Chief Eddings, last night", Mike said to me.

"Yeah? And?", I asked.

"Well, I was just getting to that part", he said, and looked at Hal. "He probably told you that he's pretty skeptical that they can do anything about it, right?"

Hal nodded and said, "Yes, he did. He called me after they asked me to drop off the tape and said they'd watched it and that, because the camera didn't actually catch the guy spray-painting the wall, they don't have any proof that he actually did it. That, yes, it's evidence, but it's circumstantial evidence that probably wouldn't even get a look by a judge."

"That really sucks the big one", said Joe.

"Hey,", I said, "you never know. Maybe he'll try it again, somewhere, and actually be on camera or get caught in the act. If so, there'll be some pretty decent evidence that the guy's, like, a repeat offender and that might help to put him away."

Hal nodded a little skeptically, but said, "Hey, by the way, these guys did an outstanding job of cleaning the wall, too. It's like it never even happened."

"Yeah?", asked Bob, looking from me to Parker. "Elbow grease?"

"Little trick I learned", said Parker. "Baking soda and a little water – but it has to be enamel paint or it won't work. If it is, the paint peels right off."

"No shit", said Joe.

"No shit", replied Parker, just as Gretchen walked up.

"Hey, Gretchen", said Joe. "These two guys got all the paint off the Center's wall. Came right off, I guess."

"You did?", she asked, looking at each of us. "You use the baking soda thing?"

"Yep", said Parker.

"What is this? Some kind of secret society that knows about this baking soda trick?", asked Joe. "I never heard of it."

"I guess you're just not all that well-rounded, Mr. Joe", she said. "Got some gaps in your knowledge."

"Oh, he's got a lock on knowledge gaps", said Marquardt, and that brought a silently-mouthed "Fuck you" from Joe and the Geezer knuckle-knock from the rest of us.

Gretchen looked at me and raised her eyebrows. I nodded. We were good to go with Suze.

We ordered. We ate. Shit was shot for a few minutes afterward and Marquardt finally decreed the daily meeting had come to a close.

"Oh – J.D.", he said, as we were all standing up and fluttering twenties onto the table. "We've got to get to that cutting and baling. We're already late and we gotta move quickly or we'll lose that field. We've gotta get it out of there before the first freeze and the weather gods say that we should be okay for a few days – but only 'til about next weekend. After that, it's supposed to get cold."

"You do it whenever you want to, Bob. Even this weekend, if you want."

Bob thought for a minute and said, "I just might get a couple of guys over there tomorrow or Sunday to cut it. Then, the raking and baling should be done by Wednesday. That'd give us a few days, just in case."

"You got it – just send 'em over", I said.

I looked at the clock on the wall and saw that it was eight thirty-five. We had about ten minutes before we had to leave.

Once we got outside, Parker and I leaned up against my car, waiting.

We saw Gretchen come out the back door. "Hey, guys!"

We met her halfway and Parker said, "What's up, kid?"

"Well, nothing – I just wanted to thank you guys, again, for doing this. And, listen, I wanted to go with you all, this morning – I've planned on going - but I hadn't realized that Artie's made appointments with several of our suppliers, today, and I have to be here for those meetings. I hate like anything to miss being with her, but she told me not to worry – that her 'knights in shining armor' will take good care of her."

"More like knights in a dirty Subaru but, yeah, kid – don't you worry 'bout a thing. We got this."

"Suze said there were some demonstrators out front the other day."

"Ah, just a bunch of people with nothing better to do", said Parker. "Not a problem. We pretty much ignored 'em."

"Yeah", I said, "and that's probably all it'll be today, too. Don't you worry?"

"Okay", she said. "But I do. Anyway, I told Suze to take the rest of the day off when you all get back here. She'll take the car home and come back to pick me up when I'm done."

"Too bad you guys have only one set of wheels between the two of you. That's gotta be a pain in the butt", said Parker.

"Yeah, it kind of is, Bill", she said, shrugging.

"Any idea if she's going to stay around here a while?", I asked.

"Well, when she first got here, she said that she was going to have the procedure done and probably head back to Ohio a few days afterward. But, in the past couple of days, she's started talking about getting a place of her own – here. She seems to like it around here."

"You'd keep her on, here at the place?", I asked.

"Oh, most definitely", said Gretchen. "She's a great worker and the people like her. Plus, she says she's doing really well on tips. I guess she's got a little money in the bank – not much, but enough to pay first, last and security on an apartment, if it's reasonable enough."

"Enough for a car, too?", asked Parker. "Or does she have one back in Ohio?"

Gretchen smiled and said, "Oh, she's already thought of that. She says that, if I'll give her a couple of days off, she'll fly back and get it and drive it out here."

"Doesn't she have a place in – where is it again – Chillicothe?", I asked.

"Yeah, but I guess it's a furnished place. And it's on a month-to-month, so all she has to do is leave, really."

"She'd have to get a furnished place here, too, then. I mean, if she doesn't have any furniture and all."

"I've got a few things in storage", she said. "Some of the stuff left over from Mom's place when she died. A convertible sofa, a couple of tables, some chairs, I don't know – but, enough to get her going. Plus, I wouldn't mind getting out from under those storage fees."

Just then, the back door opened again and here came Suze.

"What?", she said, when she saw the three of us looking at her.

"Well,", said Gretchen, "I was just telling the guys that you might be staying around here for a while."

"I think that'd be great, Suze", I said. "This is a pretty cool area. You'll fit right in. Hell, you already do.”

She laughed and said, “I’d fit in a helluva lot better than I do with those bible-thumpers out there in West Buttfuck. I gotta tell you, those people are stuck back in the 1950s – or what I’ve heard about the 1950s. And, judgmental? They’re the worst.”

“I’d imagine your tats are quite the hit, then”, said Parker, nodding at her arm, though it was covered again, today.

“Oh, yeah – the sleeve makes a big hit at the church socials”, she laughed. “Gives ‘em apoplexy. It’s funny, but most of the guys my age have tats and nobody thinks a thing about ‘em. But a woman? No way.”

“Alright”, I said. “Not to break up this little tete-a-tete, but we’d best be on our way.”

“Right”, said Parker.

“Okay”, said Gretchen. “Honey – I’m sure everything’s going to be just fine. Don’t worry.”

“Oh, hell – I’m not worried, Gretchen. I just want to get this thing over and done with. Come on, boys, let’s mount up.”

And Gretchen gave her a hug and said, “Okay – I’ll see you in a couple of hours. J.D. – you’ll call me when you’re on your way?”

“Yep. Fear not.”

A minute later, we were heading down Route 9.

It was quiet in the car for several minutes, then Suze said, “I suppose those assholes will be outside, again.”

“Yeah, probably”, I said.

“And we’ll do it just like we did the other day”, said Parker. “Exactly the way we did it. I’ll walk you in and J.D. will wait in the car. Instant replay.”

“I might walk out a little weird, afterward”, said Suze. “They told me they can do it with a local anesthetic or they can knock me out. I told them that I wanted the local. So, I don’t know if that means I won’t feel my pelvic area for a while, or what. You know, like at the dentist – you can still talk after he numbs you, but you don’t feel your mouth for a little while.”

"Don't worry, kid – I won't let you fall or anything if that's what happens", said Parker.

"Cool. And they said I should rest for a couple of days afterward, too. And I might have some bleeding, which is probably TMI for you guys. But I guess I'll be good as new in a couple of days. I'm pretty tough, though, so maybe I'll take tomorrow off and be back at work on Sunday."

"Do whatever feels right, but don't overdo it", I said.

"Yes, Dad."

Great. I guess I really am getting old.

A few minutes later, we saw the Planned Parenthood up ahead on the right. And, like on Wednesday, there were some protestors outside. Actually, maybe there were a few more, today. Yeah, there were. There were probably close to thirty people there.

"More people today", said Parker.

"Yeah", Suze and I said at the same time.

And, just like on Wednesday, they came toward the car when we drove in and shouted and all that. This time, though, there were more signs – some of them looking like they were professionally printed and not just done with big Magic Markers and spray paint.

"Okay, Suze – you ready?", Parker asked as I pulled to a stop out front.

"Oh, yeah – let's do this thing", she said.

Parker opened his door and said, in his best cop voice, "Back up! Now!" And the protestors retreated enough for him and Suze to get out. Again, they weren't violent – just loud.

"Thank you", he said, as the two of them joined up and headed toward the building, the protestors walking along with them on either side of the sidewalk. Again, I heard, "Baby killer!" several times and "No to abortions!" and stuff like that.

Once Parker and Suze were inside, I sat there looking around. I kind of wondered about those professional-looking signs – like, if it was an organized group or something. Finally, I got a pretty decent look at one of them and, at the bottom of it, under 'Stop Abortion Now!', I saw the words 'Moms for Liberty'.

Hmm, I thought. Must be some kind of organization. Or not. Maybe it was just a bunch of local mothers who more or less banded together and gave themselves a name.

One of the women carrying one of those signs walked toward me and, I gotta say, she looked pissed. A lot more so than the others, anyway.

Even though the car windows were closed, I heard her yell, "Girls! Come here! Girls!", and a few of them – carrying the same sort of sign – began to converge on the Subaru.

The 'leader' – or so she seemed – came around to the driver's side window and yelled some pretty nasty stuff at me. I could even see some spittle in the corners of her mouth. Wow, I thought – she's pretty wound up.

As I looked around, I saw that six or seven other women – her compadres, obviously – were more or less surrounding the front and sides of my car. Jeez, I thought again, calm down, calm down.

Then, the leader banged my windshield with her sign, which pissed me off. I started to open the door to get out – I wanted to rip that sign right out of her hands and, and, and…well, I didn't quite know, but….

"Sheila!", I heard. "Sheila! That guy's coming out!" And, 'Sheila' or whoever it was, looked toward the front door and took off around the front of the car and made a beeline toward Parker, who was making his way down the sidewalk.

'Sheila' marched right directly up to Parker, holding her sign up in front of her. She was blocking his way.

All of a sudden, Parker's hand shot out and he knocked the sign right out of her hands, sending it flying onto the grass.

"Don't you *ever* get in my face!", he yelled. "Now – get the *fuck* outta my way!" I mean, there was most definitely some implied violence on his part – but it was only implied. Well, other than sending her dumb sign flying and yelling at her, that is. She backed up and let him by. He stared a hole in her as he passed.

He got to the car, opened the door, then turned around to face the group, again. He looked directly at the one called Sheila and said, loudly enough to be heard, "Don't you *ever* try that again."

And he got in and slammed the door.

"Crazy fuck", he said, still staring at her. "Get us outta here."

I pulled forward down the driveway, looking at the protestors in my rear-view. "They're calming down", I said. "At least they're not chasing us."

"Those assholes couldn't run across the room", he said, taking a couple of deep breaths.

I pulled out onto East-West Arterial and headed east.

"There are some crazy ones, there, today", said Parker. "What the hell?"

"I think they might be part of a group, an organization", I said. "Some of 'em had professionally made signs and I saw something at the bottom of one of them. It said, 'Moms for Liberty'.

"' Moms for Liberty', huh? What the fuck kind of liberty are they talking about? They didn't want me to have the (finger quotes) liberty of walking down the fucking sidewalk."

"Well, there *is* that", I said. "And one of them – I heard a couple of them call her Sheila – the one that got up in your face - anyway, Sheila smacked my windshield with her sign. And I was about to get out and do something about it when I saw you coming back down the sidewalk."

"What were you gonna do?"

"Damned if I know", I shrugged. "By the way, you sent that sign flyin' – good shot!"

"Lucky shot", he said, "Just happened to catch it just right. But it was pretty cool, wasn't it?"

"I'll say. Okay, look – there's the Denny's. Wanna go in?"

"Hell, yeah, son – that's the plan, isn't it? As soon as my stomach stops turning over, I'm down for some pecan pie."

"With whipped cream on top", I said.

"Is there any other way?"

Ten minutes later, we were at a booth, eating pie and drinking coffee.

"Y'know", Parker said, "as good as this pie is, it'd be better if we hadn't eaten breakfast an hour or so ago. I might have to keep it to just this one piece, today. What're you doing?"

"Hold on", I said, looking at my phone. "I wanted to see if this Moms for Liberty thing is real or just a bunch of locals. And I found something. It's their – I dunno – their mission. Wanna hear it?"

"Sure", he said, reaching for his mug.

"Okay, listen. It says, 'Moms for Liberty welcomes all that have the desire to stand up for parental rights at all levels of government'.

"It goes on to say that the founders saw (finger quotes) 'how short-sighted and destructive policies directly hurt children and families. Now they are using their first-hand knowledge and experience to unite parents who are ready to fight those that stand in the way of liberty."

"The fuck's that supposed to mean?", asked Parker.

"I don't know, but that's what it says. It says that it was founded in Florida, so it must be a real thing, not just something around here. Maybe these people are part of a local chapter or something."

"Bunch of screaming meemies, if you ask me. At least that's what we saw a few minutes ago. Shit."

"Obviously, right-wing", I said.

"Ya think, there, Captain Obvious?"

"Bite me."

Just then, my phone rang. Suze's name came up.

"Suze?", I asked, by way of answering. "You done already?"

"Yep, but listen – one of the nurses, here, wants to give you another way in to pick me up. That way, we don't have to go through that crowd again. It's, like, the back of the place or something. Here – let me put her on."

And, before I could say anything else, I heard, "Hello, sir. My name is Wendy and I'm one of Suze's nurses and - "

I interrupted her by saying, "Is Suze okay? I mean, well, is she good?"

Wendy chuckled and said, "Oh, she's just fine, sir. She's up and ready to go. But I don't want to put her through anymore, today, so let me give you the simple directions to our back door."

"Okay. We're just east of there on Arterial."

"Okay, good. Just before you get to our building, you'll make a left on Wilson. Go to the first little turn on your right – it's an alleyway, really. Turn into it. Go past the backs of a couple of buildings and you'll see our blue door on your right. We'll be waiting there for you."

"Okay – you ready now?"

"Yes, sir."

"Give us five minutes."

"Got it."

I told Parker what was happening and we left a twenty on the table – more than enough to cover a couple'a pieces of pie and coffee.

"She's good?", he asked me as we headed out.

"Yep."

A few minutes later, we'd turned down the alleyway and saw the blue door on our right.

The door opened and Suze was sitting there in a wheelchair. When they saw us, two nurses helped her out of it, walked her down the two steps to the car, opened the back door and made sure that Suze was comfortable.

"Okay, honey", said one of them. "You just take it easy the rest of today and tomorrow. And don't forget to take these as instructed on the label." And she handed Suze a little container. "You'll be just fine."

Suze thanked them and closed the door.

"Hi, guys. Fancy meeting you here in an alleyway", she said, tapping Parker on the shoulder.

"How'd it go? How're you feeling?", I asked.

"Ah, it's not something I wanna do again but, all in all, it went just fine. It was a lot quicker than I expected and they made me lie on a bed for a little while afterward.

Then, I don't know – a few minutes ago - one of the nurses came in and sprung me."

"You don't look any worse for wear", said Parker, turning in his seat to look at her.

"Ah, I still feel a little utzy, but no pain, though. Come on, J.D. – get us the fuck outta here, will ya?"

I turned the car around and we headed back down the alleyway. As we drove past the front of the building again, the demonstrators were still there, milling about.

"Have any trouble with them?", Suze asked, looking over in their direction.

"Nope", said Parker. "Piece of cake."

I made the turn onto Route 9 and we were off to The Coffee Spot.

CHAPTER 12

As soon as we turned onto Route 9, Suze said, "I'm calling Gretchen" and she put the phone to her ear.

Suze told her that she was fine and it had all gone smoothly and she was glad it was all behind her and all that. Then, she said, "But, listen, Gretchen – they told me that I shouldn't drive, today, so maybe I'll just hang out at the restaurant 'til you leave. Shouldn't be too long, right? Oh. Uh-huh. I see. Well, shit, I guess I can find something to do 'til then. But you think we'll be outta there by four-thirty?"

I looked over at Parker. "What's the deal?", I asked her over my shoulder.

"Hold on, Gretchen. Gretchen says she still has to meet with a couple of her suppliers this afternoon and, well – you heard me – I shouldn't be driving, so I guess I'll hang out there 'til she's ready to go home."

"Tell her you'll call her right back", I said.

She looked at me in the rearview mirror, but said, "Did you hear that Gretchen? Okay, call you right back."

"What?", she asked.

"Here's what I'm thinking", I said. "You could come back to the farm with Parker and me and just hang out there this afternoon. Gretchen has to go pretty close to my place on her way home and she can just run by and pick you up."

"Your farm", she said, still looking at me in the mirror.

"Yeah – we'll kind of show you around a bit, but you shouldn't be walking too much, so we can just hang."

"Y'know", said Parker, "it's turned into a pretty nice day – must be in the sixties. We could even sit out on the porch and whatever."

"Yeah - and I can introduce you to the kids."

"The kids?", she asked.

"Yeah – my two horses – Zeus and Ceres. You'll get a kick out of them." A beat later, "Hell, yeah – when we get there, I'll just drive down to their field and you can get out and say hello."

"You have horses?", she asked.

"The most insane-lookin' horses you've ever seen", said Parker. "Big as houses and blacker'n the ace of spades. Outstanding specimens."

"I didn't know you had horses, J.D. I've always loved horses, but I've never had one or anything. Can you ride 'em?"

"Hell, yes, you can ride 'em. A couple of the best riding horses this side of the Pecos."

"Okay, yeah", she said. "Let's do that. I mean, if it's okay and I'm not putting you out or anything."

"Not at all, kid. And, like Parker said, we can sit around on the porch and shoot the shit."

"Alright, let me call Gretchen back." And, of course, Gretchen thought that was a great idea and said that she'd be at my place a little before five.

After they disconnected, Parker said, "Hey – there's an apple pie sitting on your counter, isn't there?"

"We just had pie, not an hour ago", I said. "But, yeah – it hasn't been touched. You like pie, Suze?", I asked her, looking at her in the rearview.

"Of course, I like pie", she said. "Who doesn't like pie?"

"Look", said Parker. "We only had one piece of that pecan, back there, so a little more apple won't hurt, y'know? I mean, we can wait a while after we get there, but we ain't gonna have too many more nice days to do that. You know, sit around on the porch and scarf."

"You've got a point", I said. "Suze – you up for that?"

"Why not?"

Thirty minutes later, we pulled into my lane.

"Wow – this is a real farm, isn't it?", asked Suze, looking around. "This your house?", she asked. "Well, duh – obviously it is. Nice."

"Let's drive down to the kids, first, okay? That way, you won't have to walk."

We drove past the garage, Parker's truck and my dually and I pulled to a halt a little to the left of the barn, right in front of the kids' gate.

"Wow", said Suze, leaning up between Parker and me when she saw Zeus and Ceres in the middle of their field.

"Come on – let's go say hello", I said. "You okay to walk a few feet?"

"Hell, yeah. Let's go."

We got up to the gate and, as they saw us approach, both horses made their way toward us.

"Hey, kids – I want you to meet a new friend. This is Suze. Suze, this is Zeus and this is Ceres", I said, pointing at them.

"Wow!", she said again. "They're huge!"

"Both of 'em are a little better than eighteen hands."

"I don't know what that means", she said, "but, Jesus, are they big!"

"Wanna make two friends for life?", I asked her, reaching over and into the treat can and pulling out a couple of handfuls of treats. "Here – give 'em each a couple of these."

"Oh, I don't know", she said, tentatively. "I mean….."

"Here – just hold these in the palm of your hand", I said, handing her a couple of treats. "Then, just hold your hand up to Zeus' mouth. He'll take 'em gently - honest."

"Oh-kay", she said, putting her hand up in front of Zeus. And, just like the gentleman he always is, he took the two treats very, very gently.

"Here's a couple for Ceres", I said, handing them to her.

Same thing.

"Wow", she said for a third time. "I can't believe I just did that. Can I touch them? I mean, can I pet 'em?"

"Hell, yeah – just put the back of your hand up to their noses, first, so they can smell you and check you out. Then, sure, just rub their foreheads. They like that."

And we all stood there for the next five or so minutes, with Suze gaining confidence with each passing minute. Pretty soon, Ceres had turned so she was parallel with the gate and Suze was scratching her neck and back.

"She seems to like that", she said.

"She loves that. But, now, she's gonna expect that every time she sees you."

Then, Ceres turned a little further and offered her butt to Suze, who kept scratching. Note: Everybody likes their butt scratched, no matter how many legs they have.

"Can I really see her again? See them again?", Suze asked.

"As often as you'd like, kid. Every day, if you want to. These kids love the love and they really like people, so, yeah. Come on over, any time."

Suze turned her attention back to Ceres and I could tell that she was absolutely fascinated. It was good to see. And it was as honest and innocent as it gets. The little girl in Suze came out, which is something that I knew she tried to keep hidden. Undoubtedly, for defensive purposes. It made me happy and I smiled over at Parker, and he nodded.

That's the thing about horses – that they don't judge. They don't care if you're the President of the United States or if you pick roaches out of your Raisin Bran. If you're nice and honest and respectful to them, they'll return the favor. That's the only judgment they use.

"Look", said Suze, still scratching. "Know what's interesting?"

Parker and I both looked at her.

"That Ceres, here, doesn't care that I just had an abortion or that I have an armful of tattoos or that my hair color comes out of a bottle. She just likes the way I'm scratching her butt."

See?

"That's how horses roll", I said. "They don't judge. Well, unless you're an asshole, that is."

"I'll try not to be an asshole, Ceres", Suze said to her, smiling.

My phone rang.

Ron.

"What's up, dude?", I said to him.

"Listen, you got a minute?"

"Um, sure. Parker, too?"

"Yeah."

"Okay. Wait – hold on. Let us call you back in, like, three minutes, okay?"

"Roger." And we disconnected.

Parker was looking at me, with Suze standing between us, still playing with Ceres. I nodded.

"Hey, listen, Suze", I said. "Parker and I gotta jump on a call in a minute and we're gonna run up to the porch for it, okay? Can you just hang out with the kids for a few minutes and we'll be back in a flash?"

"Oh, absolutely", she said, with a smile. "I can stay here all day."

"What's this about?", asked Parker as we made our way to the porch.

"No idea. He just asked me if we had a minute."

After we'd sat down at the table, I hit Ron's number.

"Yo", he said, answering.

"What's up?", I asked.

"Well, I hear that somebody did a nice job of cleaning some shit off the wall at the People's Center, yesterday."

Parker and I looked at each other. "Huh?"

"Yeah, I hear somebody cleaned some graffiti off a wall. Did a nice job of it, too."

"Where'd you hear that?", Parker asked him.

"Well", said Ron, "now that I have your attention, there's something I gotta tell you guys."

"What?", I asked.

"Okay, now - and this is very hush-hush. Like, top fucking secret, dig?"

"Okay", we both said at once.

"Listen – I've got a guy. He's not really, truly, a Feeb guy – he's a contractor. But he's working for us, for me."

"A contractor", said Parker.

"Right. See, this whole exploding extreme right-wing megillah has got us running too lean. We don't have enough real agents to do what needs to be done. They're – we're – spread just too thin. So, we've contracted with some guys – some guys and some women – who've got experience in this type of thing, this type of intel gathering."

"You mean, like, ex-military intelligence and ex-law enforcement counterterrorism people?", asked Parker.

"Yep, precisely."

"Okay", Parker said.

"Yeah. And, anyway, I'm running a guy over there in your neck of the woods. And he's in the process of getting in tight with a small, but expanding, group of these knuckleheads."

"Keep going", said Parker.

"I was trying to", said Ron. "Anyhow, my man – to get in real good with this group – did something, the other night. Something that would put him in solid with the pseudo-leader or whatever the fuck he is."

"Wait a minute", I said, putting two and two together. At least I thought I was. "You mentioned the graffiti. Are you telling us that it was your guy who did it?"

"That's exactly what I'm telling you", said Ron. "And, from what he tells me, when he reported back to the group that he'd done it, they all got little woodies. Made him, like, a little hero or something, to a few of the guys in that group who were sitting in a bar the other night."

"Jesus", I said. And Parker laughed out loud.

"Ron, my boy – my hat's off to you", he said. "Running a friggin' asset. You ever done that before?"

"Well, that's classified, dude. You know that" said Ron. And, a beat later, "But, no –
not really." And he laughed. "Guess there's a first time for everything, though, right?"

"Alright, listen", Ron continued. "We got this guy a job with a local garbage hauler out
there. And that's how this whole thing went down. I guess he picked up from the
Center and saw that they were playing that movie – what was it? – 'Yentl'? And he
saw his chance to make a splash with his boys. So, he went over late at night and
spray-painted that shit on the wall."

"Jesus", I said again, because I didn't know what else to say.

Ron laughed and said, "Hey – I understand that whoever cleaned that shit off the wall
did a damned good job of it. My guy was back there, this morning, and said it's like it
never even happened."

"I got a special trick", said Parker, winking at me.

"I had an idea it was you guys", said Ron. "Sounds like something you guys would
do."

"Oh, hey", I said. "By the way, it looks like your guy got away with it, too. The CCTV
didn't catch him in the act and the local police are just taking a wait-and-see attitude
about the whole thing. But they're increasing patrols around places like that and
synagogues and so on."

"Yeah, I figured that", said Ron. "Anyway, I really don't think there's anything for you
guys to do about any of it, right now. I just more or less wanted you to know."

"Thanks, I guess", I said.

"But - and there's always a 'but', isn't there?" Ron said. "But, if it's okay with you guys,
I'd like to give my guy your contact info. I don't know how it might work, but maybe
y'all should get to know each other. Maybe you guys can help do a little – I dunno,
detective work? - for him if he needs it? You're good at that."

"Hell, yeah", said Parker. "I'm just itchin' to help get rid of this scum."

"Parker's right", I said. "We ran into a bunch of right-wing kooks a couple of times, this
week. Those people are not doing anybody or this town or this area or this country
any good. We're in, dude. Just let us know what you need."

"Alright, good. That's what I figured. Now, I'm gonna give this guy – the name he's
going by is Lou, Lou Schmidt, by the way – I'll give him your numbers and maybe

you'll hear from him and maybe you won't. I dunno, it'll be up to him. But I'll tell him that we've worked together on a few things on the down-low and have brought a certain type of justice to some real assholes, so he should trust you."

"Okay", I said. "Tell him to call anytime."

"I will. And if you see a strange number pop up on one of your phones, just know that he'll probably be using a burner, so either answer it or let it go to voicemail and he'll leave you some kind of message."

"Got it", said Parker.

"Alright, gentlemen", said Ron. "Nice doing binness with you. I'm sure we'll talk again in the next couple of days. Oh – if he does call you, let me know ASAP, will ya? He's supposed to check in with me but he doesn't always do that. Not when I want him to, anyway."

"Roger", I said. "Later, dude." And we disconnected.

Parker and I just looked at each other.

"This is fucking weird", he said.

"I'll say it's fucking weird."

Just then, we looked up and saw Suze walking up the lane, toward the house.

"Suze!", I yelled to her. "You're not supposed to be walking that far! Let me come down and drive you up here."

"Don't be a dick, J.D.", she yelled back. "I can walk a few hundred fucking feet."

Parker and I both stood up because, I guess, it felt like something we should do.

"Now", she said, walking up the steps to the porch, "didn't y'all say something about apple pie?"

———————————————

As that was happening, Flint Stone was back, for the third afternoon, at the Annandale Arms Apartments. And, today, Gallagher had joined the crew, taking the place of a guy whose back had gotten screwed up carrying the bricks. And, because Gallagher's job had been a short one, Stone had called him and, luckily, he was available.

By now, all of the old bricks had been taken out – the good ones having gone into Stone's dump trailer and the pieces into the dumpster. Stone was figuring to take the trailer to the brickyard the following morning to collect some long green while the guys worked at the job site.

He had ordered three pallets of new bricks and, thankfully, they'd been delivered a little while ago. He'd tell the guys that they would break a little early today and get to laying the bricks in the morning. They wouldn't finish the job, tomorrow, but would get a lot of it done. Then, they'd break for the weekend and, if they were lucky, could finish it up on Monday, maybe Tuesday morning. He'd drive the guys pretty hard on Monday, though, because if he finished up a day early, well, that would be a good thing.

Gallagher walked over to Stone and asked, "Got a sec?" And he nodded his head away from the workers.

"Yeah, sure. What's up?"

"I just got a call from Frank and he wants to set up a meet with all the guys – the whole group."

"Okay, when?", asked Stone.

"Well, he wants to shoot for Sunday. Sunday afternoon. Can you make that?"

"Sure, I guess so. What time? Oh - and where?"

"Two o'clock. And one of the guys – you haven't met him, yet – name's Oscar – Oscar's got a small farm with a barn on it. Frank wants to meet there."

"Where is it?", asked Stone.

"Not far – up outside of Milan. I can get you the address and your GPS'll take you there. I've been there, once, and it's really easy to find. But, it's, like, set back off the road so people can't see a bunch of cars and trucks parked everywhere. That might raise questions if you know what I mean."

"Got it. Yeah, sure. I can make it. The wife's spending the weekend up outside of Albany with her kid sister, so I'm free."

"Cool", said Gallagher. "I'll let him know that you're in. I gotta call a couple of the other guys, now – the guys you met the other night - and let them know. We've got, like, a phone tree thing, where Frank calls a couple of us and we call the other guys."

"Good idea", said Stone.

"Yeah, I thought so – it was my idea."

And they fist-bumped.

<h1 align="center"><u>CHAPTER 13</u></h1>

While the three of us were sitting on the porch, doing the pie thing, I filled Suze in on the history of the farm and how I came to be here and how Parker had been a mainstay here ever since the advent of dirt or thereabouts.

"Oh, shit – the pumpkins", he said, suddenly. "Christ, I'd forgotten about the pumpkins. I'd better get down there and finish 'em up so we can get 'em to the Center, tomorrow. I told Hal we'd have 'em by then." And he stood up.

"Right", I said, as he headed down the step.

"Catch you in a few", he said.

"Pumpkins?", asked Suze as she watched him walk toward the garage.

And I went on to explain the whole dealio and how Parker was kind of the Geezers' resident 'artiste'. And that he'd promised Hal that he'd carve a couple of jack-o'-lanterns for the People's Center.

"That's a funny name", she said.

"What name?"

"The Geezers."

"Well, they are. Or, we are."

"Yeah, but you're pretty much on the low end of Geezerism, aren't you?"

"Geezerism is a state of mind, my dear, not the body", I replied.

"Gotcha. Hey, do you mind if I ask you something?"

"Not at all – what?"

"Well, to be honest, I'm a little tired after that thing, this morning. Do you suppose it'd be possible if I could take a nap, somewhere?"

"Oh", I said. "Oh, sure. Not a problem at all. You want a bed or a couch?"

"I dunno – couch'll do, I guess. Hell, it's just a little nap."

"Okay, come on", and I led her into the house, through the kitchen and into the living room.

"Voila", I said, doing my Vanna White thing indicating the couch.

"Okay, cool", she said. Then, she spied 'The Legend of Sleepy Hollow' lying on the coffee table. "Oh, man – that's one of my all-time favorite stories. Ichabod Crane and the Headless Horseman."

"You know that story's written about the area right around here – pretty near to where we are, right now, actually."

"Huh. How d'ya like that?", she said, idly thumbing through the book. "I've always thought that the idea of a headless horseman was cool as fuck. Guy comes out of nowhere and scares the shit out of people, then just disappears again. Like, did-that-really-happen-or-was-I-seeing-things type of deal."

"Yeah", I said. "Me, too. Great concept, huh?"

If she only knew,

Then, I said, "Alright, I'm gonna leave you alone, now – probably head down to the garage to see how Parker's doing. If you need anything, just hit me on my phone – don't go walking down there. You're supposed to rest."

"Yes, Dad", she said, sitting down on the couch. "Maybe I'll read this story again", holding up the book.

"Whatever. And I'll come and get you up before Gretchen gets here."

"Cool. By the way, I love your horses."

"Like I said – any time." And I headed out.

When I got to the garage, Parker was working diligently on his carving. It looked like he was in the home stretch.

"' Bout done, huh?", I asked.

"Just about", he said, not looking up. "These things'll be ready to deliver tomorrow."

They looked great, too – the two faces of drama. The way he'd carved them, they were three-dimensional. Nice touch.

"Hey – what do you think of that phone call from Ron?", he asked. "He's runnin' the dude that painted that shit on the wall. Fuckin' nuts, huh?"

"I know, right?"

"And I had no idea that the FBI was in the business of hiring private contractors to do some of its intel work." He spun one of the pumpkins around, looking at it, then said, "But, I guess if the military's doin' it, why shouldn't the Feebs?"

"I wonder if we'll hear from the guy. What's his name? Schmidt? Yeah, Lou Schmidt."

"That's just the name he's using but, yeah."

"I don't know why we would hear from him, though. I mean, what can we do?"

"I dunno", he shrugged. "Nothin', probably. Okay – these are ready to go. How do we wanna do this? Take 'em to The Coffee Spot in the morning and give 'em to Hal or take 'em over ourselves?"

"I don't know. Tell you what – I'll bring them with me in the morning and we'll ask Hal what he wants, okay?"

"Yeah, cool."

Just then, my phone dinged with an incoming text. I looked at the screen. "Oh, hey", I said, "it's Gretchen. She says she'll be here in ten minutes. Must've gotten away earlier than she thought."

"Cool. Where's the kid?"

"Suze? I left her reading the 'Headless Horseman'. She said she was gonna take a nap, but I don't know. We'd better go on up and see."

As we walked into the kitchen, Suze was sitting there at the table, reading.

"Just finished it", she said, holding up the book.

"I thought you were going to take a nap", I said.

"I did, too, but I got involved with this." And I told her that Gretchen was on her way.

"Nice. But I gotta tell you guys, I really enjoyed being here, this afternoon. It's a great place, J.D. And I've fallen head-over-heels in love with Zeus and Ceres – especially Ceres. She seems like a girl after my own heart."

"Well, like I said, come by any time at all. Every day or once in a while – I don't care.

And I know the kids would love to see you.”

“How’re you feeling?”, Parker asked her.

“Oh, fine. Maybe a little on the weak side, but a helluva lot better than I thought I would. I’m just so goddamned glad to get that all behind me. You guys can’t imagine the weight that’s been lifted.” And she smiled sweetly.

A couple of minutes later, we heard Gretchen toot as she pulled into the lane and the three of us traipsed out to meet her.

When we all met up, Gretchen hugged Suze and asked how she was and all that and Suze answered that she was fine and all that.

“I want you to take tomorrow off, though”, Gretchen said to Suze.

“Ah, no reason, Gretchen. I feel good.” But, when she saw the look on Gretchen’s face, said, “Tell you what – I’ll come in for the breakfast rush and then split. I’ll only work for – what? – two, or three hours? Then, I’ll go home, okay?”

“Well, let’s see how you’re feeling in the morning, then we’ll decide”, said Gretchen.

“Okay, Mom.”

After a few more minutes of niceties and hearing a little bit about Gretchen’s meetings, earlier, they got into the car. We all bade our farewells, Suze thanked us again, and she rolled down her window and shouted down to the kids, “I’ll be back real soon, you guys!” She waved at them. And they both looked up.

“Oh, hey – J.D. Know what would be cool?”, she said, looking up at me.

“What?”

“If you did, like, a headless horseman thing with one of them. Probably Zeus.”

“Yeah”, I said, pretty taken aback, “that would be cool. Maybe someday.”

And Gretchen turned the car around and they headed out.

“Holy shit”, I said to Parker.

“Yeah, holy shit”, he said.

My phone rang. I didn’t recognize the number but, after Ron’s call, I thought I should answer it.

"Hello?"

"Yeah – is this J.D.?"

"Yes. Who's this?"

"Umm, a friend of Ron's. Name's Schmidt."

"Oh. Yeah, he told us about you. Hey – my buddy, Parker's, here with me. Can I put you on speaker?"

"Can anybody else hear us?"

"Nope – it's just us."

"Okay, but I only got a minute." I put it on speaker.

"Okay", I said. "This is Parker", and Parker grunted something.

"Look – Ron told me you guys are solid. That I can trust you. That true?"

"Yep. Absolutely", I said. "And we really like –"

"Okay, fine", he interrupted. "Look, I want to run into you guys, somehow, just so I can put faces with the names and voices. And I know that you're the guys who cleaned that shit off the wall, right?"

"Uh-huh."

"Here's the deal. I'm just getting in with these other guys and, unless I'm with them, I'm just doing my job and laying low the rest of the time. I don't really spend much time in public. And, well, tomorrow I'm scheduled to pick up the shit from the People's Center again."

"Tomorrow's Saturday", said Parker.

"Yeah, I know, but we're short-handed, right now, and we're doing pick-ups six days a week, instead of five, so I'm working tomorrow."

"When are you gonna be there?", asked Parker.

"I'd imagine right around noon", said Schmidt.

Parker and I looked at each other and I mouthed "Pumpkins" to him and he nodded.

"We have to drop some stuff off there, tomorrow", I said. "And we can be there anytime, so noon works for us."

"Right around then", he said. "Give or take a few minutes."

"Okay. Now, what - ?"

But he'd already hung up.

"How d'you like that?", I asked Parker. "Wonder why he wants to meet us?"

"Like he said, he wants to put faces to names. Makes sense, really. Wants to know who he might be dealing with."

"You think we'll be dealing with him? How would that happen and why?"

"I have no idea, kid."

"Hell, this is all becoming some big undercover thing", I said. "For the life of me, I don't think there're any guys around here who are all that dangerous. I mean, it's not like Wolfe and those guys."

Wolfe was the oligarch-slash-illegal arms guy we'd dealt with a few months back.

"No, but you never know. There are a helluva lot of these groups around, these days, and I think it's just a matter of time before there's some real violence, somewhere." He shrugged. "At least that's the thinking of the DOJ. Remember, they put out that big domestic terrorism thing, a little while back."

"Yeah, but around here?"

"You never know, kid. But where there's smoke, there's fire. And ain't nobody wanna get burned by it. At least, that's probably what Schmidt's thinking."

I thought about that for a couple of beats and said, "Yeah, probably."

"Yeah, for sure", he said. "Undercover work is rough and I'm tellin' you that from personal experience. Okay, so – those pumpkins. Let's tell Hal that we'll drop 'em off around midday and we'll take 'em in and set 'em up and we'll keep an eye out for the garbage truck."

"Roger. By the way – they look good, man – real good", I said, nodding at the jack-o'-lanterns.

"I'm hell on wheels with a knife, kid", he said, winking.

———————————

Right then, Frank Branson was pulling into his driveway on Kilmer Road in the East Park section of Hyde Park. He saw Sheila's car in the driveway and parked his panel truck next to it. He didn't have any jobs planned for the weekend and was looking forward to a few cold ones, dinner and a good night's sleep. Oh - and the meeting on Sunday.

He locked all the doors in the van and felt the hood of Sheila's car as he walked past it. Still a little warm – she must've gotten home just a little before me, he thought. He walked in through the door in the garage, laid his tool belt on the workbench and removed his boots – Sheila hated it when he tracked dirt into the house. He walked the two steps up to the kitchen door and went in.

"I'm home!", he yelled.

"Be right down!", he heard her yell from somewhere upstairs.

He reached into the fridge and pulled out a Genesee Cream Ale – a 'green hornet' - and set it down on the counter after taking a mighty swig. Then, he went over to the sink and washed his hands.

"How many times do I have to tell you not to wash your hands in the sink?", asked Sheila, coming into the kitchen. "You make a mess. Go into the bathroom."

"Too late", he said, smiling and giving her a peck on the cheek as she walked up to him and slapped him playfully on the shoulder.

"You're incorrigible", she said, heading back to the fridge to pull out a beer for herself. "Patio?", she asked.

"Nah – I think it's too cool for that. It was pretty nice, today, but it's cooling off pretty quick. Let's go into the den."

A couple of minutes later, they were both sitting in their usual chairs and Frank hit the remote. It was already tuned to Fox News, but he muted it for the time being. "So, how was your day?", he asked.

"Well, alright, I guess. A few of the girls and I went over to that Planned Parenthood place in Poughkeepsie and milled around for a bit. I did have a guy slap the sign out of my hand, though. Scared the hell out of me."

"Wait – what? A guy attacked you?" Frank's head spun toward her.

"Well, no, not really *attacked* me. But when I walked up to him, he just reached out and knocked my sign and it fell out of my hand."

"Still", said Frank. "Who the hell was he? Got any idea?"

"Nah, just some guy dropping a girl off at the place." She took a swallow of her beer. "Goddammit, Frank, that place oughta be shut down. I can't imagine how many babies they're killing there."

"Death house", said Frank, now looking at the screen. "Almost time for Bret Baier", he said, pointing at the TV with his chin.

"Oh, by the way", he continued. "We're gonna have a meet on Sunday over at Oscar's place. All of the guys, I guess – even a couple of new ones that we recruited recently. We could be up to twenty, twenty-five guys by now."

"Okay. And, I tell you, sweetheart", she said. "There are a lot more of us out there than people realize. I'm finding the same thing with Moms for Liberty – we're adding women all the time. They're good people, too."

The commercials were over and the logo for 'Special Report with Bret Baier' came on.

"I'm not really liking this guy, anymore", said Sheila, taking another sip. "I think the lefties have gotten to him."

"Ah, yeah – but he's still on our side. But, you're right – he says some things that just aren't true or only have a kernel of truth to them." He shrugged, "Gives us a chance to catch up on the news, though."

And he unmuted it.

The lead story centered around several states beginning to enact their own anti-abortion laws, a couple of them fashioning their bills after the one that Ohio had adopted.

"See that?", asked Frank. "Perfect examples of states' rights. Those idiots in Congress can't get a goddamned thing done, but down on the state and local levels? Different story, lately."

"Never happen here, though", said Sheila. "Not with that radical piece of shit in our state house. She's already made it legal, here. People'll be flocking into this state to get abortions and that's why our only option is to get these clinics to shut down."

He nodded.

"I gotta tell you, Frank. Except for our group, today, most of those people looked like they just didn't have anything else to do – so they came and walked around. We need people with fire in their bellies at those buildings – people that aren't afraid to get their hands dirty, if you know what I mean."

He muted the TV again and said, "Y'know, maybe I'll bring that up at our meeting on Sunday. See if any of the guys would be interested in going to one of those places. The problem is, most of the guys work during the day."

"Mmm", she said.

"But maybe we can do something on the weekends. They open on the weekend?"

"Nope. Just during the week. They're closed on Saturdays and Sundays."

Frank took another swallow of beer, while another annoying Big Pharma commercial was on the tube. He thought about what Lou had done at the People's Center and he was beginning to get the germ of an idea.

"Closed on the weekends, huh?", he asked. "Listen, I got something buzzin' around in my head. Let me think about it a little more – but maybe there's something we can do."

"Really?", asked Sheila.

"Yeah, maybe", he said.

The commercials were over, he unmuted the tube again.

CHAPTER 14

When I walked into The Coffee Spot the next morning, I spotted Suze, standing next to a booth, taking an order. The place was full, as it often was on a Saturday morning, even at this early hour.

She saw me and I gave her a thumbs-up and raised my eyebrows questioningly. I wanted to know how she was feeling.

She gave me a wink and a thumbs-up in response.

Good.

As I was sitting down, Gretchen walked up, filled my mug and topped off the other guys'.

"Hey, Bill", she said, tapping Parker on the shoulder. "I'm afraid to say it, but I don't think our jack-o'-lantern's going to make it to Halloween. It's starting to, um, relax. And we're still better than a week away from Halloween."

"I was afraid that might happen", he said. "I think it's because it's pretty warm in here. Too warm for it, anyway." He took a sip of coffee, then said, "Ah, I'll get you another one."

"You will? Oh, that'd be great", she said.

"Yeah – I'll pick up another one, carve it up a bit and bring it in the first of the week. That okay?"

"Perfect", she said.

"Hey – how's Suze?", Joe asked her.

"What do you mean, how's Suze? She's fine – she's right over there, see?"

"Oh, yeah", said Joe.

"Why do you ask?", Gretchen asked him, knowing that the abortion thing was a secret, just between the four of us. I didn't think Joe meant anything by his question, but maybe Gretchen was a little flummoxed by it and just a mite on the defensive side.

"Why do I ask? Because she seems like a good kid and I was just wondering how she likes it around here. You know, working here and all."

"Oh. Well, she says she likes it a lot – you know, the area and all. Says the scenery's a lot better than in Ohio and the people seem nicer. And she says she likes her job, too, and she's already got a few regulars. From what I understand, she's even thinking of moving here."

"Good to hear", said Joe, nodding.

"You guys ready or do you want a few minutes?", she asked.

"Give us five, okay?", said Bob.

"You got it. Oh – by the way – Artie's whipping up apple-cinnamon waffles, today. I had a bite – excellent. So, if that tickles your fancy, just let me know."

"I'm down for those", said Mike.

"Yeah, me, too", said Hal.

"Look, I guess we might as well order, then", said Bob.

We all ordered and then, as Gretchen was heading toward the kitchen, Bob said to me, "J.D. – I'm planning of having my guys come over and mow your field, this morning, if that's okay. Yesterday, being so nice and warm undoubtedly dried out whatever rain had fallen on it and today's supposed to be real nice, too."

"Not a problem, Bob. Your guys know what to do. We might have to run out for a little while, but you don't need us."

"Nope - and we should be ready to lay in your ninety or so bales by Tuesday if you fellas can help us stack it up in your loft."

Parker and I looked at each other and he nodded. "Works for us", I said.

"Good." And, changing the subject, he looked toward Mike and asked, "Hey, Mike – you involved with that big Halloween thing, downtown, next weekend?"

"Ah, just a little. I was at a meeting the other night and, well, it isn't most of those folks' first rodeo, so I think it'll come off just fine, just like it always does. The council will have some tables and chairs set up in front of the building, and I'll be around, but, honestly, I'm only peripherally involved."

"It gets bigger every year, doesn't it?", asked Hal.

"Yeah, I guess it does", Mike replied. "I just know the kids love it and it means real good business for the shops in town.”

“How many people are you expecting?”, asked Hal.

“Oh, I don’t know”, said Mike. “Looking at next weekend’s forecast, it’s supposed to be clear and cool, so…..maybe a couple thousand? That’s about what we had, last year, maybe a little more.”

“Oh, hey”, I said, looking at Hal, “speaking of Halloween, we’re going to bring those jack-o’-lanterns over to the Center, this noon. It’ll be open, right?”

“Oh, yeah”, said Hal. “We’ll be serving lunch, just like always. Unfortunately, though, I can’t be there. I promised my wife that we’d drive over to Woodstock, this morning. She likes to go through the shops and we generally grab lunch while we’re over there. But you don’t need me, anyway, do you?”

“Nope, not at all”, said Parker. “We’ll get ‘em all set up and all anybody has to do is turn on the little lights that’ll be inside ‘em. We’ll put ‘em on either side of the stage and screen, right?”

“Yep. And you can find a couple little tables to put them on”, Hal said.

“Cool. Got it.”

Just then, the kitchen doors swung open and here came Gretchen with our tray. She set it on one of those little folding things.

“Clear some space, you guys” and we all moved things around so she could set our plates down.

We all tore into our vittles, with four of us having Artie’s waffles – which, I might add, were outstanding.

As usual, any conversation while the feed bags were on was more or less verboten. There’s a time to talk and there’s a time to eat. And seldom does the twain ever meet. That’s the Geezer way, anyhow.

As we were laying down our entrenching tools and pushing our plates away, Suze walked up to the table.

“Wassup, you guys?”, she asked.

“Hey, Gretchen says you really like it around here”, said Joe.

"Yeah, I do. I do, a lot. I'm thinking of moving here, like, permanently."

"You should", said Bob. "Now, I don't know about Ohio, but I know this area and, from where I'm sitting, it's one of the best places I know of."

"Yeah, I'm kinda finding that", she said. "Look, I gotta go get this order in, but I just wanted you guys to know that that fella who was in here the other day – you know, with that flyer – well, he was here again today."

"The guy from the school board?", Mike asked.

"Yep. Only, today, he was here by himself. No lady."

"Anything interesting to report?", I asked.

"Nope. He just ate and split. Oh, he made a couple of phone calls, but they sounded like he was talking about his business – he told somebody to be at such-and-such an address at nine to repair a router or something. Stuff like that", she shrugged. "Okay, I'm off. Duty calls. Just wanted to say hello." And off she went.

"You ever go to those school board meetings?", Joe asked Mike.

"Ah, I've been to a couple of them over the past couple of years, but I usually try and stay away. They generally go on forever – even worse than our council meetings - and not all that much gets done."

He took a sip from his mug, then said, "As a matter of fact, they had to adjourn the last one because it went on so long that they didn't get through their entire agenda, so they're holding a special meeting this coming Tuesday to finish it up. Maybe I'll stop in to that. I kind of want to see what that new guy's like. You know, see if he's a turd in a punchbowl or if people are really listening to him."

"I can't imagine he'd get any traction with that CRT thing, though", said Hal. "Not in this community, anyway."

"You never know", said Mike. "We're living in some weird times, now."

And we all nodded sagely.

A few minutes later, the meeting broke up and we all headed out, waving our sayonaras to Gretchen and Suze.

"You won't forget that pumpkin, will you, Bill?", asked Gretchen from halfway across the room.

"Nope – I'm on it."

And she blew him a kiss.

When we got outside, Parker said that he was going to stop at Williams' on the way back to the farm to pick up a pumpkin. "Theirs will probably be bigger than the ones they're selling at Tops and I don't wanna have to drive all the way down to Crockett's if I don't have to."

"Cool", I said. "Meet you back there."

Just then, the back door opened and Suze appeared.

"Hey, you guys! Got a sec?", she shouted.

"Sure", I said, and she hurried down the steps toward us.

"Got some news", she said. "I didn't wanna say anything to the rest of the guys, but guess what?"

"You're pregnant again", said Parker.

"No, you asshole", she laughed, backhanding him on the arm. "I think I found a place to live."

"You did? Already?", I asked.

"Yep. Gretchen and I've been talking about it and she said that the guy who manages the Town Green Apartments, on the edge of town – sort of near the fairgrounds, I guess – anyway, that guy comes into the restaurant pretty often and she kind of knows him. Well, I guess he was in yesterday morning, after we left for my thing, and she asked him if he had any apartments available. And he did – one. I guess the people who were in it moved out, recently, and he hadn't advertised it, yet."

"I know that place. I mean, I've driven by it. Pretty nice", said Parker.

"Yeah, that's what I hear. Anyway, I called the guy yesterday afternoon after we'd gotten home and told him I'd take it. It's a one-bedroom."

"Wow – good for you", I said. "You can afford it, right?"

"No, J.D. I can't. I'm just gonna squat in it 'til he throws me out. Of course, I can afford it. I've got a little money in the bank and I'm making somewhat decent bank, here. And I don't have to worry about food." She pointed with her thumb toward the building.

"Plus, like I think Gretchen told you, she has some furniture in storage and I can use that."

"That's outstanding", I said. "Good for you. And I think it's great that you're moving here."

"Well, Ohio sucks – especially nowadays. And, yeah, I really like it here. I'm psyched."

"What about wheels?", Parker asked her.

"Well, that's next on the list, but I'm gonna have to wait a few weeks to do anything about that. I gotta build up a little cash stash – enough for a decent down payment on a fairly decent car or truck. I don't want some beater, like that one I have back in Ohio. I'm thinking of giving that to a friend of mine. With what I'm bringing in, I figure I'll be good to go in another couple of months, maybe a little less. Gretchen said she'll put it in her name – I don't have shit for credit - and I'll give the payments to her every month."

"Sounds like a plan, but what are you going to do about getting to and from work and all?", he asked. "And anywhere else you want to go?"

"Well, Gretchen'll pick me up and drop me off, every day, and she said that I can use her car, once in a while, but we'll have to work that out as it comes."

I thought for a few seconds, then came to a decision.

"Tell you what, Suze. I've got a real nice truck back at the farm that's generally just sitting around. What if I let you use this", nodding toward the Subaru, "until you can get your own? And I'll just drive my truck."

"Good idea", said Parker, nodding sagely, the way Parker often does.

"Huh? Really, J.D?", Suze asked, her eyes going wide.

"Yeah, sure. Makes all the sense in the world, doesn't it? No reason for me to have two sets of wheels and you not have any. Plus, the insurance I've got will cover you, too."

"Well", she said, "it would only be for a few weeks. Promise."

"I know. Whatever."

"Oh, that is just so wonderful!", she said, actually clapping her hands.

"By the way, when are you moving in? I mean, you've gotta sign the lease and all. When's all that gonna happen?"

"We're going to run up there, this afternoon, after we're done here and do the lease thing."

"Okay - and how about moving the furniture?", asked Parker. "Like, when do you actually move in?"

"I don't know, just yet, but we'll find that out, this afternoon, when we meet with the guy."

"Okay, just let us know when that'll be", said Parker. "We can use J.D.'s and my truck to move the shit from the storage place."

"Oh, that's great, Parker, thanks, but I don't think it'll be necessary. See, the manager guy says that he's got one of those "Two Guys and A Truck' or something franchises and Gretchen said she'll hire him to do it."

"Okay, but if you need us, we're here", he said.

"Cool, big thanks. But, listen, I gotta get back inside – I've been out here too long", she said.

I reached into my pocket and pulled out the Subaru key. "Here – you might as well take this, now. I'll catch a ride with Parker."

"Really, J.D.? That is so fucking cool!", she said, taking the key.

"Yep. Just don't wreck it, okay?"

"Promise", she said, and she gave me a big bear hug.

"Go on", I said. "Get back to work."

And she smiled, held up the key and trotted back up the steps.

"Good", said Parker. "Real good."

On the way back to the farm, we stopped at Williams' and, after several minutes spent perusing the pumpkins, Parker finally chose one.

Then, we headed home.

When we got there, we could see two of Bob's guys out in the hayfield. They each had tractors and mowers and were moving up and down the field. When they spotted us, we all waved. They were good guys and they'd been around a couple of times over the summer.

Around eleven-fifteen, Parker hunted me down in the house and said, "We oughta make for the Center, pretty soon, right?"

"Yep – I was just coming to get you."

"Listen – let's both drive", he said. "After we leave there, I think I'll head home. I got a shit-ton of laundry to do and I figure I'd better do it, today."

"Cool."

"I already put the pumpkins in my truck, too – one on the floor and one in the passenger's seat. If we both went in my truck, you'd have to sit in the bed."

"Very funny."

"Okay", he said. "Let's mount up."

Twenty minutes later, we both pulled into the parking lot at the People's Center. Getting out of his truck, Parker walked over to the dumpster and looked in.

"Hasn't been here, yet", he said.

So, we each grabbed a jack-o'-lantern and went into the building.

There were a number of people in there, sitting at various tables, eating their lunch.

"Ooh, here are the jack-o'-lanterns Hal told us about", said one woman. "How exciting."

And, as if on cue, all heads turned toward us.

"Hi, folks", I said. "We're just going to set these up on the stage and be out of your hair in two shakes." I looked over and saw Parker placing tables at each side of the stage.

"Bring 'em up here", he said, and I did.

"Excuse me", I said to the group after the pumpkins were in place. "I don't know who needs to hear this, but there's a little light in each one of these. All somebody has to do is reach in and flick the little switch."

Thank God, they pretty much ignored me and I wasn't accosted by several elderly women coming up to see a demonstration of how to turn the switches on and off.

We headed back outside and shot the shit for a few minutes, waiting on Schmidt and his truck.

About five after twelve, we saw him coming down the road.

When he pulled in, he looked our way and gave us the 'hold-on-a-minute' sign. Then, he drove up to the dumpster, grabbed it with the truck's mechanical arms and tipped it over the cab and into the big box behind it.

He turned the beast around and stopped as he got to us, the big air brakes hissing loudly.

As he came around the front of the truck, we could see that he was probably around six feet tall and slim, though he had some pretty decent-sized shoulders. He was wearing a red baseball cap (I looked for the telltale MAGA embroidery on the front of it, but it wasn't there). His hair – what we could see of it – looked reddish, too, as did his beard.

"You guys Spencer and Parker?", he said, walking up to us.

"I'm J.D. Spencer and this is Bill Parker", I said.

He put out his hand and we both shook it. "Good to meet you. Listen, I don't have much time, but Ron said that I could count on you if I need you, right?"

"Yep", I said. "We're totally on your side on this."

"Good. Now, long story short, I'm getting in pretty good with a group of yahoos that are playing tough-guy militia shit. And I don't know if they mean it or they're just playing. A couple of 'em seem a little hard-core, but I'm not so sure about the rest. But, nowadays, you never know."

"Assholes are coming out of the fucking woodwork", said Parker.

"You're the one that used to be a cop, right?", Schmidt asked him.

"Yeah. Detective. Did some undercover, too."

"Then you know what it's like."

Parker nodded.

"Okay, without going into too much detail, we don't think – at least at this point – that, with the exception of – *maybe* – a couple of their hard-core leaders, we'll never get enough to charge these guys with. But we've gotta find a way to (finger quotes) 'discourage' these assholes and send them home with their tails between their legs. And leave this shit alone. Somehow. And that's why Ron turned me on to you guys. He said you might have some ideas, though I don't know what those'd be. You gotta tell me."

"That's all he said, right?", I asked, hoping that Ron hadn't spilled the beans on the whole ninja horseman thing.

"Yeah, he just said you guys might be able to help."

"We'll be glad to", said Parker. "You just gotta keep us in the loop as much as you can. And point us in the right direction, if it comes to that."

"I'll do that", said Schmidt. "What is it you guys do, anyway? Ron said it was kinda off-the-wall."

"That's classified, son", said Parker, with a wink.

"Okay, I got it. Alright, look – there's gonna be a meeting, tomorrow afternoon. At some guy's farm. And, I guess, a whole shitload of guys – maybe a couple dozen – are gonna be there. Oh, the guy who seems to be running things is a guy named Frank. Ron did a little homework on him and found that his last name's Branson. And, I guess his wife's got her own gig, too. Like she runs the local chapter of something called Moms for Liberty or something."

"Moms for Liberty?", I asked. "We ran into some of them, the other day, protesting something."

"Protesting what?", he asked.

"Ah, it was some anti-abortion thing", I said. "Wasn't much, but when you said the name, it just rang a bell. You don't know Branson's wife's first name, do you?"

He thought for a minute. "I think it's Sheila or Stella or something like that. I can find out if you want me to."

"Nah, that's okay", I said. "Just wondering."

"Alright, I gotta go. I'm on kind of a tight schedule", said Schmidt. "Oh, here – let me give you my real phone number. If I call you, it'll probably be on a burner but, if you need me, call this number." And he gave it to us and we both put it into our phones.

We all shook hands again and he said, "Keep in touch." And he went back around the front of his truck, got in, gave us a little wave, and headed out, the beast under him belching smoke.

<h1 style="text-align:center"><u>CHAPTER 15</u></h1>

After Schmidt pulled out, I said, "Interesting." Parker looked at me and raised his eyebrows, as in what-do-you-mean?

I answered, "That it sounds like that woman we saw at the clinic might be this guy, Branson's, wife."

"Yeah, that's what I was thinkin', too", he said. "Sounds like two assholes in happily wedded bliss." A second or two later, he said, "Schmidt seems okay, I guess."

"Not much to judge him on but, yeah." Then, "I wonder if we're really going to get involved in this."

"Could be. Sounds like it, anyway", he said.

"Look, I think we should call Ron. Tell him about meeting Schmidt and all. But let's do it from back at the farm. I don't wanna be standing here in a parking lot."

"Okay", he said. "Meet you back there."

Fifteen minutes later, we reconnoitered on the porch. It had turned out to be another very nice day and Bob's guys were still cutting.

"Ron, right?", I asked and Parker nodded as we walked up onto the porch. I reached for my phone and hit Ron's number.

A few seconds later, we heard, "Ha! I figured I'd hear from you two rascals. You meet my boy?"

"Yep", I said. "We just left him a few minutes ago. We were at the Women's Center and he drove in and did the dumpster thing. We set it up that way."

"What'd you think?"

"Well", I said, "it sounds like you've got us roped into this thing, right?"

Ron laughed and said, "You got it, chief. Look, like I said, we're running far too lean around here and we're paying an arm and a leg to these contractors – guys like Schmidt. So, we can use all the help we can get and, like he probably told you, we don't even know if we can do anything, legally, with these assholes. Not unless they break some law. But we gotta try and pour some water on their fire."

"And you're thinking that maybe we can help. And you're also thinking that, just maybe, the ninja horseman might be able to help, too, if I'm not mistaken", I said.

"Bingo, my liege. Maybe. I'm thinking that, if we can somehow throw the fear of God – or your demon – into one or two of these guys, maybe we can send 'em back under their rocks for a while. Whether we'll ever be able to really clean it up is another matter."

Parker and I looked at each other, then he said, "Schmidt seemed to indicate that one of the muckety-mucks of one of these local yahoo groups is married to some babe who runs a thing around here called Moms for Liberty. That true?"

"Yeah, the Bransons, Frank and Sheila", he said. "Real right-wing zealots. The husband runs his own little contracting company and, from what I've been able to find out, the wife is just involved with that group - and Moms for Liberty's on our radar in several parts of the country. They seem to be getting all up in there with local school boards and shit, trying to run their curriculums. Or is it curricula?"

"Yeah", I said, "and I guess she and a bunch of her cronies were at our local school board meeting, last week. There's another meeting, this coming Tuesday night, and Mike said he's going."

"Good", said Ron. "See if you can get with him before then and give him a little background – but only a little - and see what kind of intel he comes back with."

Mike had been involved with a couple of our cases and he and Ron knew each other through them. As a matter of fact, at one point, we'd decreed Parker and me and Ron and Mike to be 'the four horsemen'.

"Yeah, there's a little more to it, too", I said. "I guess a new guy on the school board's yapping about this CRT thing and wants it removed from the schools."

"CRT isn't even real", said Ron. "But, yeah – we're coming up against that all the goddamned time. Man, people can be so stupid, can't they?"

"There seems to be a whole lot of stupid going around, these days", said Parker.

"Ya think?", asked Ron.

"Hey", I said, "Schmidt told us that Branson's called for some kind of gathering-slash-meeting, tomorrow afternoon, like, around three o'clock. He said that there might be a couple dozen guys show up."

"Yeah, that's what he told me, too. He's gonna report back about whatever goes down but, man, would I like to get some photos of some license plates. You guys busy, tomorrow?"

I thought for half-a-second, then said, "Wait – are you insinuating that Parker and I should go there and take pictures of those guys' vehicles while they're there? What are you – nuts?"

"No, of course not. However, since you brought it up….."

"What?"

"Well, let's just say that you wanted to help out. I could overnight you a simple little toy – a motion-sensor camera. And, say you received it. And, say, you guys just might be driving past the place that the meeting's being held at and, just maybe, you affixed that aforementioned camera to a thing, directly across the road from the guy's driveway. That way, I'd get pics of license plates up the wazoo as they were all driving out. Knowhutahmean?"

"I see", I said and Parker nodded sagely. "Ron - you think there's something directly across the road where we could place that?".

"Oh, yeah – we got a Google Earth shot of it. See, the driveway – it's more like a little road, actually – leads from the west side of the road down to the house and the barn and what-have-you. But, directly across from the entrance to the driveway is an old stone fence. I gotta think that you could kind of tuck it in between a couple of rocks. It's really tiny – only about an inch-and-a-half long and three-quarters of an inch in diameter. Really small."

"Okay", said Parker.

"Oh - and it's got a transmitter in it, too, so we can snare the pics right out of the ozone. You wouldn't have to go back and fetch it."

"Got it", Parker said, "but aren't we cutting it a little too close, timing-wise? I mean, if you overnight it, you sure it'll get here in time for us to run up there and do that?"

"I can get it to you first thing in the morning – like, by around nine o'clock. That'd give you a few hours to run up there. And, it's not all that far, is it?"

"Nah", said Parker. "Only about fifteen minutes from here. If we get it, like around the time you said, we should have it set up and be back here by ten, ten-thirty. Plenty of time."

I raised my eyebrows and tilted my head, as if to say, "Okay – if you think so."

"You got the address?", Parker asked him.

"Yeah. So, you're gonna do it?"

"Guess so, dude", I said, looking at Parker, who nodded. "Yeah, we'll do it. Now – the address. I'll put it into my notes."

"Okay – it's 525 Field Road, Milan, New York."

"Got it", I said, typing.

"Alright, good", said Ron. "I'll get the camera off to you, right now. And do me a favor – shoot me a text when you get it and another one when you've got it in place, okay?"

"Roger", I said. "Oh - and, on the instructions, just tell them to leave it, that it doesn't need a signature, okay? I don't want it showing up before we get home from our morning meeting and the guy doesn't leave it because nobody signed for it."

"Okey-doke got it – catch you guys later. And, thanks." And we disconnected.

"Okay", I said to Parker. "I guess we're really in."

"Yep", he replied.

Down in the East Park section of Hyde Park, Frank Branson was sitting in his living room, watching the Wisconsin/Ohio State game, in between answering phone calls coming in from his 'phone tree' guys.

So far, with four of the five guys reporting in, he counted fifteen 'yesses' – guys who'd be showing up at Oscar's tomorrow afternoon. Throw out two or three of them who probably wouldn't show, anyway, and he figured about twelve, plus him, Oscar and the four phone tree guys – or, about eighteen, total. And that didn't include anybody that Eric would bring in.

Where the hell was Gallagher, anyway?, he thought, as he walked into the kitchen to grab a brew from the fridge. As he did, he heard Sheila's car door close, out in the driveway. She'd been at the store.

He went outside to help her carry in the groceries and, and as they got back into the kitchen, his phone rang. It was Gallagher.

"Gotta take this", Frank said to Sheila. "Yo, Eric. Whaddya know?"

He listened for a few seconds, then said, "Eight? Ah, that's great, man. Good job. I figure with you and those eight guys, added to what we already have, there'll be between twenty-seven and thirty guys show up. Biggest meeting ever."

He listened for a few seconds, then said, "Yeah, boy. I'll say. Guys are really wantin' to get involved, now. Feels good, man. Oh, hey, listen – Schmidt's gonna be there, right? Good. Yeah – I wanna give him a shout-out for that thing he did on that wall. That took guts, man, and initiative. If the other guys see him gettin' an attaboy, maybe they'll start thinking of stuff they can do, too, y'know?"

He took a swallow of his beer and said, "Look – one of the things I wanna talk about, tomorrow, is that Halloween thing up in Rhinebeck, next Sunday. I think we oughta do a little something to make a little splash, make some noise, y'know? Anyway, let's talk about it, okay? Good. Okay, guy, cool. Catch you at Oscar's."

"Sounds like you've got a good-sized group showing up, tomorrow", Sheila said, as she was putting away the groceries. "Congrats, honey. Good job."

"We're getting there, I think", he said.

"Oh, I heard you mention that you guys are thinking of doing something up at the Halloween Parade next Sunday......"

"Yeah", he said. "We're thinkin' about it. I'm not sure, yet, what it'll be. Maybe we'll just show up, en masse and, you know, sorta show the colors. Carry a couple of signs. I don't know yet – but that's why I wanna talk about it with the guys."

"Well, we're going to be there, too", she said, meaning the Moms for Liberty. "Our plan is to set up a table, somewhere along the parade route, and hand out literature and bumper stickers and pins and all that."

"They gonna let you do that? Set up a table?", Branson asked.

"Well, no, not really. But it's public space, right? And we have our First Amendment rights, don't we? I figure that, if we don't set it up in front of somebody's business, but we put it, like, along the street near the Farmer's Market – which is public property – we'll be fine."

"How many women you gonna have?"

"Oh, probably at least a dozen, maybe a few more."

"Cool", he said.

Then he laughed and said, "Trick or fucking treat, Rhinebeck."

––––––––––––––––––––

The next morning dawned chilly, with a cooler-than-usual breeze coming out of the north. It was clear, though, and that was good. The wind would help the newly-mown alfalfa to dry quicker and, maybe, Bob's guys could start raking and baling by this afternoon.

I put on my new Patagonia jacket and headed out the door.

As I walked down the lane toward my truck, I spied the kids standing at the gate. I guess when they saw me coming that far down the lane toward them, they figured that I was heading their way, ostensibly to hand them each a few treats. Which, of course, I did.

And I also noticed that their winter coats were really coming on, now. The days had gotten a lot shorter and their onboard sensors had noticed that and had triggered their hair growth. One thing, though – because of their breeding, they weren't the sort to get really shaggy in the winter. The Thoroughbred in them saw to that. But, still, they were hairier than they had been a couple of weeks ago.

The treats doled out and a few scratches given to each horse, I split for breakfast.

When I got there – being the last to arrive, as usual – the conversation was basically centered around Joe.

From what I gathered as Gretchen came over, filled my mug and briefly put her hand on my shoulder by way of welcome, Joe was holding forth.

"Yeah, I took stage lighting in college", he said. "You know, basically learning how all the circuitry and dimmer boards worked and so on, how to use gels to make the colors you'd want – all of that. I was one of the main honchos in what we called the 'light crew'. Matter of fact, I even designed a couple of shows, myself."

Because I hadn't seen any of that coming when I walked in, I just sat there, listening.

"Hey – J.D.", said Bob. "Just to catch you up, Joe's going to be working with the high school's drama department in helping them put on one of their shows. What is it again, Joe?"

"Oklahoma", he said.

"Oh, hell – I know 'Oklahoma'", I said. "We put that on when I was in high school. Actually, I was in it. I played 'Slim', who was a buddy of – holy shit! - Will Parker's." My head snapped over to Parker. "I never, ever thought of that, until right this minute – that I played a guy who was friends with the character that has the same name as yours."

Parker laughed and Mike said, "What goes around, comes around, I guess."

"Yeah – how 'bout that?", I said. "Okay – sorry, Joe – I interrupted you."

"That's cool. Cool story, too. Anyway, yeah – I'm gonna be helping them out with the lights. I'll do kind of a rudimentary design. Hell, it'll have to be rudimentary – it's been nearly fifty years since I did that. But I think it should be fun."

"I think it's great that you're doing that, Joe", said Hal. "You know, giving back and all."

"Yeah", said Joe, "but I gotta admit that I'm doing it as much for me as for the kids. I get bored, just sitting around in the evenings – that's when they have their rehearsals and do the set building and lighting work - and this'll give me something to do. Should be fun."

"Good morning, gentlemen", we heard as Suze came gliding up to us. "Just stopped by to say hey. How y'all?"

We all made noises that we were well.

Then, she asked me, "J.D. Any possibility that I could come by in a little while to see the horses?"

"Sure", I said. "But aren't you working?"

She leaned forward and, in a mock conspiratorial tone, said, "Gretchen wanted me to have today off, but I told her that I'd come in for the early rush, then split."

"Ah, she's gettin' soft in her old age", said Joe.

"You'd better not let her hear you say that, pardner", she said. "She'll short-change you on the home fries."

Joe mockingly zipped his lips.

"Sure, kid. Fine with me. Parker?"

He shrugged his acquiescence.

"Okay, look", she said. "I oughta be out of here by nine – should be at your place a little after that, okay?"

"Yep - and I know the kids'll be glad to see you, too."

She gave me a thumbs-up and said, "Okay – catch the rest of you guys tomorrow" and off she went.

"So, she met your horses, huh?", asked Mike.

"Yeah – I'd told her about them and she swung by the other afternoon. It was, like, mutual love at first sight." I wanted to get off this subject, pronto, and not have the guys ask me too many questions about why she was there.

So, like an asshole, I looked at Joe and sang – rather quietly but also quite horribly – "Ohhhh-klahoma where the wind comes sweepin' down the plain."

"Aw, Jesus", he said. "Get the hook."

Nothing more of any real import was discussed during breakfast, but Bob did say that his guys would be over – they were probably there, already.

The Geezers knuckle-knocked the day's meeting to a close and we all went our separate ways.

When I drove into the lane behind Parker, I glanced over at the porch and saw a package leaning up against the kitchen door. Good, I thought.

Once we were parked, I told Parker that I thought the camera was here and we went up to check it out.

And, sure enough, in the padded envelope, there was a tiny black tube, all wrapped in bubble wrap, with a little set of instructions packed in with it.

"Let's go into the kitchen and check it out", said Parker. "It's fucking cold out here."

A couple of minutes later, we had it figured out. It couldn't have been any simpler, either. You just point the camera where you want it to shoot and turn on a little switch on the side of it when you're ready to go. Piece of cake.

"Okay, what is it – right around nine?", said Parker, looking at the clock on the wall. "I guess we could run up there just about any time."

A text came into my phone.

Suze: "5 minutes".

"Suze says she'll be here in five minutes", I said. "What do we want to do about her? I'm not sure I should leave her alone with the horses. She hasn't had enough experience, yet, and she probably doesn't want to just stand at the gate for close to an hour."

Parker said, "Hell, she can come with us, can't she?"

"What are we going to tell her about what we're doing?", I asked. "I mean, this is kinda spy shit, right?"

He thought for a minute, then said, "Look, dude – why don't we fill her in a little bit about what's going on? She's cool as ice and you know she hates these motherfuckers just as much as we do."

"Well, how much do we tell her?", I asked.

"Tell her the truth about what we're doing – that we're helping a buddy in the FBI to get some intel on some fucking douchebag right-wing extremists. But all we're doing is placing that little camera in among some rocks. She'll be cool with that."

"Yeah, I guess", I said. "I just don't know if she should really get involved. I mean, she's just a kid and all - and she's been through a lot, lately."

"She won't be getting involved. We're just taking a nice little ride and placing a camera where it might do some good. That's all."

"Okay. I guess."

A few minutes later, Suze drove in – it was odd seeing my car coming down the lane - and I called her into the kitchen after she'd gotten out.

"What's up, you guys?", she asked, as she sat down.

"Well, look", I said, and went on to explain just a little bit about our buddy, Ron, and what he and his associates were doing, concerning some of the new and newish right-wing extremist groups.

"Fucking A", she said, "and you guys are helping him? Like deputies or something? That's so cool."

"Well, no", I said. "It's nothing official, we're just doing this on the DL. We figure it's the right thing to do."

"Got it."

Then, Parker pulled out the little camera and explained that we were on our way up to a place outside of Milan where a meeting of one of those groups would take place, this afternoon. And that we were going to stick the little camera in a stone fence across from the driveway, so Ron could get pictures of the license plates of vehicles driving in and out.

"Oh – spy shit", she said. "Let me see that." And Parker handed her the camera. "Aw, man, this is cool as shit – real James Bond stuff."

"Yeah", said Parker, taking it back. "You ready to do this?"

We nodded and I said, "Let's take my truck. It's got a back seat."

CHAPTER 16

We made our way north on Milan Hollow Road, turned east on Salisbury Turnpike and intersected with Field Road. Following the wise words of our GPS, I turned left on Field. That done, it informed us that our destination was two-point-four miles ahead.

The road was kind of woodsy and we saw several old stone fences on both sides of the road. We spotted what appeared to be a dirt road running off to our left, just as the GPS alerted us that we had arrived.

"Slow down and drive past it", said Parker, as Suze leaned forward between us in the back seat. As I did, all three of our heads snapped to the left to see if we could spot anything of interest. We didn't. The dirt road went down a little hill and wound around to the right, hidden by trees.

"Okay", said Parker, "go up a little ways and turn around, then go past it again".

I did.

"Still nothing", he said, looking to his right. "Okay, go on up about a quarter-mile or so, then turn back around." After we did that, he said, "Now, pull over to the shoulder, put your flashers on and pop your hood."

"Dude", said Suze, "we're still a hundred yards from where we wanna be, aren't we?"

"Yeah, but don't you think it'd look just a little suspicious pulling up right in front of the driveway?", he said. "Nah, this way, we'll look like we've got a problem. You guys get out and be looking under the hood and I'll go a few feet into the woods, hustle up there and come up behind the fence. Then, I'll stick the camera in. Go on, put your flashers on."

The three of us piled out, with Suze and me staring stupidly under the hood, while Parker took off at a trot.

Two minutes later, he got back to the truck via the same route, and said, "Alright, let's get outta here."

"Got it?", I asked him.

"Good as gold."

"Okay, hold on", I said, reaching for my phone. I texted Ron, "Done. Will call in a few."

A few seconds later, I got a thumbs-up emoji from him.

When we got back to the farm, the three of us headed for the kitchen.

I got three sodas out of the fridge, sat down, pulled out my phone again and hit Ron.

"Yo", he said, "Got it?"

"Yep", said Parker. "I aimed it right at the driveway and turned 'er on."

"Hold on", said Ron. A couple seconds later, he said, "Yep – there it is."

"You can see the driveway?", I asked him.

"Well, no – I can't see through the camera – the aperture only opens when there's motion and, then, only to take a shot. I can see, though, that the transmitter's working. Now, all we have to do is wait."

"Oh, okay. Hey, listen, Ron – we've got a friend here with us. Her name's Suze and she's Gretchen's niece. From Ohio."

"Hi, Ron", she said.

"Hi, Suze. Nice to meet you. I feel like I know your aunt – we did a big thing for her, not too long ago. So, what are you doing there? And, guys – I take it she's cool?"

Suze and I both started talking at once, but I motioned to her to wait a second.

"Dude – she's one of us. I mean, really. We haven't filled her in on too much, yet, but that just might happen."

"You mean about the nin– ", Ron started to say, but I instantly interrupted him by saying, "One thing at a time, man. And, no – not that."

"Not what?", Suze asked.

"Never mind, kid. There's a time and a place for everything. Now, Ron – Suze is as adamant about stopping these right-wing mofos as we are, aren't you, Suze?"

"Oh, fucking-A, yeah. Listen, um, Ron – like J.D. said, I'm from Ohio and I've seen all this shit up-close-and-personal. It's ridiculous and it's just gotta be stopped. Either that or these nitwits are gonna take us back to the last century. Or worse. So, yeah – I'm down with whatever you guys are doing."

"Hey – Parker and I are from the last century", I protested.

"Yeah - and it shows, too", she said.

"Ooh, suh-nap!", said Ron. "I think I like this chick already. Alright, look – I gotta go, but thanks for doing that, today. I think we can i.d. a bunch of guys because of it."

"Yeah, sure", said Parker. "And you're gonna get a download from Schmidt after this meet-up, right?"

"Yep, that's the plan. I don't know if it'll be tonight or not, but by morning, at the latest. Want me to let you know what he says?"

"Oh, by all means", said Parker. "And, listen – anything else you need, just let us know, right?"

"Absolutement, mes amis. You know I will. And, Suze – nice meeting you. But watch your wallet around these two old farts. They'll make you lighter by your entire bank account if you're not careful."

"I think I can hold my own", said Suze, smiling at both of us.

"Yeah – she knows Krav Maga", I said, "so we're gonna be careful."

"Holy shit, Suze!", said Ron. "You know Krav Maga?"

"Yeah, a little. Enough to hold my own and then some", she said.

"I've always wanted to learn that", he said. "I even looked into it once."

"Why didn't you do it?", she asked him.

"Because I'm lazy", he said. "Maybe someday. Alright, you guys – I'm out." And he disconnected.

"Seems like a nice guy", said Suze.

"The best", I said.

"And he works for the FBI?"

"Yep. He's an ace hacker turned Feeb guy. It's a long story."

"Huh", she said, taking a swallow of her Coke.

"Alright", I said. "You wanted to hang out with the kids for a while, right?"

"Oh, for sure. Can I go down there, now?"

"Yep, but do me a favor – don't go in with them, just yet. I'll come down in a little while and go in with you – give you a little horsemanship lesson, okay?"

"Oh, I'd love that", she said, getting up from the table. "Alright – see you guys in a few." And she walked out the door.

"What about you?", I asked Parker.

"Ah, I think I'll run down to the garage and work on Gretchen's pumpkin for a little while. I'd like to get it to her tomorrow. You?"

"I'm going in and catch a little of the Giants game."

____

A little before two o'clock, cars and trucks began streaming into Oscar Jensen's farm.

When Frank Branson drove down the lane in Sheila's car – he hadn't wanted to bring his truck, with his name painted on the side – he noticed a good dozen or more pickups, panel vans and cars already parked. He noticed Gallagher walking toward the barn.

"Hey, Eric!", he said, as he got out of the car.

"Yo, Frank."

"Looks like we're gonna have a pretty good turn-out." And they shook hands.

"Looks downright righteous, dude", said Gallagher.

Guys were milling around the big open door to the barn, talking and smoking and laughing. As Frank walked past them, there were high fives, handshakes and 'nice-ta-see-yas'.

Inside the barn, Jensen had laid hay bales in a large circle for the men to sit on. Frank walked up to him and said, "Great job, Oscar - and thanks for all this, today. Y'know, your place is a perfect spot to have a meeting – nothing can be seen from the road and we can easily fit a whole bunch of guys in here."

"Glad to do it, Frank. My pleasure. And I figure this old barn oughta be used for somethin'. By the way, if we wanna use it during the winter, we'll have to bring in a couple of space heaters."

"We can do that, Oscar." And he saw Lou Schmidt over against the wall, talking with a couple of guys. "I gotta go talk to Lou for a sec – we'll start this thing in a couple of minutes, D'you mind rounding up the guys?"

"Not at all, Frank. I'm on it."

Walking over to the little group Schmidt was in, Frank welcomed the guys, then said, "Lou – can I talk to you for a sec?"

"Sure, Frank", he said and the two of them stepped away.

"Look – I didn't wanna blindside you with this, but if you don't mind, I'm gonna tell the guys about your little spray paint thing the other night. Give you a little attaboy. I think it'll help to psyche up the group and serve as a little example of what they might be able to do themselves."

"I think that's a great idea, Frank. But, do me a favor – don't mention me by name. Not that I don't trust these guys, but loose lips sink ships, know what I mean? I just don't want guys maybe blabbing my name around. I mean, I know they'd probably mean well, but you never know who might hear my name. That okay?"

"Oh, sure, Lou. And, yeah – you're probably right. What we don't need is the cops sniffing around any of us. So, I'll just mention that (finger quotes) one of our group – one of (more finger quotes) The Group – did it and it can serve as an example of what they can do."

"Yeah, that's cool", said Schmidt.

Over in the doorway, Eric Gallagher was introducing Flint Stone to a bunch of the other guys as Oscar was trying to herd everybody into the barn and onto the hay bales.

Oscar's task nearly accomplished, Branson walked into the center of the circle of bales, not unlike a circus ringmaster.

"Alright, you guys", he said loudly. "Huddle up. Come on – sit down. Let's get this show on the road."

About thirty seconds later, all the guys were sitting and Branson began by thanking all of them for being here today. He knew it meant taking a good chunk out of their Sundays and that some of the guys had had to drive quite a distance to get here.

"But, by being here", he said, "you've demonstrated two things. First, that you feel –

like all of us feel – that this country's going down the tubes in a hurry and is being
taken over by left-wing socialists, the Blacks and the Jews, not to mention the
foreigners who're flooding in. America's in danger of not being America, anymore. And
that's just unacceptable."

He took a swig from a water bottle, then continued, "Second, that you're committed.
Committed to the cause. And it's happening all over the country – we see it on the
news all the time. From the Pacific Northwest to Florida and everywhere in between,
people are starting to rise up. They're rising up to take our country back. And that's
why we're here – to become a part of that movement. And we're gonna have to be the
ones to do it, too because the federal government is completely infiltrated with Soros-
backed traitors – people who want to see the America we know and love smashed
and burned to the ground. And we're just not gonna take that, are we?"

There was a semi-rousing round of No's, with some guys a little or a lot more
vociferous than others.

"Now", Frank continued, "what are we gonna do?"

"Kill the motherfuckers", came a voice from the group, but whoever said it was sitting
behind Frank and he didn't see who it was.

"No", he said. "That's the absolute worst thing we could do, right now. Maybe, if it ever
really comes to a revolution, but not now. That'd bring the feds - and the cops – down
on us like a ton of bricks. They'd probably send us all to Gitmo. Now, I have an idea
that I'd like to lay on you guys but, first, let me tell you about a little thing that
happened a few nights ago. It's the type of guerilla tactic that I think we can do and
that we can get away with. And, just maybe, it'll give you guys some ideas of your
own."

He took another swallow of water while turning to look at the circle of men around him.

"The other night, one of our group tagged a building. Actually, it was the People's
Center, down in Rhinebeck. On their movie night, the Center had shown 'Yentl' – that
Barbra Streisand flick that's all about Jews. Anyway, one of our members found out
about it and, in the middle of the night, went over there and spray-painted 'Fuck Jews'
in big red letters on their wall."

"Righteous", came one voice. "Fucking-A", another. Frank saw two guys high-five
each other and a number of smiles and head nods around the circle.

"Now,", said Frank, "they cleaned it off before it got on the news or anything, but still –
it was a gutsy move. It showed the type of thinking and initiative that I think can not

only make a powerful statement but that we can all use if we use our imaginations and have the courage to do it. Right?", he asked the group.

"Who did it?", one of the guys asked. Schmidt sat there with a poker face, not giving the merest hint that it was him.

"Well, I'm not gonna tell you", said Frank. "I don't want any of your names – our names - being bandied about. You never know if it'll get back to the law or not. And I don't want any of us getting arrested. It's just a guerilla thing. Oh - and if any of you do anything like that, please tell me so I can give you what? A big bear hug and a thank you? Yeah, but that's about it. Because that shit's gotta be done on the down-low, okay?"

He could feel a general consensus in the room, but he also knew that the guys were chomping at the bit to do something more than tag a fucking building.

"Now", he said, "I think I have an idea of how we can make a real splash. You ready?"

All of the guys' eyes fell on him.

"Next Sunday, they're gonna have their annual Halloween parade and festival, down in Rhinebeck."

Head nods, pretty much all around.

"Well, here's my idea……"

And, for the next couple of minutes, he laid it out for them.

It came down to as many of the guys as possible showing up, en masse, and marching right down the street with the rest of the marchers. They'd just jump into the parade and walk along. But – he wanted all of them to dress alike, much the same as the guys had done down in Charlottesville a few years ago and those guys up in Idaho at that gay pride parade, a few months back. And, they'd wear masks.

"You know, a lot of the groups - like the Proud Boys and the Oath Keepers – do that and it really makes a statement. Now, I'm thinking of camo pants and jackets. There", he said pointing, "like Steve, there's, wearing. Stand up, will ya, Steve?" And Steve stood up and took an exaggerated bow, causing laughter around the circle.

"I'd imagine most of you have something like that – or can get it at Dick's, right across the bridge, so that's what I'd like to do, okay?"

He turned in a circle and got head nods and thumbs-up. One guy said, "Dick's has camo face masks, too – the kind that covers your whole head except for your eyes. Also, you can get 'em on Amazon and they'll be at your house in three days."

"Thanks, Andy", said Frank. "I think, if we can all get one of those, that'd be great and would also really hide our faces."

"What about rifles? We gonna carry them?", asked another guy. "They're legal to carry in New York."

"Good question, Jason", said Frank, turning to him. "Here's my thinking: I don't think we should. For one thing, it's a kids' event and I'm afraid carrying guns would really hurt our cause, maybe even with the people who feel like we do."

"I thought we were trying to make a statement", said a bearded guy in a ball cap. "You wanna make a statement, we all show up packin' and that'll really make a statement. Plus, we've got Two-A rights to do that." A couple of the other guys nodded in agreement.

Frank shrugged and said, "I just think it would hurt us more than help us. But I guess because we're kind of a democracy here, why don't we put it up for a vote?"

That got head nods, too.

"Okay – all in favor of carrying long guns, raise your hand."

A number of hands went up and Frank went around the circle, counting.

"Okay – I've got twelve for. Now, against?"

He went around again.

"Fourteen against. Plus me, that's fifteen. It's real close, but that's the vote", he said. There was some grumbling, but not much.

"What about handguns?", asked Gallagher, who was sitting next to Stone.

"Hey, man," said Frank, "if you've got a permit to conceal carry, you've got a right to do that. As far as I'm concerned, that's entirely up to you."

He looked around the room again, then said, "Okay, we good?", and there was general agreement.

"Now, the parade starts in front of the firehouse, at the corner of Market and Center at two o'clock. I think we should get there, maybe, half an hour before that – say, one-thirty. And, I think we should park a couple of blocks away – either along the street or in one of the business parking lots – along either Livingston or Chestnut. If you don't know where that is, just use your GPS. Then, we'll meet up on the north side – the back side - of the Farmer's Market – and that's on Livingston, just west of Center. Just a short walk."

He continued, "Then, we'll walk as a group through the Farmer's Market – they'll have a big deal going on, there, with all kinds of shit happening. Anyway, we'll walk through all that and join the parade along East Market. We'll just step into the parade, en masse, and walk to the end. Y'all with me?"

Again, there was general agreement.

"Okay, so, I'd say that we'll make quite a statement, just walking along with all those kids and some of their parents. The whole town'll be watching the parade and they won't be able to fucking miss us – a couple dozen guys, all dressed up in camo and wearing masks."

"What about signs?", came a voice from behind him.

"Signs. Good question." He paused for a minute, then said, "I think, yeah. Just no open profanity. That'll get us busted, right away. Oh - and no swastikas, for the same reason. But Confederate flags, Trump signs, Two-A signs, White Lives Matter signs? That kind of thing? Yeah, all that is fair game."

He looked around the barn. "Anything else?"

Silence.

"Okay, then, gentlemen – I think we've got a plan. And I want to thank each and every one of you for being here, today, and for being a big part of The Group. Oh – that's our little informal name – (finger quotes) The Group. And, for that, we have to thank that man – Flint Stone", and he pointed at him, which got Stone a few thumbs-up.

"Hey – Flint Stone - like the cartoon?", one of the guys said.

"Yeah", said Stone, indicating Gallagher with his thumb, "and this here's Barney Rubble", which got a lot of laughs and one guy yelled, "WIL-MA!", which brought more laughs.

"Now", said Branson, trying to get everybody back on track, "you guys are all true believers and the guys at the forefront of rescuing our great country. Somebody's gotta do it andand it might as well be us, right?"

Head nods and a couple of fist-pumps.

"Look, if it's okay with Oscar, I'd like to meet here, again, the Sunday after next. Next Sunday's the parade. So, a week after that, same time. Oscar?"

"You got it, Frank. Not a problem."

"Thanks, Oscar. Alright, that's all I've got. So, I'll see you all next Sunday. And we'll fucking trick or treat all over Rhinebeck. Scare the shit out of a lot of people and maybe get a bunch of followers, too. Okay, that's it. Thanks." And, as he walked out of the middle of the circle, the guys started standing up and milling about.

"Oh", yelled Oscar, "leave the bales right where they are! I don't wanna bust my ass moving them all again."

It took nearly half an hour for the parking area to clear out, what with guys talking and all that.

And, as they all turned out onto Field Road, Ron's camera got every single one of their license plates on film.

CHAPTER 17

After we'd gotten back to the farm, I gave Suze a mini-horsemanship lesson with the kids while Parker was in the garage carving the pumpkin.

I explained that horses are prey animals and the fact that, when their adrenaline hits, they don't have a 'fight-or-flight' instinct like predators – i.e., humans. They only have the 'flight' instinct, meaning that they'll move, run, or jump away from what they perceive as danger. And that's important when being up close-and personal with horses.

I also explained that horses communicate in 'Equus' – their own language - and that it's incumbent upon us to learn that language as well as we possibly can. It's in the head, the neck, the legs and hooves, the tail, the attitude and, most importantly, it's in the eyes. I went on to explain that they're herd animals and all that that entails.

I was happy to see that Suze was really paying attention to my little lesson. It meant that she really wanted to learn and just wasn't paying lip service.

Finally, she asked the question that I knew she'd ask: "Do you suppose that I could ride Ceres, sometime?"

And I gave her the answer that I knew I'd give: "Of course. And I'll give you a couple of riding lessons, too. Nothing fancy, but certainly enough to keep you as safe as possible and to ride a horse the way a horse is supposed to be ridden."

"What's that mean?", she asked.

"Well, it's several things", I said. "But the majority of riding takes place between the rider's ears." She looked at me funny and I said, "It's all about making the mental connection between horse and rider. Don't worry – I'll show you what I mean. When you do that, that's when the magic happens – you begin to move as a single unit. It's very cool."

She chuckled and said, "I had no idea. The few times I've ever ridden a horse has been on a trail ride and you just kind of sit there and one follows the other and it's all real simple."

"Well,", I said, "it is fairly simple if you do it right."

My phone dinged with a text.

It was from Ron. "Got a minute?"

"30 secs – will call", I answered.

"Come on", I said to Suze. "Let's go get with Parker. Ron wants to talk to us."

The three of us sat down at the kitchen table and I hit Ron's number.

"Yo", he said.

"Yo", the three of us said in unison. "Suze is here with us", I added.

"Cool. Hey, Suze" he said and she answered with a 'Hey' of her own.

"We got pictures of over two dozen license plates, thanks to you guys putting that camera in. And your Federal Bureau of Investigation will be forever in your debt. Or something like that. Anyway, we split up the pics between the four of us to run down DMV and arrest records to find out who these bozos are. I took the last half-dozen because, using my extraordinary powers of deduction, figured that the leader or leaders would probably be among the last ones to leave."

"What'd you find?", asked Parker.

"Well,", said Ron, "we haven't gotten through all of them, yet, but it seems that most of the guys we've seen, so far, are just regulars schlumps. None of 'em have any real arrest or conviction records, really. Oh, a few misdemeanors, here and there, but nothing that really sticks out. We're pretty sure that, just like in a lot of places across the country, these are mostly knuckleheads who watch too much Fox News and listen to too many ultra-right-wing blabbermouths on the radio."

"Yeah, that's what I figured", said Parker.

"However, I did find a little something interesting about the driver of the last car out."

"What?", I asked.

"Well, the guy – his name's, um, Frank….Frank…here it is – Frank Branson. But the car isn't registered to him, it looks like it's registered to his wife. And her name is Sheila. And they own a house in Hyde Park, New York. Actually, I guess it's in an area called East Park because that name is in parentheses here on this screen."

"Plus,", he continued, "when we entered her name into the system, the algorithm popped that she's supposedly tied to a somewhat-radical women's group, called the Moms for Liberty. They started down in Florida and are trying to fuck with school systems and abortion clinics and the like."

"Hey – wait a minute", I said. "The other day when we were down in Poughkeepsie at
- " and I stopped when I saw Suze looking at me. Oops, that's right, I thought. Her little
'thing' is a secret.

"What?", asked Ron.

Nobody said anything for a few seconds, then Suze said, "Ron, look - I'm'a level with
you, here. The other day, these guys took me down to Planned Parenthood. And you
can probably guess why, too."

"Oh", he said. "Oh", as he figured it out.

"Yeah,", she said, "that's now pretty much illegal back in Ohio and that's really the
reason I came here."

"Oh", he said again. And a couple of seconds later, he said, "Look – good for you. It's
your life and you can damned well do what you want with it. Absolutely no judgment
on my part, kid. Really. Honest."

"Well, thanks", she said.

I jumped in with, "Anyway, Ron – while I was sitting in the car, waiting for Parker to get
back from taking her into the building, I got accosted by a bunch of anti-abortion
protestors. A few of them had, like, professionally printed signs and one of them came
right up to my window, holding her sign and yelling at me. And I saw the words,
'Moms for Liberty', printed at the bottom of it."

"Okay", said Ron.

"Anyway,", I continued, "when Parker started back toward the car, one of the women
yelled to the one who was at my window and called her 'Sheila'. Twice, if I'm not
mistaken. And I'm just wondering if that Sheila is Sheila Branson."

"Hmm", said Ron. "Could be, I suppose. I mean, how many Sheilas are in Moms for
Liberty in your neck of the woods, right?"

We all digested that for a few seconds, then Parker said, "What I'm hearing and
thinking, here, is that Frank is probably a big muckety-muck in this ragtag gang of
yahoos and his wife is associated, somehow, with the Moms for Liberty. That'd make
sense, I guess. A couple of right-wing activists, both under the same roof, with him
doing his thing and she doing hers."

"Plus,", I said, "I think – I *think* – she might've been the woman with that flyer, the other day, Suze. The one you waited on."

"You mean the one with the 'No CRT' thing?", she asked.

"Yep – that one. I actually hadn't thought of that before now because I didn't get that good of a look at her while she was in the restaurant. But, maybe, they're one and the same. And didn't Mike say that the guy she was having breakfast with was the new guy on the school board?"

"Yep – that's what he said", replied Parker.

"Wait", said Ron. "You say she's actively involved with your school board stuff, too?"

"Well,", I said, "I don't really know if she's actively involved, but I think she's the one who had breakfast with a school board guy and she did have one of those flyers."

Ron said, "Moms for Liberty. Sheila Branson. School board guy. It's kinda making sense."

"Hey – Mike said he's going to the meeting on Tuesday night, didn't he?", asked Parker.

I nodded.

"Look", he said. "I think, maybe, it'd be a good idea to fill Mike in on some of this. He's been with us before on some of our (finger quotes) cases and it might behoove him to have some background on this babe - and, probably, even her husband, right?"

"Fine with me", said Ron. "Mike's a solid dude. Plus, he's one of the 'Four Horsemen'."

"Yep. We'll get with him, tomorrow", I said.

"Well, lady and gentlemen – this has all been quite enlightening", said Ron. "Now, at least we know that the Bransons are in cahoots – which makes sense – duh. And, that they're both involved with some of this right-wing shit. Maybe – or probably – even movers and shakers in their own local organizations. Let me get with my guys and download all this to them."

"Okay", I said. "What do you need us to do?"

"I'm not rightly sure, m'man. Not at the moment. But keep your eyes and your ears open. Listen - I gotta go, now. Schmidt and I have a three-hour window when he contacts me and that window opens in ten minutes. And, honestly, I gotta pee and run all this by my guys."

"TMI on the first part of that", said Parker.

"By the way", said Ron. "I'm gonna tell Schmidt what we talked about, too. You know, that the team of Branson and Branson may be an important cog in all of this. He knows Frank, but I doubt he knows about the wife."

"Hey – you got an address for the Bransons?", asked Parker.

"Yeah – it's, um….twenty-seven Kilmer Road. Like I said, in East Park or Hyde Park."

"They're one and the same. East Park's just a neighborhood in Hyde Park", said Parker. "Okay, thanks."

A couple of seconds later, we disconnected.

"I'm sorry about blowing your cover", I said to Suze.

"Ah, no problem, dude. Like I said, it was just one of those things. I really don't want to broadcast it to the world, but I'm not ashamed of it, either. It's just fine that Ron knows. Really."

"You know, I was just thinking", Parker said, looking at me.

"What?"

"I was thinkin' that it just might be a good idea to take a run by the Branson place. A little recon mission."

"Ooh, I like the sound of a recon mission", said Suze. "Sounds all undercover, like."

Parker looked at her and said, "Yeah – you might as well come, too. You're kinda in this, now."

And I gave a one-man Geezer knuckle-knock.

"When do you want to do it?", I asked him.

"I dunno. Tomorrow?"

"When do you get off work tomorrow?", I asked Suze.

"Usually a little after two – after the noon rush."

"Okay, then. Let's do it tomorrow afternoon", said Parker.

"Sure", I said. "Suze – tell you what. We have to go down Route 9 to get to Hyde Park, anyway. Why don't we pick you up at the restaurant and go from there? We'll drop you off on the way back."

"Alright", said Parker, standing up. "I gotta go finish that goddamned pumpkin."

"I'd better go, too", said Suze, also getting up from the table. "I want to run by my new place and see if the landlord's delivered my stuff, yet."

"You going to stay there, tonight, if he has?", I asked.

"Nah", she said. "I figure that I'll just take my time getting it all situated. I'll just camp out with Gretchen 'til that happens. And, if I'm lucky, that'll only be a couple of days."

"Hey", I said to Parker. "I'm probably gonna take a wee snooze on the couch. Don't bother telling me when you leave. I'll just catch you in the ayem, okay?"

"Yeah - and I'll take the jack-o'-lantern with me and bring with me in the morning." Then, the two of them walked out the door.

And I went into the living room and plopped down onto the couch.

Down in the East Park section of Hyde Park, Frank and Sheila Branson were sitting and having drinks in the living room, the Falcons-Saints game on the tube in the background.

He'd already told her most of the details of the meeting and how happy he was that so many guys had shown up.

Then, he proceeded to tell her their plans for next Sunday's Halloween Parade. About how they were all going to try and dress in camo, along with masks. And how they were just going to enter the parade, en masse, from the Farmers' Market. They figured that that would make a statement.

"No guns, though, right?", Sheila asked.

"No – no long guns. I'd imagine a few of the guys have concealed carry permits so, sure, they can have them, if they want. But this is kind of The Group's introduction to the community and I think having weapons at what, basically, is a kids' event, would raise too many hackles. Actually, though, we put it to a vote and the 'no rifles' side won out by only a few votes."

"I agree with you about the guns, dear. If something should go wrong and one went off and hurt a kid or a parent, the law would come down on you like an avalanche. There's certainly a time and a place for that, but not at this event."

He nodded and took a swig of his beer. "My thinking, exactly."

"You say that your group's going to enter the parade from the Farmers' Market?", she asked.

He nodded, "Yup."

"Well, like I said, we're going to set up a Moms for Liberty table right along in there, too, since it's public property and nobody can really kick us out. You guys will have to walk right past us."

"I guess we will, won't we?", he said.

"Look – I'm expecting, maybe, two dozen mothers. Maybe a few more, maybe a few less. I think it'd be cool if you texted me just when your group's going to come by and we'll all make two parallel lines that you guys can walk through. Know what I mean? Like a gauntlet or a receiving line, and we'll all applaud and cheer for you."

"You mean like when a football team comes onto the field and cheerleaders line up on both sides and wave their pompoms?"

"Exactly."

Branson chuckled and said, "Yeah. Yeah – that'd be cool. It'd be sort of like our grand opening. After all, it's the first time we'll have done anything in public."

She nodded and said, "Are you going to have signs and placards?"

"Well, I told the guys they could do whatever they want – just no swastikas."

"Good idea."

"I'm gonna get another beer. Another one of those?", he asked, standing up and starting across the room.

"I'd love one", she said, handing him her glass.

I was jolted awake by my phone ringing.

Opening my eyes, I noticed that it was already dark, out, and whatever game I'd had on the tube was obviously over, because three ex-players-turned-studio-guys were sitting there laughing and talking.

I saw Ron's name on my screen.

"Yo", I said.

"Hey. Just thought you'd like to know that I spoke with Schmidt a little while ago."

"Yeah?"

"Yeah - and he filled me in on the details of that meeting."

"What happened?", I asked, now sitting up and my head clearing.

"Long story short, it looks like The Group - and it's now officially 'The', capital T, 'Group', capital G. That's what they've named themselves."

"The Group."

"Yeah. Anyway, the plan is for The Group to show up at some Halloween parade that's happening next Sunday in downtown Rhinebeck. I guess it's a pretty big annual deal."

"Yeah, I've heard a little bit about it."

"Anyway, the yahoos are gonna get all spiffed up in camo and masks and just kind of enter the parade, en masse, and walk along with it. And I guess there's supposed to be, like, twenty-five guys."

"Isn't it, like, a kids' parade?", I asked.

"Hell, I don't know, but I suppose so, right? I mean, Rhinebeck isn't New Orleans or Key West. So, yeah, it's probably a kids' thing. Anyway, I guess these guys aren't carrying firearms, unless guys have concealed carry permits, but signs and placards are okay."

I shook my head. "I can't believe we're even talking about having guns at a kids' thing. What the fuck?"

"Right? Anyway, I don't know what effect having a couple dozen geeks walking in the parade will have on anybody, but I can't imagine people'd be too thrilled with it."

"Do the local cops know about this, yet?", I asked.

"Nope, but that's on my agenda for first thing in the morning. I'm gonna call the police chief – I think his name is Eddings, Marty Eddings, it says here. I'm gonna call him and give him this little bit of intel. Let him figure it out. But, we're gonna have a couple of guys come up from our White Plains office and blend into the crowd. Take some pictures, keep their eyes on things – that sort of stuff."

"What time is The Group supposed to start marching?"

"According to Schmidt, the parade starts at two o'clock and they're all gonna meet up starting around one-thirty. So, probably a little after two."

"I think Parker and I should be there, too", I said.

"Probably a good idea. And, dude – do me a favor – keep this close to the vest, okay? We don't want a bunch of people finding out about it and organizing to start some shit with these dickwads. What we don't want is a confrontation right there in the middle of your little hamlet."

"Got it. We'll probably just tell Mike. And you might wanna tell the police chief to kind of keep it on the D-L, too. Like, no riot gear and stuff."

"I'll mention it to him, natch", said Ron. "But the one thing we find is that local cops do not like us butting in on their stuff. It's sort of like a 'Get off my lawn!'-type thing. But, yeah – I'll mention it. Okay – gotta split."

"Ten-four", I said and disconnected.

I was hungry, so I turned off the tube and went into the kitchen.

Y'know, I thought to myself, a nice grilled cheese sandwich and some tomato soup would really hit the spot, right now.

So that's what I did.

<u>CHAPTER 18</u>

The next morning was blustery, with a chilly north wind and low, scudding clouds.

For the first morning since I'd been here, I went down and gave each of the kids a flake of alfalfa. The grass in their pasture had gone dormant for the winter and they'd eaten it down as far as they could.

Welp, I thought, as I tossed the flakes into their feeders, I guess this'll be every morning and every evening chore for the next several months. They both thanked me by burying their heads in their feeders and chowing down.

When I got to The Coffee Spot, I saw Parker and Gretchen over at the little table by the wall. He'd set the new jack-o'-lantern on it and the old one was sitting on the floor. I walked over to them.

This was my first look at it and I saw that he'd carved it to look like a cartoon character. The smile was crooked and it looked as if one eye was winking – as if it had just told a joke or something. Like the last one, the carving was precise. It looked good.

"Nice", I said. "Looks like something out of 'The Simpsons' or 'South Park'."

"I was gonna do 'Mister Hankey and the Christmas Poo', but thought better of it", he said. "After all, it's not Christmas, yet."

"Don't you even think that Bill", said Gretchen, back-handing him on the arm. "No – this looks very, very nice. And happy, too."

"Want me to carry the old one out to the dumpster?", I asked her.

"Oh, no, J.D. But you can take it into the kitchen for me. Artie said he's going to make it into a pie and give it to Bill. You know, as kind of a 'thank you' gesture."

"We gonna have pie, son", Parker said to me with a grin.

"Listen", she said, lowering her voice, "Suze tells me that she's going on a (finger quotes) recon mission with you guys, this afternoon."

"Um, yeah", I said. "It looks like we're working on another little thing."

"Like with Wolfe?", she asked, referring to the recent situation involving the guy who, for a few weeks, anyway, owned the restaurant and, ultimately, how the ownership of it had transferred to her.

"Well, something like that – only different", I said.

"It's not dangerous, is it?"

I chuckled and said, "No – not at all. Just a little something where a few people have gotten a little too far out over their skis."

"Is your ninja horseman going to get involved?", she asked, having seen that in action.

"No idea", I said. "But, maybe."

"Okay, but you just take care of my little girl. She's been through a lot, recently."

"I think Suze is fully capable of kicking ass and taking names later if it would ever come to that", I said, as Artie came out of the kitchen and walked toward us.

"Gonna make you a pie, there, Parker", he said. "You like it spicy or not?"

"Spicy's good", said Parker. "I guess. Hell, any kind of pumpkin pie's good. I'm not really all that fussy."

"Okay, I'll whip up a little something special for you and have it ready for you when you come in tomorrow." And he bent down and picked up the pumpkin. "Nice size – it'll make for a big pie."

"Gee, thanks, Artie", said Parker. "This means a lot."

"Ah, it's nothing, man. Gonna be fun, actually." And he turned and headed into the kitchen.

We headed back to the table and Gretchen said, "I'll be right there to fill up your mug, J.D."

As we sat down, the morning's discussion was about the weather. Specifically, in the morning paper, there was a piece about the 'Old Farmers' Almanac' predicting plenty of snow, rain and mush for the winter. There'd be a real cold snap in late January, but February would bring warmer temperatures and more rain than snow. At least that's what I gathered by listening to the guys' comments.

"Ah, hell", said Joe. "That thing predicts the same thing every year. I mean, it doesn't take a weather genius to tell us that there'll be snow in January. Besides, their so-called predictions are so loosey-goosey that they're always right if you wanna look at it that way.”

“No, but it’s fun to play along with it”, said Hal. “I think it’s nice that it’s held up for so long, especially in the internet world.”

Gretchen walked up and filled my mug and topped off the other guys’ before heading back to the kitchen.

“Speaking of the weather, J.D.,” said Marquardt, “the guys are going to bale and get that hay out of there, today. Supposed to, maybe, rain tomorrow. And I told them to go ahead and put ninety bales up in your loft.”

“Oh, we’ll help ‘em do that”, said Parker.

“No need, Bill. I sent three other guys along, this morning. We’ve got plenty of manual labor on-site. They know where it goes, so let them do it. Hell, they’re thirty years younger than you guys – let ‘em earn their money.”

“I really appreciate that Bob”, I said. “I don’t want Parker to tax that frail, old body of his.”

“Bite me, Junior”, said Parker.

A couple minutes later, Gretchen came back and we ordered.

“Hey”, I said, when a thought suddenly hit me. “Where’s Gordon? He hasn’t been here in weeks.”

“Oh, yeah”, said Mike. “I spoke to him the other day. Forgot to tell you – he’s been having problems with his sciatica, lately. He said he’s getting better – he’s been seeing a chiropractor – but, for a while there, he said it hurt to stand too long, sit too long, walk too far – all of that. I guess he was really laid up for a couple of weeks. But he said that he’s going to try and make it here one morning, later this week.”

“Sciatica sucks”, said Joe. “I had it, one time. Not for the faint of heart.”

‘How’s Shirley? Did he say?”, I asked.

“Oh, I guess she’s fine. He said she likes playing nurse. The only complaint he had was that she was fixing all of his meals for a while and you know what that means.”

“Diet shit”, said Joe, and Mike nodded.

“Double whammy”, said Hal. “Bad back *and* bad food.”

A minute or so later, Gretchen showed up with her big tray and began doling out our grub. As that was happening, Hal said, "Hey – I have an idea. I have to run up to Red Hook after I leave here. Why don't I get an order to go and drop it off at Gordon's place? I have to drive right past it."

"Excellent idea, Hal", said Mike and we all gave it the ol' Geezer knuckle-knock.

"What's up with Mr. Gordon?", Gretchen asked. "I haven't seen him lately."

Mike reiterated what he'd told us and that we figured that Shirley was starving him half to death.

"And you want to take him a breakfast, is that right, Hal?", she asked.

"Yeah, I thought it'd be a nice gesture."

"Tell you what", said Gretchen. "Let me fix up a thing for him. You know – I'll get Artie to whip up some waffles and throw in several sausages and a ton of home fries and all that. And tell him it's a get-well gift from The Coffee Spot."

We all confirmed that that was a good idea, picked up our entrenching tools and dug in.

Once we were finished and were ready to leave, Gretchen handed a big bag to Hal. "Don't spill it", she said.

As we were all flocking to the door, I said to Mike, "Can you spare a minute? Parker and I wanna fill you in on something."

"Sure", he said.

The three of us met up next to my truck and, over the next few minutes, we told Mike what we'd – including Ron – found out about The Group and that they were planning to break into the parade next Sunday.

"Oh, shit", he said, after hearing the whole story. "Are you kidding me? We've got, like, a pseudo-militia around here? And they want to turn a kids' Halloween parade into a political event? What the hell is wrong with these people?"

"Ron says it's happening all over the country, Mike", said Parker. "It's just fucking nuts."

I went on to tell him that, this morning, Ron's going to call Chief Eddings and give him the skinny on what was planned.

"Ah, Jesus – but I suppose that's a good thing", said Mike. "Eddings'll probably want to beef up the police presence. You know, call in guys on their day off and so on. But, goddammit, this is just wrong, just so wrong. All of it." He stared off into the distance. "In Rhinebeck, of all places."

"I know, dude. Plus, there's more", I said, wincing.

"More? What – more?"

I'd already told him about Frank Branson, and now, I had to tell him about Sheila Branson.

So, I did.

I told him that she was, probably, the local ringleader of a Moms for Liberty group and what that group had been doing around the country, especially with school systems. And that she'd undoubtedly been the one who'd been having breakfast with that new guy on the school board, the other morning.

"Mark Fisher", said Mike. "Shit."

"You said you were gonna go to the meeting, tomorrow night, didn't you?", asked Parker.

"Yeah. Yeah, that's my plan. Do you suppose she'll show up with her group?"

"Of course, she will", said Parker. "That's red meat to those folks."

"Well,", said Mike, "the one good thing is none of the other members of the board buy into that nonsense. At all. So, no matter what Fisher proposes along those lines will get voted down, no doubt."

"Yeah, but if these Moms for Liberty get any traction at all among parents, the board could have quite a mess on its hands", I said. "And, now that I think about it, I'd say that there's a better than even chance that this Branson chick will alert the media – that seems to be their M.O. in different places. Then, it could turn into a real cluster fuck."

"Yeah, it sure could", said Mike. "Look, I'd better get with Eddings, too, this morning, and tell him about that meeting, tomorrow night. Maybe he'll even have to dispatch a few guys to that – if for no other reason than to keep the media out, if they show up."

"Can they do that? Keep the media out?", I asked.

"I really don't know the rules, as far as that goes. I do know that if it's a closed session, nobody can come in. But I think this is scheduled to be an open session."

"Do you know the school board president?", Parker asked him.

"Yeah, a little. Nick Patel - and Nick's a pretty good guy, too. Smart as a whip. I suppose I should call him, too, to give him a heads-up. Then, he'll know what he can do about an open or closed session. But he should know about this Moms for Liberty outfit."

Parker and I both nodded. Then, Mike said, "Shit. I was kinda hoping to cruise through today. My calendar's pretty empty and I was looking forward to a quiet day, maybe leaving early. Now, I'm not so sure about that."

"Sorry to be the bearers of bad tidings, dude", I said.

"No – no, don't worry about it", he said. "We've just gotta come up with a way to nip all of this shit in the bud, before any of it gets out of hand."

"We have an inkling of an idea – at least as far as the Bransons go – trying to form itself in our heads", I said. "As a matter of fact, Parker and Suze and I are going to take a little recon mission past their house, this afternoon."

"Suze? Did you say Suze? What's she got to do with this?"

I knew it wasn't my place to tell him about her abortion, so I didn't. I just said, "Ah, she was over at the farm, hanging with the horses, when Ron called the other day and asked us to plant that camera. So, she thinks all of this is pretty exciting. But, Mike, that kid's sharp. And smart, too."

"Plus, she knows Krav Maga", said Parker.

"What the hell is that?", Mike asked.

And Parker explained a little bit about it and how it could be extremely useful in certain situations.

"You're not gonna put her into one of those situations, are you?", Mike asked, with a certain amount of concern in his voice.

"Hell, no, Mike. I don't even know why you brought it up, Parker. You're just scaring the poor man."

"Oh, I'm already plenty scared", said Mike. "About all of this shit."

"Do us a favor, okay?", I asked him. "Call me after you've spoken to Eddings and the school board guy. I want to hear their reactions."

"Sure. But I can tell you, right now, that their reactions won't be good."

A minute or so later, we all drove off, Mike to the town council building and Parker and me to the farm.

When we got there, we saw that Bob had sent two tractors and two balers over and both were working the field.

"Marquardt's not fucking around getting that hay baled, is he?", said Parker. "With two rigs, those guys'll be done before noon."

"I know he's worried about the weather", I said. "And I don't blame him. It's looking pretty ominous, right about now." The sky was a battleship grey and the wind was freshening.

One of his guys, who wasn't out in the field, walked up to us and said that they'd be bringing the next load up to the barn and would put it into the loft. And that they wanted to be done with the whole job by noon and would hustle the hay back to Bob's and get it under a roof before the rain came. If it came at all.

"That's the trouble with this time of year", Parker said to him, "you can't ever tell if those clouds'll bring rain or not."

"Better safe than sorry, though, huh?", the kid said. "There's a lot of money sitting out there in that field, right now, and if that shit gets wet, that's money down the drain." Then, he walked off to resume doing whatever he'd been doing.

Down at the Annandale Arms Apartments, Flint Stone was also concerned about the weather, along with something else.

He figured that the job could be finished today, if the guys hustled. But the last thing they needed was rain while they were trying to point up the bricks. And, if the rain came now, it could continue into tomorrow, which would throw his whole schedule into a cocked hat.

As he walked to his truck to get another trowel, so he could be yet another hand in finishing the job up quickly, Gallagher walked past, pushing a wheelbarrow full of fresh concrete.

"Dude", said Gallagher, with a smile, "gettin' your hands dirty, huh?"

"Ah, shit, Eric. I wanna get this job done before it starts raining. I figure another hand'll help things along a little."

"No doubt, but I think it'll hold off for a couple of hours. Don't sweat it, man – we'll get 'er done. Hey, by the way, I haven't had a chance to ask you what you thought of the meeting, yesterday."

"I thought it was great, man. I can't believe we've got so many guys, now. I think things'll start to happen if we play our cards right."

"Yeah", said Gallagher, "and I think that the thing, next Sunday, will put us on the map. At least around here."

"About that, Eric", Stone said, and his tone had gotten serious. It was the other thing he was concerned about.

"Yeah? What about it?"

"Well, to be honest, the wife and I are kind of planning to take the kids there. To the parade. They were in it, last year, and really had a ball. Got all kinds of candy and saw a bunch of kids they know and all that. They're really looking forward to it."

"Oh", said Gallagher. "How old are they, again?"

"Well, Justin's eight and Marie's seven. And, to further complicate matters, my wife is going all out on their costumes, this year. I think she's making a pirate's costume for Justin and some kind of Disney character for Marie."

"Oh. Oh, shit", said Gallagher.

"Yeah, oh, shit", said Stone. "I don't know what to do."

"Can't your wife walk along with the kids? You could always meet up with 'em a little later – you know, after the parade or something."

"Well,", said Stone, "I've been thinking about that but I'm not all that sure my wife'll buy into it. She's got it pegged like a (finger quotes) family thing, like we did last year."

"I see. Fuck, dude – what're you gonna do?"

"Like I said, man, I just don't know. But, to tell you the truth, I'm kinda leaning toward the family thing. The Group'll have plenty of guys – it's not like I'll really be missed, y'know? And, I was thinking that, if I did that – the family thing – that I could still wear my camo and all. Sort of represent, but not march along with you guys."

"Have you mentioned this to Frank, yet?", asked Gallagher.

"No, not yet. Hell, man, I'm not even sure what to say. Well, other than what I just told you."

Gallagher thought for a minute, then said, "I think you gotta tell him, man. And, probably, the sooner, the better, y'know?"

"Yeah – it's just that I'm really new to The Group and this is the first big thing we've done and I might look like I'm chickening out or something. And I kinda don't want to piss him off."

Gallagher nodded, then said, "Well, look at it this way, dude – if you've got a choice of pissing off your wife and family or Frank, I think I'd probably go with Frank. You gotta live with your wife. Tough call, though. But, yeah – call Frank and tell him what you just told me. He'll either understand or he won't. You just gotta do what you gotta do, y'know?"

"Yeah. You're right. I mean, this is just the first thing we're doing. I'm sure there'll be more. And, who knows? Maybe I can even redeem myself by coming up with some idea of my own, like the spray paint thing that Lou did."

"Yeah, that was pretty epic", said Gallagher. "Listen - don't worry, kid – I've got your back on this, as far as Frank and the guys go. For real."

Then, he looked down at the wheelbarrow and said, "Alright, I don't want this shit to start setting up. I think this is just about the last load." And he grabbed the handles and pushed it toward the porch.

Stone was still upset, but felt a little better after bouncing it off Gallagher. He knew that Gallagher was pretty tight with Frank and that he'd put in a good word for him when he had the chance.

Fucking Halloween parade, he thought.

____

Back at the farm, Parker and I were up in the hay loft, checking out the alfalfa stash.

Over the summer and, including today's load, we had amassed close to two hundred bales. Given that the kids went through a bale about every couple of days, our supply should last us until – hopefully – sometime in April, when they should be able to start grazing, again, and next year's hay would be coming out of the ground.

I looked at my phone and saw that it was one-forty.

"Hey – we'd better get going if we're going to pick up Suze at two", I said.

"Let's do it", he said and started down the ladder to the ground.

"We gotta take my truck", I said. "Back seat and all."

We pulled into The Coffee Spot's parking lot right at the stroke of two and I said, "Why don't you stick your head in and see if she's ready."

Thirty seconds later, the two of them came out the door and headed to the truck.

"What's up, kid?", I asked Suze as she hopped into the back seat.

"Nothin', but I had a good day, tip-wise, so that's good, huh?"

"'Yep", I said, as Parker slid into the front seat.

"Put your seatbelt on", he said to her over his shoulder.

"Yes, Dad", she said, doing as instructed.

"Okay – what's the address, again?", I asked.

"Twenty-seven Kilmer Road", said Parker. "And it's probably in Hyde Park."

I plugged the address into my GPS and said, "Yep. Got it. Off we go."

And I turned out of the parking lot and headed south on Route 9.

Next stop: the Bransons' house.

CHAPTER 19

As we were heading south on Route 9, also known as Albany Post Road, we passed through the little hamlet of Staatsburg and then, a few miles further, the Vanderbilt Mansion and Historical Site was on our right-hand side.

"That's an amazing place, Suze. You'll have to come down and take a tour of it, sometime."

"Jesus, it looks like the White House or something", she said, craning her neck to see it through the trees. "You mean this was a guy's actual house?"

I laughed and said, "One of them. He had mansions like this in New York City, Newport, Rhode Island and down in North Carolina. He had more money than God."

"He was God back in those days", said Parker.

"Yeah, he made his money in shipping and building railroads and stuff like that", I said. "The dude owned just about everything."

"Wow", she said.

A few minutes later, we made a left on East Market Street. "This turns into Crum Elbow Road in a minute", I said.

"Crum Elbow Road? What kind of name is that?", Suze asked, more or less rhetorically.

"In a one-quarter mile, make a left onto Matuk Drive", the GPS lady announced.

We did that and she had us make a right on Thurston Lane, then a left onto Kilmer. "Your destination will be on your right in two-hundred yards", the voice informed us.

"Okay, slow down", said Parker. "The houses are pretty few and far between, out here, but they seem pretty middle-class."

Matuk, Thurston and Kilmer were all pretty much single-lane roads, surrounded by mature trees on both sides. All of the properties looked rather large – about an acre - and they all had fairly long driveways leading to the houses.

"It's coming up on the right", I said. "Should be the next house."

And there it was, a two-story job with a two-car garage attached to it. It was also on the corner of Kilmer and Matuk, which seemed to be a big loop with a couple of small streets, including Kilmer, leading off of it, according to my GPS.

"Stop in front of it", said Parker. "There are no cars in the driveway, so maybe nobody's home."

There was a centrally-located front door, with a large picture window to our left of it - presumably, the living room. There were another two, smaller, windows to our right of the door and four identical windows on the second floor. It was a nice, neat house, but pretty rudimentary. By that, I mean that there was nothing overly special about it. It had a couple of areas where the Bransons had landscaped plantings, but nothing really stood out.

"Turn right up there", said Parker, meaning the corner of Matuk, "I wanna see the side and back of the place."

I did and we spotted a redwood patio off the back of the house, raised a couple of steps off the ground. The back and side yards were fairly large, with a stand of trees running across the rear of the property.

"We should be able to park right along in here", said Parker. "And, you guys could make your way to the front door pretty easily and unseen. I don't think you wanna fuck with the patio."

"Yep. Simple ingress and egress", I said.

"What are you guys talking about?", asked Suze.

"The ninja horseman", Parker said, offhandedly.

"What the hell is the ninja horseman?", she asked.

I knew that, eventually, this was coming and that, eventually, we'd probably fill her in. I guess that time was now.

"Um", I said. "You just read 'The Legend of Sleepy Hollow', didn't you?"

"Yeah."

"Well, think of a twenty-first century version of the headless horseman. And you kind of cross him with Robin Hood."

She was quiet for a few seconds, then said, "Okay – I'm completely lost. What the hell are you guys talking about?"

"Well, it's like this, Suze", I said. "A few times in the past several months, we've found some people that were screwing over some other, innocent, people. And, in just about every case, what they were doing was really small potatoes in the grand scheme of the legal world. In other words, the law probably wouldn't go after them and they'd skate on their pretty assholic deeds."

"Assholic", she said.

"Yes. Of or pertaining to being an asshole. You can look it up."

"Okay."

"Anyway, 'The Legend of Sleepy Hollow' gave me an idea. What if there was, like, a twenty-first century version of the headless horseman, like I said a minute ago? And, what if he showed up on a horse, one night, at one of these assholes' houses? And scared the living shit out of the asshole? And, what if that particular horseman also delivered an ultimatum to the asshole that stated that, unless the asshole repaired the damage he'd done, that horrible things would befall him?"

"You mean a guy", she said. "A guy on a horse."

"That's exactly what I mean. And, the guy and the horse both look like demons from the depths of hell."

"Demons from the depths of hell. And that's you guys?", she asked.

"Well, not to put too fine a point on it, but it's me and Zeus. So far, anyway, Parker's been in charge of transportation. But - and this is important – we do a ton of homework ahead of time. We find the chink in the armor of the asshole. And we hold that like a sword over his or her neck and if the asshole doesn't obey our orders – the ninja horseman's orders - that sword will fall. Hard and fast."

"You and Zeus", she said, looking at me in the rearview mirror.

"Yep."

"What about Ceres?"

"She comes along for the ride", said Parker.

"For the ride", said Suze.

"Yeah", he said. "We put the kids into the trailer and drive over to near the mark's house, then we offload Zeus, J.D. climbs up on his back and goes and makes his visit."

"Are you fucking kidding me, right now?", she asked.

"Nope. Not at all."

"Holy fuck." And she sat back against the seat.

"Gretchen's seen the ninja horseman", I said.

"She has?"

"Yep. And the ninja horseman was the lynchpin in her being able to take ownership of The Coffee Spot."

"Really."

"Yep, really. That was a very complicated and weird-ass case, too, but it all worked out just the way we envisioned it. And planned it. And, executed it."

"You two old farts did that?", she asked with a laugh.

"It's a long walk from here to The Coffee Spot, young lady", I said.

"I'm just shittin' you", she said. "I think I'm impressed. I mean, I still don't understand what all you're talking about, but if you guys helped Gretchen to get the restaurant, big kudos to y'all."

Parker turned in his seat as I began to drive away, thinking that we'd been sitting there long enough. He said to Suze, "What we're talking about right here, right now, is possibly – or probably – making a visit to the Branson place. You know, he's like a bigwig in his new right-wing goon squad, right? And she's the lead dog in the local chapter of Moms for Liberty, which is also a hornet's nest of rabid right-wingers. So, just maybe, we can kind of persuade them to cool their jets a bit."

"I've been thinking about that", I said. "We know that (one-hand finger quotes, because I was driving) The Group is planning on breaking into the Halloween Parade next Sunday and marching along with the kids and their parents."

"And,", I continued, "we think that there's a better-than-even chance that the Moms for Liberty group's gonna show up at Tuesday night's school board meeting and probably disrupt it, somehow. So, we think that these two lovebirds deserve a visit."

"But wouldn't you have to do that tonight, if you wanna stop her from going to the school board meeting?", she asked. "Or, sometime this week, if you want to affect that Sunday thing."

"Yeah, that's kind of our quandary", I said.

Parker piped up with, "See, right now, we don't really have a 'hammer' on 'em."

"A hammer?", she asked.

"That's where our detective work comes in, you see. We have to dig around their backgrounds and various things in their lives – either past, present or future – that, if revealed either to specific people or the general public or whatever, would really put a crimp in their lives. That's what really scares the shit out of 'em – not just the ninja horseman."

"And you haven't done your homework, yet", she said. She had a habit of making her questions sound like declarative sentences.

"Correctamundo."

It was quiet in the truck for a minute and then Suze asked, "Why do you call it the ninja horseman?"

I laughed and said, "I have no idea. It just sort of popped out of my mouth, one day, and we've been using it ever since. Doesn't mean anything, really. Except, I guess, like a ninja, you don't see him coming and you don't see him leave. He's just there and gone, scaring the living shit outta you during those few terrifying seconds."

"Cool name, though", she said.

I had just turned back north on Route 9, then said, "We've gotta get to gettin' on this hammer thing, y'know? I mean, we could probably just scare the hell out of them, but I'm not sure that would put a stop to their shenanigans. And, it's too damned bad that we can't do it this week. But I guess we'd be better off doing it right, stopping them over the long run, than fucking it up and have our little thing go over like a fart in a windstorm."

"Yeah", said Parker.

"We gotta get with Ron – maybe he can find out something", I said.

"Ron's pretty cool, isn't he?", asked Suze.

"Ron's a good man", I said. "The best. Look – maybe we'll call him when we get back to the farm. See what he might be able to come up with.”

A few minutes later, I pulled into the parking lot of The Coffee Spot, right next to the Subaru.

With her hand on the door handle, Suze said, “Listen - you guys gotta cut me in on this. I’ve come this far, I wanna be a part of whatever you’ve got planned. You have to promise me that.”

Parker and I looked at each other and nodded.

“Deal”, I said. “I don’t know exactly what that means, but you’re in, kid, okay?”

“Sweet”, she said and opened the door. “If you find out anything, give me a buzz, alright?”

“You got it.”

As I backed out of the spot, I said to Parker, “Why not, right?”

“Yeah, I guess”, he said. “As long as she keeps her mouth shut.”

“She’s pretty cool. I think she’ll hold things pretty close to the vest. I’m not quite sure what to tell Gretchen, though. Or, even if we should.”

“Oh,”, he said, “I think, once we figure things out, we should fill her in. After all, she knows exactly what we do and how we do it. We’ll just have to assure her that Suze’ll be safe. And we’ll have to make good on that promise, too.”

“Yep. Okay, good.”

Once we’d gotten back to the farm and gotten the truck parked, we headed for the kitchen. Just then, it started sprinkling. I looked over at the field and saw that all of Bob’s vehicles and equipment were gone.

“Looks like the guys just made it”, I said, nodding over toward the field.

“Good thing, too”, said Parker. “That stuff’ll get moldy if it gets wet, then it isn’t good for anything. Except maybe cows.”

“You want something to drink?”, I asked, as we took command of the kitchen table.

“I’ll take a Coke if you’ve got it”, he said, and I grabbed one and a Diet Sprite out of the fridge.

"Let's call Ron", I said, as I sat down. I hit him on speed dial.

"Yo", he said, after the second ring.

"Hey – Parker and I are sitting here and want to fill you in on a little recon mission we just took."

"Shoot."

"Well, we drove past the Branson place. Nothing extraordinary about it, but doing a ninja horseman thing would be a piece of cake. Easy in, easy out. No close neighbors."

"Cool."

"Yeah, but what we don't have is a hammer, y'know? Not like we had with Wolfe or Silver or Conway or those other dickwads. And we need one – probably for both of 'em, Branson and the missus."

"Funny you should mention that, my liege. We've been gathering some intel on them and a few of the others in that little cabal of roaches."

"Yeah?", I asked. "You find anything, yet?"

"Well, yeah – a little bit. And what I'm gonna tell you about our boy, Frank Branson, should bring a big smile to your kissers."

"What?", Parker and I asked at the same time.

"Well – hold on, here it is – it seems that Branson was in the military for a few years. Three, to be exact. And he was attached to the 2nd Infantry Division – that's the outfit whose main focus is on helping to provide support and combat readiness over in South Korea."

"He was in Korea?", I asked.

"Yeah – he was a private, first class, and was stationed at Camp Humphreys, the massive main U.S. base just south of Seoul, in a place called Pyeongtaek. And, from what his records show, he and another soldier were on perimeter guard duty, one night, and, somehow, they'd gotten drunk."

"Aw, Jesus", said Parker, rolling his eyes.

"Yeah, but that's not all. I guess the guys were guarding some remote, dark area of the fence line, when - and I don't know what they were thinking – but they fired off several rounds at a pack of stray dogs on the other side of the fence. According to one of these reports, the other guy – his name was John Ellis – said that they thought the base was being attacked by some kind of special forces unit."

"Had that ever happened?", I asked.

"Camp Humphreys been attacked? Hell, no. Nobody's gonna send a handful of guys to attack just about the biggest fucking base in the U.S. military. Anyway, here's what happened……a few minutes after hearing the gunshots, a couple of MPs drove over there to find out what the hell was going on. And, when they confronted Branson and Ellis, they noticed that they were both drunk as skunks and - and I quote – 'observed in a compromising position and not in the proper manner of uniform'."

"Holy shit", said Parker.

"Yeah – holy shit", said Ron. "Anyway, our two heroes were taken into custody and thrown into the on-base brig."

"You're reading from a report, right?", I asked.

"Yeah, yeah – of course. First thing we did was run a scan on him and found that he'd been in the military. Then, because we're the Eff Bee Fucking Eye, we can get all of that shit. And, in looking at his military record, all of this popped up."

"Okay – go on", said Parker. "What happened to them? Branson and the other guy."

"Well, now – Branson was brought up on charges, but I don't know about the other guy. Probably he was, too, but I don't give a shit about him.

"It says here", he continued, "that Branson was charged with - and was convicted of – violating Article 112 of the Uniform Code of Military Justice. That's what the military uses – the UCMJ. Anyway, Article 112 is being drunk on duty. Plus, he was charged with Article 15 – which is DUI – I guess he'd been driving a Jeep while he was patrolling. And, Article 134, which reads "prohibited conduct that is of a nature to bring discredit upon the armed forces or is prejudicial to good order and discipline".

"Jesus", said Parker. "That's bad."

"I'll say it's bad", said Ron. "As a matter of fact, according to this, the camp's head honcho had to meet with and apologize to several local South Korean politicos, who were freaked out by gunfire coming out of the camp. Danger to civilians and all that."

"What happened to Branson?", I asked.

"He spent thirty days in the brig, was given an administrative, or, general discharge, fined three months' pay and lost his rights to the GI Bill. In other words, they kicked him out of the military. Oh - and his driver's license was suspended for two years and, as part of his separation agreement with the Army, was ordered to undergo treatment at a VA facility for the drinking thing."

"What about the 'compromising position' and being out of uniform and all?", asked Parker.

"I don't know", said Ron. "but I'd imagine that falls under that Article 134 charge, along with all that other shit."

"Wow", I said, thinking through the ramifications.

"Ya like that, huh?", said Ron.

"Hammer time", said Parker, with a somewhat evil smile.

"Okay, now that I've gotten your attention, there's more."

Me: "More?"

"Yep - and it's about the missus."

"Sweet", said Parker. "Let 'er rip."

"Well, Sheila Branson was born Sheila Stark and grew up in a little town in upstate New York – Auburn, New York."

"I know of it", said Parker. "Used to be a state prison, there, but I don't know if it's still in business."

"Okay", said Ron. "Anyway, we found out that, after she graduated high school, she went to nursing school in Syracuse and got her degree in Practical Nursing. Then, she went to work back in Auburn, at Auburn Community Hospital which had a special deal with the VA. And, you'll never guess who she met there, when he was undergoing therapy."

"Frank Branson", I said.

"Ding-ding-ding!", said Ron. "I guess he was from that area, too – a little town called Weedsport and Auburn had the nearest VA thing."

"But, wait – he could still get VA benefits with a general discharge?"

"Yep", said Parker. "If you get a dishonorable discharge, you can't, but a general discharge – which nobody wants, by the way – still gets you that benny."

"Okay, so", continued Ron, "I guess they fell in love or something. At least, they did the dirty, at least once, because Ms. Stark appears to have had an abortion at Auburn Community Hospital on August 6, 1994. She was twenty-two at the time."

"You found that record?", I asked.

"Dude – give us a little credit."

"Right. But this is huge!" I glanced over at Parker and he looked like the cat who'd just eaten the canary.

He said, "Okay – Branson got drunk on duty, shot at some poor dogs, got caught with his pants down around his knees and got tossed from the Army."

"Yep", I said. "And ol' Sheila – she of the rabid anti-abortion stance – had one of those, herself."

"That's pretty much it in a nutshell, you guys", said Ron. "Okay, listen – although I love chatting with y'all, I gotta go. Another meeting with the boss. Let's catch up later, though, okay?"

"You got it, man", I said. "And thanks for this dirt. It's exactly what we need."

"It's what I'm here for. Now, I beg your leave. Ciao." And he disconnected.

"Holy shit", I said to Parker.

"Yeah, but it's really good holy shit", he said.

CHAPTER 20

"So", I said. "What are we gonna do?"

Parker said, "Well, I think we know about what we're gonna do, but I guess the question is when?"

I thought for a few seconds, then said, "We probably oughta do it soon. But there's no way we can get our shit together before that school board meeting tomorrow night and, yeah, we could do it before the parade but, for some reason, something's telling me we should wait until those things happen before we do it."

"Well, you're right about the school board meeting", said Parker. "Plus, we don't even know for sure if Branson's gonna be there or if there'll be any kind of falderol. Didn't Mike say that he was gonna ask the board president if it could be a closed meeting? And, if that happens, the Moms for Liberty babes might mill around outside or something, but that's probably about it."

"Yeah", I said. "Also, I really don't want to rush into this – any of it. I'm thinking that we should just watch what happens over the next few days and take it from there."

"I don't disagree."

"So, I guess we just file all of this away and keep our eyes open and ears to the ground and see where it takes us."

"Yep. Guess so." And he stood up and said, "Alright, I'm gonna head out, but let's be thinking about what we want from those two. I'm kinda thinkin' that – well, I don't know – that they just somehow resign from those groups and lay off the radical shit."

"Yeah, for sure", I said. "We just have to get all of that nailed down. We'll talk about it, again, tomorrow, 'k?"

"You got it, Chief. See you in the ayem." And he headed out the door and made for his truck.

Down in the East Park section of Hyde Park, Sheila Branson picked up the phone and dialed Mark Fisher's number.

"Hello?", he said, when his phone rang.

"Hi, Mark. Sheila Branson, here."

"Oh, hi, Sheila."

"Are you busy?"

"Well, we're about to have an early dinner, but I probably have a couple of minutes. What's up?"

"Well, I just wanted to talk about that school board meeting, tomorrow night."

"Okay. What about it?"

"I just thought you should know that we'll probably have over thirty people, there. Not only a bunch of us from Moms for Liberty, but a number of other concerned parents.

We've been making some phone calls and quite a few people seem to be on our side."

"Oh, that's great, Sheila. Nice work – real nice. However, there's a good chance that the board president will call for an executive session, meaning only the board members. There might not be any audience allowed in, depending if we vote to open it to the public at the end of our session."

"What? Is that even legal? What about the sunshine laws?", she asked, obviously pissed.

"Well, when I spoke with him, earlier, he said that he feels that we, as a board, have to discuss several things in private. He says that that way, we can discuss what he called my 'sensitive issues' amongst ourselves. Then, once we've come to some sort of agreement, put those issues out in front of the public."

"It's his way of hosing you, Mark. You know damned well that they'll gang up on you and you'll get slaughtered. And the public won't have any say until it's too late."

"Well, yeah – that's what I was thinking. And I argued strongly that we should have an open meeting, first, to allow the public to give their views, and *then* bring those issues up in executive session. Otherwise, it'll look like the board handing down an edict from on high and screw what the parents think."

"What did he say to that?", Sheila asked.

"He said I had a point. And, he said he's going to think about it a little more, overnight, and make a decision tomorrow, by midday."

"Shit, Mark. One way or the other, we're going to show up. And we'll picket and make some real noise if we can't get in. Plus, if that happens, I'll make sure the Poughkeepsie and Kingston TV stations are there to get it all on the late news. I might do that, anyway, whether it's an open or closed meeting. We have to get the word out that parents want change – real change. That our kids are being indoctrinated by a bunch of leftists and Soros-funded socialists."

"I agree with you, Sheila. And I want you to know how much I appreciate your support. And with it, I don't feel like I'm out there, all alone, screaming in the wilderness."

"You most certainly are not doing that, Mark. We're here for you. All the way."

"Thanks, Sheila. But, listen – dinner's almost on the table and I've got to run. But, let's talk tomorrow, once I hear about the meeting, okay?"

"I'll wait to hear from you, Mark. And, of course, the sooner, the better, because I'll have to get our phone tree in gear, one way or the other."

"You got it, Sheila. 'Bye, now."

And they disconnected.

"I heard your end of that", said Frank, sitting across from Sheila in the living room. "And, listen – I don't know if it would work, but maybe I could call some of the guys in The Group and ask them to show up, too."

Sheila thought for a minute, then said, "That's a nice thought, dear, but I'm kind of thinking that a group of concerned mothers might have more of an impact. You know, moms with tears in their eyes and madder than mama bears when their cubs are threatened. I think that would make for better TV, anyway, and I'm going to make certain there are cameras there."

"Well, just let me know – I could probably round up a half-dozen guys if you want me to."

"Let's just see what happens, dear, but thank you." And she blew him a kiss.

The next morning at The Coffee Spot, Suze accosted me the moment I walked in.

"Guess what, J.D.", she said, excitedly, "I'm in! I'm all in my new apartment."

"Yay!", I said. "That was quick."

"I'll say. Anyway, Mr. Shafer – he's the manager guy with the moving van – he got a couple of guys, late yesterday afternoon after you guys dropped me off, and we all went to the storage place and I picked out what I wanted and they loaded it all up and helped me get it set up in the place. I'm in!"

"That's the best news I've heard in – well, at least a few days", I said. "Congratulations. I'll have to get you a house-warming gift."

"I just wanna ride Ceres, one day", she said. "That'd be more than enough."

I smiled and said, "Then, we'll make that happen. And, soon, too."

"Excellent", she said. "Now, you go sit down and I've gotta get this order in."

The guys were discussing the weather. Go figure – Geezers talking about the weather. It had been kind of sucky the past couple of days.

"How's it looking for the weekend?", Hal asked. "There's that parade on Sunday."

"It's supposed to clear up, I guess", said Bob, our de facto meteorologist. "I'm probably gonna bring a couple of guys in on Saturday and Sunday so we can make some hay deliveries. Can't do that if it's raining and I don't know about next week."

Half-listening to the talk about the weather, I realized that we should fill Mike in on what we'd learned about the Bransons, like asap, because of the school board meeting, tonight.

Ironically, Joe picked that very moment to ask Mike, "Hey – that school board meeting still on for tonight?"

"I still don't know. I spoke with Patel late yesterday and he's still trying to decide if it should be a public meeting or they should meet in executive session."

"That new guy's kinda throwing things into a cocked hat, isn't he?", asked Joe.

"I'll say", said Mike. "Plus, according to Patel, there's that group that's stirring things up with a number of the parents. Remember the flyer? Anyway, Patel's a little worried that an open session would turn into a zoo. He's leaning toward the executive session to discuss all those matters among themselves before opening it up for public discussion. He wants to put on a united front."

"Probably a good idea", said Bob. "That's how I'd do it. Get the board all on the same page and then present it to the public." And there were nods all around.

"Hey – not to change the subject", I said, looking at Hal, "but you took that grub up to Gordon's, yesterday, didn't you?"

As I asked the question, Gretchen showed up with her coffee pot.

"Oh, yeah – yeah, I did", he said. "And you should've seen his eyes light up. I told him that he should eat it, right then, before it got any colder. So, I sat with him while he did and he and Shirley and I shot the bull for a little while. I guess he's doing a lot better. He said he's not really in pain, much, anymore and he's pretty much back to normal. He asked about you guys and said to send you his best and that he'll be back later in the week. And, Gretchen – he said to send you his *very* best and to thank you for making his day."

"Gordon's such a nice man – a real gentleman", she said. "Joe." And she looked over at him.

"What? You talkin' to me?", he said. "Like I'm not a gentleman or something?"

"I didn't say a word, now, did I?", she said, winking at him.

"Don't pick on me, Gretchen – I'm not your nose."

"Point proven", she said. "Now – what're you guys gonna have? Oh – before you order, Bill – Artie's got that pie ready for you. Don't let me forget to give it to you when you leave."

Parker gave her a smile and a thumbs-up.

"Pie?", asked. Bob. "Parker gets a pie?"

"Yeah", said Gretchen. "Artie made one out of that old jack-o'-lantern that Bill carved. It looks good, too."

"Tell you what", said Parker. "Why don't you bring it out after our breakfasts. We'll each have a piece of it for dessert."

"Pie? At breakfast?", asked Joe.

"Why not?", said Parker. "Pie's good anytime."

"He's not wrong about that", said Marquardt.

"And, Gretchen,", said Parker, "bring a plate and a fork for yourself. You gotta be in on this."

"Well, now – that's the best invitation I've had in days, Bill. I will. Now – you guys order, huh?"

We did. We shot shit. The food came. We ate. We finished.

A few minutes later, Artie and Gretchen came out of the kitchen, with Artie carrying a huge pie and Gretchen, a big bowl of whipped cream.

"Holy cannoli – that's huge", said Hal, as Artie set the pie down on the table.

"It was a big pumpkin", said Artie. "Made for a nice-sized pie. Hope you guys enjoy it. But, really – pie for breakfast?"

"Like Parker just said, pie's good anytime", said Bob.

Artie cut it into eight pieces – one for each of us and one for Gretchen, leaving one piece left over.

"That one's for you, Artie", said Parker.

"Nah – there was enough of that pumpkin left to make another little one, which I ate last night", said Artie, chuckling."

"Okay, then – Gretchen – why don't you let Suze have it while she's on her break?", asked Parker.

"Good idea, Bill", she said. "And, I've got to save mine for my break, too. I'm too busy, right now. You guys dig in, though. Enjoy." And she reached over, took her plate and she and Artie headed for the kitchen.

Fifteen minutes later, Parker and I collared Mike out in the parking lot. And, for the next few minutes, we gave him all the intel that Ron had gathered on the Bransons – dirt and all.

"Good lord", he said, when we'd finally shut up. "Talk about hypocritical – those folks should be the poster people for it. Here's this guy, Frank, who's strutting around like a military leader *after* he'd been drummed out of the Army for some real sketchy things. And, that wife of his – protesting abortion clinics when she's already had one of her own? Jesus."

"Well,", I said, "we're going to confront them with all of that – or, the ninja horseman is.

We just don't know when, but it'll probably be after the parade. But, if that meeting's on tonight, you just might see Lady Branson there."

"I'm gonna call Patel as soon as I get into the office. I'm really hoping that he calls an executive session because, otherwise……" And he let that hang.

"It'll turn into a friggin' zoo", said Parker.

"Yeah. And, either way, I told Chief Eddings that I'd call him. Patel's kind of using me as the middleman, here. He's trying to stay above the fray and doesn't want to look like he's worried about any sort of commotion. I told him that I'd do that for him. You guys aren't going to go, are you?"

"Oh, hell, no", said Parker and I agreed with him.

"We're not school board-type guys", I said. "But you're going if it's open, right?"

"Yeah, for a little while, anyway. I'm not gonna stay late, though. I just want to see what kind of a crowd shows up."

"Okay, but call me and let us know what Patel decides, okay?"

"Sure – will do. Alright – I gotta git. Catch you guys later."

An hour or so later, as Parker and I were mucking the barn and cleaning and refilling the kids' water tubs, Mike called and informed us that Patel had decided on making the meeting an executive session, rather than a public meeting. That would come in the next week or so.

"How are they going to announce that?", I asked. "That the meeting's going to be closed to the public."

"There'll be no real announcement, other than one they put up on the district's website, which he's already done", said Mike. "Plus, they'll just put up a couple of flyers on the doors to the building. I guess that's what they usually do, along with whatever that night's agenda is scheduled to be."

"Sounds like you just got out of a really shitty night", said Parker.

"Yeah, but I'm still a little concerned about whether a bunch of parents will show up. If they haven't seen the website, they might not know about the change."

"Hasn't that happened before, though?", I asked. "I mean, this isn't the first time something like this has happened, is it?"

"Oh, no – not at all, J.D. It happens every once in a while – but, you know, with what they're talking about and this whole Moms for Liberty crowd and all, it might just cause a ruckus. By the way, I've already told Chief Eddings and he plans on having a couple of squad cars on site – but at a discreet distance away. He doesn't want to rile people up, but wants a few guys there, just in case."

"Let's hope they can just sip their coffee in their nice warm cars", said Parker.

"Amen to that, Bill", said Mike.

And, after another few seconds, we disconnected.

"I'll bet that Branson babe is gonna be madder'n a wet hen when she finds out", said Parker.

"Yeah, probably", I said.

At that very moment, down in Hyde Park, Sheila Branson was madder than a wet hen.

Mark Fisher had just called her and told her about tonight's meeting being closed to the public – that was an executive session.

"They can't do that!", she said. "I mean, the sunshine laws and all that. It *has* to be open to the public."

"Now, now, now, Sheila", replied Fisher. "They can. I mean, we can do that. It's a closed session where the board discusses various proposals and issues in private. I can understand that. Now – you should know that I'm putting three proposals on the table tonight. The first one is to ban that book, *Gender Queer* from the high school and middle school libraries."

"You brought that up at the last meeting, didn't you?"

"I did. And, the second one is to bring back The Pledge of Allegiance into all of the district's schools, every morning."

"Good", she said. "I don't know why it was ever taken out in the first place. We all said it in school. Just another one of those radical left-wing things meant to denigrate our country. I tell you, Mark, they're chipping away at our liberties."

"I realize that, Sheila. You're preaching to the choir. And that's why I'm trying to do something about it. Now, the third one will probably be the most contentious – the banning of CRT in our schools. Actually, I took a lot of the wording from the bill that DeSantis signed down in Florida."

"That's a landmark bill, Mark. One of our greatest victories. And I'm glad to hear you say that your proposal mirrors it. Do you think it'll pass?"

"No, not at all. Not here, not now. But I think the other two stand a chance. And, honestly, I just want the CRT thing to begin bubbling up into the public's consciousness. And that's where your group can really be of some help."

Sheila thought for a minute, then said, "Look, Mark. We might not be able to get into that meeting, tonight, but that doesn't mean that we can't show up, en masse, to make some noise on behalf of all three of your proposals. For one thing, we've already lined up over a couple dozen people – mostly moms, but a few men, too. We'll set up a picket line, out front, with our placards and banners and all."

"Well, I suppose that can't hurt", he said. "Just be careful and be civil, okay? The last thing we need is any sort of bad press."

"Oh – speaking of the press, Mark, I believe I've convinced both local stations – the one in Poughkeepsie and the one in Kingston – to send camera crews out. I was hoping they could tape the meeting, but maybe the protest thing will be just as good, if not better. That way, I can get them to interview some of our parents. That'll make quite an impression."

Fisher kind of liked that idea – that the press might show up. That way, the message would be sent out far and wide – at least in Dutchess County.

"You don't suppose they'd wait around until after the meeting, do you, Sheila? Perhaps I could give an interview."

"That would be great, Mark, but perhaps another time. I want them to get the story on tonight's late newscasts and, if the meeting runs late, that might not happen. I'll tell you what, though – I'll make a couple of calls and talk to the people they send to the meeting and, depending on how tonight goes, maybe they'd like to do a follow-up interview with you, tomorrow or the next day."

"Oh, that'd be great, Sheila. Really great. Thank you."

"Of course, Mark. This is important. Not only to us, but to the nation. And, from what we've found, grass-roots actions like this are really beginning to make a difference. We're trying to create a wave, here, Mark. And, quite frankly, you're our point man."

"Terrific, Sheila. Now, I hate to rush you, but I have to be at an appointment in twenty minutes and it's a good fifteen-minute drive from here……"

"I understand, Mark. You go do your thing and I'll go do mine and we'll touch base, either after the meeting or first thing in the morning, okay?"

"You got it."

And they disconnected.

Immediately, Sheila called her contacts at the two television stations and gave them the decision on tonight's meeting and the protest that would take place outside of it.

And she made sure that they were made aware that she was the group's spokesperson and would be more than glad to be interviewed.

And, she thought that, if she played her cards right, this would be her formal on-air entry into the ever-burgeoning world of patriotic politics and might be a springboard into making her a media personality.

That would be so-o-o nice.

CHAPTER 21

Right around seven o'clock, after Mike and his wife, Linda, had finished eating, he said to her, "Look – I'm going to run over past the library, just to see if everything's okay." They'd discussed the school board meeting over dinner and he'd expressed his concern about the potential crowd that might show up.

Linda said, "Well, okay, dear – but just drive by, okay? If there's any trouble, I don't want you getting involved."

"Yep, that's all I'm planning to do – just drive past. I don't plan on even parking or getting out of the car. I should be back in – oh, about an hour."

Fifteen minutes later, as he was driving up North Park Road toward the school campus, he noticed that the parking lot had a lot more vehicles in it than there should have been for an executive session meeting. The lot was almost half full.

The board meetings were held in the Rhinebeck High School/Middle School Library, a free-standing building on the grounds between the two schools. The building was L-shaped, with large glass doors leading to each of the wings of it and windows running along both sides. The room generally accommodated whatever audience would show up, and that was, on average, twenty to thirty people. Sometimes, far less.

As he drove past the library, he looked to his right and saw what he considered to be a huge crowd – maybe forty or fifty people. A number of them were holding big signs attached to wooden handles and the people were waving them around. He saw a few that had the same 'NO CRT' logo that was on the flyer that Suze had brought to the table the other day.

Another few signs had 'Bring Back the Pledge' printed on them and there was even a 'Trump 2024', although 'Moms for Liberty' were the most prevalent.

Although most of the protestors - that's how he mentally referred to them – were women, there were probably a dozen men in the crowd, too.

He rolled down his window and heard some chanting, though it was fairly disorganized.

He stopped in the road in front of the building when he saw a couple of bright lights illuminate parts of the crowd. Uh-oh, he thought – the TV news people were here. He tried to see the reporters and if they were interviewing anyone but, in the crowd, he couldn't make them out.

He sat there for a minute or two, just watching and listening.

All of a sudden, he heard a woman's voice coming over a bullhorn.

"They're not letting us in!", she shouted. "They're trying to silence us - and *we will not be silenced!*" That line was met with loud shouts.

"This is *our* school system!", the woman continued, "And *we* will decide what our children learn – *not them!*" More shouting, a little louder, this time.

"*And*", she went on, "we want the Pledge of Allegiance back in *all of our schools!*" This brought a loud cheer. "Say it with me!", she yelled. "I pledge allegiance to the flag….." and the crowd joined her in saying the entire pledge.

When they were finished, she yelled, "We *will not* stand for the backroom politics of this school board! Our voices *must* be heard!"

This brought the loudest response of all and the crowd seemed to become more animated.

Mike could see some other people around the perimeter of the crowd, not joining in with the protesters. Actually, he watched them as they began to walk away toward the parking lot. Must be normal parents, he thought, and not part of this mess.

He also wished that the TV stations would turn off their lights and cameras – many in the crowd were obviously performing for them.

All of a sudden, there appeared to be some sort of melee up near the library's entrance and he saw a wire garbage can shatter the glass front door. Oh, Jesus!, he thought – this is really getting bad.

Almost instantly, he heard sirens coming from the other side of the library and blue, red and white lights illuminated the whole area. Within seconds, two police cars careened into the driveway out in front of the library.

People turned to look as the cars screeched to a halt, the whole area flooded with red and blue flashing and twirling lights. Four cops jumped out of each car, all wearing helmets with face shields and flak jackets and carrying nightsticks.

As a phalanx, the cops made for the front door, holding their nightsticks horizontally in front of them with both hands. Most in the crowd backed off to let them through, though a couple of the men tried to stand their ground, but were quickly accosted by two or three officers and forced to back up.

As the phalanx of eight cops stood with their backs to the broken door, one of them unhooked a bullhorn from his belt and shouted into it: "That's it! Disperse now! Leave the area immediately! If you don't, you will be arrested! Leave *now*!" This was met with a few who tentatively stood their ground, but the majority of the crowd began backing and walking away, with shouts of "Police brutality!" and "First Amendment!" and such being hurled back at him.

One woman, carrying a 'NO CRT!' sign stood in front of the lead officer, shouting at him, but Mike couldn't hear what she was saying. He saw the cop reach behind him and pull out his handcuffs and the woman began backing away, still shouting. After a few feet, she turned and walked toward one of the TV stations' bright lights.

Mike pulled over to the curb and got out of his car, wanting to speak with the police officers and to make sure the board members were alright, inside.

Walking up toward the library, he spotted the woman who had confronted the cop being called over by a reporter and her cameraman. Oh, God, he thought, as he got closer – it's that woman from the diner – Sheila Branson. He hung back a few feet to try and hear what was being said.

"Excuse me, ma'am", said the reporter, thrusting a microphone at Branson, "Can we have a word?"

Branson quickly tried to fix her hair with one hand while saying, "Why, certainly."

"Can you please give us your name? And spell it, too."

Branson did that and then was asked, "Are you involved with the movement that was here this evening?"

"Well", said Sheila, "I'm the local organizer for Moms for Liberty and what we want is to have our voices heard about our children's education." Branson knew enough to get her points across early and often because those would be the quotes that would make it on-air.

"And why were you here, this evening?", asked the reporter, a mid-to-late twenties woman bundled up in a coat, scarf and gloves.

"We are here, tonight, to make sure that our children are not subject to that horrible CRT – Critical Race Theory – which is full of lies and indoctrination and is being foisted on our children by people who hate America."

"Is this school system teaching that, now?", the reporter asked.

"Yes!", said Branson, forcefully. "If you read our children's history books, you'll see that they paint all white people as being demons who were responsible for so many things. Slavery was *not* an all-white issue! And our forefathers were being attacked by savages all over this land, when all they really wanted was a peaceful place to live. And they don't teach that!"

"Alright, that's enough", said a man's voice. Mike looked over and saw the cop who'd spoken over the bullhorn. "Time to break this up. You – get your camera and microphone outta here. You've got what you need for tonight. And, you" – he pointed at Branson – "I thought I told you to *move! Now, do it!*"

The cameraman turned the light off and lowered his camera, obviously pissing off the reporter. "Bret!", she said to him. "We have a right to interview this woman." Bret shrugged, having been down this road before.

"That's right – Bret. Thank you", said the cop. "You guys go on, now. And, you, lady – I'm not going to tell you again."

Mike heard her mutter, "Fuck you", under her breath, but she turned around and walked toward the parking lot, still carrying her sign.

Mike walked up to the cop, put out his hand and said, "Hey - I'm Councilman Mike Wiechowski and I just wanted to thank you for the way you handled all of this, tonight."

"Sergeant William Fain. My friends call me Willy", he said, shaking Mike's hand.

"Like I said, you did a really nice job over there. Thank you."

"Ah, we figured that that crowd didn't look like a violent one – a lot of moms and a few dads. I figured the best way to handle it was to give 'em a little authority, but not take it over the top."

"Well, it worked", said Mike. "But somebody threw that garbage can."

"Yeah, and we had a camera on 'em the whole time, but I'm afraid we might've been too far away to i.d. the person. Plus, the crowd and all were in the way. I dunno – we'll review the tape when we get back to the station, but I'm not holding out much hope. The district's insurance'll cover it and I already spoke with the custodian and he said that he'll put some plywood over it for tonight and call the glass people in the morning."

"Is the meeting still going on?"

"Far as I know, yeah", said Fain. "They were a little rattled, I guess, but I spoke with Mr. Patel for a few seconds and he said that they've probably got another couple of hours to go and he wants to get whatever they're doing finished tonight."

"I was going to go in and make sure they're all okay", said Mike.

"Ah, Councilman, I don't think you have to do that, but it's up to you. They're fine. Trust me."

"Well, alright. I guess I'll be on my way, then", said Mike. "Think this'll be on the news, tonight?"

Fain laughed and said, "Most exciting thing that's happened around these parts in days, man. Course it'll be on the tube."

"God, I wish that weren't so, Willy. The last thing we need is to give those people more airtime."

"I hear ya, Councilman, but we're noticing a constant uptick in that kind of thinking. Did you hear what that woman said? That slavery was not an all-white issue? I'm here to tell you, man, that my people surely weren't owned by no other Black folk and that's the God's honest. Listen – you have a good night, now, and get home safe, okay?"

"I will. And, thanks, again, Willy. And tell Chief Eddings that we talked. I gave him a heads-up about this crowd, tonight, when I spoke with him this morning. And he couldn't have sent a better guy – a better team."

"I appreciate that, Councilman. We all do." And he tipped his helmet with a finger and walked off toward his men.

Mike stood there for a minute, wondering how such a melee could happen in Rhinebeck. He was all for political disagreements and peaceful protests – that's the way this country worked. But, large swaths of people believing nonsense like he'd heard recently? And then, trying to control what their children were taught in school? And ignoring the real facts of history? And banning books? That just wasn't right.

No way in hell that was right.

He got back into his car and headed home. On his way, he picked up his phone.

"Yeah, Mike?", I said when my phone rang.

"J.D. – I just left the library where the board meeting's being held. And there was quite a commotion – somebody even threw a garbage can through the front door."

"Holy shit!"

"Yeah, but the cops showed up, right away, and broke it up peacefully. There were a couple dozen people wanting to get into the meeting and didn't like the fact that it was closed. And guess who was front and center?"

"I probably don't have to guess – Sheila Branson, right?"

"Bingo. And she was interviewed by News12. It'll probably be on the late news – you might wanna check it out."

I looked at the time. Eight forty-five.

"It's on at ten, right?"

"Yeah. And I'm pretty sure it'll be the lead story, or close to it."

"You okay?", I asked.

"Oh, yeah – I didn't get involved. Just sat in my car and watched until it was over. And I spoke with a Sergeant Willy Fain who was running things for the police. Actually, eight guys in two cars showed up in riot gear. They did a real nice job of breaking it up without any trouble."

"Jesus", I said, shaking my head. "Cops in riot gear at a school board meeting."

"I know, right? And in Rhinebeck, no less", he said. "This is getting out of hand."

"Yeah, it is", I said. "And we're working on a plan to, um – maybe stifle – the Bransons a bit. Haven't got it nailed down, yet, but soon, dude."

"Okay. But, now, I'm worried about the parade on Sunday", said Mike. "That group's planning on showing up, right?"

"Yeah, they are", I said.

"Fuck. Anyway – I'd imagine that Chief Eddings will have his guys out in force for it. But the last thing I want to see happen is some sort of confrontation between those guys and the cops. At a kids' event, no less."

"I know."

"Alright, look – I'm almost home, now. I'll catch you in the morning, okay?"

"You got it, dude. And thanks for calling."

"Watch the news."

"I will."

And we disconnected.

And I immediately called Parker.

"What's up?", he said. "Everything okay?" He sounded a little rattled by my late call.

"Yeah, everything's fine. I'm just calling you to tell you to watch the ten o'clock news on channel 12. I just got off the phone with Mike and he went by the school board meeting and I guess there was a little melee."

"A melee?"

"Yeah, I guess a bunch of those Moms for Liberty people showed up, en masse, and were all pissed that the meeting was closed and they couldn't get in. There was a bunch of shit going down in front of the building and somebody in the crowd threw a garbage can through the front door."

"Are you shitting me?", he asked, his voice rising.

"Nope. And, according to Mike, the cops – there were eight of 'em – rode up immediately and got the whole thing calmed down and sent the crowd home. Or, somewhere, but they all got the hell away from the library and split in their cars. But - and get this – a reporter from channel 12 interviewed Sheila Branson and it's probably gonna be the lead story on tonight's newscast."

"Ah, Jesus", said Parker. "Anything else? Anybody hurt?"

"Nope – nobody got hurt and nobody got arrested, but Mike talked to some sergeant and said that he seemed like a good guy and all."

"Fuck. What time is it?"

"Um – nine-thirty. Tell you what – why don't we hang up, now, and I'll call you a couple minutes before ten and we can watch it together over the phone. Unless you don't wanna watch it and your beauty sleep is more important."

"Asshole. Alright, call me in a few." And we disconnected.

I called Parker a couple minutes before ten.

"You got the TV on?", I asked.

"Yep. Hey – how many years are they gonna keep 'Law and Order' going? I hadn't even realized it's still on the air 'til just now."

"Hell, I don't know. I wasn't watching – did they catch their bad guy?"

"No, he got clean away. First time, ever. Hell, I don't know, dude – I wasn't really watching. Okay – here's the commercial break."

And, because we didn't really have any small talk, both of us were less than mesmerized by happy-looking people hawking medicines for diseases that only a few people get, some local yokel selling Andersen Windows and a woman – obviously the dealership owner's wife, because she didn't look anything like what could be construed as a commercial actress – screaming about the whale of a deal on a car (there was a cartoon whale spouting in the corner of the screen) people could get if they hurry in today.

Finally, the news logo came on and the anchor – some guy with overly-coiffed hair – announced, "There was trouble at a school board meeting, tonight, over in Rhinebeck. Here's Becky Snover with the report…." And, over some footage taken at the scene, she described what had happened outside the school board meeting. The front of the building and the crowd were bathed in the red and blue flashing lights from the police cars.

"I was able to interview one of the protestors", said Becky. And the picture cut to Sheila Branson, trying to fix her hair with her fingers. Her name popped up on the screen, under which read, 'Moms for Liberty'.

And we saw her say, "We are here, tonight, to make sure that our children are not subject to that horrible CRT – Critical Race Theory – which is full of lies and indoctrination and is being foisted on our children by people who hate America."

"Is this school system teaching that, now?", Becky asked.

"Yes! If you read our children's history books, you'll see that they paint all white people as being demons who were responsible for so many things. Slavery was *not* an all-white issue! And our forefathers were being attacked by savages all over this land, when all they really wanted was a peaceful place to live. And they don't teach that!"

And the shot cut away to Becky, obviously now standing in the TV station's parking lot.

"The people who were there, tonight, were quite adamant about having a much larger say in their children's education. And, it seems, they don't believe what is being taught in schools, right now, is the right thing for their kids. We'll keep tracking this story. Bob?"

And the scene cut back to the well-coifed Bob in the studio.

I hit mute.

"Well?", I said to Parker.

"Slavery wasn't an all-white issue, huh? No, I guess not", he said. "It also involved Black people – who were the damned slaves! Aw, Jesus – these people are fucked up."

"Yeah - and white people were attacked by the Indians because, why? The white people thought the land was theirs? Just because they wanted it and thought they deserved it?"

"It all comes down to white supremacy, son", said Parker. "That's the whole, bottom line, basis for all of this shit. And it's always been here, but it's been kept below the radar for, like, a long time. But now, since that douchebag became President, he's made it okay and, now, they're all crawling out from under their rocks."

"Yeah, you're right", I said.

"Of course, I'm right, but I wish I weren't. Look – we can't do anything about it, tonight, and I gotta hit the hay. This is late for me."

"Yeah, me, too. Alright – catch you in the ayem."

And we disconnected, I turned off the TV and the lights and headed up to bed, a little – or a lot – disturbed.

CHAPTER 22

When I got to The Coffee Spot, the next morning, the talk around the Geezers' table was, quite naturally, all about the melee outside the school board meeting, last night.

I guess a couple of the guys – namely, Bob and Joe - hadn't seen the newscast, but Hal had brought it up on his phone and they'd seen it by the time I joined the meeting.

"That was the babe who was in here with that friggin' flyer, right?", asked Joe. "Sitting with that new school board guy."

"Yeah, it was", said Mike.

"What is she – nuts?", asked Joe, undoubtedly rhetorically. "Saying that slavery wasn't white peoples' fault? And that the settlers were just nice people who wanted to take over the Indians' land, like, because they thought they should be able to? For nothin'? That friggin' flies in the face of the truth. Didn't she study history?"

"I think she probably did, Joe", said Mike. "But what some of these people are trying to do is rewrite history, the truth be damned."

"Why? It just doesn't make sense", he said.

I piped up.

"Yeah, it does, Joe – to them. See, there's a whole, pretty big, undercurrent of white people in America that's always been here – they've just been pretty quiet up to now. And those people are scared – scared of the fact that, within the next fifteen or twenty years, whites in this country will be in the minority."

"So?"

"So, they honestly believe that the United States should be a white country. That anybody else is some kind of interloper. And the so-called 'interlopers' are taking what those people think is, somehow, rightfully theirs."

"It's white supremacy, is what it is", said Parker. "And it's here and it's raising its ugly head – even right here in the Hudson Valley."

"Well, look what happened at the Center", said Hal.

"Exactly", I said. "That's all part of it. These people think that this country has to be white and it has to be Christian."

"I've seen it, too, right in my own business", said Bob. "I've got a couple of guys from Guatemala working for me. Oh, they're official H-2A temporary agricultural workers – they've got the paperwork and all. Been working for me for a couple of years, six months at a time. Actually, they're about ready to go home again for the winter. But, a couple of weeks ago, they pulled in to get gas in one of our trucks and a couple of guys started harassing them and calling them 'beaners'."

"What happened?", asked Hal.

Bob shrugged and said, "My guys just sort of ignored them, but they told me they were scared. And, not only that, they were insulted."

Gretchen walked up to refill our mugs.

"You guys talking about that thing, last night?", she asked.

"Yeah", was the general consensus.

"That woman that was interviewed on the news was the one that Suze waited on last week - you know that, right?"

"Yeah", was the general consensus again.

"Suze says if she comes in here again, she's not going to wait on her. Actually, we were all talking about it in the kitchen a little while ago and Suze isn't the only one who won't wait on her. They pretty much all agreed on that. You know, we've got several non-Anglos working here, as well as Grace, who heard that comment about slavery and about hit the roof."

"That kind of puts you in a tough spot, though, doesn't it?", Mike asked her.

"Well, yeah, kinda", she said. "And I have to 'fess up. I actually called Irv and told him about it and asked him what he thought I should do."

"What'd he say?", asked Hal.

"Well, he said that if that situation came up when he owned the place, he'd stand behind his people. And he'd tell her, right to her face, that he wouldn't want her kind in here. I guess he saw the news, too, and was pretty upset at what he saw."

"Is that legal?", asked Joe. "Not serving her?"

"According to Irv, it is, but I haven't really checked. I guess he'd done it a couple of times, before, with some troublemakers and he'd told them - and I quote – 'Fuckin' sue me. Now, get out.' And, of course, they never did – sue him, that is."

"Is that what you're going to do?", asked Parker.

"Well, I probably won't use that exact wording but, yeah, I will tell her that she's not welcome in *my* establishment."

"What about the other guy? The school board guy?", asked Joe.

"I haven't thought about that but, no – I don't think I can keep him out. But his eggs might be a little cool when we set them down in front of him", and she winked, which caused us all to smile and give her the ol' Geezer knuckle-knock.

"Alright", she said. "What're you guys gonna have?"

And we ordered.

Right then, down at the Annandale Arms Apartments, Flint Stone and Eric Gallagher were making one last pass around the property, having finished the actual job yesterday afternoon, but wanting to make sure the place looked good and that they hadn't left any equipment or tools behind.

Also, Flint had had an early appointment with the building's manager for him to check on the job and sign the work order so Stone could send his invoice to the owner. The manager had told him how nice it looked and so on and so forth. Plus, he signed the paperwork, which was the whole point of the exercise.

After he'd left and the guys were heading to their trucks, Gallagher said, "Hey – saw Frank's wife on the news, last night. Pretty cool, man."

Stone said, "No shit? Why was she on?"

Gallagher explained about the school board meeting and what had happened and that Sheila Branson is one of the movers and shakers in the local chapter of Moms for Liberty.

"I guess both of 'em are involved in the movement, huh?", asked Stone. "Frank and his wife."

"Yep. Seems that way. Hey – have you made a decision about Sunday?", he asked, referring to whether or not Stone would join The Group at the Halloween parade.

Stone looked down and said, "Yeah. Yeah, I have. Listen – as much as I'd like to be there with you guys, I just hafta do the thing with the kids. Like I said, it's a big deal to them. And, with the wife, too. I told her, though, that I'm gonna wear my camo. You know, to represent."

"Yeah, I get it", said Gallagher. "Maybe we'll look for you and fall in behind or in front of you and your kids. That way, you'd still be involved."

"That'd be cool", said Stone, "but don't wait on me. You guys do what you gotta do when you gotta do it."

"Ah, I'll mention it to Frank, anyway – see what he says."

"I appreciate that, man."

––––––––––––––––––––––––

Over in Hyde Park, Sheila Branson had just seen herself again on the morning news. The station had run the same story as it had the night before. And her phone rang.

"Good morning, Sheila", said Mark Fisher.

"Why, Mark – good morning!"

"I just saw the newscast on channel 12. And I thought you did a great job with that interview, as short as it was."

"Thanks, Mark. It would've been longer, but a cop walked up and made them turn the camera off."

"Figures", he said.

"How was the meeting? I've been dying to hear?"

"Well, good and bad, really. I got them to consider reinstating the pledge and I think that might pass, but I really don't think getting rid of that book will fly, though they all committed to reading it before our next meeting. The CRT thing, though, is a no go."

"Why? That's the most important issue we're facing."

"I know that and you know that, but they don't know that. Anyway, it got shot down almost before I finished my pitch. And that's where I believe you and your group can help, big time."

"I totally agree, Mark. And we tried last night, but those cowards wouldn't let us in. But don't you worry – we'll be there in force at the very next open meeting. I want that place crammed into the walls with *our* parents. Oh, and by the way, we'll be setting up a table and handing out literature at the Halloween parade, this coming Sunday. Our hope is to sign up some people, there, too."

"Excellent, Sheila – maybe I'll see you there. We're taking the kids – who are over-the-moon excited, by the way."

"Oh, Mark – you'll have to stop by our table. I'd like to introduce you to some of our members and maybe even take a few pictures with you. I could do a little p.r. thing and, maybe, get it into the *Journal* or the *Freeman*."

"Well, sure – I guess, but I really won't be able to hang around. I have to be marching with my two trick-or-treaters."

"I understand but, please, do stop by."

"Promise." And, a beat later, "Okay, Sheila – I've got to get to work, now. Just wanted to check in and thank you for what you did, last night."

"I only wish they'd given me more airtime. I had - and have – a lot to say."

"I know you do, Sheila. And, with folks like you, we're going to see to it that some real changes are made."

And, after another couple of mutual admiration niceties, they disconnected.

Then, Sheila went to the TV station's website and downloaded the short video of the piece that had aired last night and this morning.

That done, she sat at her computer and sent it as an email attachment to the other local members of Moms for Liberty, as well as the organization's leaders, down in Florida. Plus, she sent it to a shirttail connection of hers that worked down in the city at Fox News.

If nothing else, she thought, I'm going to make a name for myself. Truth be told, she was all about making Sheila Branson famous and a household word. Her dream was to be interviewed on Fox by either Hannity or Ingraham. This might go a long way toward her achieving that.

When Parker and I had gotten back to the farm after breakfast, I mentioned that, somehow, we had to come up with a plan.

"Yeah, we do", he said. "Let's go into the house and toss some shit around."

"Okay, I'll make some coffee."

"Give me fifteen minutes – I wanna muck the kids' place. I'll just top off the water tubs – no algae trying to grow in 'em when it's this cool. That's a summertime thing."

"Want some help?"

"Nah, I got it. You go make the coffee and I'll be in in a few."

Twenty minutes later, we were sitting at the kitchen table.

"Too bad we don't have any pie to go with this coffee. Hell, even some of them cinnamon donuts from The Golden Potato would hit the spot."

"The Golden Russett", I said. "And I've gotta run down to Crockett's a little later and pick up some stuff. I'll grab a couple of pies and, maybe, even get some donuts. Gotta drive right by the place."

He nodded and took a swig of his coffee. "Now – what the hell are we gonna do?"

"I dunno", I said. "But, after that thing, last night, I don't think we should sit on our thumbs for too long, right?"

He nodded. "I know. And we talked about waiting until after the parade on Sunday, but I don't want that to turn ugly – which it very easily could."

"Yeah, I know."

We sat there, both of us staring out the window for several seconds, each of us taking a sip out of our mugs. While doing that, I had a little idea.

"Okay, I might have a little idea."

"Spill it."

"What if.....what if we sent them a warning - the Bransons – about it not being a good idea to screw with the parade on Sunday?"

"You mean, like the ninja horseman showing up at their place between now and then and delivering his stuff?"

"Well, something like that. But maybe with a twist." I was still running it around in my head.

"A twist", said Parker.

"Yeah. Okay – hear me out on this. I'm not sure about it, but maybe it's an idea. What if we waited until we knew they weren't home – like on our recon mission, the other day. And, what if we delivered a single piece of paper to them, warning them that, if Branson goes ahead with his plans on Sunday, some horrible thing will befall them – him and his wife."

"Huh?"

"Yeah – just go with me on this for a minute."

Parker shrugged. "Okay."

"I'm thinking that we could write a note – on the parchment and in calligraphy, just like always – that instructs him, in no uncertain terms, to change his plans. And we sign it something like, 'The Stranger from Hell'. Yeah – just a single sheet of paper. And, maybe we could stick it to their front door – or some door – with an old knife. Like, 'The Stranger from Hell' had stopped by their house and stuck the note to the door with a knife. Like in the old days – like you've seen in the movies. Yeah – something like that. No ninja horseman, yet – just us driving by and sticking the thing to their door."

"No ninja horseman?", he asked, with a healthy degree of skepticism. "Dude – that's our ace in the hole. That's what scares the shit outta people."

"I know. But, here – we stick the note on the door. And it says something like I just said – that something horrible will befall them if he goes ahead with his plan. And, if he *does* go ahead with things, *that's* when the ninja horseman shows up and all hell breaks loose – including exposing both of their past – um, indiscretions. We don't use that as a deterrent – we just let loose with it. You know, blast it out everywhere. Expose 'em both in public."

"So, in other words, the hammer isn't a deterrent, it's a punishment. Is that what you're saying?" I could see that Parker was now with me and his gears were turning.

"Yeah. Yeah, that's it."

He took another swallow of coffee and stared out the window again.

A few seconds later, he said, "Not bad. But that addresses Branson. What about his wife?"

I thought for a couple of seconds, then said, "Well, the same note can also address her."

"How?"

"Well, it can just tell her to quit the Moms for Liberty, can't it?"

"Weak", said Parker. "Well, kinda weak. I mean, what's her deadline for doing that and how are we gonna know if she really does quit? It's not like it's some legit organization – just a bunch of parents and shit, right?"

"Well, yeah", I said. "There is that."

"But, dude – I like where you're going with this. I think it'd be great to put the kibosh on those assholes showing up on Sunday. And, if you word that note correctly, it might have some effect. I dunno. But it's worth a try. We just have to think about the wife, a little, is all I'm sayin'."

"Okay", I said. "Let's be thinking about that for a little while. Maybe we can come up with something."

"When are you going to Crockett's?", asked Parker.

"I guess about now."

"Want me to ride shotgun? Not much going on around here."

"Why not?"

Fifteen minutes later, we were heading south on Centre Road and came upon the intersection where The Golden Russett was located.

"Let's wait and stop on the way back", I said and Parker nodded his acquiescence.

My phone rang.

Ron.

"Dude", I said, putting it on speaker. "We're driving down to pick up some vittles for the kids. What's up?"

"Pie wouldn't be on the shopping list, would it?", asked Ron.

"Wouldn't think of it", I said.

"Okay, you guys. Because we're the FBI, we heard all about that little scuffle at your school board meeting, last night. And, also because we're the FBI, I saw that little interview with your buddy, Branson's, wife. Nice family, huh?"

"I'll say."

"Well, look – I talked with Schmidt a few minutes ago and he confirmed that Branson and his little gang of Meal Team Six guys are a 'go' for that parade on Sunday."

"Yeah, and we're trying to figure out a way to put the skids to that", I said.

"Okay, tell me about it in a minute. But here's what else Schmidt told me. He told me that Branson told him that his wife and a bunch of those Moms for Liberty people are gonna set up a booth or a table at the parade, too. Hand out literature and shit like that."

I looked over at Parker and we both raised our eyebrows.

Ron continued, "I had a little meeting with my boss, a few minutes ago, and he's a little concerned that, with both of those groups showing up, there might be a possibility for some trouble."

"What are you guys gonna do?", asked Parker.

"Well, nothing – other than have a few agents in the crowd. Maybe three or four. But, neither of these groups have broken any laws, yet, so we can only watch, really."

"Well, oddly enough, my friend, Parker and I have been discussing the possibility of trying to put the skids to The Group's little thing. But we were having trouble trying to figure out how to deal with the missus. This might just be it."

"Spill."

And, over the next couple of minutes, I laid out the basis of the idea I'd had a little while earlier." Ron, of course, was very well versed in the ways and means of the ninja horseman.

"So, you stick a note to their door and tell them, basically, to back the fuck off, right?"

"Yeah. And, now, we can tell what's-her-name – Sheila – that she'd better cancel her little dealio, too. Now, because we'll be addressing both of them, that idea works."

"And if they don't, the ninja horseman chews 'em new assholes, right?", asked Ron.

"Precisely. And we let the world know about their pasts, which would probably ruin them in their own little groups."

We all agreed that we might be on the right track and that I would take a shot at writing the note when we got back to the farm. Then, I'd run it by both of them and take it from there.

Ron asked me to call him as soon as I had the note written and I told him it'd be a couple of hours but, yeah, we'd call him back.

By the time we hung up, we were pulling into Crockett's parking lot.

CHAPTER 23

Once inside the store, I'd ordered our usual fifty-pound bags of grain and bran, along with a bag of salt with trace minerals and a small tub of on-feed electrolytes. Parker went directly for the baked goods table.

He came over to the register with baked goods in each hand.

"I got us a strawberry-rhubarb and made an executive decision on the other one. It's a crumb cake. I figured it looks good, so....."

"Oh, that's new", said Emily, the young woman behind the counter. "Barbara just made that yesterday for the first time. She'll be interested to hear how you like it."

"We'll be back with a complete report", I said. "It looks real good."

"By the way, she did a lot of canning, this summer, so we should have fresh fruit pies all winter long."

"You guys just keep 'em coming and we'll keep on takin' 'em home", said Parker.

We got the feed loaded into the bed of the truck and the pies loaded into the back seat and headed home.

We drove in silence for a few minutes and I glanced over at Parker and he had 'that look' on his kisser. He was not happy.

"What?", I asked.

"You can't stop running water", he said, after a few seconds.

"Huh?"

"Neville Brothers. 'Sons and Daughters'. It's a song – great song. And, in it, they sing that line. Means that the world and everything in it keeps moving forward, keeps moving along. Everything – like running water. You can try to stop it, but it'll always find a way."

"Mmm", I said, nodding, knowing that he had more to say.

"It's like these assholes – the Bransons and those other dimwits. They're trying to take this country back to a time that doesn't exist, anymore, and probably really never did. They're trying to stop the world from moving forward. Probably because if they *can* take it backwards, they can rebuild it the way *they* want it. White. Christian. Nationalist. Shit that the guys who made this country in the first place would never stand for if they were here, today. Hell, that's why they revolted. To get away from that kind of suppression. They wanted freedom and they got it. And, now, these douchebags are trying to whitewash everything and turn the country into some sort of fucking redneck, bible-totin', gun carryin' revival meeting."

"But you can't stop running water", I said.

"Precisely. It's just fucking nuts and it's gotta stop."

"Yeah", I said. "But all we can do is what we can do. We're not going to change the world. Maybe, though, if we play our cards right, we can change our little corner of it. Or stop it from happening around here. At least a little."

"True dat", he said. "Hey – we're almost to The Golden Potato. Wanna stop?"

"Golden Russet. But, nah, not really. We've got these pies and all and - wait – what's that?", as I came to the four-way stop adjacent to the store.

"What's what?"

"That sign. That flyer – over there on their bulletin board next to the door."

"Oh, fuck", said Parker. "It's one of them 'NO CRT' things. Pull in."

"Yep", I said, as I came to a stop in front of the store. "Come on."

We got out of the truck and walked along the wooden boardwalk-slash-porch and I reached up, took the flyer down and opened the door.

"Hey, guys", said Craig, as we walked in. He's the young fellow who owns the store with his wife, Jenny.

"Hey, Craig", I said, walking up to the counter. "Um, did you know this flyer was outside on your bulletin board?" And I laid it on the counter.

He looked at it and said, "Ah, Jesus – no. I had no idea it was there. Somebody must've put it up earlier today. It wasn't there when I got here, this morning. Here – let me throw it away."

And he took the flyer, folded it into quarters and tore it into pieces. "There", he said, throwing the pieces into the garbage can. "You know, I can't believe people around here are into this. Did you see that thing on the news, last night? Over at the school board meeting?"

"Yeah, we did", I said and Parker nodded. "Friggin' nuts."

"I'll say", said Craig. "You know, Jenny and I are from upstate – near Syracuse. And I was talking to my dad, this morning and told him about the thing on the news, and he said the same thing is happening up there. That parents are trying to run the schools. And, my dad said - and I quote – 'Those morons can't find their own asses with both hands and a road map and they want to tell us what should be in our schools? Eff 'em.' Only he said the word."

"Your dad sounds like a good man", said Parker.

"Oh, he's got his moments", Craig said with a smile. "Hey – thanks for bringing that in. Jenny and I'd better check that board all day long."

"Sure. And, hey – as long as we're here, how about four of those cinnamon donuts?"

"Absolutely. And they're on the house. That sign might've driven a bunch of my customers away. It's the least I can do to thank you."

"Well, okay", I said, "but just make it two donuts. I'll split the difference with you."

"You sure?"

"Oh, yeah. You've got mouths to feed and bills to pay. And we probably don't need the extra calories, so that'll work out just fine, thanks."

And, we took our donuts, said our see-ya-laters to Craig and got back into the truck.

"These things are the best", said Parker, taking a bite.

We drove the rest of the way home, scarfing fried cakes and bitching about all the things we'd been talking about.

As I pulled into the lane, I said, "Look – I think I'll run up and take a shot at that note we might want to put on the Bransons' door, okay?"

"Good idea", said Parker. "I'm gonna go into the garage and screw around on the workbench. I've got an idea for another metal sculpture."

"Oh, yeah? What is it?"

"Not gonna tell you, just yet. Like I said, it's just an idea. I've gotta see if I can do it and, if so, exactly how. And I think better when I'm hammering and bending metal. Even if nothing comes of it, I just need the mental work, right now. I gotta get over this being pissed. You can't do things the right way when you're pissed and we've got some work ahead of us. Gotta clear the brain a little."

"Okay, got it", I said. "Once I get a first draft of the thing, I'll bring it down and we'll go over it, okay?"

"Yep. Oh – why don't you take the pies into the house and I'll unload the kids' stuff."

"Sure you don't want some help with that? Shit's heavy."

"Nah, piece of cake. I'll just back the truck up to the barn and toss 'em where they belong. No problemo."

Ten minutes later, the pies were sitting on the kitchen counter and I was sitting at my computer, up in my office, prepared to write.

Okay, now. It has to be short and sweet. Well, not sweet at all, but pithy. One time, when I wrote one of these, Parker called it 'pithy', which I thought was kind of a weird-ass word, so I looked it up. It means 'concise and forcefully expressive'. The word 'pithy' is strange, though, because a word like 'pithy' sounds like – well, I don't know – anything but concise and forcefully expressive.

Come on, Spencer – concentrate.......

Actually, this was gonna be easy.

I typed.

Frank and Sheila Branson......

Do NOT go ahead with your plans for Sunday.

Do NOT attempt to befoul a day meant for children.

For, if you do, forces beyond your understanding will visit you.

And the results will not be pleasant.

Heed these words well.

Very well.

~ *The Specter from the Darkness*

There – that oughta do it, I thought.

Plain and simple. And, if I do say so myself, rather pithy.

I printed it out, grabbed the sheet of paper and headed down to show it to Parker.

I found him at his workbench in the garage, banging away at a piece of metal.

I think I scared him when I walked in because he jumped and said, "Oh, it's you."

"Yep. And I just wrote that thing. Here – take a look at it." And I handed him the sheet of paper.

"And you're gonna do the calligraphy thing on that special paper, right?"

"Yep."

"And we're gonna stick it to their door with some kinda old-looking knife, right?"

"Si."

"I think it's good", he said, after he'd read it. "I mean, you've pretty much said it all, right here. And I like the word, 'befoul'. Good one. And you've called our boy 'The Specter from the Darkness'. Not bad. I'd say we go with it."

"Pithy, huh?"

"Yes. Yes, it's pithy. Now, about that knife…..". And he began looking around at the various tools on the wall and the workbench. My late stepdad, Bill, had probably kept every tool he'd ever handled and they were hung on pegboards all over the garage.

Toward the back wall, there were several knives in sheaths that were hanging from hooks.

We walked over and surveyed them. Some were pocket knives, some were fish filleting knives, and some were just plain old knives, from what I could see.

"Look", said Parker, reaching up to the left and pulling one down. "A friggin' Bowie knife."

He pulled it out of its old leather scabbard and held it up for us to see. He gently ran his thumb along the blade. "Not very sharp", he said. "But I guess we really don't need sharp, do we? We're just gonna stick it into a wooden door and this'll suffice for that."

"I think it looks really cool", I said. "I mean, it looks like something out of the old days, doesn't it? The leather on the handle sure has seen better days, but I guess that's what we're going for – something from out of the past."

"Yeah", said Parker. "I think this oughta work real well. If you don't mind parting with it."

I chuckled and said, "I think I'll manage without it."

"Okay, then. When do we wanna make a run by Branson's?"

"What's today – Tuesday?", I more or less mused. "Too late to do it today. Probably tomorrow, right? Sometime in the afternoon….but how are we gonna know if the missus isn't home? Frank'll probably be out working, but she might be at the house."

"I dunno", he said.

I thought for a second, then said, "Hold on. I've got an idea.….Look, we know that Sheila must've busted her ass to be on TV, last night. I mean, that reporter could've picked out anybody to interview, but it was her, so I'd say that ol' Sheila made herself very available."

"Oh-kay."

"What if.….what if, to make sure we get her out of the house, we have Suze call her and impersonate the reporter who interviewed her and tell her that she wants to do a follow-up story? And that the station would like to get the piece on their early evening newscast. Sheila won't know the woman's voice from last night, so if Suze says she's her, it won't be a problem."

"And", I continued, "Suze'll tell Sheila that she and her cameraman are pretty busy, right then, so she'll ask if they could meet her somewhere that'd be convenient for both parties. If she says yes, she'll meet the so-called news crew, we'll know that she'll be out of the house."

"That could work", said Parker. "We'll just have to clue Suze in and have her kind of wing it when it comes to a meeting place. The reporter doesn't know where she lives, so Suze'll have to ask her and, then, pretend that they're too far north of there. Then, she'll just have to come up with some place. Doesn't really matter where."

"Exactly. And it'll probably have to be mid-afternoon when we do it, because Suze doesn't get off work 'til the lunch crowd has left. And that'd still be in time for the early newscast." Parker nodded.

"Okay, look", I said, "I think we oughta get ahold of Suze, like, now, and fill her in on all of this. She doesn't know about the note or anything. Or, the ninja horseman – or, 'The Specter from the Darkness', for that matter."

"Yep. We should see if we can get her over here. It's too complicated and complex to do over the phone."

"Hold on", I said. "Y'know, we haven't dusted off the ninja horseman in, like, months. What if we ask Suze to come over, this evening, and we'll not only fill her in, but we'll introduce her to the Specter."

"You mean do the whole ninja horseman thing?", he asked.

"Yeah, exactly. It'll give me and Zeus a chance to practice a bit and Suze might get a kick out of it. Or, it'll scare the shit out of her. Or both."

Parker nodded and said, "Not a bad idea. And we can do it pretty early, too – it's gettin' dark early, now – like, around seven-thirty."

"Okay, let's do that", I said. I pulled out my phone and said, "I'm gonna call her." And I hit her number.

"Hello?"

"Hey, Suze – it's J.D. and Parker."

"Oh, hi, guys. What's up?"

"Listen, we're working on a plan that we hope will put the kibosh on the Bransons' plans for Sunday."

"Plans? What plans?", she asked.

"Oh, right. You don't know all that yet, do you?" And I took the next couple of minutes explaining that Frank and his band of bozos are planning on disrupting the Halloween parade on Sunday and that his wife and her little coven of right-wing witches are gonna set up one of their Moms for Liberty booths or a table or something. And that we're gonna try and stop all of that from happening.

"Huh", she said, mulling it all over. "How're you gonna do that?"

"Well, that's why we're calling. We were wondering if you could come by the farm, this evening, and we can spell it all out for you. Plus, you just might meet somebody that'll blow your mind."

"Blow my mind? What are you guys – matchmakers?"

We both laughed and I said, "Nope. Not at all. It's just somebody – or some *thing* – that you'll never forget."

"That I'll never forget, huh? You mean, like, you'll have Ryan Reynolds there?"

"Who?", we both asked.

"Never mind. You guys are both too old. But, yeah. Yeah, okay – I'll be there. What time?"

"How about you get here right around seven-thirty? That work?"

"Yeah, I can do that. And, I gotta tell you, I'm kinda intrigued by all this. Especially meeting somebody I'll never forget. That'll be a first. Pretty much everybody I've ever met is forgettable. Oh – present company excluded, of course."

"Good catch", I said. "Okay, see you later."

And we disconnected.

"Well, alrighty, then", said Parker. "Guess we're on for tonight. You got all your gear?"

"Yep. It's all in the closet."

"Good. So, I'll plan on getting here around seven, maybe a couple minutes before. And I'll get all of Zeus' tack ready and put it on the sawhorse. Then, around seven-fifteen, we'll get all of Zeus' stuff on him and you all mounted up."

I nodded and said, "Okay - and why don't we do it like we did it with Mike? Why don't you and Suze go into your office in the barn and you close the barn door behind you. Then, I'll come up and toss the bag of rocks at the door and back off. Then, you guys open the door and, voila – there's the ninja horseman bearing down on you."

"Got it. Good plan. You got rocks and shit?"

"Yep – on the floor of the closet. I think I'm all set."

"Alright, then. Now, I'm gettin' excited. I'm not pissed, anymore. Well, I am, but you know. At least we have a plan to move things forward. I'm gonna head out, now. I gotta stop at Tops on the way home and pick up some stuff. And I'll be back later, okay?"

"Yep. And I'll go up and take a stab at writing that note in calligraphy. That way, we can show it to Suze. Here – hand me the knife and I'll keep it with the note and we can show her that, too."

We headed out, Parker to his truck and me to the house, note and knife in hand.

Forty-five minutes later, after two or three rather feeble and highly unsuccessful attempts at writing the note in calligraphy on the antique paper, I was satisfied with the finished product. I laid it and the knife on the desk.

I figured that I'd better grab something to eat – it'd probably be a little too late to eat after the evening's festivities. So, I made a ham and Swiss on rye, tossed a pickle onto the plate, grabbed a bag of chips and a soda and carried it all into the living room.

Shit, I thought. The Series doesn't start until tomorrow.

So, I turned on CNN and almost unbelievably, they had a panel that featured some mouthy babe who was somewhere to the left of Lenin and a guy who'd recently gained notoriety for wanting Congress to declare the United States a 'Christian' nation.

This is bullshit, I thought. I knew enough about journalism – having spent over a decade in the newspaper business – to know that what I was looking at was nothing but a cheap-ass ratings ploy on the part of CNN.

Good God, I thought. How this network has tanked over the past few years. It's gone from a first-class news gathering and reporting organization to nothing more than reality television.

All in the name of money.

Fuck that, I thought, and turned off the tube.

Silence was better than that shit.

CHAPTER 24

Actually, after a few minutes, I turned the TV back on, mostly out of boredom, I guess.

I went to the 'Guide' and scrolled through the scores of channels' offerings. And, after seventy-some-odd channels, I realized that ninety-nine percent of what was being offered was mindless bullshit. Even the National Geographic channel had 'The Science of Stupid' followed by 'Banged Up Abroad'. Good God.

Anyway, the time marched on and, around six forty-five, I went upstairs to get ready.

I opened my closet and pulled out my black jeans, black turtleneck and black boots. I put 'em on, along with my lightweight black gloves. Then, I pulled out my Achiou balaclava with the black see-through mesh face covering – my face couldn't be seen while I was wearing it. I hit the switch on the little red LED lights that would rest right at my eyebrow level, giving people the impression that I had glowing red eyes. The lights worked. Yay.

Then, I pulled out Zeus' black fly mask. It also had two tiny red LED lights affixed to it, that rest just centimeters above his eyes, too, giving off the same impression of glowing red eyes. I hit the switch and those lights worked, too.

I put on the balaclava, but kept it up on my head, not covering my face, just yet. And I ran the lights' wires and the controller down the front of my sweater. Good.

I'd put a small braid in Zeus' mane and run his controller wires through it so I could turn them on and off with ease as it would rest on the top of his neck.

Then, I reached into the closet and pulled out my black Medieval Witcher's cloak. It was long – almost to the floor - but split up the front and back so I could easily ride in it. It had an oversized hood that I'd eventually pull up over my head. There were big, oversize sleeves that afforded ease of motion.

I pulled out two canvas sacks from the floor of the closet. They each had a drawstring to close it. In one, I placed a couple of large rocks. That would act as the ninja horseman's calling card. The other would hold the note or missive or whatever you call it that I would deliver to our 'mark' – in this particular case, Suze.

Then, I went into the office, grabbed a simple sheet of paper and wrote 'Hi, Suze!' on it. That way, she'd get the effect of receiving the message that the mark – in this particular case, the Bransons – would get if and when Zeus and I visited them. I put a rock into that sack, too, laid the note on top of it and pulled the drawstring closed.

Back in my bedroom, I pulled the balaclava down over my face, put the cloak on and got everything all situated. Then, I turned on my LED lights and pulled the hood up over my head.

Ready.

And, as I always do, I walked into the master bedroom. It had been Mom and Bill's room before they both passed and I'd left it just as it had been when they were living in it. Actually, Mom had lived in the room by herself for the last year or so of her life. Bill had passed first.

That room has a full-length mirror in it and I always check myself out before I go on one of my ninja horseman jaunts, just to make sure everything looks right. And, also, to get psyched.

By now, there was almost no light in the sky and the room was almost fully dark.

I swept into the room and strode over in front of the mirror.

And there he was.

A vision from the darkest depths of chaos.

The image was hard to make out. In the darkness, it was difficult to define its edges because the black-on-black vision of the outfit, combined with the darkness surrounding it, made it hard to define.

But those red eyes, hidden deep under the hood, made my blood run cold, just like always.

I just stood there, staring at the vision before me.

It was evil.

It was black as night and hulking. It was hard to tell if it was real or a mirage. It was a nightmare, not moving. It just stood there.

And it meant business.

Like the threat of death.

And, just like always, I marveled a little at the fact that a pretty mild-mannered guy like me could morph into something as chilling as what I saw before me.

But there he was, staring directly at me from out of the darkness. What the Bransons would come to know as The Specter from the Darkness.

Okay, I thought. I'm ready.

So, I turned off the lights, not wanting to waste the batteries, pushed the balaclava back up onto my forehead and swept back into my bedroom. Note: When one is wearing a Medieval Witcher's cloak one sweeps from place to place.

I grabbed the two sacks and Zeus' tricked-out fly mask and, as I was turning to sweep out of the room again, I heard Parker's distinctive 'toot-toot' as he pulled down the lane. Good. Right on time, I thought.

As I walked down the lane to meet him, I yelled, "Yo!"

"Yo, yourself!", he yelled back, trying to see me coming in the faint light of the rapidly-ebbing dusk. "Oh, there you are."

"Yep."

"I'm gonna go down and get Zeus' stuff out of the tack room", he said, walking over to move the sawhorse into a better spot. "Set your stuff down next to this", as he got the sawhorse where he wanted it.

I did and said, "Okay, I'll go down and get Zeus and meet you back here."

"Ten-four."

A couple of minutes later, the three of us – Parker, Zeus and I – were together. When I went down to fetch my boy, I'd told Ceres that we'd be right here – that we weren't going anywhere and not to worry. A flake of alfalfa tossed at her feet sealed the deal and we left her happily munching away.

I put Zeus' hackamore, or bitless bridle, on him while he was still in the pasture and hooked the lead rope to it. Now, all I had to do was to put his fly mask on, run the lights' little wire up between his ears and affix it to his mane with a little braid.

Which I did while Parker got his saddle and saddle pad on him.

Two minutes later, our tasks complete, Parker looked at his phone and said, "Okay, seven-twenty. Suze could be here any time, now. Why don't you get up on Zeus and go up around the other side of the house or the garage or something so she doesn't see you when she drives in."

"Yep", I said. "Okay, give me a leg up." Once up on Zeus' back I said, "Okay – hand me the two sacks." And he did.

"Alright", said Parker. "I'll go down into the barn. Want the lights on in there?"

I thought for a second, then said, "Yeah – they only throw light out about ten feet in front of the door. When we come up and I toss the sack at the door, Zeus and I'll go twenty or thirty feet back up the lane. Y'all won't be able to see us the minute you open the door. But you will in another two or three seconds because I'll goose ol' Zeus pretty good and we'll be on you before you know it. Oh - and keep the lights on, now, so Suze can see where she's supposed to go when she gets here."

"Got it." He looked to his right, up the road. "Look – headlights. That's probably her, so you'd better get a move on."

"Roger. See you in a few." And I nudged Zeus with my heels and we turned and trotted up the lane, hanging a left between the garage and the house. Then, we slowed to a walk and camped out behind the garage.

At that point, I pulled the balaclava back down over my face and pulled the hood up over my head. The only thing left to do was turn on our two sets of lights. I was holding the two sacks in my lap, my right hand holding them in place.

I saw the sweep of Suze's headlights cross the house and turn into the lane. I heard her park next to Parker's truck, get out and close the door. The thought crossed my mind that my trusty old Subaru was home again, if only for a short visit.

Parker yelled to her and told her to walk down to the barn.

A few seconds later, I heard the big barn door squeak on its track as he slid it shut.

Alrighty, then. Just about ready. I'd give them a minute or two to get situated and then do my thing. I'd given Zeus his head and he was grazing on some of the grass at his feet.

'Well, son – you ready?", I asked him as I pulled his head up. Then, I reached up on his neck and turned his lights on. Then, I reached up under my sweater and turned my lights on. We were good to go.

We walked around the garage, again, and down the lane toward the barn.

We got up to within about ten feet of the big wooden door and I could hear their voices.

No time like the present, I thought, as I grabbed the sack with the two rocks. I windmilled it twice and, on the third time, let it fly right at the door.

BLAM!

Jesus, that was loud, I thought. And I turned Zeus on a dime and we trotted forty or fifty feet back up the lane. Then, I turned him around so we faced the barn again.

The instant that I saw the door begin to slide open, I nailed him in the sides with my heels and we shot forward.

By the time the door was fully opened and I saw Parker's and Suze's silhouettes, we were fifty feet away and closing quickly.

Suze looked up at whatever she was hearing or seeing coming toward her and I saw her mouth open. Zeus gave a mighty snort as we rushed toward her like a freight train, red eyes blazing, my cloak flowing and Zeus' hooves thundering.

Nightmare.

She screamed.

A second later, I pulled hard on Zeus' reins and had him stop and go up onto his hind legs, not twelve feet in front of her. And, God love him, he stayed up there for nearly four seconds, while I just stared straight at her, my head nearly fifteen feet off the ground.

She screamed again, only louder, this time. She was trying to backpedal away from us, but Parker grabbed her and held her in place.

I windmilled the second sack, but only once and let it fly directly at the ground in front of her feet.

She looked down at it. She looked back up at me, a look of terror on her face.

"Open it", I said, in the gravelly stage whisper that I use on these occasions.

She looked down at the sack, then back up at me.

And I had Zeus sky again. And, yep, he stayed up there forever, this time, too. I kept staring directly at her.

When he got back down onto all fours, I whipped his head around and nailed him into a slow gallop back up the lane and into the darkness.

"Oh, my GOD!", she yelled. "What *WAS* that? What -?!? Oh, my GOD!"

By now, I'd slowed Zeus and we turned and walked slowly back toward the barn. I reached down and turned Zeus' lights off and then, mine.

"Better open it", I heard Parker say.

In the lights from the barn, I saw Suze bend over and pick up the sack. She reached into it and pulled out the piece of paper just as we entered the barn lights' spill again. She looked up at me.

"Hi, Suze", I said. "What's the note say?"

I could see that her hands were shaking a little as she unfolded the note.

"It – it says, "Hi, Suze", she stammered.

"Well, there ya go", I said, pushing the balaclava up onto my head. Then, I jumped down off of Zeus and walked him over to the two of them.

"J.D.!", she yelled, a little louder than was necessary, I thought. "What the hell was that?!? What did you just *do*?"

"Ms. Suze", said Parker, "meet the ninja horseman."

"I don't believe this. I just don't fucking *believe* this! This is just plain fucking *nuts!*", she said.

"Did we scare you?", I asked her.

"Scare me? You *fuck*! I thought I was gonna have a heart attack or faint dead away or something. I had no fucking clue that this is what you guys were talking about." She took a deep breath and shook her head.

"Zeus – is that really you?", she asked, a few seconds later, putting the back of her hand up to his nose. He nuzzled it.

"You guys", she said. "You fucking guys."

"Alright", said Parker. "Let's get Zeus home and this shit put away." And he walked over to loosen Zeus' cinch. "I'll get the saddle and you guys get his mask." He handed me the lead rope and I hooked it to Zeus' bridle.

"Here, Suze – you grab Zeus and walk him over to the gate", I said, passing the lead rope to her. "I wanna grab a flake of hay for him. Meet you there."

"I-I've never walked him before - and it's dark", she said. I knew that she was still a little freaked out, but walking a monster like Zeus would give her her confidence back. He's a good boy and he'd be a perfect gentleman.

"He'll show you the way", I replied. "and I'll be right behind you."

Five minutes later, the three of us two-leggeds were walking back up the lane toward the house, Suze firing off questions and me answering them the best I could. Basically, she wanted to know where the idea came from. And I told her 'The Legend of Sleepy Hollow', only we'd brought the headless horseman into the twenty-first century.

She fell silent, thinking about that.

Parker broke the silence. "Strawberry-rhubarb?"

"You got it, chief", I said.

"Huh?", said Suze.

When we got into the kitchen, I set the pie and three forks down in the middle of the table.

We all sat down and Suze said, "Well, that's it? You gonna cut it, or what? And you'd better bring over some plates while you're up."

I grabbed three Diet Sprites out of the fridge and sat down. Suze looked at me like I had two heads.

"Well, dig in", I said, and Parker did just that, plunging his fork right in the middle of the pie like a boss.

"Don't need no plates", he said. "Help yourself."

"Oh, I get it", she said. "You guys are fuckin' heathens."

"Yup", said Parker, around a mouthful of strawberry-rhubarb.

"That is most excellent!", she exclaimed, stabbing her fork into it and shoveling a large piece into her mouth.

We scarfed and shot the shit for the next few minutes, mostly answering Suze's questions about the origins of the ninja horseman. And, of course, we had to regale her with the tales of a couple of our 'cases', namely, PJ Conway and Gene Wolfe/Yevgeny Volkov. And, with that one, she got the behind-the-scenes low-down on how her aunt had come to take ownership of The Coffee Spot. And, how her great-aunt's name got to be associated with the new park that's being built next to it.

"So, you guys are sorta like that Charles Bronson character in those old 'Death Wish' flicks – only nicer."

"Well, we've never hurt anybody", I said.

"Yet", said Parker, out of the corner of his mouth.

"Honestly, Suze, we're more like Robin Hood, in a way. We see to it that assholes who've somehow cheated innocent people - and will probably get away with it – are made to see the error of their ways and, basically, reverse their thievery or whatever. It's more of a soul-searing justice than what Bronson's character did."

"I see. But, now, like with the Bransons and those people, who have they cheated? What have they stolen or whatever?"

"Well,", I said, "to the best of our knowledge, they haven't really cheated or stolen from anybody. But what they're doing is trying to steal certain freedoms – like the long-standing right to abortion, for instance. And, also, with the shit they're trying to pull in the schools, they're attempting to steal important parts of kids' educations and, therefore, deprive them of the truth. And, really, the truth is a very important freedom in this country. At least, it always has been."

"Those fuckers are also white supremacists, kid", said Parker. "You know that. All wrapped up in some bastardized version of what they think is Christianity. Or try to pass off as Christianity, anyway. It's fucking nuts.

"Yeah, but it's all over the country", she said. "And you can't do anything about that, can you?"

"'Course not", Parker replied. "But we might be able to do something about it here – where we live. Remember, you can only control what you can control. And we've got no control, at all, over anywhere but right here."

I said, "I wouldn't call it so much 'control', as I'd call it 'affect'. We can't affect anything but what we can affect, right here in our little burg, our surroundings."

Parker shrugged and said, "Yeah, okay. Maybe that's a better word. Whatever. But you see what I mean, don't you, kid?"

"Yeah, I do", said Suze.

"Oh", I said, standing up. "I gotta run upstairs for a sec to get that piece of paper we're gonna leave at Branson's house tomorrow. And we'll lay our plan on you – you're a part of it." And I headed out of the kitchen.

"Me?", Suze asked.

"Yeah", I heard Parker say as I went up the stairs. "You're gonna be a little telephone actress tomorrow."

I came back down and showed Suze the note I'd penned in calligraphy.

"Cool", she said, looking at it. "Where'd you get this old paper?"

"He's fuckin' old", said Parker. "Brought it with him from elementary school."

I said, "Bite me, grandpa" as Suze read it.

"Well, that's pretty short and sweet", she said. "Nice handwriting, too. But where's the ninja horseman in this?"

"He won't be involved in this part of it", I said. "We're just going to stick this note to their door with this", and I pulled out the old Bowie knife.

"Oh, far out", she said. "Can I see it for a minute?" And I handed it to her.

"Now, let me explain what's gonna happen." And, over the next couple of minutes, explained the phone call she'd make to ensure that Sheila would be out of the house when we show up.

"You're gonna do it in broad daylight?", she asked. "What if somebody sees you?"

"They won't", said Parker. "None of the neighbors are close enough to see. Plus, I'll take a clipboard with me and walk up to the door like I'm a contractor or I need directions or something. And I'll hold up the clipboard as I stick the thing on the door. You know, to kind of mask it, just to play safe. Then, I'll just hustle my bustle back to the truck and we'll split, one-two-three."

"What time do you get off work, tomorrow?", I asked her.

"Oh, two, two-thirty. Right around there."

"Okay, we'll pick you up at two-thirty and, once you get into the truck, you'll make your phone call. Remember, you'll be that reporter who interviewed her the other night and you want to do a follow-up."

"Yep. And I'll tell her that I'm up north of her, somewhere, and why don't we meet in the middle."

"Bingo", I said. "Tell you what – ask her where she is. The reporter wouldn't know that she lives in Hyde Park. Tell her that you're up in Red Hook and ask her to meet you in the parking lot of the Mills Mansion in Staatsburg. She'll know right where that is – on the Old Post Road. Tell her three-fifteen, three-thirty. That way, we'll know that she'll be outta the house by the time we get there."

"Okay, I can do that."

"We'll go over it again, tomorrow."

Suze nodded and put down her fork.

"Speaking of tomorrow, gentlemen, I've gotta get up early in the morning. So, if y'all don't mind, I'm gonna head home, now. This has been quite a night and the adrenaline's worn off and I'm gettin' mighty tired."

"I'm'a head out too", said Parker, standing up.

"We did a pretty good job on that", I said, pointing to the pie, of which only about a quarter was left.

"I left that for tomorrow", said Parker.

And, ten minutes later, they'd both left and I had carried my ninja horseman stuff upstairs and put it all in the closet.

It was then that I realized how exhausted I was.

CHAPTER 25

The next morning dawned grey and chilly. The thermometer in the kitchen window said forty degrees.

Jesus, I thought. After spending a few decades in LA, this was definitely not something I was used to. And it was only going to get worse from here. Yikes.

I put on my new down jacket and headed out the door, yelling and waving to Zeus and Ceres as I made my way to my truck. By now, their winter coats were almost in full effect and they didn't seem to even notice the chill. Lucky bastards.

When I pulled into The Coffee Spot, I noticed that most of the cars had some kind of flyer stuck under their windshield wipers. I pulled into my regular spot and took the one off the car parked next to me.

Aw, man - it was one of those 'NO CRT' flyers.

I took it in with me and the guys were already there, naturally.

I waved to Gretchen and saw Suze, down at the other end of the place, taking an order.

As I sat down, I tossed the flyer onto the table, just as Gretchen walked up with her coffee pot to fill my mug.

"Did you guys see this?", I asked. "They're on most of the cars and trucks, out there."

There was a general consensus that they hadn't seen it and that's when Gretchen piped up.

"Just happened a few minutes ago", she said. "I happened to look out the window and saw that babe – you know, the one that was in here, last week, the one that was on the news – putting 'em onto cars. So, I went out the front door and yelled at her to knock it off and to get the hell out of here."

"Did she?", asked Joe.

"Well, yeah, but not before flipping me the bird with a pissed-off look on her face. I just stood there, watching to make sure she got into her car and left. And, when she did, she peeled out and threw gravel all over the place. What a piece of work she is."

Parker and I exchanged glances and he gave a little nod.

Just then, Suze walked over and said her hellos and asked what was up when she saw the looks on all of our faces.

Gretchen picked up the flyer off the table, showed it to Suze and told her about what had just happened.

"You mean that lady that was in here, the other day, with that guy?"

"Yep", said Gretchen. "The very one. Listen, do me a favor – run on out there and grab these things off the windshields, okay? I don't want our customers to see this garbage. It might reflect poorly on us."

"Sure. On my way", said Suze, turning and heading for the door.

"Why do you guys suppose she's picking on us?", asked Gretchen.

I jumped in with, "I don't think she's just picking on The Coffee Spot, kid. It's just that there are a number of vehicles, all in the same place at the same time. I'll give you even money that she – or her compadres – do it in Topps' parking lot, too, along with a bunch of other places."

"I think J.D.'s right, Gretchen", said Bob. "They're just trying to get as many of those things out there as they can. And your place fits the bill."

"Well, I don't like it, one little bit. These people are nuts, trying to whitewash history."

"You know, they're even trying to downplay The Holocaust", said Hal. "Holocaust deniers are popping up all over the place and, for some reason, the media lets it happen and actually interviews some of these creeps."

"It's all about ratings, dude", said Joe. "Hell, all the media companies are owned by big-ass multinational conglomerates, nowadays, and those bastards don't care about nothin' but profits. They'd put Hitler on if he was still alive. Shit, they made that fucking moron President because he made for good TV."

"Alright, you guys", said Gretchen, "why don't y'all order and change the subject to something a little more uplifting? This is bumming my high."

"Well, we're certainly not here to do that, darlin'", said Bob with a smile. "I'll start….I'm gonna have scrambled eggs, bacon and home fries – bring me the sorta burned taters, too. Whole wheat toast."

And we went around the table and we all ordered. Naturally, Gretchen didn't write anything down – she never does.

"I'm a little concerned that those people will show up at the parade on Sunday", said Mike. "Honestly, it's a perfect spot for them, too, what with all those kids and their parents."

"Can anything be done?", asked Hal.

"Well, no – not really", said Mike, shrugging. "You know, First Amendment and all. But I know Captain Eddings will have his guys out in force, in case there's any brouhaha."

"God, it would be terrible if that happens", said Bob. "For cryin' out loud, this is a kids' thing. It's supposed to be fun."

"Well, let's just hope for the best", said Mike and we all agreed in our own little ways.

The door opened and here came Suze with a handful of those flyers. She held them up so we could see, then she went behind the counter and tossed them in the trash.

"Suze seems to be fitting in real well", said Bob. "Nice kid."

Nothing earth-shattering happened after that. Gretchen brought our food. We ate it. Marquardt adjourned the meeting with a unanimous vote signaled by the Geezer knuckle-knock. Twenties floated into the middle of the table and we all got up and marched for the door.

I was purposely the last one out, waving Suze over and telling her, "Pick you up at two-thirty."

"I'll be ready", she said.

"Listen – have you mentioned any of this to Gretchen, yet?"

"Well, no. Was I supposed to?"

"No. But I think that, pretty soon, we should fill her in a bit. She's quite a fan of the ninja horseman. We'll talk about it later, okay?"

"Sure, dude. Whatever. And I'd feel better not hiding anything from her."

"Good. Later…." And I walked out the door.

When we got back to the farm, Parker walked up to me and said, "Listen – I think we should take the Subaru down to Branson's, this afternoon. That big dually of yours kind of stands out and the Subaru looks more like it belongs in that neighborhood, y'know?"

I thought for a second and said, "Yeah, probably. Yeah, you're right. Okay, we'll just drop the truck at The Coffee Spot and have Suze drive the car."

"I call shotgun", he said.

"Me? Sitting in the back seat of my own car? I don't think so."

He smiled and said, "Okay. One time – rock, paper, scissors. Ready?"

I put my fist out and moved it up and down as he said, "One….two….three….shoot!"

I flashed two fingers. He put out a fist.

"Fuck", I said. "Best two out of three?"

"Nope. Besides, you'll like the view from back there."

Around two o'clock, I went up to my office and grabbed the Branson note and the Bowie knife.

When I got back downstairs, I went hunting for Parker and found him in the garage, bent over a piece of metal.

"You finally figure out what you're gonna do?", I asked him.

"Yep. And you can't see it 'til it's finished."

"Whaddya mean, I can't see it? How come?"

"Because, my fine feathered friend, it's for you. It's for this place."

"Really?" Hmm…intriguing.

"Yeah, really. I've got it all figured out and it oughta be done in a week or so. Then, we'll do the great unveiling, okay?"

"Okay, but where's it going to go? I mean, like, where'll we put it?"

"Haven't quite figured that out, yet, but I've got a couple ideas. Say – it's about time to blow this pop stand, isn't it?"

"Yep. And I've got the note and the knife."

"Cool. Give me two minutes and I'll be out. And, why don't we take my truck? It doesn't suck down gas like yours."

"Deal."

Twenty minutes later, we pulled into The Coffee Spot and spied Suze over by the employees' entrance - and Gretchen was standing there with her.

"What are you guys doing with my little girl?", she asked as we walked up to them. "Seems like a big mystery."

I told her that we were just gonna take a little ride and we'd be back within the hour. And that, yes, we owed her an explanation. And that we'd like to do that asap.

"Suppose you could stop by the farm when you're finished here, today? We should be back here by, oh – three forty-five. And, then, maybe we can all make a trek back to my place."

"Well, yeah – I suppose so", said Gretchen. "But I have a feeling this is gonna be one of those things that involves your ninja horseman or something."

"And you probably wouldn't be wrong in thinking that", I said.

"I'm coming, too", said Suze. "I wanna see Ceres again."

"Okay", said Gretchen. "Just come and find me when you get back and I'll leave then."

"Deal", I said. "Okay, let's mount up. Suze – you're driving because we think the Sube will fit in better in that neighborhood than my truck and there isn't really room for three of us in Parker's."

Gretchen headed back up the stairs to the back door and we went to the Subaru.

When Parker opened the front passenger's door and got in, Suze said, "What – you're not riding in the front seat of your own car, J.D.?"

"We did a rock-paper-scissors thing and I lost the shotgun spot", I said, climbing in behind Parker. "You know, I've never even been in this back seat. Not bad."

"Not good, either, I'd imagine", said Parker, stretching out somewhat luxuriously in the front seat.

"Okay", I said. "Suze – time to make your phone call. You remember what you're supposed to say? And where you wanna meet her?"

"Yeah – the Mills Mansion in Statesburg, right?"

"No – Staatsburg – like 'ah'."

"Okay, Staaaatsburg, Got it. You got the number?", she asked, reaching for her phone.

"Yeah – hold on." I pulled it up on my phone and hit the number, then I passed it up to Suze. "Here."

A couple of seconds later, she said, "Uh, yes – Mrs. Branson? This is Libby." She rolled her eyes as she made up the name on the spot. Dumb move on our part not to have thought of that ahead of time.

"Yes – I'm the reporter who interviewed you at the school board meeting, the other night. Remember me? Good. Hey, listen – we'd like to do a follow-up with you, if that wouldn't be too much trouble. And we'd like to get it onto tonight's newscast."

She listened for a few seconds, then said, "Oh, good. Where are you?" A couple of seconds later: "Oh, dear. My cameraman and I are up in Red Hook. You don't suppose you could meet us halfway, do you?"

Suze smiled and said, "Good." She paused for a couple of seconds, then said, "Okay - I'm thinking that the Mills Mansion in Staatsburg would be about halfway for both of us. Do you know the place? Good. Well, we should be able to get there right around three-thirty. Would that work for you?"

She gave us a thumbs-up and said, "Okay, we'll get there a couple of minutes early, so you'll see our news van in the parking lot. Just drive on over to it, okay? Good, Mrs. Branson. Looking forward to it." And she disconnected and handed the phone back to me.

"Well done", I said and Parker gave her a high-five. "She'll have to split her house by, like, three-ten, to get there on time. We're right on schedule."

"Okay, let's roll", said Parker.

We headed down Route 9 and I remarked that we'd probably actually pass Branson going the other way and we all laughed.

"Maybe I should toot at her", said Suze. "And we'll all wave."

Pretty soon, we'd turned onto East Market, which became Crum Elbow. Again, Suze remarked at what a dumb name that was. Finally, once we were on Thurston, Parker said, "Slow down – Kilmer's coming up on the left."

As we slowly approached the Bransons' house, Parker said, "No cars in the driveway. Good. Okay – just stop in the street, out front, and I'll run up and stick the thing in the door."

"Did you remember your clipboard?", I asked.

"Fuck, no. Forgot it. That's okay, it'll only take me a couple of seconds. Hand me the shit."

And I handed him the note and the knife. "Stick it in the note somewhere that it won't screw up the message", I said.

"Okay, thanks for the heads-up, genius. Alright, I'll be right back."

And he opened the door and walked quickly up their front sidewalk and up three steps. Oops, I noticed – there was a storm door covering the actual wooden front door. Fuck.

Parker opened the storm door and stabbed the note into the inner door, carefully letting the storm door close, so the knife wouldn't break the glass. However, that meant that the storm door had to stay open a few inches.

He walked quickly back to the car and got in. "Okay, let's split", he said.

"What about that storm door?", I asked.

"Actually", said Parker, "that's probably a good thing. That way, when one of 'em gets home, they'll notice the door open a little ways and that'll guarantee that they'll see the note."

"Yeah, okay – good", I said. "Hit it, Suze. Just pull a U-ie and go back the way we came."

As we drove north on 9, we all looked to our left when we passed the Mills Mansion, but, of course, we couldn't see the parking lot from the road – it was over a quarter-mile away.

We pulled into The Coffee Spot and I said, "I'll go fetch Gretchen. Be right back."

Five minutes later, we had a little convoy heading back to the farm: Parker and I in his truck, Suze in the Sube and Gretchen in her aging Altima.

"Think it'll work?", I asked Parker.

"What – the note? I dunno. Maybe. But I'd imagine they'll think it's kind of random. I mean, it'll be coming out of the blue and there's really no context. But maybe they'll consider it for what it is – a warning shot."

"Well, really, that's all it is."

"Yep."

We all sat around the kitchen table and I made a pot of coffee. As I poured hers, I said to Gretchen, "Here's a switch – me pouring your coffee."

"Don't slop it is all I ask", she said. "You'll notice that I never spill a drop. It's all in the wrist."

Over the next several minutes, we filled her in on everything – all of the things the Bransons were involved in and all of their activities. We even told her about the dirt we'd found out about them. And that all led us to what we'd done this afternoon.

"Oh, for the love of God", she said when the three of us had finished. "I just can't believe things like this are happening around here. First, we get an oligarch, now we get these....these....I don't know – people that want to take the country back to the dark ages.

Which led me to my sort of go-to postulation that so much of it is centered in white supremacism and the fear those people have that the country is changing in ways that are good for it, but is bad for them. And that a form of white supremacy has been part of this nation's history ever since the first Pilgrims set foot on Plymouth Rock. And that it's been ingrained in so many people, for so many generations, that they don't even see it in themselves. So, they dance around it and place blame wherever they feel they can – especially in those that champion progress. They want to *regress*, not *progress*.

And, that ever since that guy came down the escalator in 2015, they've had a champion for their cause. And, because he's never had anyone really stand up to him and make him pay for his many morally- and legally-corrupt transgressions, they feel that they're free and clear to mimic his attitude, as well as some of his actions.

"And that's the way I see it", I said, by way of getting down off my soapbox.

"Well, that's as good an explanation as any", said Gretchen.

"He's right on, from where I'm sittin'", said Parker. "Hey – anybody wanna try that new coffee cake or whatever it is that we got down at Crockett's yesterday?"

"Nah", said Suze, getting up from the table. "If you don't mind, I'm gonna go down and hang out with Ceres and Zeus for a little while."

"I think I'll pass, too", said Gretchen. "I've gotta get home. I'm tired. But, hey – you guys – thanks for filling me in on all of that. You said the ninja horseman might show up?"

"Well, we'll have to see how the Bransons and their groups react to the note", I said.

"You can bet your bottom dollar", said Parker to her. "that those assholes'll still go through with their plans. I can see that plain as day."

"Well, we'll just have to see, but I agree with you, dude", I said. "But let's just see how the next few days play out and take it from there."

With that, Gretchen stood up, thanked us, again, and took her leave, telling us that she'd see us in the morning. She yelled and waved to Suze on the way out.

"Coffee cake?", Parker asked me.

"Well, hell, yeah. We gotta make sure it's not poison."

He got it from the counter and brought along two forks.

We dug in.

"Hmm….not bad", he said, his mouth full. "Not bad at all."

It was good, too. But, in all honesty, I felt like eating coffee cake in the late afternoon was just a little weird. I'd always thought of it as a morning thing. And I said so.

"Hell, man – open your mind a little. You eat pie in the morning – why not coffee cake in the afternoon?"

"Good point", I said. "Now – what did you say you're creating, down in the garage?"

"I didn't. But nice try, though."

CHAPTER 26

The Mills Mansion, high on a hill overlooking the Hudson River, was inherited by Ruth Livingston Mills, wife of financier and Thoroughbred racehorse owner, Ogden Mills. Originally purchased in 1792 by Ruth's great-grandfather, in 1894, the Mills' decided that the house – their summer home – was far too small to accommodate their large parties and the number of guests who visited with regularity.

So, in 1895, work began on more than tripling the size of the house, from twenty-five rooms to seventy-nine rooms. When construction was complete, in 1897, the project had cost the Mills' a then-whopping $350,000.

And, whether or not it was the Mills' plan, the building looks very much like the White House, with six large white columns dominating the front entrance.

There are several good-sized parking lots designed for visitors to the mansion, which offers guided tours, year-round. Plus, the pathways and out-buildings on the 192-acre property draw thousands of visitors each year. Picnics along its tree-lined pathways are an everyday occurrence during the spring, summer and fall.

When Sheila Branson pulled through the property's massive front gates at 3:17 that afternoon, she headed for the parking lot closest to the mansion, figuring that that's where the News10 van would be waiting for her. She was a little surprised to find that wasn't the case.

So, she drove to the next nearest lot. No dice. Then, a third one. No news van.

She then figured that, maybe, Libby and her cameraman had gotten delayed for a few minutes. Oh, well, she thought, I'll just go back to the main lot and listen to Joe Rogan for a few minutes. Not only was he pretty funny, his views on American politics had increasingly paralleled hers.

Unbeknownst to her – or to me – back in LA, Ron had noticed that I had been dumb enough or unwitting enough to use my own cell phone for Suze to call her. Rookie move, thought Ron, watching the numbers flash onto his screen. The FBI had recently purchased Pegasus software from the Israelis and Sheila Branson's number had been plugged into it, along with her husband's and several other members of The Group. Pegasus was the bomb, doing all kinds of magical, secret things with cell phones.

When Ron had seen my number pop up on her phone, he used some Pegasus magic to wipe it from Sheila's history. That way, there'd be no trace that I – or Suze – had called her.

After looking at the time and realizing that Libby was now over twenty minutes late and she hadn't heard from her, Sheila pulled out her phone. She looked at her 'Recent Calls' but, for some reason, Libby's number wasn't there. Odd, she thought. She scrolled down to see if, by chance, it had gotten out of order on her screen. Nope – she went all the way back to Monday and there was no phone call from a strange number.

She sat there another minute or so, then decided to call the TV station. Maybe they'd be able to shine some light on Libby's present whereabouts. After finding the station's number on Google, she called it.

"Good afternoon, News10 – how may I help you?", intoned a pleasant woman's voice on the other end. Sheila noticed that she had an rather pronounced accent.

"Uh, yes. Good afternoon. Maybe you can help me – I'm supposed to meet Libby and your news van at three-thirty at the Mills Mansion in Staatsburg. She wants to do a follow-up interview with me. And, now, it's nearly four o'clock and they aren't here. I was wondering if you know where they are or if you can give me her phone number so I can call her and check."

"Oh, sure – just let me look up her number and that way you can call her, directly. What did you say the reporter's name is, again?"

"Libby. I don't have her last name."

"Okay." Several seconds passed and, then, the woman asked, "Is she new to News10, do you know?"

"I don't think so – I've seen her on TV a number of times."

"That's funny, because we don't have anyone by the name of Libby anywhere in our directory."

"What? What do you mean?", Sheila asked.

"Well, ma'am – I'm sorry, but there just doesn't appear to be anyone by that name working at News10."

"Well, I just spoke with her, not an hour ago. She called me."

"Gee, ma'am, I just don't know what to tell you. Did she call you on your cell phone? Perhaps her number's there in your recent call log."

"It's not. And I don't know why. Okay, maybe I got her name wrong. What's the name of your reporter that was up in Red Hook, this afternoon?"

"Let me check the dispatch log", the woman said. Another few seconds went by and she said, "Gee, ma'am, we have no reporters or news vans in Red Hook, today. There's one in Kingston and one down here in Poughkeepsie, but none in Red Hook. Are you sure she said that she was from News10?"

"I'm absolutely sure – do you think I'm an idiot?" Sheila was now beginning to burn. "For Christ's sake, she interviewed me the other night and she called *me*! Are you new or something?"

"Well, no, ma'am. I've been here for several years and I can assure you that, to the best of my knowledge, we've never had a reporter named Libby. Now, if you'll excuse me, I have to take some other calls."

"And I think you're an idiot!", Sheila half-screamed into the phone and hit the 'End' button.

Jee-zus *Christ!*, she thought. Another goddamned immigrant! I should've known the minute I heard her voice that she'd be an idiot. And *this* is why something has to be done. These immigrants can't do their goddamned jobs and American-born citizens are out there scrounging for work.

She put her car in drive and, if the vehicle had had more power, would've left rubber in the parking lot. And, when she pulled out onto Route 9, almost into the path of an oncoming car and the driver had laid on his horn, she rolled down her window and flipped him the bird.

Fuck you, she thought. You're probably just another goddamned immigrant or lefty piece of shit.

She'd cooled down a bit by the time she pulled into her driveway and noticed that Frank's van was there. As she got out, he surprised her by walking over from the front of the house.

He had a piece of paper in one hand and a big knife in the other.

"What the hell, Frank?", she asked, closing the car door. "What are you doing with that knife?"

He had an odd look on his face and held out the piece of paper.

"This was stuck to our front door", he said. "With this knife."

She took the paper from him and read……

Frank and Sheila Branson……

Do NOT go ahead with your plans for Sunday.

Do NOT attempt to befoul a day meant for children.

For, if you do, forces beyond your understanding will visit you.

And the results will not be pleasant.

Heed these words well.

Very well.

~ The Specter from the Darkness

She read over it again, having more or less glanced at it the first time through.

"What the hell is this?", she asked.

"Damned if I know", said Frank.

"And it was stuck to the front door with that knife?"

"Yeah – the wooden door. And the knife kept the storm door from closing – I noticed it was open, a little, when I drove in. When I went over to check it out, I found this stuff."

"Well, what does it mean? And who is this 'Specter from the Darkness'?", she asked.

"I have no idea. But let's go in the house. It's cold out here. Maybe we can figure it out."

Five minutes later, they were sitting in the living room, Frank with a beer and Sheila with a glass of wine.

"Okay, so – ", he began, but Sheila interrupted.

"Wait. Before we get into that, let me tell you what just happened to me." And she proceeded to describe her experience with the reporter and her trip to Staatsburg and the fact that the reporter hadn't shown up and that some immigrant bimbo from the TV station had never heard of the reporter before.

"You mean the one that interviewed you the other night?", he asked.

"Well, yeah – supposedly. On the phone, she said her name was Libby, but they have no record of a Libby working there."

"What time is it?" And he looked at the clock. "Look – it's almost five. Why don't we turn on that station and watch their five o'clock news? Maybe she'll have a story and we can find out her name, because I guess it's not Libby."

Several minutes later, the anchor blabbed something about a food drive that was happening in Poughkeepsie and tossed it to a live shot, saying, "And here's Caitlin with the story….."

"That's her!", Sheila said. "She's the one that interviewed me."

Just then, a strip appeared across the bottom of the screen, reading, "Caitlin Carnes, News10".

"Caitlin Carnes?", said Frank. "She certainly ain't no Libby."

"Fuck!", said Sheila, probably a little louder than was necessary. "What the fuck, Frank?"

"Well, I don't know, honey – but maybe you've been had."

"Why, though?", she asked. She took a big gulp of wine and, then, said, "Oh, shit. I got lured out of the house."

"Oh, my God, you're right", said Frank. "Somebody scammed you into leaving the house so they could stick that note on the door, right? That's what happened, didn't it?"

"Aw, Jesus, Frank. I feel like such an idiot."

"Hell, don't feel that way, honey. Some asshole played a dirty goddamned trick on you. You were doing what you thought was right and this….this…..this shit happened", he said, holding up the note.

"What's this all about, Frank?"

"I don't know. I just don't know." He took a swallow.

"Who do you suppose it is?", she asked. "This 'Specter' person?"

"I have no idea. At first, I was thinkin' that, maybe, we've got a spy in our group. Somebody that knows about our plans for Sunday. But this is addressed to both of us

– you and me. So how would a spy in The Group know about your plans?"

"They wouldn't. Unless one of your guys is married to one of my women", she said. "Is that possible?"

"It's possible, I suppose", he said. "Do you have a list of your members?"

"Of course. I have all of their phone numbers. And, of course, their last names."

"I've got a list of my guys, too. But I had each of them write their names with their phone numbers, so I'm not sure I'll be able to read some of the names very well. Some of these guys aren't what you'd call 'A students'."

"Let's get the two lists and compare them", she said.

"Right now? Honey, I've been working all day and I'm tired. Couldn't this wait 'til after dinner?"

"Don't you care, Frank? Don't you care that we've been threatened? Because that's what this is – a threat. Something about a force visiting us and the (finger quotes) 'results will not be pleasant'. That's a goddamned threat, Frank. Here. In our house. And you want to put it off? What's the matter with you, anyway?"

"Okay, okay. Fine. You're right. Okay – I've got my list in my office. I'll go get it."

"And I have mine in the bedroom." And she stood up.

"Okay, let's go get 'em. But, first, you want another drink?"

"Of course, I do", she said, handing him her glass.

Fifteen minutes later, sitting next to each other on the couch, with their two lists lying on the coffee table in front of them, they'd gone through them, trying to match last names.

Nope. Nothing. No names matched.

"You suppose any of 'em are shacking up?", Frank asked.

"I have no idea", said Sheila. "Maybe, but almost every one of my members is married. Hell, we're Moms for Liberty, not Whores for Liberty. Most of 'em have kids. Well, a good many of them do, anyway."

"So, we don't know anything more than we did when we started", he said.

"Nope." She took another drink. "Alright, I'm hungry, but let's call for delivery. I just don't feel like making dinner, tonight."

"Pizza?"

"Fine. Anything. But I don't like this, Frank. I don't like this, one bit."

"Either do I."

____

Back at the farm, Parker had left for the day and I was doing something, but I don't remember what it was.

My phone rang.

Ron.

"Dude – what's up?", I said.

"You've gotta work on your spy shit, son."

"Huh? What're you talking about?"

"You used your own phone to call that Branson chick."

"Yeah, so?"

"So, that way, you left a trace. Simple thing for her to just call that number back – your number – and find out that you're the one who called her. Could've screwed up everything, but fear not – your helpful Eff Bee Eye fixed it for you."

"Oh, shit – you're right. I didn't even think about that."

"That's what I figured."

"You said you fixed it, though. How? What'd you do?"

And he explained the whole Pegasus software thing to me. About how he can, basically, take over any phone in the world, if it's not encrypted. And, even then, the Feebs' computer geeks can sometimes get around those, too.

"You mean you can listen in on just about any conversation you want to?"

"Not only that, dude, but I can turn on the speaker and listen to people talking even when they're not on the phone. Which isn't all that great if, say, the guy we're listening to is in a bar or at a concert or something – there's a ton of background noise. But, otherwise, it works like a charm. Plus, we can read all of the phone's texts and emails. Even download 'em."

"Whoa."

"Yeah, so, using that software, I was able to delete your number from her phone. As far as her phone is concerned, the call never even happened."

"Oh. Wait. Hold on. Run that all by me again. Do you mean to tell me that you can Big Brother in on any phone?"

"Yeah, but only if we jump through some legal hoops and get a judge to approve it. Which we've done with those mongrels out by you. Well, at this point, the Bransons, anyway. And Schmidt, because he's one of us and we need a record of what he talks about with any of those other guys. You know, for future evidence and shit."

"Huh. Does Schmidt know?"

"No comment, but don't mention it to him. And, listen, dude – this is all top-secret shit, okay? You can tell Parker, but that's it. Nobody else. I'm putting my neck on the line, a little, just telling you – but that's nothing new, right?", and I could almost hear him smile.

"My lips are sealed", I said. "Well, except for Parker."

"Good. And it might be a good idea for you to get a burner or two, too, just in case you have to call any of those people again. Those can be traced back, too, but it would take some pretty sophisticated shit to be able to do that. None of which those bozos have."

"Okay, I'll pick up a couple in the morning."

"Cool – but let me know their phone numbers, 'k? That way, I can plug into 'em and see what's what, if I need to."

"You got it. Anything else?"

"Not really, I guess."

"Okay. Hey, listen – we put that note from the 'Specter from the Darkness' on the Bransons' front door today. Parker stuck it into the door with an old Bowie knife."

"Yeah? You told me that you were gonna do something like that, but not exactly what or when. Can you send me a copy of it?"

"Sure. I'll text it to you as soon as we're done here. Anyway, it warns the Bransons that they oughta cancel their plans for Sunday or something rather disturbing will happen to them."

"And that would be a visit from our friend, right?", asked Ron.

"Yep - and if and when that happens, that's when we'll let 'em know that we know about their past – um, indiscretions - and that those indiscretions are now being made public. Of course, if they change their plans, that won't have to happen."

"Cool. Very cool. Think it'll work – your note?"

"Honestly, I have no idea. But, hey – after what you just told me – "

Ron interrupted me, saying, "I can glom onto their phones and see what's what."

"Yeah – if you could do that, it might help. I don't know exactly how, but it might give us a good indication of how seriously they're taking the note."

"I'll do that. But I won't do it in real time – I don't have the time to do that. But I can have their calls recorded and either I or one of our guys can go back and listen to 'em when we have time. Plus, we'll have a record of their texts and emails and we can go over those, too."

"Excellent", I said. "And you'll keep us posted on what you find out."

"Ten-four, my liege. Okay – I gotta go. Text me that thing, okay?"

"Right now."

And, as soon as we disconnected, I texted him what I'd written to the Bransons.

Fifteen seconds later, I got a thumbs-up emoji in return.

I couldn't wait to tell Parker about Ron's new ability with peoples' phones. And what he'd done to erase my bonehead move.

Could it wait 'til morning? Well, yeah – I supposed it could. But……

I picked up my phone and called him, even though it was a little late.

Down in Hyde Park, over extra cheese, pepperoni and onions, the Bransons talked about – of course – who'd stuck the note on their door and how that person or those persons had learned about The Group's and the Moms for Liberty's plans for Sunday.

Having hit a roadblock on that subject, Sheila told Frank about another little thing that had happened today. That, when she was putting flyers on cars' windshields at that diner on Route 9, some babe had come out and chased her off.

"Dammit, Frank – I've got First Amendment rights", she said. "I can put notes any goddamned place I want to put them. That's guaranteed under the Constitution, which is being trampled on all over the place, nowadays."

"What'd she say to you", Frank more or less mumbled, his mouth full of pizza.

"She told me to get the hell out. To get off her property."

"Did you?"

"Did I what?"

"Did you get off of the property?"

"Well, yeah, I did. But I was actually in there last week – I had breakfast with Mark Fisher, and the place seemed to be full of lefties. Plus, half their damned staff is immigrants. Black, brown – you name it."

"How'd you know they were lefties? Hey – pass the salt."

"Ah, Frank, you know", she said, handing him the shaker. "I can smell those bastards from a mile away. I don't like that place. And I especially don't like my First Amendment rights trampled on by some lowlife waitress. Hell, it wasn't her business *what* I was doing."

"Mmm. Got it." He looked at her and put his arm around her shoulders and gave her a squeeze.

"Well, hon, look", he said. "I know you've had a shitty day and I wanna try and make it up to you, somehow. So, I'm gonna meet some of the guys at Maude's after work, tomorrow, and maybe I'll mention it to them. Who knows? Maybe one of the guys'll try and do something like Schmidt did at that People's Center up in Rhinebeck. You know, just leave a little calling card or something. Would that make you feel better?"

She smiled and said, "Aw, that's awfully sweet of you, dear.

Frank returned her smile, let out a semi-stifled belch, and said, "There's my girl."

CHAPTER 27

At The Coffee Spot the next morning, the early conversation centered around a piece in the local North Dutchess 'Daily Voice' that Marquardt had so generously brought with him.

It seems that Readers' Digest had compiled a list of the signature sandwich from each of the fifty states. The fact that the choice for New York State was pastrami on rye with spicy brown mustard was quite well received by the Geezers.

"Nothing better in this world than a good pastrami on rye", said Joe. "But a lot of it's in the mustard. Gotta be hot enough to offset the taste of the grease from the pastrami. And, of course, pastrami better have some grease to it – otherwise, it's dry as a bone."

Nobody could honestly argue with that, so we didn't.

"What's California's?", I asked, interested in what they thought my ex-home's choice would be.

"Um, let's see….", said Bob. "Here – French dip."

I considered that and said, "Good French dip is hard to beat, too – especially if the au jus is good." And that drew a round of nods, too. See, with these guys, it'd be hard to come up with a bad sandwich.

"Oh, wait", said Marquardt, looking down at the paper, "here's one for you. It says that the signature sandwich of Massachusetts is the Fluffernutter." And he looked up at the group, the look on his face a combination of disbelief and disgust.

"Fluffernutter?", said Joe. "You gotta be friggin' kidding me, right now."

"Nope, that's what it says", replied Bob.

"That's gotta be the most disgusting sandwich in the history of the world", said Parker. "I wouldn't eat one o' those with your mouth, Joe."

"I don't mind Fluffernutters", said Hal. "But I wouldn't go out of my way to get one."

Just then, Gretchen walked up, pot of coffee in hand. "Go out of your way to get what, Hal?", she asked, topping off our mugs.

"A Fluffernutter sandwich", he said.

"A Fluffernutter? What made you say that? Ugh!"

Bob explained the crux of the conversation to her and she said, "Massachusetts? There's gotta be some mistake. People in Massachusetts have more taste than that. Don't they?"

"Would you ever serve Fluffernutters here?", asked Mike with a smile.

"Here? Oh, God, no. Not on your life, Mike."

Bob chimed in with, "Says here that, in New York State, pastrami on rye with spicy brown mustard is the thing."

"Well, there you go", she said. "And, I'll have you know, that we make just about the best pastrami sandwiches this side of the Hudson. It's just that you guys are never in here at lunchtime, so you wouldn't know."

"I love pastrami sammiches", Joe more or less reiterated and the rest of us more or less nodded our agreement.

"Well, alright", said Gretchen. "Tell you what. If you guys are up for it, I can have them whip up some of them, right now, and you can each have one. You know, to test them out."

"Pastrami sandwiches for breakfast?", asked Hal.

"Why not?", Joe answered. "It all ends up in the same place."

We all kind of looked at each other, then Bob gave a tentative Geezer knuckle-knock. And, before you knew it, we'd all joined in.

"Well, good", said Gretchen. "Six pastrami on ryes, coming right up. Oh - and you'll love our mustard, too. We use Hoffman's brand and it is simply the best. Oh - and our pickles rock, too. I'll be right back." And off she went to the kitchen.

Frank Branson was sitting in his home office, returning some calls from perspective clients. He was still wondering whether or not to be upset about the note that was stuck to the door, yesterday.

Actually, he was pissed because, now, he'd probably have to hit that knife hole with some spackle and, then, probably next spring, re-paint the goddamned thing. Ah, it probably needs it anyway, he thought. Been a couple of years.

He put all that out of his mind – or tried his best to – while he was making his calls.

By a little after eight, he'd set up two appointments for a little later in the morning. One, a somewhat simple, though time-consuming, one to point up a ten-foot by six-foot brick wall at a house up in Millbrook. The other one was fairly close to that, too – about five miles away in Amenia. That woman wanted her gutters fixed – they'd pulled away from the house and, according to what she'd said, probably needed to be re-fastened to the ends of the rafters. Simple job of drilling through the fascias into the rafters and putting in some wood screws.

He called Gallagher.

"Hey", he said when Eric answered. "Wanna take a ride? I gotta run by a couple of places and quote on jobs. A couple of easy ones. And I kinda figured you'd be the guy to help do the work."

"Yeah, sure – why not? Where are they?"

"One's in Millbrook and the other one's a few miles away in Amenia."

"Yeah, okay. Tell you what – you tell me what time and I'll meet you out in front of that Williams Lumber place in Pleasant Valley. It's on your way."

"Good. Okay…." and he looked at the time. "How about nine-fifteen? I told the guy in Millbrook I'd be by his place around nine-thirty."

"Got it."

"Oh - and I gotta tell you what happened, here, yesterday. It's kinda freaking me out a bit."
"Yeah? What?"

Frank considered telling him, right then, but decided it would be better to do it in person.

"I'll tell you when I see you."

"Okay - whatever, man. See you in a few."

And they disconnected.

Gretchen was absolutely right about The Coffee Spot's pastrami on rye.

The six of us tore into them like men who'd just gotten rescued from a deserted island.

"This is outrageous", said Joe, taking a slight pause in his chuffing a couple of minutes into the meal. "And the mustard really makes it."

"Y'know,", I said, "maybe we've been too – um – conservative in our breakfast choices. We almost always order about the same things. At least I do. I'm beginning to think that maybe I should branch out a little – try some new things, like this."

"Yeah, but this is lunch stuff", said Parker. "They probably don't usually have it for breakfast. Didn't Gretchen say that she'd get the guys to whip these up special for us?"

"Yeah, I guess she did, didn't she?"

"She did what?", came Suze's voice from behind me. I hadn't seen her coming, but she was obviously stopping by to say hello.

"Oh – hey Suze", I said. "Look – Gretchen had these pastrami sandwiches made up special for us this morning. And they're beyond excellent."

"You guys are eating pastrami for breakfast? Ew."

"Y'oughta try it, sometime. It'll put hair on your chest", said Parker.

"Yeah, that's just what I need, thanks. Hey, J.D. – how's my girl?", meaning, of course, Ceres.

"She's just fine and dandy. She told me to say 'hey' to you when I left her a little while ago."

"Maybe I'll come out a little later and hang out with her. Would that be cool?"

"Any time, kid – you know that. Just show up whenever you want to."

She patted me on the shoulder and said, "Great. Now, I gotta get this order in", and walked toward the kitchen.

When we'd finished and Bob had adjourned the meeting, I'd caught both Parker's and Mike's eyes and gave a little nod toward my truck. They got it.

Once the other guys had left and the three of us were standing there, I said, "Alright – a little intel." And I proceeded to tell Mike about our putting the note on the Bransons' door, yesterday. And that Suze had been with us, having been filled in on the dealio.

And that Gretchen knew, too.

"Think they'll listen to it – the Bransons?", asked Mike.

"We don't know. Maybe, maybe not. But we had to give it a shot."

"Ah, I hope so. Otherwise, it could turn into a complete clusterfuck on Sunday."

"Well, we'll probably have a pretty good idea as we get closer." A thought hit me. "Which reminds me – I should pick up a burner or two. I used my phone to call Sheila, yesterday, remember? I thought of that last night", I said, looking at Parker. "Well, that was a bonehead move. She could've called that number right back and that could've blown our cover."

"Aw, Jesus", said Parker, shaking his head. "I shoulda thought of that. I must be gettin' rusty."

"Yeah, well, anyway – I talked to Ron about it and, somehow, he was able to scrub my number from her phone. Some kind of FBI magic, I guess. It's like it never even happened, as far as she's concerned. There's no record of the call, now."

They both nodded, cogitating on that.

"Look – guys", said Mike. "I've got an early meeting at the office, so I'd better get going. But, do me a favor – keep me up to speed in real time if you hear of anything. I've gotta let Eddings know, so he can plan what he has to do on Sunday."

"Isn't he kind of wondering where you're getting your information, Mike?", I asked.

"Well, I'm sure he's kind of curious, but he hasn't pressed me on it, yet. Catch you guys later. You'll call me, right?"

"Yep."

As Mike was mounting up, I told Parker about Ron' new Pegasus system, but told him that that info was completely on the d-l and that's why I hadn't mentioned it in front of Mike.

"Holy crap – it sounds like real Big Brother shit", he said.

"Ya think? Now, where do you suppose I can get a couple of burners?"

"Hell, I've seen 'em for sale at Topps. Pretty much any place sells 'em, nowadays. Even some of the c-stores carry them. But make sure you get the kind with prepaid time on 'em."

"Alright, I'll stop by Topps on the way home and see. You're heading to the farm, now, right?"

He nodded and said, "Just buy the cheapest ones you can find - the kind that act strictly as phones. You don't need the internet shit. If you spend over twenty bucks, you're getting taken. Plus, get, say, like ten dollars' worth of time put on 'em. That's probably the lowest amount you can get."

"Got it. Catch you back there."

And we both got into our trucks and headed out.

____

Around eight forty-five, Frank Branson was about to leave the house. That'd get him to Williams' Lumber in Pleasant Valley right around the time he was to pick up Gallagher.

He knew that Sheila was still upset about what happened yesterday and she said so. "Dammit, Frank – this note really has me bothered." She held it in her hand. "I mean, somebody went to quite a bit of time and trouble to write it in calligraphy on this antique-type paper. This isn't some goofy hand-written note – some thought went into it."

"I know, honey. And I feel the same way. I just don't know what to make of it or what to do about it. You don't know anybody who does calligraphy, do you?"

"Oh, get real, Frank. How the hell would I know something like that?"

He shrugged. "Yeah, right. Listen, I'm gonna pick up Eric Gallagher on the way up to do those quotes. I'm gonna run it by him and see what he thinks. After all, he's sort of my second-in-command and he should know about it."

Sheila nodded. "Yeah, probably."

She waited a few seconds, thinking, then said, "Look – we're still going to do our things on Sunday, right? I mean, we can't let some stupid note stop us from doing what needs to be done. This whole movement can't stop because some creep stuck a note on our door."

"Oh, definitely, we'll go through with them – with both of our things. They're important. I'd just like to find out who did this and make him wish to hell he hadn't. I wanna make the sumbitch pay."

She put her fist out and he joined her in a fist-bump.

"Know what I think?", she asked. "I'll bet it's the deep state that's behind this. More of this Soros shit. Next thing we know, Blackhawks will be hovering over our house and guys'll be coming down on ropes. That's what I think. Jesus, it's getting bad."

"Could be", he said, though he knew that his wife sometimes got out over her skis on the whole deep state thing. He wasn't even sure that was a real thing. Maybe, but probably not.

He was more concerned with the feds. Which, deep state or not, were really the ones they had to watch out for.

Because the feds were more interested in going after people who were true patriots than tracking down real criminals.

And that's why the crime problem is so bad, now – because the feds are ignoring it and spending their resources on trying to suppress real, honest-to-goodness, dyed-in-the-wool Americans who are really trying to save this country, instead of doing what they're supposed to be doing – stopping crime. Plus, everybody knows that most of the crimes, today, are being committed by Blacks and immigrants. And most of them are illegal. And, yet, nothing is being done.

But undoubtedly, he thought, whoever had done the note-to-the-door thing wasn't with the feds. That isn't what they do. And if it wasn't the deep state – which probably doesn't really exist – then who was it? That's what made it so hard to understand.

"What are you going to do, today?", he asked her, opening the door to the garage.

"I'm meeting a bunch of the girls up at Planned Parenthood. Think I should tell them about the note?"

"I wouldn't, if I were you. Why get them all riled about something they can't do anything about? I'd just keep that quiet, for now."

"Okay, you're probably right. But if we find out who did it, I think we should all go, en masse, after this guy."

"You sure it's a guy?", he asked.

"Well, or woman. Whatever."

And she walked across the kitchen and gave him a kiss on the cheek as he left.

On the way up to Pleasant Valley, Frank had been listening to Charlie Kirk's show on the radio.

This morning, Kirk was, once again, decrying the Democrats' immigration policies and he said that they were aimed at diminishing and decreasing the white demographics of America. It's not about white privilege, he said, it's just that this nation was founded on the principles designed by Anglos and, if the country really wanted to stay true to its roots, bringing in more and more non-whites will only further dilute the founders' principles. And that's exactly what the Democrats are doing and it has to be stopped.

When he pulled into the parking lot at Williams Lumber, Frank spied Gallagher leaning against a concrete column in the pick-up area.

He pulled up to the curb and turned the radio off as Gallagher climbed into the truck.

"What's up, kid?", Gallagher said, as the two men fist-bumped.

"You ever listen to Charlie Kirk?", ask Branson.

"On the radio? Yeah, sure – once in a while. Why?"

"Ah, he was just on as I was driving up here and he was talking about the Democrats' crazy friggin' immigration policies. That the hordes of non-whites that they're letting into the country are changing the demographics of the country – and quickly, too. Pretty soon, dude, us whites'll be in the minority." He shook his head.

"Yeah, well, dude," replied Gallagher, "it's happening, alright. And it's gonna get worse if something isn't done, pretty quick." He looked out the window. "Fucking nuts, is what it is."

He waited a beat, then said, "Hey – you were gonna tell me about something that happened, yesterday."

"Yeah, right. I tell you, it's weird, man", said Frank, pulling out onto Route 44 and heading north. "When I got home, yesterday afternoon, I saw that my front storm door was open a little. So, I went over to check it out – you know, to close it and all. But when I got there, I saw this big freakin' knife stuck in the wooden door."

"A knife?" Gallagher looked over at Frank.

"Yeah. And it was stuck into a piece of paper."

"Go on."

"Yeah, well, I pulled the knife out and looked at the paper. And there was a note on it. And, dude – it was like antique paper, know what I mean? Kind of yellowed and, well, old-looking. And the fucking note was written in calligraphy."

"Calligraphy? What's that?"

"Oh, shit, you know – like the old-time handwriting. All fancy-like, with fancy-type letters and all."

"Okay. What'd it say?"

"Here's what's kind of freaking me out a bit. It was addressed to both me and Sheila. And it said that we should not go ahead with our plans on Sunday. You know that Sheila's Moms for Liberty's settin' up a table at the parade, too, right?"

Gallagher nodded, "Mm-hmm."

"Well, anyway, it said that we shouldn't go ahead with our plans because, if we do - and let me get this right – forces beyond our understanding will visit us. And that the results will not be pleasant."

"What?!?"

"Yep, that's what it said. And it was signed, the specter from the darkness."

"The specter from the darkness? What the fuck is that?!?"

"I dunno, man. I don't have the faintest."

"Are you shitting me with all of this, right now?", asked Gallagher.

Branson shook his head and said, "Nope. Not even one little bit."

"What. The. Fuck", said Eric.

"That's what I said. And, hell, man – it's kinda freaking Sheila out, too. I mean, it's really freaking her out."

"Who the hell knows about our plans *and* Sheila's plans? Well, other than you and me?"

"It wasn't you, was it? You didn't do it, did you?", Frank asked, looking over at him.

"What – have you lost your fucking mind? Of *course*, I didn't do it. What the fuck, man?"

"I know, Eric, I know. I mean, I just had to ask because we have our plans and Sheila and her girls have their plans but, really, the twain don't meet. Far as I know, only you and me and her know that both our groups'll show up at the same time. Hell, we even looked at both of our lists of people - our members - and ain't none of 'em married. Well, not to each other, anyway. So, I don't know how the info leaked. But it damned sure did."

"Well, then – who the hell is this – what'd you call it again?"

"Specter from the darkness."

"Yeah, this specter from the darkness. Who the fuck can it be?"

"That's the sixty-four-thousand-dollar question, my friend. Hey – look, we gotta start looking for this house. I think we're close. Look for Hart's Village Road. I think it's up here on the left."

<h1 style="text-align:center"><u>CHAPTER 28</u></h1>

When I got back to the farm, I noticed that the garage door was open. I figured that Parker must be in there.

I parked the truck, grabbed the bag of burner phones off the seat and went in to see what was what.

I saw him fiddling with what looked to be an electric space heater. He was brushing the dust off of it.

"Space heater?", I said. "Where'd that come from?"

"Ah, it's been up in the little attic, here. I thought it was up there, but I hadn't seen or used it in a couple of years. Not since Bill died. I'm trying to see if it still works." He inserted the plug into an outlet above the workbench and said, "Let's see."

A few seconds later, we saw the coils in the front of it begin to glow.

"So far, so good", I said.

We watched it for a few more seconds and began to feel the warmth coming from the front of it.

"Yep. Works", he said. "Good. I'm gonna need it out here. Gets cold as fuck in this garage."

I looked over at the end of the workbench and saw a large sheet of canvas covering what was, obviously, his latest project. It was pretty big. "How's that coming?", I asked, pointing at the thing with my chin.

"Good, I think. Real good. So far, it's exactly as I envisioned it. I oughta have it finished in a couple of days."

"And you're not gonna tell me what it is."

"Nope."

"But it's for me."

"Yep. For this place, this farm, actually. Hey – are those the burners?", he asked, looking at the bag in my hand.

"Yeah. I got a couple of them. Y'know, we probably won't need them, but I guess they're good to have in case we do."

"Yep. And that was real fucking boneheaded of me not to think of that when we called Branson. I must be slippin'."

"No harm, no foul", I said.

Just then, a gust of wind hit and a whole slew of leaves swirled around outside the big, open doorway.

"Lotta leaves", I said. "What do we do with 'em? I mean, do we rake 'em up or what?"

"Nah – leave 'em. They're good for the land. You know, they decompose over the winter and actually fertilize the soil. Why people rake 'em up off their lawns and, then, when springtime comes, they put fertilizer shit all over their lawns, is beyond me. They had all the fertilizer they needed lying right there. Which reminds me – it probably wouldn't be the worst idea to rake some up and toss 'em in the garden. We'll clean up whatever's left of 'em next spring. Plus, we'll save on fertilizer."

"Good idea. Maybe I'll do that, now."

"Yeah – toss a couple loads into one of the poop carts and just dump 'em in the garden and kick 'em around a little. Take you half an hour, tops."

"We got a rake?"

"Yep. Right over there, next to the shovels."

"Hey – that thing's working pretty well", I said, nodding at the heater. "You can feel it getting warmer in here, already."

"Uh-huh. Bill always bought good stuff. He figured that, if you spend a few more bucks upfront, on good stuff, you'll save money in the long run by not having to replace it so often. Here's proof of that. That damned thing's probably seven or eight years old. Works like we just took it outta the box."

I grabbed a rake that was leaning up against the wall and headed down to the barn to rustle up a poop cart.

____

"You know, Stone's not gonna be at the parade on Sunday", Gallagher said to Frank as they pulled away from the house in Millbrook, having gotten the one-day job for five-hundred. They'd do it tomorrow – shouldn't take all day, either.

"He's not?", asked Frank. "How come?"

"He said that his kids are all hot on marching in it and so's his wife. He said he'd catch holy hell from her if he wasn't with 'em. He did say, though, that he'd rock the camo – you know, to represent."

"Y'know, dude – we don't know Stone all that well, do we?", Frank asked.

"Well, I do – pretty much. He's a solid guy. Why?"

"Well, again – that note and shit. You don't suppose – ?"

"That it's Flint?", Gallagher scoffed. "No way, man. Nope. He's as upset about all this shit as we are. Nah, it ain't Stone."

"Well, I'm not a hundred percent convinced. I mean, he's new and all. And, now, with the first thing we're doing, he's not gonna show? After what that note said? Ah, dude – I got my doubts."

Gallagher shook his head.

There was silence in the van for a few seconds, then Frank said, "Wait. We're gonna get together up at Maude's tonight, aren't we?"

"That's the plan."

"Listen – I want you to call Stone and tell him to be there, too. Tell him he's needed. I've got an idea that should prove, once and for all – to me, at least – that he's clean."

"What's your idea?"

"You'll see. Later."

And, as they passed the little sign heralding the entrance to the little hamlet of Amenia, Frank said, "Watch for South Street."

There was a 7-11 up on the right and Branson said, "Hold on. I'm gonna run in here for a minute. I wanna pick up a burner phone. With that note and all, I'm not trusting anybody, right now. And I sure as hell don't want the feds listening in to any of my phone calls."

"Shit, dude – they ain't gonna do that. I mean, no offense, but you're pretty small potatoes."

"I know, but better safe than sorry."

"It's your money, man."

And Frank turned into the c-store's parking lot.

____

A couple of hours later, Suze showed up at the farm.

I'd done the leaves-into-the-garden thing and Parker had just finished working for the day on his new piece and we were in the process of tossing a bale of alfalfa down from the loft when we heard her car drive in.

"Hey! We're in here!", I shouted to her.

"What're you guys doing?", she asked, walking into the barn.

"Gettin' a bale down for the kids", said Parker, from up in the loft. "This oughta last 'em a couple'a days. Back off – this thing's gonna bounce."

And, when he pushed it over the edge, it did, indeed, bounce. Note: You do not want to be standing anywhere near a hundred-pound bale of hay when it's tossed down out of a loft or other high perch. You never know which way it's going to bounce and you can lose a leg in a hurry.

I got the bale situated in a cart and pushed it over to where we kept the hay we were using, over near the 'inside' part of the kids' in-'n-out of the barn. Now that the grass was gone in their pasture, we generally put their feed into two large indoor Rubbermaid tubs, next to their water tub.

"Can I do it?", Suze asked.

"Can you do what?", I responded.

"Feed them. Can I put the hay into their feeders?"

"Sure – why not? Just put a flake in each of those tubs."

"What's a flake?"

I showed her, just as Parker walked up to us. "There ya go", he said as she doled out the hay. "Y'know, once you feed 'em, you're required to muck 'em, too. It's the rule."

"Huh?"

"Ah, he's just shitting you, kid. Don't mind him. Why don't you call 'em – Zeus and Ceres?"

"Call them?"

"Yeah – just shout their names. When they hear their names from in here, they'll know that grub's in the offing and they'll hot-foot it right in here."

"Okay", she said. "Ceres! Zeus! Soup's on!"

And we heard them coming before we saw them, their big hooves pounding out a trot. Suddenly, there was Ceres, followed closely by her brother.

"It's not like he's being gentlemanly, letting her go first", I said. "She's just a chow hound who'll pretty much eat anything that won't eat her, first. She's like, 'Outta my way, bro!'".

Both kids dove into their feeders, paying us zero attention.

"I guess we won't be doing any horsemanship thing with them, today, huh?", Suze asked. "It's their dinner time."

"Yeah, sorry, kid. I forgot about that. But you learned a bit, anyway, today, didn't you? You learned what a flake of hay is and how we feed 'em. And, of course, that nothing gets between your girl, Ceres, and her food."

"And to get outta the way of a falling hay bale", said Parker. "That's important, too."

"Yeah, you're right – I did learn something today", she said. "I've never done anything like this, before, so it's all new and all of it is a learning experience."

"There you go", I said.

"Hey – you guys up for some coffee cake?", Parker asked. "There's over half of it left, up there in the kitchen."

We all decided that that sounded good, especially because it was getting downright cold out here.

"I'll make some coffee", I said and Suze nodded that it sounded like a good idea to her, too.

When we sat down at the table, the two burner phones were sitting on it.

"Burners?", asked Suze. "Why've you got burners?"

And I explained the bone-headed move I'd made in letting her use my phone to talk to Sheila Branson. That all Branson had to do was to check her phone and call back and she'd have me dead to rights.

"Oh. I never thought of that", she said.

"We didn't either. But it's all fixed, now. My number's disappeared from her phone."

"Disappeared? How?"

"Well, honestly, kid, I can't tell you that. I wish I could, but I can't. But my number's gone from her phone."

"Is this some kind of woo-woo spy shit?", she asked.

"Something like that."

We sat around for another half-hour or so and shot the shit, then both Parker and Suze announced that they had to split.

"That's good coffee cake", said Parker, standing up, "but I like pie better."

"No doubt", I agreed. "We might have to take a run down to Crockett's tomorrow, to re-stock the larder."

He gave me a thumbs-up and, within a couple of minutes, they'd both gone their separate ways.

____

A little after five-thirty, five of the guys from The Group – Al, Mark, Lou Schmidt, Gallagher and Flint Stone – were on their first pitcher of beer when Frank Branson walked in. There was a chair waiting for him.

"Fuck, it's getting cold out", said Branson, as he shrugged off his canvas jacket and sat down.

"Ain't nothin', yet", said Al. "S'posed to be a cold winter."

"Where'd you hear that?", asked Gallagher.

Al shrugged and said, "I dunno – ain't they all?"

This group of guys paid pretty close attention to the weather as they all were in the contracting business or something close to it. The weather affected their businesses and nobody in their right mind really wants to work outside in cold, nasty weather. Schmidt, driving a garbage truck, couldn't care much one way or the other.

Shit was shot and beer was consumed for a little while, then Frank got down to business.

"Okay, we all set for Sunday?", he asked.

They all nodded and Mark said, "Far as I know, man. We ain't gotta do anything but show up, right?"

"Well, yeah – but I wanna make sure everybody's there on time, so we can huddle up and march in as a group. I don't want any stragglers with their thumbs up their asses wandering in too late. I want us to look like – well, a militia. You know."

It was then that Flint Stone spoke up.

"Um, Frank. Guys. Look - and I told this to Eric the other day – my kids and the wife have been planning on walking in this thing for weeks, now. Costumes and everything. And when I mentioned to my wife that I couldn't be with them because I was gonna walk with some (finger quotes) friends, she 'bout hit the fucking roof."

The other guys looked at him, with a couple of them nodding just a little, as if they may have understood Stone's predicament.

"Anyway, guys. I hate to do this, but if I don't go with my family, I might not have a family to go home to. The wife said - and I quote – 'If you aren't with me and the children on Sunday – well, I don't even want to think about that'. So, I had to tell her that I would be with them. They're my life, guys. I'm sorry."

Al laughed and said, "What she meant, my man, is if you ain't with 'em, then you got no chance of getting laid again before Christmas." And they all laughed, even Stone.

"Isn't that bad enough?", he asked, and took a swallow of beer.

Frank looked over at Gallagher and then said to Stone, "Look – Flint. I understand and I think the other guys do, too. I mean, you can't fuck up a family just to march with us."

"I am going to wear my camo, though", said Stone, brightening a bit. "You know – to represent. And, who knows? Maybe once we all get there and the parade is going on, maybe she'll let me join up with you guys for a while."

"Well, do what you gotta do", said Frank. "But, listen – you really wanna make it up to The Group? Do something that'll really impress all of us? You know, like Lou, here, did at that place for the old people?" He took a swallow while looking at Stone.

"Well, yeah, I suppose. Sure. What is it?"

"Look – you know my wife's one of the leaders of the Moms for Liberty around here, right?" And the guys all nodded.

"Well, the other day, she was putting flyers on the windshields of some cars in the parking lot of a diner – they were some of those 'NO CRT' flyers."

"I'm with her on that", said Al. "Fucking schools are teaching that all over the goddamned place, now, and it's hurting the kids. And the country. You go, girl." He raised his mug.

And, for the next couple of minutes, the discussion at the table centered around the subject of critical race theory and how most of it was lies to make white people look bad. And, with all the immigrants and non-whites flooding the country, now, kids might grow up to think white people are bad and that the other races are the good guys. Not good. Not good at all.

Finally, Frank said, "Well, anyway – when Sheila was putting the flyers on those cars - and it's her First Amendment right to do so – some waitress or something came out and screamed at her and made a big fucking fuss. She actually threw my wife off the property. Can you imagine? Stomping the fuck all over the First Amendment that way?"

"Plus", he continued, "Sheila's been in that place before and figures it's full of lefties. How she noticed that, I don't know, but she's a damned good judge, so I'll take her word for it."

"What's the place?", asked Mark.

"It's called The Coffee Spot – over on Route 9, just south of Rhinebeck."

"Oh, yeah – I know the place", said Al. "Right-hand side of the road, heading south, right?"

"Yeah, I guess so", said Branson. "I've prob'ly been by it a hundred times, but never paid it any mind."

Then, he turned to Stone.

"So, here's what I'm thinkin', Flint. I'm thinkin' that, maybe, a nice brick through their front fucking window might be just what the doctor ordered."

"Ooh", said Al. "I kinda like that." And the other guys nodded their agreement.

"A brick through their window", said Stone.

"Yep. A simple brick flung right through the window", replied Branson.

"And you want me to do it", said Stone and it wasn't a question.

He looked over at Gallagher, who smiled back at him, recalling the conversation in the truck, earlier.

"Well, man,", said Frank, "if you can't be with us on Sunday and you really want the guys to respect you……"

"I see." He thought for a minute, then said, "Yeah. I guess I can do that. Just fling a brick. Hell, I haven't thrown something through a window since a bunch of us used to go around doing that in high school."

"You did that?", asked Schmidt. "We did, too." And they high-fived across the table. "Good times."

"Yeah, I'll do it", said Stone. And the other guys all raised their mugs in salute.

"When should I do it?", Stone asked, looking at Branson.

Frank shrugged and said, "No time in particular, but you'll probably wanna do it before Sunday. That way, when I get the guys together before the march, I can tell 'em that, unfortunately, one of our guys can't be with us today, but he pulled off a real nice move – what? – a couple of nights ago. That'll get 'em psyched, too. Oh - and I won't mention your name. I'll just say it's one of our members. Maybe one or two of the other guys might put two and two together, but I won't mention your name. You know, for legal reasons and all."

Stone nodded thoughtfully and took a swallow.

"What time do they close? The diner", he asked.

Nobody knew, so Frank picked up his phone and called Sheila to ask her if she knew, having been there before.

"She's not sure, but said that she knows that they're only open for breakfast and lunch – that they probably close in the late afternoon. So, really, it's probably closed, now."

Stone considered that, then said, "Look – I told the wife that I probably wouldn't be home 'til eighty-thirty, nine o'clock, tonight. I can probably stretch that a bit if I call her and tell her that I'm stopping somewhere to pick up some dinner for the two of us. We don't usually eat 'til after the kids go to bed. So, if I do it tonight - around nine – suppose that would work?"

"It's a little early – might be a little traffic passing by", said Branson. "But if you just drive in, fling the thing out your window and book it, I don't see why not. Just make sure there's not too many cars going by. If there are, put it off for later or another time."

"Anybody got a brick or a rock in your truck?", Flint asked the table.

"I got a couple of bricks in mine", said Frank. "I'll give you one when we leave."

Stone nodded and raised his mug.

"Hey – this is almost empty", said Al, picking up the pitcher and standing up. "I'm buying, in honor of Flint's – um – contribution to the cause."

CHAPTER 29

At eight-forty, Flint Stone called his wife, a hot pizza in a box next to him on the passenger's seat. Extra cheese, sausage, onions and jalapeno peppers – just the way she likes it. A red brick was between him and the box.

"Hi, hon. Listen – I'm on my way home and I just ordered a pizza. I have to pick it up in fifteen minutes, so I'll be home a little after nine, okay?" Just a little white lie, he thought.

"Well, I'd complain that you're going to be a little late, but you saved yourself by bribing me with pizza. I just got the kids down and I think I'll pour myself a glass of wine."

"Okay, great", said Stone. "See you in a few. Oh - and pour me one, too."

He disconnected and looked along the somewhat darkened road. The diner was up here on the right……

Thankfully, probably because there was a light rain falling, the traffic was almost nil. He'd only passed a couple of cars over the past mile or so and only saw one pair of taillights in front of him, nearly a mile away. He should be good.

There it is. He slowed down.

Just before he turned into the parking lot, he doused his lights, leaving his wipers going at a slow clip. He pulled into a parking spot and put his truck in park so his brake lights wouldn't show. He looked around and saw that there weren't any other vehicles in the lot. He looked up at the roofline and didn't see any cameras.

Cheap bastards, he thought. If I had a place like this, you're damned straight I'd have cameras.

There was a spotlight on each end of the building, their light washing over the front of it, but that was to be expected.

He looked both ways, up and down the road. A single car was coming north and one had just passed heading south.

He backed his truck in front of one of the big plate glass windows that ran along the front of the building, putting the gearshift quickly into 'Park' again. The cab should just about shield him from anybody going past, but he knew that the chances of anybody looking over here at just that moment were about a million to one.

He reached over in the darkness and fumbled around for a second or two before grabbing the brick. There it is – got it.

He opened the door, jumped out and quickly closed the door again, not wanting to be lit up by the dome light. He ducked down.

The entire front of the place was windows, starting about seven feet off the ground from where he was standing. The windows were separated by sections of concrete and stucco, each approximately a foot wide. He had his pick of them.

Hell, he thought, this one right in front of me is as good as any. He looked both ways up and down the highway again. No cars that he could see.

Now!

He stood up and, a little like the outfielder he'd been on his high school baseball team, flung the brick.

The entire window didn't shatter because it was obviously treated glass, but a hole almost twice the size of the brick was dead center in the middle of it. Plus, spider web-like cracks emanated from the hole almost to the edges of the window. He'd heard something crash inside, meaning that the brick had hit something else in its travels.

Having expected it, he didn't freak out when he heard the *very* loud alarm go off. He also knew that the alarm was probably tied in to the cops. No matter. They couldn't be here for several minutes at the earliest and he'd be halfway home by then.

He jumped into his still-running truck, put 'er into 'Drive' and pulled to the edge of the parking lot, his lights still off.

Nothing coming.

He turned south, in the direction of his house and, as soon as he'd hit the macadam, turned his lights back on and set his wipers to the next highest speed.

He actually chuckled to himself, thinking about the evening's earlier conversation about him and Schmidt both breaking windows back when they were kids.

He pulled out his phone and, with one hand on the wheel and one eye on the road and one on the phone, scrolled down to Frank's number. Good thing the road's straight along in here, he thought. Ah - found it.

He tapped the 'text' button and wrote, "done!"

Then, he sat back, took a deep breath and savored the aroma of the pizza sitting on the seat next to him.

____

A little before ten o'clock, my phone rang, scaring the living shit out of me while I was reading in bed.

The screen announced that it was Suze.

"Suze – what is it?"

"Oh, J.D. – somebody threw a brick through the restaurant window!"

I sat up. "What? When?"

"Yeah, a little while ago – I guess around nine o'clock. Fuck!" She sounded shook.

"How do you know? I mean, how'd you find out?"

"Gretchen called me as soon as she hung up from talking to the cops when they called her. I guess the window was alarmed and it alerts the cops when something's wrong and they had to call her to tell her and to come down and unlock the door so they could get in."

"You're there now?"

"Yeah, me and Gretchen and several cops. But here's the deal – there's a big fucking hole in the window and it's raining and, well, we're trying to figure a way to get a sheet of plywood or something up, tonight. Gretchen said we can get a glass guy in here, tomorrow, to get it fixed, but – "

"Got it", I interrupted her. "Hold on." I thought for a couple of seconds. "Wait – there's a couple sheets of plywood in the garage, up along the wall. Let me get one of 'em, along with my Skilsaw and a couple other tools and some nails and screws and shit and I'll head right down there. I probably oughta call Parker, too. He's better at this stuff than I am."

"Oh, J.D – really?", she said, sounding understandably relieved. "Oh, that would be wonderful! Let me go tell Gretchen. She's pretty upset, y'know."

"I can imagine", I said. "But tell her not to worry, we'll get 'er fixed up for the night. Just give us a little while. Gotta go."

I disconnected and called Parker.

"What's wrong?", he asked, answering.

I told him what had happened and what I was going to do.

He said, "Let me get my clothes on and I'll meet you there. Take me – oh – twenty, twenty-five minutes. Oh - and don't forget the electric screwdriver. And some sheet metal screws – doesn't matter what size, just not real small ones, okay? I'm kinda hoping we can screw the thing in, but if we have to nail it, that'll work, too. But, fuck, huh?"

"Yeah. And I gotcha."

"See ya in a few."

I got dressed, went down toward the garage and, while walking down there, made a list in my head of the things I had to rustle up.

I found the plywood and wrestled it into the bed of the truck, which I'd backed up to the big garage door. Then, the Skilsaw and the electric screwdriver. And, because Parker was nothing, if not organized, found a chest with all kinds of screws and nails in it, all sorted by type and size. I grabbed a handful of sheet metal screws and some wood screws and a handful of fairly large nails and put them into a coffee can that was sitting on the workbench. Oh – the hammer. I found that and added it to my bunch of stuff.

Five minutes later, I pulled out onto the road, satisfied that I had everything we'd need.

When his phone had dinged, Frank and Sheila Branson had been watching Greg Gutfeld on Fox. Branson didn't think he was at all funny, but he usually had some guests that were pretty good. They were discussing Hunter Biden's laptop, though the Bransons didn't really get what so many people were up in arms about. To them, it was just a distraction from all the real problems that needed to be solved.

Frank looked at his phone and saw that he had a message from Flint Stone. "done!", it said. He smiled, pleased that Stone had had the 'nads to go ahead with it.

"Hey, honey – get this", he said. "Stone just did a little payback at that shit-hole diner you had a problem with."

"Really?", she asked, muting the TV. "What'd he do?"

"He put a brick through their fucking window." And he picked up his can of beer in a toast.

A smile slowly came to Sheila's face and she said, "He did, did he? Well, how d'you like that?"

"I like it pretty good. Ain't no crowd of lefties gonna mess with my wife." He leaned forward and his Barcalounger folded back into a chair. "I think this calls for another one, don't you?"

She held up her empty wine glass and said, "Absolutely." And, as he walked over to where she was sitting, she stood up and kissed him on the lips. "Thank you, sweetheart", she said. "That was so thoughtful of you."

"I might've earned a little something extra, tonight, don'tcha think?", he responded, going in for another kiss.

"I wouldn't be surprised, my good knight." And she kissed him right back.

____

By the time I got to The Coffee Spot, the rain had just about quit, with only a fine mist in the air.

There was still a police car sitting there, though its lights were off. I also spotted Gretchen's car and the Subaru. No sign of Parker, yet, though.

I parked right in front of the broken window, seeing the hole and the spiderwebs emanating out from it. Smart to have shatterproof windows, I thought.

The cop was standing just inside the door just as I entered. He looked at me, then realizing that I was supposed to be there, nodded at me. I returned the nod. And, backing up to let me in, he said, "Alright, Gretchen – I'll head back to the station and write up the report. You can pick it up in the morning – your insurance guy'll need it."

"Thank you, Ed", said Gretchen. "And thanks for getting here so soon."

"I don't know who'd wanna do this, Gretchen", he said. "Seems like a stupid act of vandalism, from what I can see. Maybe some kids", he shrugged.

"Yeah, probably. Thanks again, Ed."

"Hope your night gets better", he said. "We'll have some guys drive past here a few times, overnight, though I think it's probably a one-and-done. Night, folks." And he walked out.

I saw Parker's headlights turn into the parking lot and said, "Parker's here. Let's take a look at what you've got here, Gretchen." And I walked over to the booth next to the window.

Gretchen and Suze both walked over to me and each of them gave me a hug.

"Oh, J.D. Thank you, so much, for coming. I was about at my wit's end", said Gretchen. "Look at this mess!"

Suze busied herself sweeping the pieces of glass off the table and into a dust pan. Then, she reached over for a broom that was leaning against the counter. "Let me get all this shit up", she said. "It's actually not too bad."

"Yeah, but look – the brick broke our pie shelf", said Gretchen. "There's broken glass and pie all over the floor over there."

"No sweat", said Suze. "I'll get the place cleaned up. You and J.D. worry about the window. Hey – here comes Parker."

And he walked in through the front door.

"What the fuck?", he said, by way of introduction.

"Somebody threw a brick through our window, Bill", said Gretchen.

"Yeah, I know. J.D. – you bring all of that stuff?"

"Yep – it's all in the truck."

"Okay, let's go bring it all in and get that thing boarded up."

And, for the next twenty minutes, we did just that. We put the plywood on the inside of the window and Parker drilled a few holes and used the sheet metal screws to attach it to the aluminum window frames. We'd had to cut it down to size but, other than some extra sawdust on the floor, that posed no problem.

"That oughta be good", said Parker, once we'd finished. "You gotta get a glass guy in here, tomorrow, though."

"I'll call somebody, first thing", said Gretchen.

"Good. But I'd say you're good for now. That plywood'll hold real well."

"It'll look like shit in the morning, though", said Suze. "And we'll probably lose that booth for tomorrow, too. I mean, who wants to sit next to a plywood window? And, hey – isn't this Ms. Jenkins' booth?"

"Yeah, it is", said Gretchen.

"Huh?", I asked.

Gretchen gave a little smile and said, "Yes. Ms. Jenkins comes in every morning at seven on the dot. Been doing it for years."

Suze said, "Oatmeal, fresh fruit and whole wheat toast. Dry."

"Yep", said Gretchen. "See, she's like you Geezers. Comes in every day. You'd probably recognize her if you saw her."

"She that little woman who wears overalls like Marquardt?", asked Parker. "She always sits facing us."

"Yep – that's her", said Gretchen. "Ah, don't worry. I'll set her up and comp her breakfast. She'll like that a lot."

Looking around, Parker asked, "Where's the brick?"

"Right here", said Suze, taking it from behind the counter and handing it to him.

Parker turned it over in his hands a couple of times and, then, pronounced, "Just a brick. No markings or nothing. No clues here."

"Who do you think might've done it?", I asked Gretchen. "Any ideas? Maybe Ed was right. Maybe it was just a random act of vandalism."

We all stood there for a few seconds, then Suze said, "Hey – didn't you say that you pissed off that Branson babe, the other day?"

"Well, yeah – we all talked about it. But all I did was chase her out of here."

"That's probably enough", said Parker.

"Really? You think she did it?", asked Gretchen.

"I wouldn't put it past her in the least", I said. "Or, just maybe, she told her husband about it and either he or one of his dimwit friends did it."

"That'd be my guess", said Parker. "Although we don't have any evidence that it was. But, just think – you've never had something like this happen before and, now, just a couple of days after that little thing, bingo – broken window."

"Well, you've got a plan for them, right?", she asked.

"We do", I said. "And this just might be one more reason."

"What's this world coming to?", asked Gretchen, shaking her head.

"I don't know", said Parker. "But it ain't good."

"Well, there's nothing more we can do here, tonight", said Suze. "So why don't we all get outta here?"

"You're sure you're okay?", I asked Gretchen.

"Oh, I'm fine", she said. "Just a little freaked out, is all."

A thought hit me. "Listen – let's not mention anything about the Bransons and all, tomorrow morning. Like, with the guys. Let's just all put it down to vandalism, okay? Let's keep our little secret a secret."

They all nodded, thinking about that.

Five minutes later, after all the lights were turned off, the door was locked and we were all heading to our vehicles, Parker said to me, "Oh, man – I wanna fuck them up." And he held up the brick.

"Yeah – me, too. Their time is coming."

And Flint Stone went to bed feeling confident that he'd passed Frank's test.

CHAPTER 30

Naturally, the next morning, The Coffee Spot was abuzz about the broken window. Everybody who entered couldn't help noticing the plywood up in its place and, of course, asking what had happened.

Earlier, Gretchen had gotten the staff together and, though she'd told them the truth – that somebody'd thrown a brick through the window – she thought it best to tell the customers that a passing vehicle had hit a rock in the road and had sent it flying, enough to crack the window. And that it was being replaced a little later today.

Which it was, Gretchen having gotten ahold of a local glass company who promised to have a couple of guys here this morning, hopefully between the breakfast and lunch rushes. Gretchen had texted a couple of photos of the window to the company and they estimated that it'd probably take less than an hour to get a new one put in.

Anyway, all of the customers bought the stone-from-the-road theory and life went on as usual. Of course, Ms. Jenkins was rather upset, that booth being her favorite and all, but Suze smoothed it over by sitting her in the booth next to her favorite and comping her breakfast.

All of the Geezers, on the other hand, knew the truth, with Gretchen coming over and she and Parker and I relating all the gory details, including the fact that we had our suspicions that it was somehow related to that Branson woman who'd been in here with the 'NO CRT' flyer several days ago.

"How do figure that?", asked Joe.

"Well, because the other afternoon, I chased her out of the parking lot", said Gretchen. "She'd been putting those flyers on our customers' windshields. She gave me the finger and peeled out of here, throwing gravel everywhere."

"The hell's the matter with these people?", asked Joe. "They seem to be all over the damned place, lately - like flies on shit. Oh - not that I meant this place, Gretchen", he said, trying to redeem himself after that clumsy simile, "but you know what I mean."

"You're absolved, Joe", she said. "And you're right. I mean, that thing at the school board meeting and the desecration of the People's Center and, now, probably this. I just don't know what's going to happen if it continues. Look - I've gotta run into the kitchen. Catch you guys in a few."

When she'd left, Bob said, "Something's gotta be done, but I just don't know what that is. The First Amendment allows them to say and write and broadcast just about anything they want, but I don't think the framers had this type of thing in mind."

"I don't know, Bob", said Mike. "Some of those fellas weren't the saints they've been made out to be. And they all had some pretty diverse opinions on a lot of issues, the Constitution notwithstanding."

"But you can't yell 'Fire!' in a crowded theater", Bob said. "And it seems as if some of this nonsense is coming up right next to that line."

"I agree, one-hundred percent", said Mike. "But, like you said, I just don't know what can be done about it. That whole movement seems to be snowballing. And it isn't healthy, especially as far as our democracy is concerned."

"It's that asshole carny barker that was in the White House. That sumbitch started it all", said Joe.

I piped up. "Oh, he didn't start it, Joe. It was there. It was all there, but it's been percolating below the surface for decades. He just made it okay for those people to come out from under their rocks. And it goes all the way back to just after the Civil War, when a lot of slaves were given land. You know – the forty acres and a mule thing and all that. A whole lot of poor white folks thought that they were being dissed while slaves were given the keys to the kingdom. And that feeling's still there with a lot of people."

"Exactly, J.D. And the Great Migration made the whites up north feel the same way", said Hal. "Like something was being taken away from them that they thought was God-given or something."

Just then, I saw Parker's eyes widen as he looked at the door. He shifted his gaze to me. And, when he did, he jutted out his chin in that direction.

I couldn't help turning around and, when I did, I saw Frank Branson standing at the take-out counter.

What the hell?

I spun back around in my seat and looked, wide-eyed, at Parker.

"What?", asked Bob, looking from us to the guy at the counter. "Who's that?"

I quietly said, "That's the Branson woman's husband."

Naturally, although I hoped it wouldn't happen, all of the guys turned to look at him, though they did display a certain modicum of surreptitiousness. I snuck another look and saw that he was facing away from our table, so he didn't see the 'gawk' coming from it.

"What the fuck is he doing in here?", Joe asked in a stage whisper.

"Looks like he's getting a coffee and a couple of donuts to go", Bob said quietly. Bob was sitting next to Parker, so he had an unobstructed view of Branson.

"Okay, he's walking out", said Parker.

Just then, Suze came rushing over.

"Did you see that?", she said, quietly enough to not be heard by the other customers. "Fucking Branson." Her eyes were wide.

"Yeah, we saw", said Parker.

"Lotta goddamned nerve, if you ask me", she said. "I wanted to go up to him and do a little Krav Maga on his ass."

"A little what?", asked Joe.

"Never mind", she said. "Some people, though, huh?"

We all nodded in agreement and she headed off to the kitchen, looking into the parking lot and seeing Branson climb into his truck.

———————————————

Twenty-five minutes later, Frank Branson pulled into the parking lot of Williams Lumber in Pleasant Valley. He was going to pick up Eric Gallagher and they'd do the pointing up of the fence job this morning.

He saw Gallagher standing there, sipping his coffee and pulled up to the curb.

"Wassup?", Gallagher asked him as he climbed into the truck.

"Here – want a donut?", Branson asked him.

"Sure. Special occasion?"

"Well, yeah. It is a special occasion. Flint Stone sent a brick through that diner's window last night."

"He did? Hot damn! I wasn't sure he had it in him. I thought he might, but I wasn't sure", said Gallagher, putting out his fist for a bump.

"Yep. He texted me around nine, last night. Said he'd done it."

"Sooo-weet!", said Gallagher, taking a bite of the donut. "I like glazed donuts. How'd you know?"

"Wild guess. And, you'll never guess where I got 'em."

"Where?"

"That diner."

"What? You're shittin' me."

"Nope. I just thought I'd stop in there, this morning, and see for myself. And, yep – they got a big ol' piece of plywood covering the spot where the window was. I took a picture of it and sent it to Sheila, too. She was psyched. I guess some bitch from there really dissed her."

Gallagher chuckled and said, "I'll be damned."

"Yep. He's cleared himself in my eyes, anyway. And it'll give us another thing to tell the guys on Sunday to get 'em psyched for the parade. I'd really like to see more of that stuff, to be honest. I wanna make a mark on this area."

"I think the parade's gonna be a good start", said Gallagher. "People're gonna know we're here."

"Yep – they are."

On my drive back to the farm, my phone rang. Ron.

"Dude", I said, "you're up early."

"Long night. Gonna crash in a few, but I wanted to run something by you."

"Shoot."

"Frank Branson got a text, last night, from some guy named Fred Stone. All it said was, 'done' – small 'd' in 'done'. And Branson texted back a thumbs-up. By the way, I guess this Stone is a contractor or something, out in your neck of the woods. Got any idea what that could've been about?"

"Well, yeah, maybe", I said. "I think so. Somebody threw a brick through a window in The Coffee Spot last night. Gretchen called me and Parker and I went over and put a sheet of plywood over it. Happened around nine o'clock or so."

"Well, I figured something might be afoot – that's the kind of message that rings some bells around here. I think, though, that Branson must've gotten himself a burner. In the last couple of days, the only calls and texts that he's made or received have been about his business. That, and a couple of things back and forth with the wife. Nothing about 'The Group', though."

"Huh", I said. "Think they're still going ahead with that thing on Sunday?"

"Schmidt says they are. He says that they're all gonna meet up in one spot and walk, en masse, to the parade and enter it from the Farmer's Market. You know where that is? I got it here on a map and it looks like it's right in the middle of town."

"Yeah, it's a big parking lot right on Market Street, the main drag. North side of the street."

"We're gonna have a couple of agents in the crowd taking pics. Actually, I think there's only gonna be one agent – a woman. There's talk that the other guy's gonna be assigned to something else that day. Either way, we'll have at least one agent on the ground. You won't know who she is or they are. Oh – plus Schmidt, of course, but he has to stay in character."

"But you haven't heard any chatter about them making trouble, have you?", I asked.

"Nope. Just the normal shit about how they're gonna make a real statement by prancing around in their paramilitary gear. Fuck, man – these guys act like a bunch of little kids who get to wear their Cub Scout or Little League uniforms or something. It'd be a friggin' joke if they weren't so dead-set on screwing things up."

"I heard where a bunch of those militia types who stormed the Capitol have gotten sent to jail", I said.

"Fu-u-uck. Slap on the wrist. What? A couple of months, here? A few months, there. Yeah – a couple of 'em got longer sentences but, for the most part, they're gettin' nothing. Not for trying to violently overthrow the government - and hurting a bunch of people. It's a freakin' joke, if you ask me or the people I work with. A lot of time, money and effort went into hunting these assholes down and it's like, 'Thanks, but we're pretty much just gonna sweep this under the rug'. A lot of folks around here are pretty demoralized."

"I can imagine", I said.

"Yeah, whatever. Alright, son – I gotta go. Gotta catch some shut-eye. Let's keep each other posted on anything we hear, though, okay?"

"Of course. Listen – before you go, we're still planning on the ninja horseman visit if this thing with the Bransons – both of them – comes off. You know that, right?"

"Well, yeah – that's what you said. It's really kinda too bad, though, that you couldn't do it ahead of time. You know – maybe put a stop to it."

"I know", I said. "I've been thinking about that but, with that note and all, I think the dye is pretty much cast."

"Yeah."

I thought for a second.

"But, you know, maybe a visit on Saturday night, with a note warning them, again, not to go ahead with their plans for Sunday wouldn't be the world's worst idea."

"Well, that's kinda what I was thinking. Maybe the horseman could scare the shit out of 'em enough for them to call it off. But, then again, if you do it Saturday night - and that's what, day after tomorrow? – you think they'd have enough time to call around and tell people it's cancelled? I mean, even if they do decide to cancel it after your visit. That'd be pretty late and would be cutting it awful close."

"Yeah, but it might throw a monkey wrench into the works. It might cause confusion among the ranks. And – it might even get them to keep their presence at the parade a little more subdued. Ya think?"

"I don't know, man", said Ron. "I guess I could argue it either way."

"Okay. It's just an idea. Let me think about it and run it past Parker. See what he thinks. I'll let you know what we come up with. But I'll give you a few hours to get some rest."

"Thanks, man. But let me know asap, 'k? Once you know?"

"Deal."

And we disconnected just as I was turning into the farm.

I saw Parker pushing a poop cart into the barn, obviously ready to do some mucking. When he saw me coming down the lane, I flashed my lights a couple of times to get his attention. As in, "Hold up – I gotta talk to you".

Once I'd parked and alit from the truck, he said, "What's up?"

"Just got a call from Ron. I guess a guy named Stone texted Branson around nine, last night, and pretty much admitted to being the guy who threw the brick through the window."

"So, it was one of his goons, huh? Doesn't surprise me one bit."

"Yeah. And, listen – we got to talking about this Sunday thing and he asked me if we're still gonna do the ninja horseman thing if they go through with it."

"Of course, we are", he said. "That was never a question, was it?"

"Oh, hell, no. But I got to thinking - and I mentioned this to him, just thinking out loud – what if the ninja horseman paid the Bransons a visit on Saturday night? And gave them a second warning telling them to call off their shit on Sunday? I wonder if it'd make a difference."

Parker thought about it for a few seconds, then said, "So – the actual ninja horseman shows up on Saturday night, tosses 'em a note giving them a second warning. Only this time, it's live and in living color. And, then, if they still go through with their shit, we hit 'em with the hammer – the shit about their pasts on, like, Sunday night, right?"

"Yeah. Or Monday. I'm thinking that Monday night might be better because who knows if they're gonna go back home after the parade? I mean, maybe there'll be some big goon get-together or something. Plus, maybe the Bransons will be on their guard on Sunday night, if they really believe that 'the specter from the darkness' will come a-visiting. By Monday night, maybe it'll be more of a surprise."

"Yeah, I can see that. But, are you sure you wanna introduce 'em to the ninja horseman twice? We'll lose a bit of the element of surprise if we do it a second time."

"Dude,", I said, "I still think the horseman's scary enough to do it twice. Hell, it scared you twice, didn't it?"

"Well, yeah, kind of. Pretty much, honestly. I mean, it's not something you wanna see twice. And, of course, you're in and out in a flash and it's not like you're hanging around for them to really figure out what's happening. So, yeah – I guess twice would be okay."

"I think we should do it."

"Night after tomorrow", said Parker. "Yeah, okay – why not? It might fuck up their plans – if not completely, then enough to make 'em think about it. Throw 'em off their game a little."

"Alright", I said and put up my hand. Parker gave me a high-five.

"I gotta think about a note", I said. "Should be simple, real simple. Like, 'This is your final warning' – something like that.

"Yeah - and you might wanna add, 'Call off your plans for tomorrow', just so there's no question or confusion."

"Good idea."

I looked over at the kids' pasture and they were wandering around, trying to find some grass that was long enough to eat.

"Hey, you guys!", I shouted. "Wanna go for a ride a couple of nights from now?"

They didn't pay any attention to me, whatsoever.

Then, Parker said to me, "Hey – what about Suze? She's been a part of this, so far, and I think we oughta at least tell her what's up, don't you?"

"Yeah, we probably should. She deserves it. Plus, if we don't, we might piss her off and she'll do a Krav Maga thing on us."

Parker chuckled and said, "Yeah, we don't want that. But, listen – do we just tell her what we're gonna do or do we take her with us?"

"Well, I dunno. We should probably give her the choice. But if she does come with us, she'll have to stay in the truck. We've got our thing down to a science, by now, and another person'll probably just get in the way. And that's the last thing we need."

"Agreed."

"Okay, so we're good with telling her. I gotta call Ron back a little later and tell him our plan. He worked all night, I guess, and he needs to sleep for a few hours. Let me call Suze and ask her to stop by, this afternoon, after work. We'll run it by her then."

Parker nodded and I reached for my phone and hit her on speed dial. It started ringing, then I said, "Shit – she's probably busy, right now. I should've waited 'til later."

Suze picked up on the third ring.

"J.D. – everything okay?", she asked by way of answering.

"Oh, yeah – everything's fine. Look - I know you're busy, right now, but Parker and I were wondering if you can stop by the farm on your way home from work, this afternoon. We wanna run something by you."

"Well, yeah – sure. No problem." I could hear restaurant noises in the background. "I get off a little before three. I can be at your place around three-fifteen, three-thirty, okay?"

"Yep. Perfect. See you then."

We disconnected and I said to Parker, "She'll be here a little before three-thirty. Now, I think I'll run up and type up that little note. Should only take me a couple of minutes, then I'll run it by you. Then, once we're happy with it, I'll do the calligraphy thing. Might as well get it out of the way."

"Alright", he said. "I've gotta go muck the barn and do the water thing. The nice thing about the colder weather is that the water seems to stay a little cleaner than it does in the heat of the summer. I only have to change it out every other day, right now."

"Yeah – I noticed that, too. Cool. Alright, catch you in a few."

And, with that, I headed for the house.

CHAPTER 31

Well, that was easy, I thought as I printed out the message I'd just written.

I read it over…….

Frank and Sheila Branson…….

This is your second and final warning.

Do NOT go ahead with your plans for tomorrow.

You have two choices:

- **Call off your plans and continue to prosper; or,**

- **Continue with them and suffer the consequences**

Choose wisely.

~ The Specter from the Darkness

Fine, right?

Simple and straightforward.

I took the sheet of paper and headed down to round up Parker, who was probably still in the barn.

Actually, he was pushing the poop cart back into the barn after having dumped its contents into the big roll-off container that resided around the corner of it.

"Yo!", I yelled.

"Let me put this away and I'll come meet you in the office", he shouted back.

He had a little electric space heater in one corner of his office and it took the chill off the fifty-something-degree day. I sat down in the chair in front of his desk.

"Let me see it", he said, sitting down. I handed him the sheet of paper and he read.

"Looks fine. Short and sweet. I like the choices idea, too. Sorta puts it all on them."

"That's what I was thinking", I said. "So, if you're cool with it, I'll do the calligraphy thing in a little while."

"Yep, cool." And he turned in his chair and picked something up off the floor. "Here", he said, turning and setting a brick on the desk. "Let's use this in the note sack instead of a rock. It's the brick that went through Gretchen's window." He smiled and said, "Just a little poetic justice."

"The Bransons won't know that, though", I said.

"No – but we will."

At that, I smiled. "Done."

"You hungry?", he asked. "Got some ham and Swiss and some rye bread here in the fridge." He had a small refrigerator behind his desk.

"Half", I said. "Then, I think I oughta lunge the kids for a little while to get the kinks worked out and burn off some energy, considering we're gonna do our thing tomorrow night. Oh, hey – tomorrow, we'll have to run down to Crockett's and pick up a couple of pies. You know, for our post-event celebration."

"Good idea", he said, fetching the sandwich fixin's out of the fridge. "Plus, we should probably pick up a couple of bags of grub for the kids, as long as we're down there." He busied himself slapping the sandwiches together. "Which reminds me, I gotta toss down another couple of bales. We're into the last one, down here. Soda?"

"Sure – Coke."

He'd also found a jar of pickles in the fridge and we ate.

When we were finished, I said, "Okay – I'm gonna go lunge the kids, now."

"Cool. I'll toss the hay down, then I'll go work on that project in the garage. It's just about done."

"Can I see your work in progress?"

"Nope."

"Alright, be that way. Sure you don't want help with the hay?"

"Nah, I got it", he said.

And I stood up and walked out to the kids' gate.

"Hey, you guys – wanna run a bit?"

They walked over to meet me, thinking that – strike that – *hoping* that it was treat time.

"Nope. Not yet", I said. "We're gonna go play for a few minutes."

And I walked out to the middle of their pasture and, when I turned to face them, they knew what was up.

I quickly raised my right arm and made a little 'Tch!' sound with my mouth. And, just like I knew they would, they began trotting to their right, in a counter-clockwise direction. I made the noise again, quickly raised my arm again and took a step toward them. They got it and they both put the hammer down.

I galloped them in that direction three times around, then I stepped to my left – as if I was cutting them off - and quickly raised my left hand, making the little noise again. And, yep – they turned and took off in the other – the clockwise – direction.

Again, three times around. Then we repeated the entire sequence several times for about the next ten minutes. I could see that they were having fun, too, tossing their heads and, sometimes, cow-kicking to the side. All the while, I talked to them: "There ya go! Good, you guys!". Stuff like that. I kept a smile on my face so they'd know that we were just having fun.

As big as horses are, they're always watching your face, especially your eyes. From what I understand, that's a thing that prey animals do - and, of course, horses are prey animals. And, when the human – the predator – looks like he or she is having a good time and is being non-threatening, they're gonna have a good time, too.

When I'd had enough, I relaxed and turned away from them. They knew that was the signal to stop. I stood with my back to them – again, non-threatening to a prey animal - and, pretty soon, I heard their breaths coming up behind me. Next thing I knew, Zeus was standing at one of my shoulders and Ceres was standing at the other.

I reached up and patted and scratched them both on their necks. "Good job, guys. Thanks. Now – I think y'all have earned a few treats. Come on."

And the three of us walked back to the gate.

When I got there, I opened it, closed and latched it and reached for the treat can. I pulled out a handful and went back and doled them out, one at a time. That's when I told them that, tomorrow night, we'd be taking a ride again. And that Zeus and I would take another little walk and Ceres would be staying in the trailer for a few minutes. It was all very matter-of-fact and I always do that. Whether or not they ever really understand my words, at least I know that I've tried my best to communicate with them.

And I guess it must work, because every time we'd done the ninja horseman thing over the past several months, they were always just as solid as they could be.

When we were finished – or, when I was finished – with the treat thing, I rubbed each of them on their foreheads and told them I'd see them a little later. They were cool with that.

I headed up to the house and stuck my head in the garage, spying Parker bent over his workbench.

"I'll be back down in a little while", I said.

"Cool", he replied. "Suze oughta be here before too much longer, right?"

I looked at my phone. "Yeah – about an hour. I'll hit you with a text when I've finished the note and maybe you'll come up to the kitchen and check it out."

"Ten-four", he said, not looking up from his work.

Up in my office, I pulled out a sheet of the antique paper, the ink and my calligraphy set and set to work. And, just like always, I screwed up the first two attempts. The third one, however, looked great. And, somehow, it always takes me a little longer than I think it should.

I looked at the time. Hmm – only fifteen, twenty minutes 'til Suze gets here. I texted Parker: "Ready." He hit me back with a thumbs-up.

"Well?", I asked him as we reconnoitered in the kitchen and I handed him the note.

"Excellent", he said, looking at it and then setting it down on the table. "And, oh – by the way – I should have that piece done this weekend. Maybe we can do an official (finger quotes) reveal on Monday."

"Sure. And it's for me, right?"

"Well, yeah – for you and this farm."

"Where should I put it?"

"I dunno – that'll be up to you. But it's pretty big – too big for the house, anyway, I think. Maybe the barn."

"Well, who's gonna see it if it's in the barn?", I asked.

"Maybe not in the barn – maybe on the barn. But, look – I ain't gonna say any more, right now. You'll see it and we'll figure it out."

"Okay. Want a soda?" He nodded and I grabbed a couple of Diet Sprites out of the fridge, just as we heard a toot in the driveway. I recognized it as the Subaru.

Suze.

Parker got up and motioned her into the kitchen.

"What's up, guys?", she asked as she came in and sat down at the table.

"Look, Suze.....hey – you want a Sprite?"

"Sure." And I got her one.

"Okay, Suze. Little change of plans." She looked from one to the other of us.

"Yeah. Remember, we were planning on doing the ninja horseman thing after Sunday. Monday night, actually. If the Bransons go ahead with their plans for the parade, that is."

"Okay, yeah."

"Oh, by the way – we have it on good authority from Ron that the guy who threw the brick through the window is part of Branson's cadre of goons."

"Doesn't surprise me", she said.

"Nope. But here's what we're thinking.....we're thinking that it would probably be a good idea for the ninja horseman to visit the Bransons tomorrow night, before the parade. And give them one last warning that they should cancel their plans. Here's the note we want to deliver to 'em."

And I passed her the note.

"Oh, man – this shit is so *cool*! The calligraphy on this old paper? Looks like it's right out of Sleepy Hollow days." She read it.

"Got it", she said. "And you're right – it's probably a good idea to scare the shit out of 'em ahead of time." She thought for a minute, then said, "But d'you suppose they could call it off in time? I mean, it'll only be – what? – twelve hours or so before the parade. It'd probably be quite a heavy lift for them to pass the word, right?"

"Yeah, but it could be done if they wanted to do it", said Parker. "Those guys've probably got a phone tree or something set up. And Sheila and her Moms for Liberty probably do, too. Either way, there's a good chance that this'll throw 'em off their game a little. Maybe they'll go ahead with it, but tone it down from whatever they've been planning."

Suze nodded and said, "Yeah, okay. I can see all that."

Then she looked at each of us again and said, "Dudes – this is so far fucking out. This ninja horseman thing. It's fucking *outrageous*, is what it is." Her attitude changed just a bit and she asked, "Can I come? Tomorrow night?"

I looked at Parker and he nodded once.

"Well, yeah, I guess so", I said. "But, look – if you're going to come with us, you'll have to stay in the truck. Parker and I have the whole thing down to a science, time-wise. We both know what to do and exactly when to do it. And the timing has to be just about perfect. No offense, but you might get in the way."

"Nothin' personal, kid", said Parker. "But J.D.'s right. Besides, the whole thing – from parking the rig to us blowing outta there again shouldn't take but five minutes – ten, tops."

"Alright", she said. "I'm just psyched about going with you guys. And you say that Ceres stays in the trailer while this thing is happening?"

"Yep", I said. "Right when Zeus and I are about to take off, Parker tosses a flake of hay into her hay net. And you know Ceres – food bribery works like a charm with her."

"Yeah", said Parker. "And I stand out at the back of the trailer while they're gone and as soon as I see these guys coming back, we bust a move. J.D. jumps down offa Zeus and I rush him right into the trailer. We close the doors and vamoose."

Suze said, "Well, once they're on their way, can't I get out of the truck and stand with you 'til we see them coming and then, when we do, I can jump right back into the truck?"

"I supposed that'd work", said Parker. "Just do what I tell you and don't get in the way. That cool with you?", he asked me.

I shrugged and said, "Fine with me. As long as you do what you just said."

"Oh, I am so psyched for this!", she said. "What time?"

"Good question", I said. "It gets dark real early, now. But I think we should wait 'til they're all relaxed and all. After dinner, when they're just chillin', maybe while they're watching TV or something. Like – what, Parker? – nine o'clock?"

"Yeah, if we do it right around nine, that oughta work real well. That means we'll have to leave here at eight-thirty. Takes a good twenty-five, thirty minutes to get down there."

I nodded and said, "Yeah - and we'll park around the corner from their house, right? Along that tree line so they won't be able to see the rig from their place. Then, Zeus and I'll just walk across their lawn and around to their front door and do it."

"Won't people wonder what a horse trailer's doing in that neighborhood at that time of night?", Suze asked.

"Probably not", said Parker. "Don't forget, J.D.'s truck is black and we painted the trailer black, so, with no streetlights - and there aren't any along in there – we'll be pretty invisible, as big as it all is. Plus, I'll pull up onto that grassy area between the street and the tree line – off the pavement."

"Yeah", I said, "and because it's a suburban-type neighborhood, there probably shouldn't be any traffic along in there at nine o'clock on a Sunday night."

Suze gave a big smile and said, "Ooh – I can't wait. This is just so exciting!"

"Well, it'll be a helluva lot more exciting once we get home", said Parker. Then he laughed and said, "It should be pretty goddamned exciting for the Bransons, too."

And the two of us gave the ol' Geezer knuckle-knock.

"What the hell?", asked Suze.

"That's the Geezer knuckle-knock", I said. "It's how we Geezers vote on things. If we agree, we all knock on the table."

"I can see why you guys are called the Geezers", she said, shaking her head and smiling.

"Bite me, young'un", I said. "Oh - and when we get home from our little ninja horseman soiree, we always celebrate with pie."

"Pie", she said.

"Yep", said Parker. "We gotta run down to Crockett's Feed Store in the morning and pick up a couple." He looked at me and said, "Maybe they'll have strawberry-rhubarb."

"Maybe", I said. "But aren't those things out of season, by now?"

"I dunno", he said. "Maybe they can it or something. Let's just see. And, y'know – maybe they'll have pecan."

"What's your favorite?", I asked Suze.

She shrugged and said, "Never thought much about it. Anything's pretty much fine with me. Well, except for mincemeat. That shit's rude."

Another Geezer knuckle-knock from us Geezers.

"We'll find something", I said. "And we'll celebrate when we get home."

"Sounds like a plan", she said.

"Alright, I gotta get out of here", said Parker, standing up. "I gotta stop at the store on the way home."

"If there's nothing else, I should, too", said Suze. "I gotta take a shower and get all this grease smell off me. Y'know, I smell like a friggin' kitchen when I get home."

"Hey – did the glass guys show up?", I asked her.

"Oh, yeah – I forgot to tell you. They got there around ten-thirty and they had the whole thing looking good as new a little before noon. It looks great, I guess. I mean, it looks like a window, y'know?"

"Did Gretchen pick up the police report?", asked Parker.

"Yep – she ran down to the station in between the breakfast and lunch rushes. The insurance guy came by, this afternoon, and, according to Gretchen, she should have a check within the next week or so."

"Excellent", I said. "So, now, it's like it never even happened, huh?"

"Something like that", said Suze. "But Gretchen's still pretty pissed about the whole thing."

I looked at Parker and said, "We should tell Gretchen about what's going on with the ninja horseman thing and all, tomorrow morning. Let her know that at least somebody associated with that little di-do is gonna get fucked around with."

"Yeah, let's do that", he said.

And we all got up and the two of them left.

I took the sheet of paper up to my office and laid it on the desk.

Then, I went back downstairs to see what time the Series game started.

The goddamned Astros were in it again, having beaten the Yanks. Again.

But the Mets were in it, too, and they were playing in New York. Last night, in Game One, Scherzer blanked the 'Stros for seven and the Mets won, 3-1.

Go, Mets.

CHAPTER 32

"Everything on schedule for the parade, tomorrow?", Bob asked Mike after we'd all gathered for the daily Geezers' meeting at The Coffee Spot and Gretchen had filled all of our mugs.

"Far as I can tell", said Mike. "You know that I don't really have anything to do with the planning or execution of it, this year. Last year was enough for me. Getting all those merchants and everybody else together on the same page is like herding cats. I'll be at the town council building, though. We'll have chairs and tables set up and the Legion guys are going to set up a grill thing."

"Looks like the weather's going to cooperate", said Hal. "After the last couple of days, I wasn't so sure."

The cold low that had dominated the Hudson Valley for the past three days had moved out and a high pressure system was moving in, promising clear skies and a high in the 60s for the next three or four days.

"Guess the Old Farmer's Almanac missed on this one", said Bob, who was a devout follower of it. None of us could quite understand why Marquardt, being a pretty progressive guy about farming and everything else, adhered to it like he did, but he did. Go figure.

"When are they gonna shut down the streets to traffic?", asked Joe.

"Oh, not 'til eight-thirty, nine o'clock", said Mike. "All of the booths and so on will be set up along the sidewalks, so that won't be a problem."

"What time does it start?", asked Hal.

"Well, the parade steps off at two, but the whole thing – the whole day, with stores and booths and all – starts at ten. The Farmers' Market has some kind of kick-off thing at ten. I guess they're giving out apples to the kids or something."

"You guys going to it?", I asked the table.

"Hell, no. Not me", said Joe. "I ain't gettin' involved with traffic and parking and all that. And, honestly, I could give two shits about it. I'm gonna watch the Jets-Miami game."

Hal shook his head, as did Bob. "Not my cup of tea", he said. "What about you?", he asked me.

"Ah, I don't know. I've never seen it before and I really like downtown Rhinebeck. If I can convince this guy to go along as my wingman", I said, nodding in Parker's direction, "I think it'd be fun."

Parker shrugged in the way that he does when he's agreeing with something.

"You hear of any trouble on the horizon?", he asked Mike.

"You mean from some of those right-wingnuts? Well, there have been whispers that some of them might show up with signs and placards and so on – there's always some group or other that wants to make a statement at the event – but Chief Eddings says that he'll have his guys out in force and, if anything gets a little too over-the-top, they'll step in and put an end to it. Quietly."

"Well, I hope it goes well", said Hal. "After what happened at the Center and here, the other night, I wouldn't put anything past some of those people. Something's simmering, just below the surface, if you ask me."

"And in friggin' Rhinebeck, of all places", said Joe, shaking his head.

"It's everywhere", said Parker.

Just then, Gretchen walked up to the table.

"Hey, gents – guess what? Artie's trying out one of his new things, again, this morning. Breakfast burritos. And he wants to use you guys as lab rats – er, taste-testers – again, meaning that they're on the house."

"What's in 'em?", asked Joe.

"Well, there's a choice of two. One, he's calling the 'Country Burrito'. It's got eggs, naturally, and potatoes and cheese. Kind of a vegetarian thing. The other's the 'Chorizo Burrito', with eggs and chorizo, natch, and potatoes. Oh - and that one's got cheese in it, too. I've had a bite of both of them and I think they're both real good."

"I'm down for the chorizo one", said Bob.

And the rest of us, with the exception of Hal, ordered the same thing. Hal opted for the 'Country' thing. Something about his cholesterol, which didn't make a whole lot of sense, considering.

"You got it", she said. "And I tell you what – because the burritos have potatoes in them, y'all probably don't want individual home fries with it, but I'll bring out a big plate of them and you can take what you want."

The Coffee Spot's home fries were the Eighth Wonder of the World, according to just about everyone who's ever eaten them. Cooked just right – never soggy and just the right amount of crispness - with plenty of onions and peppers and, from what I could taste, a lot of seasoned salt.

"Good idea", said Bob.

"I'll have a side of bacon, too, if you will, Gretchen", said Hal.

"Wait – what about that cholesterol thing?", asked Joe.

Hal just shrugged.

____

Down in Hyde Park, Frank Branson was getting ready to leave the house. He and Gallagher had just about finished that wall, yesterday, and it would only take another hour-and-a-half to finish it and get everything cleaned up. And he had that other job up in that neck of the woods that he wanted to start on first thing Monday, so he'd pick up Gallagher, again, finish up the job and he'd be home before noon. Ohio State-Michigan started at one and he wanted to catch it.

"When I get home,", he said to Sheila, "I wanna do the phone tree thing again with the guys. That way, we'll be able to get a final head count for tomorrow. But, really, hon – I think there'll be a good twenty-five or so of us. I should know by dinnertime."

"I thought you wanted to watch the game", she said.

"I can multi-task", he said, winking at her. "Besides, I only have to call four guys."

"You've done a wonderful job putting this all together, dear", said Sheila. "You've gone from nothing to a couple dozen men in a few short weeks. Congratulations are in order."

"Well,", he said, "it ain't been all that hard, to tell you the truth. There's a lot of people around here that wanna see some changes, some big changes. Basically, all I did was put the word out. And, after tomorrow, I'll guarantee you that we'll grow some more. Once people see us and what we stand for, I think they'll jump right on the bandwagon."

He took a last swallow of coffee from his mug and, rinsing it out in the sink, said, "And, you, too, baby. Your Moms chapter is kicking ass. Hey, that reminds me – you think any of the TV stations'll send out a crew, tomorrow? Be great if you could get on the tube again."

"I don't know, but I'm still angry about getting punked the other day. I sure as hell won't let that happen again." She busied herself wiping off the counter-top. "You're not worried about that note, are you?" She was still a little upset about that knife-in-the-door thing.

"Ah, hell, no. Matter of fact, I'd 'bout forgotten about it. I think it was just some asshole left-winger who was too afraid to confront any of us, personally. Fucking punk-ass snowflake, is what I think. Nah – we're gonna go ahead with it like nothin' happened."

"You're probably right. I'm sure you are. It's just that I still feel a little violated", she said.

"Come here", he said, walking toward her and wrapping her in a bear hug. "Don't you worry your pretty little head about a thing, little darlin'. Your boy's got this."

"That's better", she said, holding him tightly.

"Alright – I gotta git. I gotta pick up Gallagher in twenty minutes and I'm running a little late. I'll be home around noon."

And he kissed her and headed toward the door.

"Oh – I'm going to do a phone-tree thing with my girls, this morning, too."

"Yeah? How many you expectin'?"

"I'm hoping for about twenty, maybe a few more", she said.

"That'll be quite a turn-out", said Frank. "Hell – between our two groups, it'll be close to fifty of us. And that's pretty goddamned impressive. Alright, kid – see you in a little while."

And she blew him a kiss as he went out the door.

After we'd finished our breakfast - and we'd all agreed that the burritos were a hit, by the way - and our twenties had floated onto the table, I caught Gretchen's eye and motioned with my head for her to meet Parker and me outside the employees' entrance in a couple of minutes. And I indicated Suze, too. Gretchen got it.

I should mention that, although our breakfasts had been on the house, we all pitched in our cash, anyway. We'd done that the other times that Artie had used us as guinea pigs, too. Let Gretchen spread it around to the other workers or something.

I caught up with Mike as he was getting into his car and asked him to join the four of us over around the corner of the place. I wanted to fill them all in on our plans. Mike was well-versed in our ninja horseman exploits and had been a part of two of them.

When we all reconnoitered at the bottom of the steps that lead up to the back door, I told Gretchen and Mike that the ninja horseman was going to visit the Bransons, tonight, in a last-ditch attempt to get them to call off their plans for the parade, tomorrow. And, of course, that we'd already told Suze and that she was going to join us, but she'd stay in or next to the truck.

Gretchen looked at her. "Are you sure you want to do this? I mean, it could be a little bit dicey. These guys are one thing – they've done this before – but are you sure you want to get that involved?"

"Look, Gretchen", said Suze. "That Branson chick has done us wrong – three times, maybe four. The first two, she got up in my face and hassled me down at that thing in Poughkeepsie. And, just the other day, she flipped you the bird and threw stones and shit all over the parking lot. Plus, she was probably in on that brick-throwing deal, too."

"Oh, right", I said. "I spoke with Ron, yesterday, and he told me that he learned that the guy who threw the brick was one of the guys from Branson's group."

"See?", said Suze. "So, yeah – I wanna be in on this."

"You guys do all of your recon and so on?", asked Mike.

"'Course", said Parker. "Our ingress and egress oughta be a piece of cake, given the layout of the place and the neighborhood."

"Do you really think you can get them to call it off?", Mike pressed.

"Ah, I doubt it", I said. "But if we don't try, it's for sure going to happen. And, maybe our little visit might cause them to tone it down a little. Or something." I shrugged.

"And if they do go through with it", said Parker, "we're gonna come down on them like a ton o' bricks. We have dirt on both the husband and the wife. Real good, honest-to-goodness dirt, too."

"I take it you think that you're going to have to make a return visit", said Mike.

"Yep. We're planning on Monday night", said Parker. "That is, unless tonight, we somehow hit the jackpot."

"I just don't want any trouble downtown, tomorrow", said Mike. "That would be horrible for the town and, of course, for all the kids and the families that'll be there.

"You're goddamned right, it would be", said Parker.

"You going to the parade, Gretchen?", I asked.

She laughed and said, "Oh, hell, no. We're open, tomorrow, and I'd imagine that we'll be busier than usual. I know we were, last year. A lot of the families stop here for breakfast on their way into town."

"I wish I could go", said Suze. "If nothing else, just to hang out with you guys."

"Well, let's see what the morning brings", said Gretchen. "If we're not really slammed, maybe you can slip out around ten – after the rush."

"Hope so", said Suze.

"Alright", I said. "Time to break up this little shindig. Parker and I gotta get back to the farm and, in a little while, run down to the feed store. I want to take it pretty easy, this afternoon. Tonight'll be a strain, no matter how it goes."

"Do me a favor and call me once you get home, tonight, okay? Let me know how it went", said Mike.

"For sure", I said. "Will do."

"Hey,", said Parker, looking at me, "I've got an idea. Why don't we run down to Crockett's, now? I'll leave my truck here and we'll swing by and I'll pick it up on our way back. Save us some time."

"Yeah, sure. Good idea."

"I've got to get back inside", said Gretchen. "And call me, too, once you do your thing. And take care of my little girl, y'hear?" And she looked Parker and me right in the eyes. "I'm counting on you."

"You have our word", I said.

She and Suze made their way back up the stairs and through the door.

Mike said, "I gotta tell you guys – I'm a little worried about tomorrow. I know Ron's been on the horn with Chief Eddings and told him that he'll have an agent or two in the crowd and Eddings says he has his end of it all under control, but, still. Things can go real bad, real quick, you know?"

"Let's just hope for the best", I said.

"Yep. Alright, look – good luck, tonight, and who knows? Maybe you'll do some good."

"From your lips to God's ears", said Parker.

That little tete-a-tete broke up and, a couple of minutes later, Parker and I were headed to Crockett's.

____

Up in Pleasant Valley, Branson and Gallagher were busy on the wall.

"You psyched for tomorrow?", Gallagher asked Frank.

"You bet, son. I think we're gonna have a ton of guys there. Which reminds me, I'm gonna call the other three guys when I get home, this noon. And have them call the guys on their lists. You'll make your calls, too, right?"

"Oh, yeah. Fear not, man. I'm on it."

"Fuck", said Branson, as a thought hit him.

"What?"

"Ah, shit. You know I've been using this burner for the past few days, but I'm afraid I'll have to use my regular phone to make those calls. Those guys don't know the burner's number and they probably won't take the call when they see it come up."

"Ah, big deal", said Gallagher. "Don't make a big thing out of it. Just use your regular phone. Hell, you'll just be on the line for a few seconds and just say something like, "Make your calls. Tell your guys to meet up where you said to meet up at one-thirty. That's all. Don't get into any details, just in case. They'll get it. Hang up. Piece of cake."

"Yeah, I guess you're probably right."

"Chill, dude. This'll be a good thing."

"Yeah. Yeah, it will", said Branson. "Think we got enough cement here?"

"I'd say so, yeah. We just got those few bricks to do. Otherwise, we'll probably waste some. Let's make it work."

And Frank reached for the trowel.

Parker and I got back to the farm, laden with some grub for the kids and having scored a couple of pies. Good-looking ones, too.

Unfortunately, I'd been correct about the strawberry-rhubarb being out of season, but we got a pleasant surprise when we found that – according to the woman behind the counter – they had special 'autumn' pies.

One was a hazelnut pecan. And, again, according to the woman, it had a little chocolate in it, too. Natch, we had to pick up some homemade whipped cream to go on top of it. The other one was a maple pumpkin which, I guess, had maple syrup as part of the ingredients. We got whipped cream for that one, too.

We were stylin'.

Now, if tonight went well, we'd be celebrating with one or the other – or both – of them.

We hurried through the chores, with Parker taking the mucking and me doing the water tubs. We were both kind of quiet because we were both probably thinking about tonight. At least I was.

Once we'd finished, Parker said that he wanted to work on his piece for a little while – it'd help him to get his head clear. Then, he'd probably leave in about an hour or so, but would be back around seven-thirty. I actually got him to admit that he'd probably get a nap in. He had this thing about always wanting to appear that he was on duty. Must've come from his cop days.

I made no bones about it - I was most definitely going to take a nap. Probably catch a little college football on the tube and zone out while I was watching it.

Shit, I thought. I'll probably miss the Series game, tonight. The damned Astros had scored three in the eighth, last night, and had won Game Two. They and the Mets were now a game apiece.

Time went by and Parker left and I camped out on the couch. I turned on the Ohio State-Michigan game and the Buckeyes led, 14-3, in the middle of the second quarter.

As I lay on the couch, I reached over for my copy of 'The Legend of Sleepy Hollow'. Early on, when we were about to do our ninja horseman thing, I'd read the whole thing again, just to get in the mood.

I didn't need that kind of stimulation any longer. But I did hold the book on my stomach, thinking that, maybe, I'd get a little inspiration through osmosis.

Whatever, I was asleep in ten minutes.

My phone woke me.

As I sat up and looked at the screen, I saw that it was three o'clock. And Ron was calling.

"Dude", I said.

"Wassup, m'man?" He sounded pretty chipper – at least more so than he did yesterday, when he'd been up all night.

"Chillin', son. Just getting ready for tonight. We're gonna hit Branson's around nine o'clock. Oh – that reminds me – I haven't sent you the note we're gonna give him. I'll email it to you as soon as we hang up."

"Yeah, well, I'm calling about Branson."

CHAPTER 33

"What about him?", I asked.

"Well, he used his own phone to make three calls a little earlier. And we traced the recipients back and found that they're members of The Group. And we also listened to them."

"You can't use those calls as any kind of evidence, though, right?"

"Of course not. We just wanted to see what they're up to. And, in each case, Branson was short and sweet. He told each of them to make their calls – we're figuring that they have a phone tree or something. And he said to tell everybody to meet up at one-thirty. Then, basically, he ended the all. A couple of the guys wanted to talk a little more but he cut 'em off. He's probably got a pretty good idea that his phone might be bugged."

"Did any of them say where they're going to meet?", I asked.

"No, but Schmidt called me a couple of minutes ago and confirmed that he'd gotten a call. And they're supposed to meet up on Livingston Street, which he says is adjacent to the back end of the Farmers' Market. You know where that is?"

"Yeah, I do. At least I know where the Farmers' Market is. Gotta be the street behind it."

"From what I gather,", said Ron, "you can get to the parade – which is on East Market Street, right? – by going through the Farmers' Market and you're there."

"Yep."

"Anyway, it looks like it's on. But you guys are gonna do your thing, tonight. You got any hope that they'll call it off?"

"Not really, but we figure it's worth a try. Hey – you don't have any idea where the wife's Moms for Liberty group is going to be setting up, do you? We think they're setting up a table or a booth or something, somewhere along the parade route."

"Nope. None of that came up. But you just may have hit on something. If Branson's got a phone tree set up, she probably does, too. I'm gonna get to her phone, right now. See if she's making any calls. Plus, I'll be able to see her recent calls and, if there are several of them, I'll know."

"Good idea. And let me know, okay? In the meantime, I'll email that note to you as soon as we hang up."

"Gotcha. But what's it say? Anything spicy?"

"Nah. Just that it's their second warning and they have two choices: call off their things, tomorrow, or suffer the consequences. And that they should choose wisely. It's short and sweet."

"Got it. Cool. Alright, I'll call you when I find out anything."

"Not too late, though. Not after about seven-thirty, seven-forty-five, my time. I'll be getting ready to do my thing, right about then."

"Ten-four."

And we disconnected.

I looked back at the tube and saw that the post-game thing was on. It looked like Ohio State really spanked the Wolverines in the second half, because the final score was 31-10, Buckeyes.

I really didn't know what to do with myself for the next few hours. I'd gotten a nap and didn't want to sleep anymore. I had to eat, but it was too early for that. And my nervous energy had started percolating through my veins.

Maybe I'd take a walk. I'd done that a couple of times over the summer on pre-ninja horseman afternoons and they had helped me to center myself. Yeah, but that was in the summer, when everything was in full bloom and the hay fields were deep with hay. And I'd been able to marvel at all the denizens that lived in the fields and in the sky and so on.

Now, here we were, just about the beginning of November, when nature was beginning to settle down for its long winter nap.

Hell, I thought. Maybe I'll see something. I gotta move.

Because the day was pretty warm, I was good just putting on my down vest.

I walked out, waved to the kids whose heads had come up when they saw the motion

up here at the house, and headed for the hay field that ran northeast from the barn —
the same field I'd sat in over the summer.

The first thing I noticed was the absence of the swoosh-swoosh-swoosh noise my
legs made while walking through eighteen-inch-deep hay two or three months earlier.
And the lack of insects buzzing around. Sure, there were birds flying around, but the
robins were gone. The red-winged blackbirds, who didn't leave for the winter, were
clearly in evidence, as were the sparrows and blue jays who, just like always, were
screaming the way that blue jays do.

I looked all around the sky to see if I'd find a kestrel or a hawk or something. Nope. I
knew they stayed around for most of the winter, but their internal clocks must have
readjusted and this wasn't their feeding time, right now.

Because it was just a mite boring, I decided to walk over to the far eastern edge of the
field, where it met the woods and that old stone fence separated them. A couple of
minutes later, I found myself at the same spot I'd sat down, one afternoon, not long
ago.

The stone was cold on my butt, but not too cold.

And, because the sun was lower in the sky, right now, I could feel its warmth on my
face.

I just sat there, closed my eyes and breathed deeply.

After just sitting, quietly, for a couple of minutes, I could feel my other senses
sharpening — particularly my sense of sound.

I could hear little rustles in the leaves, thinking that it must be squirrels or chipmunks,
who were busy filling their larders for the winter. I could hear the dead and dying
leaves rustling in the breeze on all three sides of me. The sounds resonated from the
tallest trees to the smallest bushes, so it was almost all-encompassing, sound-wise.

And it was almost musical, like several drummers tapping and swishing out sounds
with their brushes on their hi-hats, their snares and their tom-toms. There was almost
a beat to it.

Hell, there was a beat to it. It was the beat of Mother Earth, conducting her music with
all of her woodland children expertly playing their individual parts. And the longer I sat
there with my eyes closed and my ears open, the more I enjoyed it. Every once in a
while, when the breeze shifted just a bit, I could hear the creek that runs along back

there. There was even a cricket or two, adding their instruments to the mix. And, when the various birds joined in with their own unique songs, it really was a concert.

I almost felt like singing, myself, just to join in with my fellow music-makers, but I thought that was just a little too much on the silly side. But I did sing – in my head. No words, mind you, just imaginary notes strung together that felt as if they belonged to the etude that was taking place all around me.

With my eyes still closed and the sun still shining on my face, I smiled. And that smile stayed right there for several minutes as I lightly swayed back and forth in time to the music.

I don't know how long I sat there, mesmerized the way I was, but it must've been ten or fifteen minutes. And I was awakened from my reverie when I felt the warmth of the sun leave my face. I opened my eyes and saw a big, white, fluffy cloud passing in front of it. It almost seemed as if it were dancing across the sky.

I slowly came back to reality, though not all that willingly.

God, that was great, I thought.

And I thought how different that experience had been from the last time I'd sat here, when the summer was at its peak and everything was quite different. But this was wonderful, too, in its own way.

And, for a few seconds, I thought about the rhythm of time. And how it's always changing and, no matter what time of year or season it is, it's always different. And it's always wonderful in its own right.

The rhythm of time.

The rhythm of life.

I finally stood up and turned around to look behind me. The forest. What an amazing and vibrant place is the forest.

Somewhat reluctantly, I headed back across the hay field, thinking that I'd most definitely have to come out to that spot again during the depths of the winter, just to experience that. I knew in my heart that I'd enjoy that, too.

As I got back to the barnyard, I stuck my head into the barn and saw that the kids had walked in and were eating their hay out of their feeders.

"Don't forget, you guys – we're gonna take a ride in a little while." They looked up at me and instantly buried their heads in their feeder again.

As I got back to the porch, I noticed that the sun was quickly dropping into the western sky. It'd be dark within the hour.

I decided to call Parker and tell him what I'd learned from Ron. Not that it was anything earth-shaking or needed any immediate action, but my nervous energy was trying to return and, well, I just wanted to call him, is all.

"Everything okay?", he asked by way of answering.

"Oh, yeah. No problem. I just wanted to let you know that Ron called and, through his Feeb magic, found out that things are still full speed ahead on the Branson front. At least on Frank's part – he's got some kind of a phone tree going on. Ron's gonna take over Sheila's phone to see if he can find out if her dealio's still a go, too."

"Okay. But you and I both know it is. These assholes wanna make a statement and they're gonna go ahead and do that. I don't even think tonight's thing will stop that."

"We gotta try, though", I said.

"Yeah, we do."

"Alright, I'll let you go. See you a little later."

"You okay?"

"Yep. I'm fine. Just a little nervous energy, is all."

"Understandable. Look, though – I gotta eat and you probably do, too. So, I'll see you in a little while."

And we disconnected.

Yep, I'd better eat. And nothing would fit the bill better than a can of tomato soup and a grilled cheese sandwich.

After I ate, I walked down to the barn, basically to check on the state of Zeus' coat. Now that his winter coat was about in full bloom, I wanted to make sure that he hadn't rolled in mud or poop and it was sticking to him or something.

He had a couple of little spots of crusted mud, but I scratched that off with my fingers. Actually, he was in pretty good shape. I checked Ceres' coat, too, though the state of hers wasn't really crucial to our mission, tonight – she'd be staying in the trailer the whole time. Hers was pretty good, too.

I told them that I'd see them in a little while and reiterated that we'd be taking a ride, later. They seemed fine with that.

As I was walking back to the house, my phone dinged with a text.

Suze. "Be there at 7:30." I sent her a thumbs-up.

I screwed around for a while, not doing much of anything worth noting, and then, at 7:30, I saw Suze's lights turn into the lane.

Once she'd parked, I shouted for her to come into the house.

"Want anything?", I asked her once she'd sat down at the kitchen table.

"Got a soda?"

"Coke or Diet Sprite?"

"Coke."

I handed it to her and we shot the shit for a few minutes, with me going over the plan, again, with her. And I reiterated that she had to stay out of the way. She was cool with that.

I told her that Parker should be here pretty soon and that I'd run upstairs and get my ninja horseman gear on and all.

"Hey", she said. "Do you suppose it'd be alright for me to go down and brush the kids?"

"Sure", I said. "I guess so. Why not? I scratched most of the schmutz off 'em, this afternoon, but if you wanna polish 'em up a bit, sure – go right ahead. The brushes and so on are in the tack room. And, if the kids are outside, as soon as you turn the barn light on, they'll come in. Just be careful."

A big smile crossed her face and she stood up. "I'm outta here. Just let me know when you want me to do anything else."

"Just keep an eye out for Parker and let him know you're in the barn. In a couple of minutes, I'll go up and put my shit on and meet you guys down there in a little while."

And she headed out the door.

I went upstairs and began pulling my gear out of the closet and setting it on my bed.

There were the black jeans, the black turtleneck and my black boots and gloves. I grabbed my balaclava and tested the lights. They were working. Then, the piece de resistance – my black hooded Witcher's cloak. Finally, I took Zeus' black fly mask down from the shelf and made sure his lights were working, too.

I reached down to the closet floor and pulled out the two canvas sacks. I'd brought the brick that Parker had given to me and put that into one of the sacks. In the other, I placed two good-sized rocks.

Then, I went into my office and fetched the note that we'd deliver to the Bransons, went back into the bedroom and put it into the sack with the brick. I'd carefully folded it in half. Then, I pulled the drawstrings tight on both sacks. I knew which one was which because, well, I could feel the difference between a brick and rocks.

A couple of minutes later, I'd donned the whole affair, including the balaclava, though I'd pulled up the mesh face mask onto the top of my head. Then, I put the gloves on.

I heard a double-toot from outside and I knew that Parker had arrived.

I put the cloak on and got it situated. Then, I pulled down my face mask, making sure the lights were in the right place. Then, I pulled the hood up over my head.

Done.

And, as I always do before one of these little exploits, I walked across the hall into Mom's and Bill's old room. Entering, I turned on my red lights. Now, to find the full-length mirror in the darkness. Actually, I really didn't need to find it – it hadn't moved in years.

So, I walked across the room to the far corner and stepped in front of it.

And there he was.

The demon from hell.

Nothing but a black apparition, the only thing reminiscent of humanity being its size.

The two red eyes stared out from deep inside the hood. Are they really eyes? Is that what they are? They're where eyes are supposed to be, but they're just tiny red-glowing embers staring back at me.

I just stared. And then, I felt it. The cold chill running up my spine.

And that always amazes me. I knew damned well that it was just me in some kind of crazy costume but, if I didn't know the truth, it would scare the shit out of me.

And that was the whole point, wasn't it?

To scare the shit out of – in this case – the Bransons.

To make them think that some demon from hell or somewhere was sitting astride a black horse of monstrous proportions - and that horse had the same kind of eyes as its rider.

And I'd seen the fear, too. I'd seen it in a dirty high school principal named Conway and his wife; I'd seen it in a crooked councilman named Hylan and his missus; a baseball coach-slash-fraudster named Vinal and his wife; a thieving real estate mogul and her second-in-command; I'd seen it in a friggin' Russian oligarch who was moving illegal arms and had tried to bury The Coffee Spot; and I'd seen the guy I used to work for who had defrauded an entire company, along with all of its employees.

So, yeah – I'd seen the fear.

And, from where they stood, it sure wasn't pretty.

But, from where I sat, high up on Zeus, it was a thing of beauty.

Because each and every one of those people were being served with a form of justice that they all so richly deserved and probably wouldn't have gotten any other way.

I was ready.

The ninja horseman was ready.

I turned on my heel and swept out of the room, pushing the cloak's hood off my head and pushing the balaclava up onto it. I went back into my room and grabbed Zeus' mask and the two sacks.

I grabbed my phone and hit Parker on speed dial.

"Yeah?"

"I'm coming down and I've got all the stuff."

"Cool. We're just finishing making the kids all clean and sparkly. I'll go get the rig ready and into the driveway and I'll have Suze put Zeus' tack on the sawhorse."

"Make sure you toss a couple of flakes into the back seat of the truck."

"On it. Okay, see you down here."

I stuck my phone into my pocket, made one last look-around and headed downstairs.

When I got to the kitchen, I looked at the clock: ten after eight. Perfect.

When I got down about to the garage, Parker had the truck hooked up to the trailer and the whole rig pointing toward the road.

Suze was standing next to the sawhorse and I walked over to her.

"Lookin' pretty scary, there, Mr. J.D.", she said.

"Yeah, you weren't quite so cavalier the last time you saw me in this get-up." I looked at Zeus' gear – it was all there. Good.

"I'm glad I'm not the Bransons", she said. And I fist-bumped her.

Parker walked up and said, "I guess we're good to go."

"Did you get the two flakes of hay?"

"Sure did. I think all we gotta do, now, is to get the kids into the trailer and blow on outta here. What time is it?"

Suze looked at her phone and said, "Eight-eighteen."

"Good", I said. "Right on schedule. Okay, let me put these sacks into the truck, then we'll go get the horses."

And, just like always, Ceres walked in, just as pretty as you please, and Parker hooked her lead rope to the clip on the wall. He'd put a little hay in her hay net, already, and she took to munching.

I put Zeus' halter/reins thing on his head, then his fly mask. I tested the lights so they were in the correct spot on his forehead, and ran the little control wires up between his ears and down his mane, where I attached them to it with a little braid. The control box was secure, right about at his withers.

Then, we put his saddle pad and saddle on, tightening the girth, but not too tight for the ride to our destination. He was ready.

Parker took him into the trailer, tying his rope to the wall.

"Welp", I said. "Let's do it."

Parker closed and latched the trailer's doors, tapping it twice with his hand for luck or something.

"Back seat", he said to Suze and she nodded.

We all mounted up and Parker said, "Well, here goes nothin'. You good?", he asked me, as he put the truck into gear and we began to move.

"Oh, yeah. Let's go scare the shit out of some assholes."

And we fist-bumped and Suze patted me on the shoulder from the back seat.

We were off.

CHAPTER 34

"I'm gonna take kinda the back way", said Parker. "I don't think we wanna be pulling this thing down 9G – it's a busy road, especially on a Saturday night. Plus, if we go that way, we'll have to pass through several populated neighborhoods and I'm afraid we'll stick out like a sore thumb."

"You going down Centre Road, then?", I asked.

"Yep. Then, we'll go west on Fiddler's Bridge to North Quaker and south on that. It intersects with Crum Elbow Road and we'll go in that way. Probably take us about the same amount of time as it would getting over to 9G and down."

"The horses seem pretty quiet, back there", said Suze. "Are they always like that?"

I smiled and said, "Oh, yeah. They're used to riding in the trailer. Hell, they rode in it all the way from LA - and that took us four days."

"That must've been quite a trip", she said.

"It was an experience, I'll say that. But they were great the entire way. You should've seen the looks on their faces when I finally pulled into the farm, that first night, and took them down to their new pasture. They thought they'd died and gone to heaven – there was actual grass!"

"Alright", said Parker. "We're all set, right? Once we get down there, I'm gonna stay on Matuk and not turn onto Kilmer, the way we went before. Matuk curves around and intersects Kilmer, again, right at the Bransons' place. I'll pull up a hundred yards or so past their property – up along that little forest along in there and get up onto that grassy area. There aren't any streetlights along in there, so we should be just about invisible."

"Cool", I said.

Then, it grew quiet in the truck, with each of us thinking about what lay ahead.

I took the opportunity to get into character. I could feel my eyebrows lowering and tensing. I worked on steeling my soul. Because this wasn't going to be J.D. Spencer who was riding up on the Bransons, this was going to be a beast from the great void.

Parker knew enough not to talk to me, anymore, and Suze must've taken the hint, too, because we rode in silence for the next twenty minutes.

"Here's Crum Elbow", said Parker, and he turned onto it. "A couple of miles and we'll hit Matuk."

Even though it was a Saturday night, there was virtually no traffic. Once we got onto Crum Elbow, we didn't see a single vehicle, other than one set of taillights, maybe a mile in front of us.

"Matuk", he said, slowing down. "At some point before we get to Kilmer, I'm gonna pull over and we'll tape the lights."

"Oh, shit – I'd forgotten about that", I said. "We got tape?"

"Yep – right there in the glove box."

I opened it and pulled out two rolls of black tape. We would get out of the truck and tape up our tail, brake and reverse lights. And Parker always doused the headlights when we got close to our destination – all to help ensure that it would be almost impossible to see the black truck and trailer.

Matuk ran straight for about a quarter of a mile and then curved to the right. Once we'd negotiated the curve, he stopped. "Wait. The dome light", he said, reaching up and turning it off. "Okay – now."

We both got out and I went to the back of my side of the trailer and he went to his. Ten seconds later, the trailer's lights went dark. Then, we did the same thing with the truck. We now had no lights in the back of us.

We got back in and he moved forward, slowly.

"Comin' up", he said. "Right-hand side. Killin' the headlights." And he turned them off.

And we all looked over as we came to Kilmer and there was the Branson house. There was a spotlight on the roof of the garage, lighting up the driveway, along with Branson's parked truck. Her car must be in the garage, I thought – if she's home, that is.

Interestingly enough, the light over the front porch was not lit. A little weird, but okay, I thought. It'd make us pretty invisible right up 'til the last minute.

We saw lights burning in what was obviously the living room, as defined by the large picture window. A couple of other windows had a little light shining through them, but that was probably ambient light from the living room. Or the kitchen. Or something.

This end – the end of the house facing us – was dark.

Parker was barely moving, maybe doing four or five miles an hour, and he was peering over to the side of the road. "Here's the tree line. I'll pull up onto the shoulder."

And he got the rig right up next to the trees, several feet off the roadway.

"You ready?", he asked, quietly.

"Oh, yeah", I said. "Suze – you wait here. If a car or anything comes by, duck your head so your white face can't be seen."

"Okay."

I grabbed the two sacks that were sitting at my feet and Parker and I both got out, making sure not to slam our doors.

He went around to the back of the trailer and opened the door, while I sat the sacks on the ground. As he climbed up into it to get Zeus, I went back to the truck and grabbed the two flakes of hay off the floor of the back seat.

By the time I got back to the rear of the trailer, Parker was backing Zeus out of it. I stepped up and stuck a flake in Ceres' hay net and the other one into Zeus'. "Okay, little angel – we're gonna take a little walk, right now. We'll be back in just a few minutes. You eat and your brother'll be right back, okay?" I gave her a pat on the neck and got down out of the trailer.

"Ready?", whispered Parker.

"Yep."

And he gave me a leg up onto Zeus' back. I got my feet into the stirrups and fiddled around with the cloak so I wasn't sitting on it – it was cut all the way to my waist in the back and I finally got it to fall down on either side of Zeus' flanks.

I pulled my balaclava down over my face and got it situated. Then, I flipped the hood up over my head. I scootched around in the saddle for a couple of seconds, making sure I was good and comfortable.

"Okay", I said. "Hand me the sacks."

Parker handed them up, one at a time. I felt for the brick. I'd leave that one on the bottom, in my lap, or really, my crotch. The other one – the one with the rocks in it – would ride on top of the one with the brick and the message.

I grabbed the reins and said, "Now."

"Good luck", he whispered. "Get right on back here." And I reached down and we did a modified high-five.

I turned Zeus and we walked up the tree line, which only took us a few seconds. When we got to the end of it, I looked off to my left, toward Branson's. I had a nice open expanse of lawn and there was only a gentle slope up toward the house. I reached down and turned his lights on, then I did the same with mine.

"Alright, son – you ready?", I whispered to Zeus. "Let's go." And I nudged him forward with my heels.

The walk across the lawn only took us fifteen or twenty seconds, then I stopped him before he got to the sidewalk running from the front steps to the driveway. I didn't want his big hooves clip-clopping on it.

I turned to our left. We were now facing the house, about twenty feet from that front step.

"Now", I said, nudging him again. And we walked a few feet forward before I stopped him.

I looked at the front storm door and was glad to see that the bottom third of it was pretty obviously aluminum. I didn't really want to break the window in it, so I'd aim low in order to hit the metal. Besides, that would make a single, quick, loud sound and probably wouldn't attract the suspicion of any neighbor who might hear glass breaking.

I looked into the picture window and could see the wife – Sheila – staring at something across the room. TV, I thought. Good. I couldn't see Frank, but I saw her mouth moving so she was obviously talking to him and he was out of my view.

Okay, I thought. Here goes……

And I grabbed the sack holding the rocks and, using the rope that was its drawstring, began to swing it back and forth at my side. Once I had a little rhythm going, I windmilled it…..once…..twice……and, on the third time, I let it fly right at the bottom of the storm door.

WHAM!

Holy fuck, that was *loud!*, I thought.

I quickly backed Zeus off a few steps, so we were about twenty feet from the porch again.

I started counting down in my head: five, four, three, two –

And the porch light went on and the front door opened, revealing a guy standing there.

Because the light was more or less in his face and we were pretty far away, we were out of his range of vision. He looked at the door – probably to check to see if it was broken or not. Then he looked down and spied the sack.

When he looked up again, I nailed Zeus in the ribs and we shot forward.

By the look in his eyes, I knew the very millisecond that he saw us. In another half-second, we were ten feet from him and I hit the back of Zeus' front legs with my toes and up he went onto his hind legs. And, when he did that, his front hooves were a good fifteen feet off the ground, his head about twelve feet high and my head up there about ten feet.

Branson looked like he'd seen a ghost.

Just as all that happened, the wife peered around the door.

And she screamed.

God love him, just like he'd done all those other times, Zeus stayed up on his hind legs for a good four or five seconds, while I did nothing but stare directly at Branson from under my hood, my red lights boring into him.

He fell back and hit the half-open front door. Of course, with his weight hitting it, it swung open all the way and he fell right on his ass, knocking his wife back as he did so. He screamed, probably not only from what he was seeing, but from falling down, too.

Instantly, I realized that he couldn't slam the door because he was lying there against it. Good.

I grabbed the other sack and windmilled it once, then let it go, directly at his crotch.

Instinctively, he reached up as if to catch it, but couldn't. It hit its mark.

"Open it", I said in my ninja horseman stage whisper.

He looked down at the object more or less lying in his lap. And he tried to back away from it like it was on fire or something.

"Open it!", I said again, a little more forcefully, this time.

Then, I had Zeus sky again and both of the Bransons screamed again.

Scream your fucking lungs out, you assholes, I thought.

Then, I turned Zeus and, nudging him a little harder, we trotted off into the darkness.

A couple of seconds later, I heard the door slam.

Once we were thirty or forty feet away from the porch, I dug into Zeus again and he broke into a canter. We hustled back to the tree line and were there in no more than a few seconds.

I pushed my hood down and my mask up onto my head so I could see a little better and there, dead ahead, was the trailer.

Parker was standing next to the door and I saw Suze standing across from him.

"Go", he said to her and she ran around to get back into the truck.

I stopped and jumped down, handing Zeus' reins to Parker, who hustled him right up into the trailer. I stood at the back door. A few seconds later, he jumped down and I closed and latched the door.

Then, we both ran around to our respective doors and jumped into the truck.

Parker fired 'er up and pulled out onto the roadway. After a couple hundred yards, he turned the headlights on again.

We knew that Matuk wound around to meet up with Crum Elbow again – it was actually a big circle - so we kept going straight on it. Just before we got to Crum Elbow, Parker pulled off to the side again and we both jumped out, ran to the back of the truck and the trailer and pulled the black tape from all the lights.

None of us had said anything, yet, and we didn't until he made the left onto Crum Elbow Road.

Then, Parker looked over at me and asked, "Well?"

"Worked like a charm", I said. "A fucking charm."

Frank Branson was shaking, leaning his back against the door. Through his haze, he had the sneaking suspicion that his bowels had let go a little when that thing hit him down there.

"Frank! *FRANK!*", his wife yelled, her hands up to her mouth and bent half over. Her whole body seemed to quake. "What *was* that?!?"

Frank was gasping for breath and he saw dark little spots swimming before his eyes. His knees began shaking and he reached out for Sheila.

"Frank!", she half-screamed, grabbing his hand. Even in her over-the-top agitated state, she could feel that his hand felt a little cold and clammy. "Let's get you over here and sit down", she said, leading him slowly to the nearest chair.

"I-I-I think I'm okay", he said, though the color had drained out of him.

When they got to the chair, he sat down heavily, still breathing hard.

"Put your head between your knees", said Sheila, pushing down gently on his shoulder.

"Nah – I think I'm a little better, now. I think I just hyperventilated."

"Let me get you some water", she said. And, although she was still terrified, she had shifted into triage mode.

"No. No water. But just bring me a drink – straight. I don't care what it is." He began to feel a little better – at least he didn't think he was going to pass out any longer.

Sheila rushed to the kitchen, found a bottle of Wild Turkey in the cabinet and poured half a glass. She drank it and refilled it before half-running back into the living room.

"Thanks", said Frank, taking it from her shaking hand with a shaking hand of his own. He tossed it back. "Another?"

She hustled back into the kitchen and brought the whole bottle back with her. She took another swig straight from it before pouring some into his glass.

"Frank – what *was* that?" Now that her husband had settled down a bit and she was pretty sure he wasn't having a heart attack, Sheila's own fear returned.

"I don't know", he said. "I've never –"

"What's that?", she interrupted, pointing over at the sack on the floor next to the door.

Frank looked over at it and said, "I don't know."

"What's that smell?", she asked, sniffing the air.

"Oh. Oh, Jesus", said Frank, remembering. "Look – I have to run into the bathroom for a minute. Can you do me a favor and bring me a clean pair of pants out of the bedroom?"

"Oh, Frank", said Sheila, standing up.

"I'm sorry", he said, somewhat sheepishly. "But when that thing hit me down there, I – uh –"

"It's okay, dear. You go in and get yourself cleaned up and I'll get you a clean pair of pants. Underwear, too?"

"Uh, yeah – okay. Thanks."

And Sheila headed for the bedroom as Frank kind of waddled to the bathroom.

Five minutes later, they had reconnoitered in the living room.

The sack was still there, lying on the floor of the foyer.

"We'd better look", said Frank, nodding in its direction. "I'll get it." And he walked over, picked it up and carried it back into the living room. He sat it on the coffee table with an audible 'thud' and they both sat on the couch.

Frank untied the heavy string and peered inside, with Sheila leaning in to look, too.

"There's a piece of paper", he said. "And a brick."

He reached for the note, pulled it out and opened it, holding it in front of him so both could see.

And, together, they read…….

Frank and Sheila Branson…….

This is your second and final warning.

Do NOT go ahead with your plans for tomorrow.

You have two choices:

- **Call off your plans and continue to prosper; or,**

- **Continue with them and suffer the consequences**

Choose wisely.

~ The Specter from the Darkness

"Oh, Frank", said Sheila, her hand going to her mouth again.

"What…is…this?", he asked. "What the fuck *is* this?"

"The note, the knife – now this!", she said. "And that *thing*! And was that a horse?!? It was a horse, wasn't it?"

"I – uh – yeah, I think so, but it all happened so fast. I thought it was gonna kill me!"

"Was it a person? A person on a horse?"

"I don't know, honey, but it must've been. But I've never seen a horse that big or – fuck! – anything like that before."

"Well, what does it mean? What does this mean?", she said, picking up the note.

"You can read it as well as I can", said Frank. "Whatever it is – whoever it is – wants us to cancel, tomorrow."

"Should we call the police? I mean, we were *invaded*, Frank. That thing *invaded* us!"

"Hold on, hold on." He took another slug of his drink. "We can't call the fucking police. Fer chrissakes, the first thing they'd ask us is about our plans and that'd fuck up the whole thing. Could, maybe, get us into some kind of trouble if they pressed us too hard. I mean, we couldn't say that our plans are to hand out candy to the fucking kiddies."

"Well, what *are* we going to do?"

"I dunno. I gotta think about it for a few minutes."

CHAPTER 35

"So – spill", said Parker as we cruised up Crum Elbow.

Suze was leaning up between the two front seats.

"Put your seatbelt on", I told her.

"I wanna hear", she said.

"Well, it went smooth as silk. Really. We walked right up across the lawn, I got us situated maybe twenty feet from the front door, then we walked up and I flung the sack. Oh – I hit the aluminum part on the bottom of the door, so I didn't break a window. And that was loud as fuck."

"Yeah – we heard it from down at the rig", said Parker. "And a couple of screams, too."

"Yeah – they both screamed. Anyway, when Zeus and I skyed, ol' Branson fell back against the door and went right down on his ass. He even knocked into his wife, who'd come to the door to see what was happening. And, when I flung the sack with the note in it, I got him right in the 'nads – or thereabouts."

"Nice", said Parker and Suze said, "Ooh, I bet that hurt."

"I don't think he was thinking about the pain, right then. He was fighting for his life – or so he thought. I had to say 'Open it' twice and I still don't know if it registered. But rather than hang around, we split. We just left him on the ground and the wife looking like she'd seen a ghost."

"He'll open it", said Parker. "No doubt."

"Think it'll work?", asked Suze.

"Who knows?", I said. "But, really, I kinda doubt it."

"Well, they'll stew in their own fucking juices, anyway", said Parker. "And, hell – they can't do anything. I mean, they're not about to call the cops and complain, right? That'd be the last thing they'd do."

"That'd be funny", I said, chuckling. "Officer – this, this *thing* showed up and I think he was on a horse. And they both had these little red eyes. And he flung this sack at me telling me to cancel our plans for tomorrow."

I deepened my voice and continued, "And what plans would those be, Mr. Branson?"

Parker and Suze both laughed at that and Parker reached over and we low-fived.

"Here's Quaker Lane", said Parker. "We oughta be home in fifteen minutes."

"Pie", I said.

"Yep – pie", said Parker.

"I like pie", said Suze.

"And you're gonna get some", said Parker.

"Hey", I said. "As soon as we get home, we gotta call Ron. And Mike. Oh, and Suze – maybe you'll want to call Gretchen. Either Parker or I will be glad to talk to her, but we don't want to spend all night on the phone."

"Why don't I call her now?", asked Suze.

"Okay."

A few seconds later, Suze was telling Gretchen that our mission had been a success and that we'd delivered the note and that we were on our way back to the farm.

I said, "Tell her it all went smooth as silk and we'll fill her in on the details in the morning."

"Did you hear that, Gretchen? Good. Yep, I'm safe. And I'm going to have some pie with these guys, then I'll go on home. I'll see you in the morning. Yep – love you."

A few minutes later, we pulled back into the farm.

"Why don't Suze and I take the kids home and you deal with the rig?", I said to Parker.

He nodded.

I climbed up into the trailer, untied Ceres, backed her out and handed her lead rope to Suze. "Hang here for a sec while I get Zeus", I said.

When I'd gotten him out, the four of us walked over to the sawhorse and I untacked him, placing his saddle and pad on the crossbar, taking his fly mask off and laying it on top of the saddle. "We'll put this stuff away in a minute", I said.

We walked the kids down to and through their gate, taking their halters off when we'd gotten them into the pasture.

"Treat time", I said, pointing at the can that sat just outside of it. We each gave the kids four or five treats.

"I'll put Zeus' tack away", said Suze. "I know right where it goes."

"Deal. Thanks. And bring his fly mask to me, okay?"

"You got it."

Soon, with everything put away, the three of us headed up to the house. She handed Zeus' mask to me.

"Hazelnut pecan or maple pumpkin?", I asked when we'd gotten situated in the kitchen.

"I don't know", said Suze. "They both sound pretty interesting."

"Bring 'em both over", said Parker.

I set the two pies on the table, tossed three forks down and got the whipped cream out of the fridge. "Sodas?" They both answered in the affirmative and I got out three cans of Diet Sprite.

"Good idea on the diet soda", said Suze. "Gotta make sure we watch our calories."

Parker plopped the whipped cream all over the tops of both pies, then said, "Dig in."

And, for the next couple of minutes, forks flew between the two pies as we each jockeyed for position on the next forkful.

"We gotta call Ron", I said with my mouth full. It came out sounding like, "Wugahcawah."

"Huh?", asked Parker.

"Ron", I said, after swallowing.

I hit him on speed dial and turned on the speaker.

"Yo", he said, answering.

"Yo, yourself", I said. "I've got Parker and Suze, here, with me."

"Hi guys", he said and they returned the greeting.

"Well?", he asked.

"Done", I said. "And it went perfectly. We scared the shit out of the Bransons, delivered the note and got outta there unscathed."

"Excellent. Good work. And, my friends, I've got a little piece of news for you, too."

"What?"

"About fifteen minutes ago, Branson's phone lit up. So, I flipped the switch on our little magical box and listened in to the conversation."

"Yeah? What happened?"

"He called that guy Gallagher who, I guess, is his second-in-command or something. Anyway, your boy, Branson, sounded pretty shaky and half-drunk."

____

And Frank Branson had called Eric Gallagher, primarily because he was freaked the fuck out.

Using his own phone, he told Sheila that he just had to make the call.

"Are you going to tell him what happened?", she asked him.

"Yeah, pretty much, I guess." He took another swallow of bourbon, straight. "I mean, this was, like, over-the-top, honey. I've just got no idea who this might be or who's behind it. I think I've gotta run it by Gallagher."

"What about tomorrow?", she asked.

"What about it?"

"Are we still going to go ahead with our stuff?" She stared at him with frightened eyes. "Oh, Frank." Frank looked at her and he could see that she was pretty pale and had some red splotches riding up her neck. She was still obviously very shaken.

"I don't know – but I think so. I mean, we can't let one….one….whatever it was….stop a movement of – tomorrow, anyway – fifty people. I mean, can we?"

"What does that mean, though?", she asked, pointing at the piece of paper on the coffee table. "What does 'suffer the consequences' mean? Jesus, Frank, whatever that was could burn our house down or come after us, physically. I didn't bargain for this."

"I know, honey. It is a little scary." He sat there for a little while, then took another glug. "You know, sittin' here, I just thought of something."

"What?"

"What if…..what if I got a couple of the guys to come over for the next few nights? You know, maybe hang around and keep an eye on the place. Sort of like bodyguards. If that thing shows up again, maybe they could blow his ass away or something."

"You mean shoot it?", she asked. She shook her head. "That won't work, Frank. The self-defense laws about home invasion – at least in this state – say that the owner can shoot an intruder – but, inside the house – not just somebody – or some *thing* – on your property."

"Well, maybe they could shoot *sort of* at it. You know, to scare it – or him – away."

"Well, we'll see. Jesus, I hate this." She took another swallow of her drink.

"Me, too. But I gotta call Gallagher, now." He hit speed dial.

"Hullo?" Branson heard rustling. "Is that you, Frank? What time is it, anyway?"

"Sorry to wake you up, man. I did wake you, didn't I?"

"Yeah, whatever. What's up?"

"I gotta tell you what happened a little while ago."

And, for the next couple of minutes, he told Gallagher about the – *thing* - and the horse and the fact that they'd both had little red eyes and that the *thing* had thrown a sack at him and it had a note inside that threatened both him and Sheila if they didn't cancel their plans for tomorrow.

"What the fuck, Frank? Are you shitting me? Wait – you've been drinking, haven't you? You're half-slurring your words."

"Yeah, I've had a couple – but not 'til that thing was here. I gotta tell you, man, it scared the living shit outta me." He didn't share the fact that it literally *had* scared the shit out of him.

"Ah, Jesus, Frank. You expect me to believe that?"

"Eric – I don't care if you do. Sheila's sitting here, right next to me, and she's as scared as I've ever seen her. It happened, man. It really, really happened. I am *not* shitting you."

"Well, alright – if you say so. And you say the note says for you to cancel tomorrow, right?"

"Yep, or we'll - and I quote – 'suffer the consequences', whatever that means."

"Oh. 'The consequences', whatever the fuck they are", said Gallagher. "Look man, we've put a lot of time and effort into this thing. And Sheila and her group have, too. Now - and this is just me talkin' – to cancel all of that just because some – I dunno – some goofball on a horse got up in your face, well, that just don't seem right."

Branson was silent for a minute, thinking.

"Hold on, Eric", he said and put his hand over the mic and addressed Sheila. "Gallagher says that a lot of people have put in a lot of time and effort into tomorrow, including you and your girls. And he says that just because that happened – just one guy – that we shouldn't cancel."

"I don't like any of this, one bit, Frank", she said. Then, thinking about it for a few seconds, continued, "But he might be right."

Branson uncovered the mic again and said, "Yeah – I just told Sheila what you said

and she agrees with you. She's still scared, but my wife is a champion." And he leaned over and kissed her on the cheek.

"So, we still on?"

"Yeah. We're still on. But, tomorrow, let's talk about this a little more. I think it might be a good idea if a couple of the guys could come over and kind of guard the place for the next two or three nights. Just in case that thing shows up again."

"Yeah, okay. Let's talk about it tomorrow. Maybe we can rustle up a few guys. We'll see."

"Alright, man. And, thanks. But I gotta tell you, we're kinda freaked. You've never seen anything like that, before. I'll guaran-goddam-tee you that."

"Sounds like it, man." But, in his mind, Gallagher wondered. Branson's story was just a little over the top. He wondered if, maybe, Branson was getting cold feet and, just maybe, he'd concocted some cockamamie story to try and put the kibosh to their plans.

"Alright, then, Eric. It's full steam ahead. I'll see you in town tomorrow."

"Yep. I'll get there a little early, just in case some guys show up ahead of schedule. Now – go to bed. And put a cork in the bottle, okay?"

"Right. See ya."

And he disconnected.

––––––––––––––––––––––––––––

Ron had given us the gist of the conversation between the two men.

"So, it's still on", said Parker.

"Yep, guess so", said Ron. "And, just FYI – I had to wipe that conversation from the official record. I still have it on my personal thing, but there's no way I want any mention of the ninja horseman getting around this place. I'd get my ass handed to me if it did. This is our little secret and your Eff Bee Eye doesn't need to know about it. It could land y'all in a heap of trouble. All of us, for that matter."

"Got it", I said. "And, thanks."

'We gotta go to that parade", said Parker. "No doubt."

"Well, don't get involved", said Ron. "Like I said, we'll have an agent or two in place, plus Schmidt. If all hell breaks loose, he knows whose side he's on, but we'd have to extricate him immediately if that happens. And, if you see him, you don't know him at all, okay?"

"Deal", I said.

"I'm coming, too", declared Suze.

"Sure, why not?", said Parker.

"Alright, you guys", said Ron. "I gotta get back to work and finish up a few things here. I wanna get home a little early tonight. I'm supposed to join in a game and it promises to be a doozy. Some dickwad team from Algeria thinks they can beat me and my partner and I wanna clean their clocks."

"Who's your partner?", I asked.

"Some guy from China. A friggin' genius. Actually, I think he works for the MSS, but he won't admit it."

"What's the MSS?", asked Suze.

"Ministry of State Security", said Ron. "The guys who are always trying to hack into our shit."

"You mean that you're partners with one of our enemies?", I asked.

Ron laughed and said, "He ain't no enemy, m'man. He's just a guy doing his job just like the rest of us. Only he works for them and I work for us. And, hey – it's all about the game, right?"

"Do you mean your computer game or the, um, intelligence game?", asked Suze.

"Both", he said, laughing. "It's all just one big game. Alright, you guys – I'll check with you tomorrow." And we disconnected.

Parker shook his head.

"What?", I asked him.

"It's all just one big game. And, y'know, he's right. All of this shit between countries is just one big game that a whole lotta people play, all trying for one-upmanship. And the people – the regular people - just get caught in the middle. Or in the crossfire."

"Don't bum my high, dude", I said. "I'm feeling pretty good, this evening."

Parker chuckled and said, "Me, too. Fuck countries and their shit. We just kicked some righteous ass, tonight."

And he held up his soda can and we joined him in a toast.

A few minutes later, Suze informed us that she had to go. She had to get up before six to get to work. And Parker said, "I gotta split, too. It's been a long day. A good day, but a long one."

"Agreed", I said.

"Look – just leave the pies there. We'll polish 'em off tomorrow", said Parker, standing up. "Better put the whipped cream back in the fridge, though. Don't want it to go bad."

"I'll get it", said Suze, standing up and taking it from the table and putting it in the refrigerator.

"Come here, you guys", I said, standing up. "We all need a group hug."

And we did just that, but only for a couple of seconds. None of us were all that touchy-feely.

Then, they left.

A few minutes later, I carried all the ninja horseman stuff upstairs and put it away, thinking that I'd probably have to use it again within the next couple of nights.

Fuck.

I wished those assholes would just crawl away, somewhere. Absolutely nothing good could come of their goofball radical ideas. They were trying to put the country into reverse.

And, if there's one thing I've learned, it's that you never make any progress if you're moving in reverse.

Oh, shit, I suddenly thought: Mike!

It probably being too late to call him, I just simply sent him a text: "Done! All went well! Will explain in the a.m.".

Then I went to bed.

CHAPTER 36

The Coffee Spot was spookier'n hell the next morning.

Well, not 'spooky' spooky, but fun spooky.

All of the front-of-the-house staff was in some kind of Halloween costume. One of the waitresses was in a black and white skeleton outfit; another was dressed up like a princess; and there was Wonder Woman, a ghost (who had a little trouble seeing out of the little eye holes), and a fifty-pound overweight Spider-Man.

When I sat down, Mike looked at me and picked up his phone, winked and nodded, indicating that he'd gotten my text from last night.

Gretchen came by, all decked out in a witch's costume, complete with a black pointy hat over a long, grey scraggly wig. When she walked over to fill up our mugs, Joe asked her, "Hey, Gretchen – you got any eye of newt and toe of frog on the menu, this mornin'?"

"Yes, my little pretty", she said. "Especially for you."

"You guys look great", said Mike. "Great idea, Gretchen."

"Well, we like to have a little fun", she said. "Plus, we know that a few families with kids'll be in a little later and we thought the kids might like it."

"Are you the good witch or the wicked witch?", asked Hal.

"Depends on who you ask, Mr. Hal. Hey, Bill – I think Halloween came around just in time for your jack-o'-lantern, over there. I'd say he's got about another day or so before it gives up the ghost."

We all looked over at the pumpkin that Parker had carved and brought in a little over a week ago and, yep, it was just this side of becoming pie filling.

"Stood up better than I thought it would", said Parker, shrugging. "Glad it made it 'til now."

"What are you going to put there, next?", Marquardt asked Gretchen. "Some kind of Thanksgiving thing?"

"I really haven't given it much thought", said Gretchen. "The table's too small for a cornucopia, which would be the logical thing, right?"

"Here's an idea", said Parker, looking over at the table. "What if we got a big wicker-type basket and filled it with Indian corn?" He looked over at me. "I saw a bunch of it when we were down at Crockett's, yesterday. Probably pick up some kind of basket, there, too."

"Oh, I like that, Bill", said Gretchen, and the other guys gave the idea the ol' Geezer knuckle-knock, albeit rather half-heartedly because it really wasn't that big a thing.

"Alright,", said Parker, "I'll stop by – probably tomorrow - and pick it all up. And I'll bring it in on Tuesday morning."

"Just bring me the receipt", said Gretchen, "and I'll pay you back."

Parker just waved off the idea.

Right then, Suze walked up to the table, dressed in an all-white judo-type affair, complete with a brown belt tied around her waist.

"Oh, look – our very own sensei", said Joe.

"Not quite, Joe", Suze said, smiling and patting him on the shoulder. "Actually, this is called a ji – like they wear in jiu jitsu. But I don't really practice that. I do Krav Maga, which is a little – or, a lot – different, really. In Krav Maga, we usually only wear a ji on special occasions, not when we're training. And today is a special occasion – it's Halloween – so, that's why the ji."

"Does the belt have any significance?", asked Bob.

Looking down at it, Suze said, "Yeah, well, it does. It signifies the level you're at."

"And what level is brown?", asked Hal.

"It's Level Five – one below a black belt."

"You must be pretty good, then", said Hal.

"I can hold my own", she said.

"Krav Maga will eff you up", Parker said to the table. "You know, it was devised by Israeli military intelligence and anybody who's proficient in it – especially a brown belt like Suze, here – will put you in the hospital before you even know what happened to you. It's rough stuff."

"Oh, I wouldn't go so far as to say that", said Suze, acting a little embarrassed, but I could see the pride in her eyes. "We just have competitions and I guess I've won my fair share."

"So, you'd better behave yourself, Mr. Joe, or Suze, here, will pull a Krav Maga on you", said Gretchen. "Alright – what're you guys gonna have?"

"I'd better get back to my station", said Suze. She bowed at the waist and said, "Kida", then headed off to do her thing.

We all ordered.

Once Gretchen had headed to the kitchen, the talk around the table centered on today's Halloween parade.

"Everything all set?", Bob asked Mike.

"Yep, as much as can be. And, because it's such a nice day, we're expecting a real good crowd. I wouldn't be surprised if over fifteen-hundred people – maybe even a couple of thousand – show up. Should be fun."

"Parker and I are going to be there for a while", I said. "I really want to see a nice, good old-fashioned, semi-small-town celebration."

"You'll have to stop by the building", said Mike. "Grab a burger."

"We'll do that."

"Anything else about any potential problems?", asked Hal.

"Not that I've heard", said Mike. "Fingers crossed." And Parker and I shared a glance.

A couple of minutes later, Gretchen showed up with the grub and we all slapped on the ol' feed bags.

Down in Hyde Park, Sheila Branson's phone rang – probably for the umpteenth time, already this morning.

She was surprised to see Mark Fisher's name come up.

"Well, hello, Mark."

"Hi, Sheila. I know you're busy getting ready for your set-up, today, but I just wanted to ask if you thought it'd be alright if I stopped by your table and, um, said a few words to the crowd."

Damn, thought Sheila. That's all she needed – another detail to deal with.

"Well, gee, Mark – I think it would be fine, just great, if you stop by. But we surely don't have any kind of p.a. system. And it'll be pretty noisy, so I don't know if you could be heard."

"Well, I've got a little mini-thing – it's got a cordless mic and a tiny, but pretty powerful, amp and speaker that runs on batteries. I could just carry it up to your booth and set it on the table. I'd just speak for a minute or so and then take everything with me again."

She tossed that around in her mind for a few seconds. It might not be the world's worst idea if a school board member actually stirred people up a little about what's going on with the schools and how things have to change. Plus, the Moms for Liberty were all about schools.

"Well, sure, Mark – I guess that would be just fine. You know that our Moms are behind you, one-hundred percent. And I think a little mini-talk – especially with so many parents in attendance – might be just the thing. What time do you think you'll want to do it?"

"Well, the actual parade starts at two, right? So, I'm thinking a little after that - say, two-fifteen, two-thirty. There should be plenty of parents around about that time."

"Yep, I agree. I think that time'll work just fine. We'll just wait for you and when you get there, we'll get you all set up and you can do your thing, okay?"

"Oh, that's just great, Sheila. Thank you."

"Thank *you*, Mark, for all you're doing for the children."

And they disconnected.

"Who was that?", Frank asked, as he walked into the kitchen.

"Mark Fisher. You know, the new fellow from the school board. The one that we Moms are holding a lot of hope out for."

"What'd he want?"

"He wants to set up a small portable sound system at our table and give a little address to the crowd about how our schools have to change. He said that, because there'll be a lot of parents around, he might be able to do some good."

"Not a bad idea", said Frank, who was still nursing a hangover and a rather sore crotch. Thankfully, his phone had been quiet, this morning, and he inwardly congratulated himself on having gotten things set up so well beforehand.

"I guess we should both drive, right?", asked Sheila.

"Nah, let's just take my truck. That way, we'll only have to find parking for one vehicle. Plus, you wanna take a table and a few of those folding chairs, right? It'll be easier just to slide those into the back of the van. We can just meet up there after the thing."

"Probably a good idea. What time do you think we should leave here?"

Frank looked at the clock on the kitchen wall.

"Well, you want to get all set up on East Market and you're gonna be right in front of the Farmers' Market, right?" She nodded. "And I've gotta meet the guys at one-thirty — just the other side of there. And we've gotta park, so, I dunno — I'd say we should be out the door no later than twelve-fifteen, twelve-thirty."

"That sounds about right", she said. "Just so we're not rushing around at the last minute, I'm going to go into my office and get those boxes of flyers and our banner and the tape and everything. I'll go out and put them in the van. Will you grab the table and those chairs out of the garage?"

"Sure. Hey — do you know where my camo gear is?"

"I'd imagine it's right in your closet where you left it."

Frank's phone rang — it was Gallagher.

"You okay?", Gallagher asked him when he answered.

"Yeah, I'm fine. We're fine. Still freaked out about that thing, last night, but we're rarin' to go, this morning."

"Yeah, well, you weren't okay, last night."

"I know. And I gotta tell you, man, that was something from out of the movies or one of those action comics. I've never seen anything like that before. And I'm still concerned about that note, but I got to thinkin' about what you said — that it was probably just some leftie piece of shit, tryin' to cause trouble."

"There ya go."

"What I can't figure out, though, is how he knows about both our plans for today. I mean, if it was just The Group - our plans - I'd say that we have a spy in our midst. Same with Sheila's group. But, for this guy – or whoever – to know about both groups is something that I just can't figure out."

"Well, let's just get through today and we can look into it a little later", said Gallagher.

"Yep, today we gotta focus."

"Amen, brother. Okay – I just wanted to check in with you. I'll see you around quarter after one, right?"

"Yep." And they disconnected.

Up at The Coffee Spot, we'd polished off our vittles and the gang was fixin' to leave. The place was a little busier than usual, with a few people standing around, waiting to be seated. We didn't want to come off looking like assholes who were hogging a table, so Bob called the meeting over a little earlier than usual.

When we got outside, Mike caught up with Parker and me.

"You say it went well, last night", he said.

"Yep. Piece of cake", I said. "Scared the shit out of both of the Bransons and we got away clean."

"What'd your note say?"

"Well, it told them to cancel their plans for today or suffer the consequences."

"Consequences?"

"Yeah", I said. "It seems that ol' Frank got drummed out of the Army for being drunk on duty and getting caught in a compromising situation with another soldier – a guy soldier."

Mike's eyebrows went up. "Really?"

"Yup. And - and get this – not long after the Bransons met, Sheila had an abortion. Ron found the records of it."

At this, Mike couldn't help but chuckle. "Great. A big-mouth anti-abortionist, a total pro-lifer, had her own abortion. And, what – her husband, Mister Meal Team Six militia leader? He gets kicked out of the service for getting sloshed on duty and caught in a compromising situation with a *guy*? I gotta tell you, these people are the most hypocritical gaggle of bozos, ever. That whole movement is hypocritical. How can they even be taken seriously?"

"Because to all of those people – not just the Bransons, but the whole movement", I said, "the ideas of truth and integrity and decency mean nothing. They want what they want and they don't care how they get it. Their ends justify any means they come up with. And screw the truth. The Bransons are just a couple of real-life examples, right here in our neck of the woods."

Mike nodded and shook his head at the same time.

"By the way, Mike,", said Parker, "we're gonna blast all of that info out into the public, too, if they go ahead with their things, today. Branson's Army shit and her abortion."

"Sort of like you did with Hylan and a couple of those other guys, right?", Mike asked.

"Exactly", said Parker. "Which reminds me, J.D. – we've gotta think about that. Like, how are we gonna blast it out there? The media, like the other times?"

"Well, yeah – I guess so. And, you're right, we really haven't come up with that part of it, yet. We'll have to get on that, later or in the morning. Oh, and Mike – here's a news flash that you probably already suspected: Ron told us that he learned that, yep, both groups are still on for today."

"Shit", said Mike. "I figured that was going to happen, but I was kind of hoping that…..well, no matter. I'll call Chief Eddings in a minute and tell him."

"I'd imagine Ron's already done that", I said, "but just to make sure, yeah – do that. Call him."

"Alright, I'd better get going. I'm due at the office building in a few minutes to help get everything set up. Really – come by as soon as you guys get there, okay? I don't know what we can do if something goes sideways, but….", and he shrugged.

"Let's just hope for the best", I said. "Maybe those guys'll just galumph along and people will take 'em as just a bunch of overgrown kids, all dressed up for Halloween."

Parker sneered and said, "And maybe the Moms for Liberty will be handing out cookies with cute little smiley faces on 'em? I don't think so, son."

"Well, we'll see", said Mike. "Alright – see you guys up there."

Mike headed for his car and I said to Parker, "A little later, we'll call Ron. I want to see if he can somehow get ahold of the email addys or the phone numbers for Frank's and Sheila's groups."

"Sure. Why?"

"Because I'm thinking that, in addition to sending the Bransons' info to the media, maybe we can send it directly to the members of both groups. That'd really hit 'em where it hurts."

"Ooh, that's cold", said Parker, smiling. "But I like it."

"We should also ask him if he can send the documentation for both of them", I said. "You know, the Army discharge thing or the record of the charges or something. And, I think he said he already has the hospital documentation for Sheila. I can't really remember, but I think he said that. Whatever – if we can get ahold of some kind of official documents, that'd kind of seal the deal, don't you think?"

"Oh, hell, yeah. But even if we can't get that stuff, I think whatever you write would start raising a whole lot of questions among their members."

"Yeah – I'd think so. Alright, look – let's get back to the farm and get all the chores done and maybe I can start to write that stuff before we leave for town."

"Deal. And while you're doing your writing thing, I can put the finishing touches on that piece."

We bumped fists and headed to our trucks.

When we got back to the farm, I walked over and told Parker that I was going to call Ron, right then. I wanted to find out, for sure, whether he had that documentation on the Bransons. I thought he did, but.....

"You think he's up already? Hell, man, it's only a little before six, out there."

'Who the hell knows? He's Ron. He doesn't have a regular clock like we do."

"Well, alright, but he's gonna be pissed when you wake him up."

I reached for my phone and hit speed dial.

"My man!", he said, exuberantly, after the first ring.

"You're up?", I asked.

"Hell, yeah, man. Haven't been to bed, yet. I've got the day off and I plan on sleeping 'til dark. Hold on – let me tell you – we just finished our game a few minutes ago and my Chinese partner and I cleaned those guys' clocks! We had 'em on the defensive all night long. Ah, man – it was a beautiful thing to see. I'm still so psyched - and, I might add, jazzed on a ton of Red Bull – that I won't be able to sleep for a couple of hours, if then."

"Sounds great", said Parker, obviously unimpressed.

"Ah, you're just jealous 'cause you're an old fart, Parker."

"Well, there is that", said Parker.

"Look, Ron", I said. "A while back, when you were doing the background on the Bransons, didn't you say that you had access to their records? Branson's Army record and the wife's abortion record?"

"Yeah. I got 'em on my box at the office. Why?"

"Well, because they're going ahead with their things, today, we want to bring the hammer down on 'em. And, like we did before, we'll send a note out to the local media and all, but we'd also like to send a note to all of the members of both of their organizations."

"No way I could allow those records to see the light of day in the media", said Ron. "No how, no way."

"Alright, maybe we just send the – wait.....tell you what – what if we *don't* send anything to the media – at all. What if we just send a note and copies of those records to their members, like via email or texts? Maybe we do just an inside thing that'll rattle their members' cages enough to throw a monkey wrench into their works."

Parker looked at me and nodded while Ron thought for a minute.

"Okay, look – I can't let Sheila's records go because of the HIPAA laws. That'd bring bad shit down on all of us. But the fact that she was a patient on those dates would skirt it. But just barely. I could give you those. But I think you'd just have to go with the dates and write about it yourself."

"Okay, yeah – I see. I can do that in a way that'll raise a whole lot of questions with the Moms for Liberty. What about the husband?"

"Actually, I found out that, if you've been discharged less than sixty-two years ago, you need the service member's or the next of kin's written request to get the records. Which, of course, we didn't do." He was silent for a few seconds. "But - and go with me on this – but, what if Branson had asked for 'em? And got 'em? And, somehow, the ninja horseman or whoever, got ahold of 'em. Maybe Branson left them lying around on his front porch or something."

"So, you're saying that it's possible that they weren't – um, illegally obtained? That, somehow, Branson got them and then they just got out into the ozone when somebody found them?"

"Yeah, exactly. I know it's a stretch, but…."

"Okay, let us think about it. But, can you send me both of their records? Just so I can read them and help me to write what I have to write?"

"Well, yeah, sure. And I can access my work computer from here at home. Give me a few to dig those things up and I'll email 'em to you. But, like I said, watch yourself with Sheila's medical stuff."

"Deal."

After we'd disconnected, Parker said, "I think you're right. I'm not sure the media would even care about that and it's probably all too complicated for 'em. I mean, these are unknown people and, really, who gives a shit? It's not like a town councilman or a principal or something."

"No, but if shit happens, today, it might come in handy, later", I replied.

"True. But, for now, anyway, I think it's a great idea to just blow it out to their members."

"Yep. Alright, let's get our shit done in the barn and see where we're at."

CHAPTER 37

"Tell you what,", said Parker, "I'll go do the barn chores and you run up and write whatever you're gonna write to send out to those mopes. When I finish in there, I'll be in the garage, working on the thing."

"Yep, okay."

And we went our separate ways.

Once I'd gotten situated at my laptop, I thought about what I wanted to write. It had to be short enough for people to read – too long and they'd probably just skim it or ignore it, altogether. But it had to have enough meat in it to really get their attention. And, hopefully, begin some form of uprising within the ranks. Plus, as Parker was wont to say, it had to be pithy.

Also, should I write two notes – one to Frank's group and another to Sheila's? Or, should I compose a piece that went to both groups, disclosing both of their secrets?

I opted for the former, primarily because the guys in Frank's group might not even know about the Moms for Liberty and couldn't care less about it. The same was true for Sheila's group, only vice versa. I figured that, in most cases, the twain never met. It was probably only in the Branson household that the two groups intersected. Anyway, that was my thinking.

So, I began with the note to The Group……

Frank Branson Is NOT What He Seems. Read On……

There. That might make for a halfway-decent email subject line.

A little while later, this is what I'd come up with…..

Frank Branson is not who you want as a leader. As a matter of fact, you should not even want him in your group. He has a couple of incriminating secrets in his background that you should know about.

When he was in the military and stationed at Camp Humphreys, outside of Seoul, South Korea, he was found guilty of being drunk on duty, driving while intoxicated, illegally discharging a firearm, and caught in a 'compromising position and not in the proper manner of uniform' with another male soldier.

He was found guilty of violating Article 112 of the Uniform Code of Military

Justice; Article 15 (drunk driving); and Article 134 ("prohibited conduct that is of a nature to bring discredit upon the armed forces or is prejudicial to good order and discipline").

He was given a general discharge from the Army and lost his rights to the GI Bill.

That is not the mark of a leader.

Furthermore, less than a year after returning home, he paid for an abortion for his then-girlfriend, now his wife.

Again, he:

- **Got drunk on duty and got caught**

- **Drove drunk, while on duty, and got caught**

- **Carelessly discharged his firearm, while on duty, and got caught**

- **Fooled around, half-naked, with another male soldier, while on duty, and got caught**

- **Got kicked out of the military**

- **Paid for an abortion**

If I were you, I would ask him about it.

And, although he may deny it, there are records to prove it. All of it.

Then, ask yourself, "Is this a person that I would trust or want as a leader?"

Be smart.

Sincerely,

The Specter from the Darkness

There, I thought. A little unwieldy, but not horrible. At least I think I got the point across.

Now, for Ms. Sheila.

First the email subject.....

Anti-Abortionist Sheila Branson Had an Abortion

Ooh, that looks cold, I thought. I mean, Jesus Christ, I'm a total believer in a woman's right to choose. After all, it's her body and her life. And, to write something like this made me feel a little utzy. I mean, if that's what she wanted to do, that was her right. Right?

But, because she was so vociferously anti-abortion and actually tried to stop other women from exercising the very same right as she had exercised, the hypocrisy was just untenable.

Now, if she'd changed her feelings over the years - and had publicly admitted to having a change of heart – that would be one thing. I couldn't really fault her for that. That stuff happens.

But, she didn't. She never admitted it. She just went through life with this holier-than-thou attitude. And that's what got to me.

So I wrote…..

Sheila Branson is a total hypocrite.

As a member of the local chapter of Moms for Liberty, there is something that you should know.

Although Sheila is adamantly and vociferously pro-life and anti-abortion – even to the point of leading regular protests at Planned Parenthood facilities - I'll guarantee you that she never told you that….SHE HAD AN ABORTION.

On August 6, 1994, a young woman named Sheila Stark (now Sheila Branson) had an abortion performed at Auburn Community Hospital in Auburn, NY. She was twenty-two years old at the time.

Has she ever told you that?

If you question this fact, just know that the records exist, in black and white.

Ask her about it.

And ask yourself, is she the leader you really want?

Sincerely,

The Specter from the Darkness

There – that looks okay, I guess.

I printed out both notes and hustled down to find Parker.

He was in the garage.

"Dude – check it out." I held out the two sheets of paper.

"That didn't take long", he said, taking them from me and looking down at them.

He read through both of them a couple of times. "Not bad", he said.

"Well, certainly not the most poetic things I've ever written, but I think I got the points across, don't you?"

"Well, yeah, you got the facts in and I guess that's all that really matters. What made you decide to write two separate ones?"

I told him and he nodded, "Probably a good idea."

I checked the time. While I was looking at my phone, my email chimed. It was from Ron. The subject line read, "Addys". Good – I now had all the email addresses that we'd need.

"Okay – Ron just sent me the addresses."

"Then I guess we're good to go, right?", Parker asked.

"Yep. Okay, let's go over this one more time…..We'll go to the parade and, undoubtedly, those people are going to go through with what they have planned. Then, we don't do anything tonight, because we're not sure if they're going to be home or not. Or, if they'll have a cluster of people show up, afterwards."

Parker nodded.

"So, tomorrow night – same time as before – we pay them a visit. And we'll deliver these two emails – but we'll print them out on the antique paper – along with a cover note from the 'Specter from the Darkness'. And, I'm thinking that, just before we leave here to head to their place, we blast out the email. That way, everything'll pretty much happen at about the same time."

"Yeah, sounds about right", said Parker. "And, if we're lucky, maybe they'll start getting calls from a few of their members just about the time you show up at their door."

"That'd be cool. All hell would start breaking loose around the Branson household." I smiled.

"Alright – why don't you go put that stuff away and we'll get ready to head to town."

So that's what we did.

About forty-five minutes later, we drove into town on East Market Street, then Parker said, "Take that fork on the left – it's South Street. We might be able to find a spot along in there. And I'd suggest we park a little ways away 'cause we don't want to get stuck in traffic later. It's easier to walk a few extra blocks than to fuck around with that."

The first street we came to was Beech and, fifty feet in from the corner, there was an empty spot and I pulled in.

"If we walk up here for three or four blocks, we'll come to the parking lot of the town council building – which, I'd imagine, is full, by now. Anyway, we can walk through there and around to the front and maybe we can find Mike."

We did that and there were four or five grills going, burgers sizzling on each of them. They had a big, long table with a red and white checked plastic tablecloth on it and three or four people were behind it, serving burgers and sodas.

We looked around and didn't spy Mike, so I asked one of the servers if he knew where he was.

"Nope. He was here a few minutes ago, but I don't know where he went. He should be back in a little while, though."

"Okay, thanks."

"Come on", said Parker. "Let's walk around a bit. Check out what some of those stores are doing."

I looked at the time. It was ten after one.

We sauntered up East Market Street, past the CVS and toward the block-long strip of stores, all of which had either tables or racks with their goods on them, out by the curb, so the foot traffic could pass by.

The street was crowded with people, too, and there were a lot of families with their little ones, all decked out in their finest Halloween costumes. It was loud. When they're outdoors, kids don't always use their quiet voices. Plus, they were all excited.

And happy. It was nice to see and experience.

We walked past Samuel's Sweet Stop and Pete's Famous Restaurant and No Sugar and Periwinkle's and Winter Sun and Summer Moon, a clothing store. The Land of Oz toy store was booming – every kid wanted to go in there or play with the stuff that they had on their tables along the street.

When we got to the corner, where Mill Street mysteriously becomes Montgomery Street, we looked over at the Beekman Arms, the famous inn where presidents and Hollywood stars have stayed over the decades.

We crossed Market at the light and decided to walk back down that side of the street.

The Rhinebeck Department Store had their expensive sweaters and winterwear in the window, then came Pegasus Footwear and a rather famous (at least, locally) store, the A.L. Stickle Five and Dime, which carried all kinds of weird and wonderful stuff.

There was a book store, a wine shop and another little restaurant that had tables set up along the sidewalk, trying to be out of the way of the foot traffic, but failing rather miserably.

Up ahead, on our left, was the large parking lot that housed the Farmers' Market.

And, there, right on the sidewalk in front of it, was the Moms for Liberty's table. We stopped, several yards away from it, and looked.

They had two tables put together, with six or eight or ten women sitting in chairs behind them. A number of others were milling around, handing out flyers. The tables held all kinds of propaganda and buttons and bumper stickers and that type of thing.

Parker nudged me in the ribs and pointed with his chin. "Sheila."

"Yup."

By now, most of the families were beginning to head east – the direction we were walking – because they wanted to get down to the firehouse, where all the kids were gathering for the parade.

"You know it's really not a parade, right?", said Parker. "Just a bunch of kids and their folks walking up the street. I mean, there ain't any floats or marching bands or anything."

"Well, yeah, I knew that. I think."

"Yeah - and the shopkeepers toss out candy to 'em when they walk by. It's usually kind of a stampede."

We walked along, more or less caught up in the rush to the firehouse.

When we got opposite the town council building, about a short block-and-a-half from the firehouse, we looked over and spied Mike.

"Let's go over there", I said.

"Good idea. I've about had it with all of these rugrats banging into me."

We walked across the street, which was closed to traffic.

"Hey", I said to Mike, as we walked up to him.

"Hey, yourselves. Glad you guys could make it."

"How's it going?", I asked him.

"Fine. Lotta people – more than last year, I think. Hey – want a burger?"

We both answered in the affirmative and, a couple of minutes later, the three of us found an empty table and sat down.

"Not bad", Parker said with his mouth full, holding up his burger.

"Hear anything about our 'friends' (finger quotes)?", asked Mike.

"Nope. You?"

"Well, I got a call from Eddings a couple of minutes ago and he said that there's a group of men gathering over on Livingston – on the other side of the Farmers' Market. And they're all wearing camo."

"Must be the Branson contingent", I said. "Did he say how many there were?"

"Not exactly, but he figured there had to be fifteen, twenty of them. He's got one of his units sitting there with their eyes on them, though."

We sat there, shooting the shit for another few minutes, then heard some noise coming up the street from our right.

Looking over in that direction, we saw three or four clowns, a Frankenstein monster, Spider Man and a fairy princess, dancing and skipping up the street, followed by a throng of kids and their parents.

"Those are volunteer firefighters", said Mike, pointing at the clowns and the other full-grown revelers. "Every year, a half-dozen or so dress up and lead the parade."

Craning my neck, I could see that the crowd of marchers was nearly a full block long, with probably over a hundred kids and adults walking and waving to the onlookers. Most of the kids carried bags to hold their goodies and a number of kids darted out to pick up this or that piece of candy tossed by people in the crowd.

A couple of short minutes later, they began passing in front of where we were sitting.

Mike suddenly stood up, looked across the street at the Moms for Liberty set-up and, spying something, said, "Oh, God. It's that Fisher guy – the new guy on the school board. And he's setting up some kind of speaker or something – like he's going to give a speech."

"Let's go over and see what it's all about", I said.

And the three of us stood up and walked across Market, weaving our way between the early wave of kids and their folks.

Walking up the sidewalk, we could see that Fisher was standing behind the table with a microphone in his hand.

"Hold up", said Mike. "Let's see what this guy says."

We stood there, a good twenty-five feet away, as Fisher began, "Friends – may I have your attention, please? May I have your attention, please?" A couple of the Moms for Liberty shouted things like, "Hey, everybody! Listen up!"

A number of people stopped along the sidewalk, turning their attention to Fisher. Most of the parents at the front of the parade, walking with their kids, just kept walking, though.

"Hello! Hello! My name is Mark Fisher and I'm the newest member of the Rhinebeck School Board."

Several more people on the sidewalk walked up to listen. At this point, he had a ragtag audience of, maybe, twenty or thirty people.

And, over the next couple of minutes, he disparaged the school system as not being responsive enough to parents' wants and needs. And that the schools were teaching left-leaning subjects and that there was far too much permissiveness as far as the children's reading materials.

"For instance,", he said, loudly, "they have books in the high school library that promote homosexuality and promiscuity. That is an abomination! Plus, our kids are only hearing one side of the slavery issue and are being taught that our settlement of this great nation was actually a bad thing! That the white settlers that moved westward were actually stealing land – when nothing could have been further from the truth!"

"Why don't you give it a rest?", yelled a male voice from the middle of the street, obviously one of the marchers. "Shut that damned thing off and let the kids have their fun!"

"Oh, it's fun you want, huh?", Fisher yelled back. "Well, there's nothing fun about brainwashing our children! And that's what's happening – right here, right now, in Rhinebeck!"

A number of the other onlookers began to boo him, having gotten their courage from the fellow out in the street. Several of them even approached the front of the table, in front of Fisher, and began to shout at him, too.

At that point, several of the Moms for Liberty jumped up and joined in the shouting match, pointing fingers and getting up in peoples' faces. Not that they were the only ones, the onlookers did the same. Within a matter of a few seconds, a crowd had gathered at the tables, with people shouting at each other and Fisher yelling, "Please! Please! Let me finish! Please!"

A woman reached over and tried to turn off his amplifier, sitting there on the table, and one of the Moms slapped the woman's hand away, which brought both sides closer together and, standing there, we could sense that violence was just around the corner.

All of a sudden, a group of men came rushing through the Farmers' Market, all dressed in camo and wearing face coverings.

"Uh-oh", said Parker, nudging me and pointing over toward them.

"Ah, Jesus!", said Mike.

The men converged on the scrum that was taking place around the table and began pushing their way through the crowd that surrounded the table.

We heard a siren coming up the street behind us. Turning around, I could see a squad car with its lights flashing slowly inching its way toward us, hugging the gutter and being careful not to come into contact with the people walking up the street.

The parade had actually stopped and parents didn't know what to do, but they grabbed their children's hands and more or less froze in place, everybody watching the melee in horror.

There was a great deal of pushing and shoving and Branson's gang of goons was shouting all kinds of epithets at the crowd. I had to admit that they were foreboding.

Parker and Mike and I moved forward, too, toward the mess. I turned and saw that the cop car was still a couple of hundred feet away.

Suddenly, one of the onlookers fell backwards, obviously pushed. In trying to keep his feet, he stumbled two or three steps and bumped into a young child – a girl dressed up as the Little Mermaid - and she fell backwards, hitting her head, hard, on the pavement.

"Tanya!", a man's voice shouted as he ran to her. "Tanya!" There was a little pool of blood beginning to form under her head.

Parker and Mike and I swung into action, pushing people away from the little girl and her dad and trying to give them room. We were joined by several others.

"Somebody call 911 – quick!", yelled Mike.

Just then, the police car stopped next to us and four officers jumped out. Out of the corner of my eye, I could see three of them holding their nightsticks out, horizontally, and pushing the crowd back onto the sidewalk.

The other officer came running past us and bent over the little girl.

"She's awake", said the dad, who was also dressed in camo. "But I think she cracked the back of her head when she fell."

"Don't move her", said the cop. "I called for an ambulance before we got out of the car. One's coming from the firehouse, right now." And we heard the siren.

The crowd of marchers dispersed almost immediately, the parents rushing their children to the other side of the street. There was much crying and screaming coming from the little ones.

This was horrible.

<u>CHAPTER 38</u>

"Daddy?", the little girl said as her eyes fluttered open. She tried to sit up.

"I'm right here, angel. But don't move. Everything's going to be alright."

She began to cry. Her father looked up and there was abject fear on his face. "Can't I hold her?", he asked the cop or anyone else who would listen.

"Not yet, sir", said the officer. "The medics will be here in just a few seconds. It's best if we don't move her until then. You can certainly hold her hand, though."

Parker moved forward and got down onto one knee next to the little girl and her dad, while Mike and I stood there, uselessly. "I'm an ex-cop, sir, and I've been down this road before." He looked up, questioningly, at the cop, who gave a little nod. "She's conscious and knows who you are - and that's a good thing. What's your name, little darlin'?", he asked the girl.

"Tanya." Parker looked at the dad and he nodded.

"Well, Tanya – that's a beautiful costume", he said to her. "I think it's the prettiest costume in the whole parade, today."

"Yes. I'm the Little Mermaid", she said.

"All good things", Parker said, glancing up, again, at the dad. He gently stroked her face. "You'll be just fine, honey. Your dad will see to that."

The EMT vehicle was only about a hundred feet away, with lights flashing, but no siren.

"Back up", said the cop to the people gathered around. "Let 'em through. Let 'em through." And the crowd parted dutifully.

I looked over at the group of guys in camo, with the three cops doing their best to disperse them, but they were outmanned and it wasn't working. Until I saw another four cops run from across the street to join them.

"You", one of the original officers said to Fisher, who had his little speaker system under his arm and was trying to make his way through the crowd. "You – stand right there. Don't move. Do not move."

"Who, me?", said Fisher, a look of fear on his face.

"Yeah – you", the cop said, walking up to him and taking him by the arm. "Come with me." And he marched him back toward the Farmers' Market parking lot.

"This is fucked", Branson said to Gallagher, who was standing next to him. "What are we gonna do?" Most of his guys were looking in their direction, obviously for some sort of guidance.

"Damned if I know", said Gallagher. "Fucking cops are crawlin' all over the place, right now. And that kid…..and that's Stone, isn't it?"

"Yeah. I got a look at him bending over her."

Once it got to its destination, the ambulance turned, so its back doors were easily accessible.

Behind it, two police cruisers pulled to a stop and another eight cops jumped out and headed over to the crowd of guys in camo, who were milling about, pretty much rudderless. There was a little yelling coming from them, but it was fairly tepid.

Two EMT technicians emerged from the ambulance and one of them came around to the back of it and opened the doors, grabbing a heavy-looking container.

"Make way", said the cop who'd been there from the beginning.

Parker backed off and walked over next to where Mike and I were standing. "I think she's okay", he said. "Maybe a little concussion and a mean-assed cut on the back of her head, but she doesn't seem to be in any danger."

One of the techs bent over little Tanya while the other said, "You the father?"

The fellow said, "Yes. Is she gonna be okay?"

"We're going to do our best, sir. Can I have your name, please?" The tech had a clipboard and she was poised to write.

"Stone. Fred Stone. And this is Tanya", he said, pointing to his daughter.

While the one tech took Stone's information, the other was busy examining Tanya. He was having her move her hands and legs and, finally, had her sit up. There was blood still running from the back of her head.

The tech reached into his medical box and fiddled around, finally pulling out a large pressure bandage and a roll of tape. Then, he went to work, trying to clean the wound a bit and getting the bandage in place.

Once he was finished, he asked, "Can you stand up, Tanya?" And he helped her to her feet.

"Yes", she said. And I was amazed by the little girl's calmness and her courage.

"Okay, stand right here. Dad – can you come over and hold Tanya for a sec? I wanna get the wheelchair out of the truck."

"Wheelchair?", asked Stone, the distress showing on his face. "Does she need a wheelchair?"

"Just procedure, sir. We want to take her up to Northern Dutchess. The doctors, there, will be able to examine her better and get that wound all cleaned up and sutured."

"Oh. Okay. Can I ride with you?"

"Sure."

"Okay - I gotta call my wife", Stone said, reaching for his phone.

He bent down and said to Tanya, "I'm going to call Mommy, now. Do you want to say hello to her?"

"Yes."

He knew his wife was up at the little park surrounding the Beekman Arms, probably sitting on one of the benches with his other daughter, who was a little too young to be part of the parade. They were to meet there when the parade ended.

He spent a few minutes explaining the situation, then said, "I think she's fine, though.

Yes, I'm sure – that's what the EMT guy told me. But she'll probably need some stitches. Here – wanna talk to her?"

"Say hi to Mommy", said Stone, holding the phone to Tanya's ear.

"Hi, Mommy. My head hurts. But I'm going to get to ride in an ambulance.....I love you, too, Mommy."

"Okay", said Stone, putting the phone back to his ear. "Like I said, I think she's fine........hold on." He touched the EMT tech on the shoulder and asked, "Do you suppose we could pick up my wife and daughter up at the corner where you turn onto Montgomery? They'll be waiting right there."

Receiving an affirmative response, he told his wife where to meet them. "Just be on the corner, waving, when we come toward you. It should only be a couple of minutes. Okay, 'bye."

Two minutes later, with Tanya and Stone in the back of the ambulance with one of the techs, the driver hit the lights and siren and pulled slowly up the street.

The three of us turned our attention to the group of guys in camo and the cops that had confronted them. I tried to spot Schmidt, but with all of them having their faces covered, it was almost impossible, especially having only seen him one time.

Suddenly I made eye contact with one of them and he gave me a little nod. Schmidt.

"That's it!", said one of the cops, obviously the one in charge. "Disperse, now! And I mean *right now*! And take off those goddamned masks, *NOW*!"

"But this is a free country", said a voice from the group. "We have every right to be here."

"And I have every right to arrest your sorry ass for disturbing the peace. Every last goddamned one of you! Now – you want that? Just say the word." And he swept his arm to include the now dozen-or-so officers standing there at the ready. At this point, all of them were wearing riot helmets. I don't know where they came from, but they must've been in one of the squad cars.

"Frank?", one of the men shouted and several heads turned toward Branson, including Gallagher's.

"Well?", asked Gallagher.

Fuck, thought Branson. He knew that several of these guys are spoiling for a fight, but that was a losing proposition. They'd probably all end up in jail – or the hospital. Better to retreat and live to fight another day.

"Come on, Frank", another voice yelled. And that riled up several of the men.

"I said *disperse*!", yelled the cop again, walking up to Frank after realizing that he must be the leader.

"You're first, pal. And take off that mask", said the officer. Frank pulled it down but stood his ground. "Buddy, you've got three seconds.....one.....two....."

"Alright, guys – let's go", Frank shouted. "These assholes don't care about the First Amendment and I'm gonna sue this town for everything it's got!"

"You go right ahead, bright boy", said the cop. "See where that gets you." And he stepped another foot or two closer to Branson.

Frank tapped Gallagher's chest with the back of his hand and said, "Come on, Eric – let's get outta here. Come on, guys, let's go. We're not wanted in this fascist hell-hole of martial law."

And he turned toward the Farmers' Market, only then noticing that the Moms for Liberty's tables had been knocked over and the women were packing up to leave.

"Sheila!", he shouted. "You okay?"

She hurried over to him and said, "What just happened, Frank? We were attacked by the police! And, look", she said, pointing over at Mark Fisher, who was still standing there next to the cop who'd taken him away.

At that point, the officer in charge walked up to the cop holding Fisher and said, "Let him go."

"But he's the one who started all this", said the cop.

"It's all over now", said the officer. "What's your name?", he asked Fisher.

"Fisher. Mark Fisher. And I'm on the school board and I – "

"You are, huh? Well, then, Mister – um – Fisher – you oughta be ashamed of yourself. A little girl got sent to the hospital because of what you started. That any way for a school board member to act? To have kids sent to the hospital?"

Fisher looked a little subdued and said, "I had no idea something like that would happen. Is she going to be alright?"

"Funny time for you to be caring about her, now, isn't it? What the hell's the matter with you, turning a kids' parade - a happy time – into some kind of political event and spewing your nonsense over a loud speaker? Huh? Are you proud of yourself?"

"Well, I, uh – "

"Yeah, you 'uh'. Get your ass out of here, right now, my friend. And we have your name, so in case things go south with that little girl, you can expect a visit from us. Let him go", he said to the other cop. "Go. Git!", he said to Fisher, who turned and quickly walked away.

"They let him go", Frank said to Sheila.

"Oh, Frank – this has been a disaster. I can't tell you how many of my group are freaked out. These are *moms*, Frank! And for them to see a little girl hurt – all because of us – well, I don't think I'll see some of them again." She began to cry.

"There, there, honey", he said, putting his arm around her. "It'll be okay."

She buried her head in his chest, saying, "I've tried so hard, Frank. So very hard."

"I know you have, honey. And this is just a minor setback, you'll see. You're fighting the good fight and it's a fight that needs fighting. You know that and so do I. We'll just re-group and take it from there. We can't give up. Not now – especially now."

He felt her head nod against his chest. "I know", she said, quietly.

"Come on", he said. "Let's go get the truck and drive back here and pick up this stuff. Come on."

And he guided her across the rapidly-emptying Farmers' Market parking lot toward the place he'd parked his truck.

They passed several of his men as they did. A couple of them gave him verbal votes of confidence and an equal number either ignored him or looked in his direction and shook their heads. He spied Gallagher and yelled, "I'll call you later, Eric."

"Sure, Frank", he replied. "Sure."

Thirty minutes later, with all of their gear packed up, the Bransons headed back down to Hyde Park.

Having witnessed a lot of that from across the street, where we'd retreated so as not to get involved any more than we already were, Parker and Mike and I just walked up the street, mostly in silence. We noticed that the whole Halloween event was breaking up. Even the stores were pulling their things off the sidewalk and taking them inside.

"Jesus Christ, guys", Mike finally said. "What a disaster."

"Yeah", I said.

"It could've been a helluva lot worse", said Parker. "Especially if those cops hadn't all shown up when they did. That saved the day. I feel bad about the little girl, though. And her dad. He was pretty shaken up."

"He was all decked out in camo, too", I said. "D'you suppose he was part of Branson's group?"

"Hell, I dunno", said Parker. "But he was walking along with his daughter and he didn't come across the parking lot with those other goons."

"Odd that he was dressed just like them, though — except he didn't have his face covered."

"Maybe he was just dressing up for Halloween and it was all a coincidence", said Mike.

Just then, we heard a blip off to our right — like a siren just being tapped - and, as we looked over, we saw another police car.

"Hey, Mike", said the driver, pulling up next to us and stopping.

"Chief!", said Mike. He walked over to the car and we went with him.

"Guys — this is Chief Marty Eddings. Marty — this is J.D. Spencer and this is Bill Parker."

We each reached through the window and shook his hand.

"You're those friends of Ron's, aren't you? He's told me about you two."

"You're not gonna arrest us, are you?", said Parker, with a smile.

"Not today, anyway", said Eddings, smiling, too. His smile took up his whole face.

Then, he turned to Mike, "That was something, wasn't it?"

"I'll say. It was horrible. But it could have been so much worse if your guys hadn't shown up when they did. They put an end to it, real quick."

"Well, I assigned my best guys - and a few of them have riot control experience. They all knew enough to look and act like bad-asses, but to not exacerbate the situation. I give 'em a lot of credit."

"What about that group of guys dressed in camo?"

"Ah, you mean The Group. Yeah, thanks to your friend, Ron, we've gotten quite a bit of information on them. The leader's a guy named Branson — lives down in Hyde Park. We think they're pretty much a rag-tag group of semi-losers — a couple of them have minor records. But, I gotta tell you, groups like that are — or can be — dangerous. I never thought I'd see the day when this town, this area, would see something like that. The world's going to hell."

"Can you do anything about them?", asked Mike.

"Not 'til they break the law", said Eddings. "And, today came awfully close. We decided to low-key it as much as possible – we didn't want a war on our hands. But we're going to be keeping a close eye on them, from here on out."

Um, we have a plan for that, Chief, I thought. But I kept my mouth shut. Parker glanced at me and Mike had the wherewithal not to say anything, either.

"Alright, gentlemen", said Eddings. "I'm going to run over to the hospital to check on that little girl. I got a report a few minutes ago that said she's doing fine and they're trying to decide whether to keep her overnight or not. I hope not – for her sake. If she's able, she'll be a lot happier if she's home with mom and dad. Alright, y'all have a good rest of your day. And, nice meeting you guys." And we waved as he drove off.

"You know, Mike,", I said, "the ninja horseman's going to visit the Bransons again, tomorrow night."

"Yeah, that's what you said. You still going through with it, huh?"

"Oh, yeah. And we've got the hammer on both of them. Each of them. And they'll know it, tomorrow night. Plus, we're emailing what we have to both Branson's and the wife's groups."

Parker piped up, "I don't think a lot of Branson's guys were all that happy with the way he handled things, back there. I think a bunch of 'em wanted a fight on their hands and they think he wussed out."

"Well, once they see what we have on him, they're gonna be even more unhappy with him, I think."

"Just be careful, is all", said Mike. "Like Eddings said, these guys can be dangerous."

"If it's anything like Friday night, it'll be a piece of cake", I said.

"Well, still", said Mike. "Look, guys – I want to get back to the town offices to see if they need any help in tearing down. So, I'm going back that way, now."

"We're parked down that way, too. We'll walk with you", said Parker.

And, after a couple of blocks, Mike walked over to a few people who were taking down tables and carrying chairs in front of the building.

We all said that we'd see each other in the morning and we headed off to the truck.

A few minutes later, we mounted up and I got us turned around and headed toward home.

"So, what'd ya think of your first Halloween parade?", asked Parker.

I thought about that for half-a-second and said, "Well, Halloween's supposed to be scary, right? Well, that was downright scary."

"Fucked up, is what it was. Assholes", he said.

"Well, maybe we can make a difference tomorrow."

"Hope so."

CHAPTER 39

About halfway home, I said, "Too bad Suze had to work. Well, too bad for Suze, but good for Gretchen. They're almost never busy in the afternoons, so I'd imagine she's thrilled. But the poor kid sounded bummed when she called."

Parker chuckled and said, "She'll be especially bummed when she hears about the little melee. I think that girl likes the action."

"Yeah." A few seconds later, I said, "Hey – we oughta call Ron."

"Prob'ly."

I picked up my phone and hit his number.

"I figured I'd hear from you guys", he said, by way of answering. "Quite the afternoon, huh?"

"Where'd you hear about it?"

"Chief Eddings called me a few minutes ago. And, so did Schmidt. You're the third call I've gotten in the last twenty minutes."

"So, you heard all about it", I said, and it wasn't a question.

"Yeah, pretty much. Eddings filled me in on the little girl - he called me as he was leaving the hospital and said that she can go home in a little while. And he said that his guys did a real good job de-escalating the thing."

"Good news about the little girl", I said. "What a little trouper she was. Cute as hell, too."

"Well, you know her old man's one of Branson's guys, don't you? His name's Stone. And, through Branson's phone, we've determined that he's the guy who threw the brick through the window, the other night."

Parker and I exchanged glances.

"Really?", I asked. "He was just walking with his daughter, today - he wasn't a part of Branson's crew. But he was sporting some camo. Wonder what that means."

"I dunno", said Ron. "Maybe the kid trumped the goons."

"Yeah – either that or maybe he had a change of heart", I said.

"Doesn't explain the camo", said Parker.

"Hell, I don't know", I said. "Ron – what did Schmidt say?"

"He said it was a complete clusterfuck. He said that they were supposed to enter the march as a group, but some nonsense was going on at a table, right near where they were walking. I guess it was the Moms for Liberty table and some guy was shouting over a microphone or something."

"Yeah", I said. "That would be Mark Fisher, that new douchebag on the school board who's trying to ban books and raising all kinds of shit about CRT and so on. And that's what he was doing there, too. A couple of the parents – people who were walking in the parade – yelled at him to shut up and several people who were just watching the thing joined in, too. And a shoving match started and that's when the little girl got knocked down."

Ron said, "Schmidt said he didn't see what started it – he was too far back in the group. But he said that they all stood around with their thumbs up their asses, wondering what to do next. He saw that Branson had a few words with a cop and, then, he told all his guys to stand down. And, basically, leave."

"That's about the size of it", said Parker.

"Here's the thing, though. Schmidt said a bunch of the guys were bitching that Branson backed down so easily. I guess they were itchin' for a fight. Or, at the very least, they wanted to march up the street as a group after the ambulance left."

"Well, the thing started breaking up, then. People started leaving", I said.

"Yeah, but these guys wanted to make a statement. They wanted to 'show the colors' – as Schmidt put it. Like, show the town that they were large and in charge. And a bunch of 'em were pissed that that didn't happen."

"Well,", I said, "at least Branson did the right thing, the smart thing."

"Yeah, but that's not what some of his guys are thinking, according to Schmidt."

"Huh", I said.

"Sounds like there's a little wedge there", said Parker. "Like some dissension in the ranks."

"Well, if Branson gets wind of it - and I'm sure he will — that could be a good thing", I said. "Or a bad thing."

"Uh-huh", said Parker.

"Look — guys — I gotta go", said Ron. "I've gotta write all this up and get it to the boss. I'm'a let you guys go, for now, okay?"

"Yeah, cool", I said. "And thanks for the info."

"Stay chilly", said Ron, "and I'll catch up with y'all later."

Once we'd disconnected, I said to Parker, "This little dissension thing could work to our advantage. If he's been thrown off his game a little, maybe tomorrow night's visit is just the thing to tear down his little domain. Especially once his troops get that email."

Parker nodded and said, "Yeah, maybe. Probably. If those assholes can read."

Down in Hyde Park, the Bransons had finished putting the table and chairs away and were standing in the kitchen.

"Drink?", asked Frank.

"A double."

They'd talked it all through on the drive home, both of them realizing that both of their forays had been just short of disastrous, Frank's worse than Sheila's, though.

Just as they'd headed out of Rhinebeck, Gallagher had called Frank and had told him that a number of the guys were pretty upset that their part in the march didn't come off. That they'd wanted to march up the street, anyway, even after Stone's little girl got carted off in the ambulance and the parade started breaking up.

"What good would that have done?", Frank asked him. "Bunch of guys walking up the street? Plus, it was pretty obvious that we were involved in that little to-do and that cop and those cops weren't fuckin' around. Hell, a whole shitload of us could've been arrested."

"Well, yeah. And actually, Frank, I think that's what some of the guys wanted."

"What — to get arrested?"

"Well, according to a couple of them, we could've been busted for disturbing the peace or something, but that's, like, a misdemeanor. I think those guys would've been proud of that, especially if it made it into the news. You gotta admit, in various spots across the country where that's happened, the guys who've gotten arrested have become sorta mini-heroes to the movement."

Frank thought about that. Shit. That was true.

"Well, maybe", he said.

"Yeah, for real, Frank. Personally, I tend to agree with those guys but, either way, I stood up for you. I told 'em that it was a stupid idea. Hell, their damned jobs could've been at risk. And those guys who have their own businesses maybe could lose work over such a thing."

"What'd they say?"

"Ah, you know – they hemmed and hawed and shit and a couple of 'em grumbled but, for the most part, they heard what I was sayin'. I think I smoothed it over."

"Well", said Frank, "a leader's job is to know when to fight and when not to fight. And the way I saw it, today we were gonna lose. So that's why I called a retreat."

"Yeah, I know", said Gallagher. "But I think it'd be a good idea for you to somehow take the bulls by the horn and address that with The Group. Tell 'em what you told me. And reiterate what I told them. But, to really get 'em a hundred-percent behind you, again, I think we gotta come up with something new. Something where we can do what we wanted to do, this afternoon. You know, make some noise."

"Alright, yeah. I agree", said Frank. "Okay – let's think on it and see what we can come up with. But we oughta do it soon, right?"

"Oh, yeah."

And, once Frank and Sheila had sat down in the living room with their drinks, they dissected the conversation he'd had with Gallagher.

In an attempt to make her husband feel better, Sheila told him that she was sure that there were only a few guys who were bitching and that most of them – especially those who'd witnessed his confrontation with the cop – agreed that he'd made the right decision.

"Shit, I hope so", said Frank. "Gallagher had a point, though. If we'd gotten arrested, we'd have gotten big ups from a lot of people in the movement. Coulda put us on the map."

"There'll be another chance, honey. Probably soon, too. For what it's worth, I was very proud of the way you handled yourself, this afternoon." She raised her glass in a toast. They drank.

"Thanks. And, other than that fiasco with Fisher, how did you guys do, today?"

"Well, a number of people stopped by and we handed out a lot of literature but, you know.....it was early on, before the parade. There's no doubt we would've done better if all that hadn't happened."

"Well, I'm sorry it did", said Frank. "Have you talked to any of your members?"

"Well, just after it happened and we were cleaning up, we had a few conversations. And the ones I spoke with, Frank, weren't at all happy about that little girl getting hurt. A couple of them told me that that wasn't what they signed up for. These are mothers, honey, and they put children first. And, to see what happened, happen, well....." and she trailed off.

"Yeah, I know", said Frank. "It was too bad. I should call Stone, too. But I'll wait 'til tomorrow to do that. Hell, his daughter might be in the hospital." He took a swallow. "And even if she's not, tonight wouldn't be the right time for that."

"Oh, absolutely", said Sheila. "And you should call, too. That's what a leader does."

"Mm-hmm", he said. "God – what a day."

"Ups and downs, Frank. Ups and downs. Don't worry – tomorrow will be a brighter day." She paused. "Should we turn on the TV?"

———————————————

When Parker and I got back to the farm, he said, "Look, I think I'll split for home. We've got nothin' going, right now, and I wanna eat and sack out early. Tomorrow's gonna be a long day."

"Agreed", I said. "And I think I'll do the same."

So, when he climbed down from my truck, he walked over to his.

"Hey", I said, calling to him. "Nice job with that little girl, today."

"All in a day's work, son. All in a day's work. See you in the morning."

Once I'd gotten into the house, I realized that I was tired, too. Probably a little more emotionally tired than physically tired, but tired, nonetheless.

Today was an off day for the Series and the Astros and Mets were tied at two games apiece. Hell, that's too bad, I thought. I could've used a little baseball tonight.

And, for some reason, I wasn't all that hungry, but I thought I ought to put at least a little something in my stomach. I slapped a few slices of ham on some bread and hit it with some horseradish mustard. That worked.

After that, I walked down to see the kids, one last time, for the night. And I found them in the barn. I turned on the lights and checked their feeders and, seeing that they were almost empty, broke a flake of alfalfa in half and dropped the two pieces into their feeding tubs. "There ya go, guys", I said.

And they moseyed on over to check it out, both heads going into their feeders.

"Look", I said. "We're gonna take another ride, tomorrow night. Same as last time. Like an instant replay. You guys good with that?"

Natch, they didn't answer me, finding the hay more interesting than my short little monologue and the ensuing question.

"Alright, good. Okay – I'm going up to the house and hit the hay. Well, not really the 'hay', like you guys have, but it means I'm going to bed, okay? We two-leggeds have weird expressions. I'll catch you guys in the morning."

And I turned, switched off the lights and headed back to the house, thinking a little bit about what had happened this afternoon and the conflicts that are going on right in our own back yard. And everywhere else, for that matter.

What a weird goddamned world, I thought. Here we were, us humans – supposed to be the dominant species on earth - and no matter where in the world you looked, we were fussin' and fumin' and fightin' about all kinds of nonsense. Stuff that really didn't make a goddamned bit of difference in the grand scheme of things.

That, no matter what we did, no matter what we are doing or what we will do, Mother Earth's gonna go along just as pretty as she pleases. The ol' girl's been through plenty of changes – big changes – over the millennia and she always comes out smelling like a rose. And she always will, in her own inimitable way.

And, we - we humans – think that we can control her and everything on her body.

What a crock.

That thinking has to be the most asinine, the most arrogant, the most ridiculous thing, ever. Patently absurd, yet we go on thinking it and we go on fussin' and fumin' and fightin' over shit that means nothing in the long run.

Horses have figured it out. All the animals have figured it out. Trees have figured it out. Insects have figured it out.

Each and every species has figured it out.

They all realize that all of Mother Earth's children are here for a reason. And that we're all connected in some way. And, through ways that none of us understand, we all rely on each other for our well-being and our happiness. Because that's how Mother Earth designed it.

Humans, on the other hand, all-too-often don't fucking understand that.

Sheesh.

I went up the steps to the back door, took off my jacket and made my way upstairs.

I read for about forty-five minutes and then called it a night.

––––––––––––––––––––

The next morning, the Geezers' table was abuzz about yesterday's parade and the fiasco it became.

Everybody, of course, was of the same mind: that it never should have happened.

And, yes, Mike and Parker and I filled the crew in on the details and Parker got verbal tips of the hat for stepping in to help with the little girl. And, according to Joe – who'd watched the late local news – she was released from the hospital early last evening.

"I'm just glad she wasn't hurt worse", said Parker. "Coulda been a whole lot worse."

The entire atmosphere of the place was rather subdued, this morning. The Halloween parade is kind of a big deal in Rhinebeck and it's something the town is proud of so, with what happened, yesterday, it was a blow to the civic pride. And that was reflected in the mood of the place.

Gretchen tried to be her normal more-or-less ebullient self and only missed by a hair.

When she came over to take our order, her pragmatism was a breath of fresh air. "Look, guys – what happened, happened. And it was a bunch of dimwits that ruined the parade for everybody. And, today, they look like the grinches who stole Christmas, if you'll excuse the mixed metaphor. Virtually everybody I've talked to in here's expressed nothing but disgust about it. They're all kind of up in arms about all of this stuff, now."

Suze walked up.

"Guess I missed all the excitement", she said.

"Yeah, if that's what you wanna call it", said Parker.

"Well, we were busy, here, and Gretchen asked me to stay around to help out, so…."

"Yeah - and pay you double-time", Gretchen said, playfully backhanding Suze on the arm.

"Well, there is that", said Suze, with a smile.

We bullshat for another minute or two and then, Suze headed off to do Suze things and Gretchen took our order.

Once we'd all spoken up, Parker said, "Oh, hey, Gretchen – we'll run down to Crockett's today and pick up that corn and stuff for your table, over there."

"Oh, that would be so nice, Bill. Thank you." And she headed off to the kitchen.

"And pie", I said to Parker.

"And pie", he said, with a wink.

Our breakfasts came and we scarfed. And, like always, there was very little conversation during that little exercise.

Several minutes later, Gretchen returned and we all passed our now-almost-clean plates to her.

"I take it everything was to your satisfaction, gentlemen", she said. "Let me take these into the kitchen and get you guys some more coffee."

"Gretchen!", Suze called from over by the register. "This gentleman would like to speak with you."

Being nosy, we all looked over and, before I was able to turn around, Parker said, "Holy shit."

And there was that guy, Stone, standing there.

"Yes? Can I help you?", Gretchen asked as she walked up to him.

"Um – can we, maybe, step outside for just a minute? I have something to tell you – a confession of sorts. But I'd like it to be private."

"Uh, yeah – okay – follow me."

And the two of them walked out the front door. Unfortunately for us nosy Geezers, they were out of our line of sight.

"What's that? Who's that?", asked Joe.

"That's the father of the little girl who got hurt at the parade, yesterday", said Mike. "Parker helped him out while they waited for the ambulance."

"Wonder what he wants with Gretchen", said Hal.

I looked over at Parker and he gave a little shrug and a half-nod.

"Look, guys", I said. "Don't ask us how we know this, but Parker and I found out that he's the guy who threw the brick through the window, the other night."

"What?!?", was the general reaction from Bob and Joe and Hal. Even Mike, because we hadn't passed on that little bit of intel to him, yet.

"Yeah", I said. "We don't really know, but we think that he might be somehow involved with that group who showed up at the parade, yesterday. He wasn't with 'em, though – he was just walking along with his daughter."

'Well, what the hell's he doing here?", asked Joe. "Maybe we oughta go check on Gretchen."

As we sat there, babbling on - rather stupefied, I might add - the front door opened and in walked Gretchen. And Stone. They were both looking at us.

"Come on", she said to him, leading the way over to our table.

CHAPTER 40

"Um, guys – can we talk to you for a minute?", Gretchen asked, as they approached.

I could see that everybody was as dumfounded as I was.

"Uh, yeah – sure", said Bob, always the leader.

"This is Fred Stone", she said, "but his friends call him Flint." She smiled at him and, rather sheepishly, he attempted a little smile, too.

"Well, you saw that Flint and I just had a conversation, outside. And, to his great credit, he admitted to being the one who threw the brick through our front window, the other night."

Six sets of eyebrows shot up.

"And, he's offered to make restitution for any of the costs we incurred", she said. "And he said that he recognized you, Bill, when he came in and he wants to thank you for helping his little girl, yesterday."

We all kind of looked around at each other, then Bob said, "Pull up a chair, Flint. Sit down and talk to us."

Parker reached over to the next table and grabbed a chair while we all scootched over to make room.

"Gee, thanks", said Stone, still uncertain where he stood. But he accepted the chair and sat down.

"I'll get you a mug", Gretchen said to him.

"Okay, I'll go around the table", said Bob. "This is Joe. And Hal. And Mike. And J.D. And you kinda already know this guy – Bill Parker." We all nodded and smiled. Why not, right?

"I recognize you two guys from the parade, yesterday, too", said Stone, indicating Mike and me.

"And, Bill – I simply cannot thank you enough for what you did for Tanya and me, yesterday. I was so scared and the fact that you talked to her - and she was able to talk back – about saved me from a heart attack. Thank you, again, sir."

"In a prior life, I trained for that sort of thing", said Parker. "And, you're welcome. By the way - call me Parker – everybody else does. Well, 'cept for Gretchen."

"So, you're the guy who tried to wreck this place, the other night, huh?", asked Joe, pointedly.

Stone looked down at the table and said, "Yeah. I am. And I'm totally ashamed of it, too. It was just so wrong."

"Why'd you do it?", Joe pressed.

'Well, it's kind of a long story", said Stone. "Alright, look – I'll start at the beginning.....I have to admit that I haven't necessarily liked the way things are going in this country, lately. So, somehow, I started listening to a bunch of those right-wing radio shows. And catching Fox News, every once in a while, too."

We all just stared at him.

Gretchen walked up and sat a mug down in front of him and filled it, raising the pot and her eyebrows at the same time, to the rest of us, who all gave a little nod. She walked around the table, topping them off.

"Hang on, ma'am, if you can", said Stone. "You should probably hear this, too. If you have a minute, that is."

"Sure", said Gretchen.

"Anyway, I got all caught up in what those people were saying and, if you listen a lot, you begin to think that they're making a lot of sense." He took a sip and looked at Gretchen. "I'm telling these guys how I got wrapped up in this right-wing stuff." She nodded.

"Honestly, I didn't know what to think. According to all that stuff, the country's in a nose-dive. And, there's, like, only one way to fix it. And that's to almost overthrow the government and a lot of the institutions. Start from scratch, almost. And, I guess I got caught up in it."

"Yes, but a lot of that stuff is wrapped up in white supremacist nationalism and some bastardization of religion and, hell – almost Nazism", said Mike.

"I know", said Stone. "And I gotta admit that I've never been around people of color or people from other countries. Hell, I was born and raised around here – spent all my life, here - and there aren't a lot of those people around here. So, I kinda got caught up in it. Plus, I thought if churches and so on were getting behind it, it must be okay. I don't really go to church. Never have, so I didn't know any better. So, I just bought into what those guys were selling. I thought, maybe they're right. Lately, I've changed my mind about it, though." He shrugged.

"What made you change your mind?", asked Bob.

"Ah, hell – I dunno. I guess I just started thinking about my life and my family and came to the realization that we're really pretty happy. And we're doing okay. That, really, I'm happy with my life. And, just maybe, all those guys are stirring up stuff that doesn't need stirring – primarily for their own good and to make a bunch of money. And I've been thinking about that ever since the other night." He shrugged and said, "I guess I felt guilty, too."

He took another sip of coffee, then went on, "See, I did that type of thing back when I was a kid in school – vandalized stuff with a bunch of guys. And it always seemed like fun while we were doing it. But, really – once I got into bed at night and thought about it, I felt bad. I mean, I didn't stop, right away – it was kinda fun. But I always felt a little guilty, afterwards. And I've had that same guilty feeling ever since I threw that brick."

I know that more than one of us Geezers could relate to a certain amount of youthful vandalism. It's a part of growing up, I guess.

"Anyway, I'd joined this group - and that's its name – The Group. It's really kind of a mish-mash of a bunch of guys – right-wing guys. And, honestly, it's just kind of getting off the ground. There's, maybe, twenty, twenty-five guys in it. And those are the guys who were at the parade, yesterday.

"I was supposed to be with them, but my wife always makes a big deal about dressing the girls up and going to the parade. And she told me, in no uncertain terms, that I was going to be with them. So, I told the guy who's more or less the leader that I'd have to pass on marching with The Group. And I think he was testing my loyalty by having me do what I did."

"You mean it wasn't your idea?", asked Parker.

"Oh, hell, no. It was Branson's idea – he's the leader. I guess his wife thought Gretchen, here, dissed her or something and he wanted to pay her back for it. That's where the brick idea came from."

Parker and Mike and I exchanged glances.

"Anyway, after that thing, yesterday – when I thought I might actually lose my little girl

- and you guys - especially you, Parker - came to help us, right away, well.....” He looked down at the table, then raised his head again. “And, when I was sitting in the hospital with my wife and my littlest one, waiting on what the doctors would say, I had a – well, I guess you could call it a revelation. That what I’d gotten involved with wasn’t me. It’s not who I am. And my wife and I talked about it for a long time when we got home, last night, and I came to this decision – that I’d leave the group and try to make amends for what I did.”

We were all silent for a while, rolling around everything he’d said in our minds. I didn’t know about anybody else, but I felt for the guy.

“Good for you”, Bob said, finally. “Good for you, Mister Flint Stone. That took guts. And what you’re doing, right here, right now, is taking a lot of guts, too. There aren’t many guys who’d lay their hearts out to a bunch of strangers like you just did.” And he raised his mug in a toast.

And we all toasted, too.

“It’s a crazy world”, Hal said, finally, and we all nodded judiciously.

“But God love ya for coming clean”, Joe said to Stone.

“Well, thanks”, he replied. “But I also want you guys to know that I’m done with that group. I mean, I may not agree with a lot of things that are going on – or even with you guys – but I don’t think we’re gonna get anywhere by tryin’ to tear things down. Seems to me that the answer’s somewhere in the middle.”

“Little story for you, Flint”, said Bob. “Look at a grandfather clock’s pendulum. It swings all the way to the left, then it swings all the way to the right. But the interesting thing is that it spends twice as much time, right smack dab in the middle than it does at either end of its swing. I think this country’s just like ol’ grandfather clock. Most people are in the middle.”

Stone thought about that – hell, we all did - and he nodded.

“Yeah, you’re probably right”, he said. “Never thought of it that way.”

He paused for a second, then slid his chair back and said, “Look, guys. I really appreciate y’all hearing me out, today. It’s something I had to get off my chest and it meant a lot to me.” He looked over at Gretchen and said, “And, Gretchen – you’ll let me know what all that cost, okay? And I’ll get it right to you.”

“Ah, it was only a few hundred dollars and the insurance took care of it. You just promise me that you'll stay on the straight and narrow and take care of that family of yours – your little girls need you - and we'll call it even."

"Oh, no. I really want to make amends. Tell you what – if you need any contracting work done around here – anything at all - you just let me know and I'll do it for you on my dime, okay?"

"Fair enough", said Gretchen, smiling.

Flint Stone stood up and said, "Real nice meeting you guys. Maybe I'll stop by some morning and say hello."

"We'll pull up a seat for you", said Bob. "Any time at all."

And Stone walked around the table and shook all of our hands, thanking Parker, again, for the help he'd given yesterday.

A few seconds later, he was out the door.

"Wow", said Mike, once he'd left. "That was something, wasn't it?"

Natch, we all agreed and probably would have sat there discussing it and all the craziness that seems to be floating around, right now, but we all had shit to do. So, Bob suggested we table the discussion for the day and reconvene in the morning. He got no arguments.

So, with all of us having knuckle-knocked the meeting to a close, Bob said, "Okay, you guys – until tomorrow. And try to stay dry, okay?" And we all headed toward the door.

"Storm's supposed to be a beaut", Bob said to me as I filed out in front of him.

It had been raining a bit when I drove over, this morning, but I hadn't thought much about it.

"Huh? We're supposed to have a storm?", I asked, rather dumbly, I guess. I hadn't paid any attention to the forecast.

"Yeah, boy. A nor'easter's headed this way and it's supposed to stick around for a day or two – later today, tonight and tomorrow. I guess, by Wednesday, it's supposed to be okay, but when one of them storms comes through, we get a ton of rain and a lot of wind. Best do indoor things, if you can."

"Oh. Okay, yeah, sure."

Shit, I thought. We're supposed to do the ninja horseman thing tonight.

When we got outside and made our way to our vehicles, I motioned to Parker and he walked over.

"Did you hear anything about a nor'easter we're supposed to be getting?", I asked him.

"Uh, yeah. But not until this morning, driving over here, when I heard it on the radio. I wanted to talk to you about it. Let's go back up there under the canopy – we're getting wet, standing here."

"What the hell's a nor-easter?", I asked him, once we were under cover. "I've only heard about 'em, like, up in Nantucket and shit. Like in the old whaling stories. We didn't have anything like that, back in Cali."

"Oh, yeah. We get one every couple of years. Storm rides up the east coast and brings the rain and wind in from the ocean. They kinda suck, really."

"Well, we're supposed to do our thing, tonight, right?"

"Yeah, but.....I dunno – I think we oughta get back to the farm and talk about it. I'm thinkin' that we might have to modify our plan, a bit."

"Fuck. Really?"

"Let's get back to the farm and talk about it."

About half-an-hour later, we were sitting at the kitchen table.

"So, look", said Parker. "If it's gonna rain like I think it's gonna rain, I don't think we oughta be doing that thing, tonight. Fuck – you wanna do all that in a downpour and a thirty, forty mile-an-hour wind?"

"Well, no."

"That's what it's supposed to be", he said.

"Hold on – I wanna look at the weather app." I picked up my phone and hit the Accuweather icon.

There was one of those little things with a white exclamation point inside a little red box. Next to it, it said, 'Storm Warning'. I read it aloud, with the major points being that heavy rains were expected, along with coastal and local flooding, high winds that would be capable of knocking down trees and damaging roofs and blah, blah, blah. And it would continue through Tuesday and most of Tuesday night.

"See?", asked Parker.

"Yeah. Well, shit." Still looking down at my phone, I said, "There's no way I want to put the kids through that, especially Zeus." I looked back up at him. "Plus, it could be dangerous. I mean, if there's lightning or thunder? That could freak him out while we're doing our thing and he could go nuts under me. That'd be terrible."

He nodded and said, "I don't think it's a big deal, really – postponing it for a couple of nights. Hell, Branson ain't going anywhere and everything you wrote and all that other shit still stands. Plus, maybe after a day or two, he'll think it was all a bogus thing and won't be expecting it, at all."

"Good point. Alright, then – should we plan for Wednesday night?"

"Yeah, if the weather clears. Otherwise, we can do it Thursday." He shrugged.

"We'd better tell Ron", I said, and Parker nodded.

He answered on the first ring and I explained the situation. And that we were postponing the thing until Wednesday night, maybe Thursday.

"A nor'easter, huh?", he asked. "Like in 'Moby Dick' or something?"

Parker went on to explain what he'd had to explain to me.

"Sorta like one of our 'Pineapple Expresses', I guess", said Ron, digesting it.

"Yeah, that's what it sounds like to me, more or less", I said. "Only, I guess there's a lot more wind."

"Huh. Well, okay – just keep me in the loop."

We promised we would and hung up.

―――――――――――――――――――――

Frank Branson was sitting in his living room, watching TV.

Because of the rain and the expected two-day storm, he'd postponed a job that he was supposed to have started this morning. Although a little rain wouldn't bother him, today, according to the forecast, the next day or so would be a total wash-out. And, considering this job would require a load of dirt, he didn't want that sitting there, getting wet and turning to mud. So, here he was, feet up and channel surfing.

He hit one of the local cable news stations and there was a story on about something that made him sit up and take notice.

It seems that two planeloads of young immigrants had been flown into Orange County Airport, over across the river, last night. There was a total of forty-eight kids, ranging in age from thirteen to seventeen and the planes had originated in El Paso.

According to the report, the Department of Health and Human Services had arranged the flights and had handed over the kids to the Office of Refugee Resettlement.

What the fuck? though Branson.

There didn't appear to be any specific destination for those getting off the plane, but it was suggested that they would be dispersed to local churches, non-profits and shelters in Kingston. After that, who knew? The report didn't say and the reporter didn't know.

Republican Councilman Ralph Estes was interviewed and he was angry about the "secret" shipping of migrants to his community. "The Biden administration is exporting its border crisis right into our backyards", he said. "This cannot stand."

"Hey, honey?", Branson shouted to his wife, who was somewhere, probably the kitchen. "Come here, willya?"

Walking into the living room, she said, "What?"

"Look at this", he said, pointing at the TV. He filled her in on what he'd just heard and, by now, the shot was back in the studio and the two anchors were discussing the story.

"Can you believe it? They're sending illegal teenagers – probably gang members – here. To Kingston. Dozens of 'em. And the reporter said that more are expected over the next week."

"Oh, for the love of God", said Sheila, sitting down on the couch. "Really?"

"Yeah - and Councilman Estes said it's like the Biden administration is exporting its border crisis right into our backyard."

"Well, he's right", she said. "We shouldn't have to put up with those people. You know they'll be nothing but trouble. And they'll probably end up costing the taxpayers a bundle. Plus, all the crime they'll bring."

They both looked at the screen and, just as the report was wrapping up, one of the anchors said that at least two more flights were expected at the end of the week, most probably on Friday evening, according to a source who wasn't authorized to speak on the matter.

"Friday, huh?", said Branson. "I've got the inkling of an idea." He paused, then said, "I gotta call Gallagher", and he reached for his phone. "Sit there – you might wanna hear this."

"Yeah", said Gallagher, answering.

Frank relayed the entire story to him, including the fact-slash-rumor that another couple of loads were coming in, probably on Friday night.

"Fuck – really?", was Gallagher's response to the whole thing.

"Yeah – it's on the news, right now", said Branson. "Listen – I've got an idea. Why don't we get a bunch of the guys – as many as we can round up - and drive over to Orange County Airport on Friday? You know – show the colors and all. I don't think there's any way we can stop 'em from coming in, but if we're there in force, maybe they'll think twice about bringing any more wetbacks into our neighborhood."

Sheila smiled from across the room.

Gallagher thought about it. "How do they get the kids – or whoever – out of the airport and to where they're going?"

"They said there were buses."

"Hmm. Yeah. What if we're there and surround the buses when they leave the airport? Like, stop 'em from leaving."

"There ya go. Good idea. And, even if the cops come and shit, they'll have to force us to leave. And, yeah – maybe a couple of guys get busted, just like they wanted yesterday. Fuck, man – something like that could even make it onto the national news. You know the TV stations – at least the local one – will have a crew there. And, if they get decent footage, it'll go out to the national networks, like Fox. That could put us on the map."

"It could, yeah", said Gallagher. "And, honestly, the timing would be right for you, too. It'd get everybody back on board – it'd show that you've still got your leadership chops.”

“Yeah, it would. Alright, Eric, look – why don’t we get together a little later and kinda plan this thing out. Then, once we’re set, we’ll contact the guys and let ‘em know, okay?”

“Well, I’ve got a fuckin’ dentist appointment, this afternoon, so why don’t we plan on talking again in the morning. That work for you?”

“Works perfect.”

And they disconnected.

“Oh, honey”, said Sheila. “I really think you’re onto something big, here. This could be big news if you guys can pull it off - and I don’t see any reason why you can’t. And, now – now with so many of us so pissed off about the flood of illegals coming across the border – something like this could make national news. I haven’t seen any group do this, yet. You could be the first.”

“Well, we just gotta make it happen”, said Frank.

CHAPTER 41

Parker and I decided that we'd better get the chores done, now, before the rain really began in earnest.

He threw three bales down from the hay loft and I stacked them over where they belonged. He mucked the kids' section of the barn while I cleaned and refilled their water tub.

When Parker got back into the barn from dumping the poop into the big roll-off container, he said, "Shit – it's really starting to come down." He shook off some rain. "Not a day fit for man nor beast."

I turned and looked over my shoulder and, yep - the kids were standing in the barn, not wanting to deal with the rain, either.

"Good point", I said.

"Y'know,", said Parker, "I think, maybe, that I'll go into the garage and put the finishing touches on that piece. It's almost done."

"When can I see it?"

"When it's done."

I knew that was coming.

"Alright, I should go into the tack room and put some saddle soap on the kids' saddles and tack. Get 'em all soft and shiny again."

So, for the next hour or so, we both did our thing. Then, I walked over to the garage and walked in the side door. Parker seemed to be cleaning up his stuff.

We agreed that we couldn't really do anything more, today, really. So, he announced that he was heading home and I said I didn't know what I was gonna do, but it would probably be something insignificant.

My phone rang. Ron.

"Yo", I said, hitting the speaker.

"Yo. Hey, listen – a little while ago, I intercepted a call between Branson and his guy, Gallagher. Fucking idiot used his own phone again."

"Yeah? What about it?"

"Well, it seems that a couple of planeloads of kids flew into – uh, let's see – Orange County Airport, the other night. You know it?"

Parker said, "Yeah, it's down about ten miles west of Newburgh. Not very big." He looked at me. "Probably less than an hour from here." I nodded.

"Well, the planes took off from El Paso and, from what I can gather, all of the passengers were teenagers. And they were from two or three countries. And, I guess HHS turned 'em over to the Office of Refugee Resettlement and the kids were taken to a few churches and non-profits somewhere in your neck of the woods."

"Okay", I said, not knowing exactly where this was going.

"Anyway, there's a rumor that another couple of flights are coming in late this week, probably Thursday or Friday. I checked it out and, yeah, that's the plan. So….Branson and Gallagher talked about it and they're fixin' to go to the airport – with their goon squad - and, somehow, disrupt things. Gallagher said they could surround the buses and not let 'em leave the airport. And that it'd probably make news. Put 'em on the map, is what he said."

"Aw, jeez", I said. "Really? They'd screw with a bunch of kids? Kids that are probably scared out of their wits in the first place?"

"Remember, jefe – these guys are douchebags. So, yeah, I wouldn't put it past 'em."

Parker and I exchanged glances and I said, "Well, it looks like we'll definitely have to do the ninja horseman thing on Wednesday night. The storm's supposed to be over by then, isn't it?"

Parker pulled out his phone and checked his weather app.

"Says here that it's probably gonna move out sooner than they thought. Probably by late tomorrow. According to this, Wednesday's supposed to be partly cloudy with only a thirty-percent chance of rain. Down to ten percent by Wednesday evening."

"Just so you know", said Ron. "I had to pass this up the chain and they're working, right now, to get a pretty good-sized contingent of law enforcement at the airport on both nights. If those schmucks show up, they won't be able to get anywhere near the kids or the buses."

"That's good", I said. "But it could be a good PR ploy for Branson. You know, a bunch of so-called patriots gathered around screaming about the border problem and how we're letting illegals - their words – into the country to rape and pillage and sling dope and all that shit."

"And you know they'll alert the media ahead of time", said Parker.

"Yeah", I said. "I don't think these guys actually want to stop these flights – maybe they do – but I think they're more interested in making a name for themselves."

"Like I said", said Ron, "Branson and Gallagher talked about just that."

"So, there's no doubt that we have to move on Wednesday night. No question. And, when we email that stuff to Branson's members, maybe it'll throw their whole thing into a cocked hat."

"If they could be stopped before some sort of fiasco happens at the airport, that would be good", said Ron. "See – we can't really do anything because those guys haven't broken any laws, yet. And there's no law against being an asshole."

"Too bad", said Parker.

Then, we disconnected, agreeing to keep in close touch if any of us heard anything.

A few minutes later, Parker pulled out of the lane and I headed into the house.

And, like I thought I'd probably do, I did a few insignificant things: I channel-surfed on the tube, finding nothing worthwhile and I read for a little while, dozing off on the couch while doing so.

When I roused myself, I wondered if I should think about kick-starting the ol' Spencer Sales Associates thing again. It was easy – easy money, too. But it was well into most schools' semesters and, even if one of them did bite, it'd probably be sometime in the Spring before anything would happen. And I couldn't really think that far ahead. Plus, even if one of them was interested in doing something soon, that might require traveling in the winter, which I was not wont to do.

So, in the course of about a minute-and-a-half, I'd expertly talked myself out of that idea. And I was quite proud of myself for doing so.

Insignificance ruled the rest of the day and night.

The next morning, it was raining like a cow pissin' off a flat rock – it had all night - and I half asked myself if I should head to The Coffee Spot. Maybe some of the other guys would beg off due to the weather. But, if I was the only one who didn't show, I'd probably never live it down, being the youngest and - ahem – probably the most able-bodied of the Geezers.

Nah – I had to go.

And I was right – the guys were all there when I got there and Gretchen was asking Parker about the native corn that he said he'd bring.

"Look", she said, pointing at the little table against the wall under his artwork, "I tossed the pumpkin and that empty vase I put there's looking downright lonely."

"I know", said Parker. "And I'm sorry, but I didn't get down to Crockett's yesterday. Maybe J.D. and I'll run down there, this morning." He looked over at me and raised his eyebrows.

"Yeah, sure", I said. "Why not? Not much we can do in this rain, anyway."

"Oh, hey", said Marquardt. "I heard on the radio, coming over here, that it's gonna move out even sooner than they thought it would. I guess a high's moving in from the Midwest and it'll chase this thing out of here by early this afternoon."

That brought a Geezer knuckle-knock from around the table, though Joe had to pipe up.

"Figures. Those weather goons always make it sound like it's gonna be a lot worse than what we actually get. You know, like with snowstorms and so on." He changed his voice a little. "'Oh, we're really gonna get it. Batten down the hatches! Stock up on supplies! Get your milk and bread! Monster storm a-comin'!' And then, we get something like four inches. Bozos miss it every time."

"Well, I'm glad they got it wrong, this time", said Hal. "We're planning on showing 'When Harry Met Sally' at the Center, tomorrow night. I know a lot of people are looking forward to it and I was afraid that, because of the storm, a lot of them wouldn't show. Now, if it really does clear, we should have a nice crowd."

Naturally, Joe had to start with the Harry-met-Sally scene in the restaurant. You know the one I mean – the Sally scene.

"Oh, for the love of God, Joe – no!", said Gretchen and that stopped him.

Suze walked up just as Gretchen said that and asked, "What's going on? What'd I miss?"

"Nothing", said Gretchen. "Just Joe being Joe."

"Gotcha", said Suze. She looked at me. "Hey, J.D. – that Subaru's a champ in this rain. Those cars are made for weather like this."

I realized that we hadn't filled Suze in on all the latest news about Branson and company, other than to tell her that we had to postpone last night's ninja horseman thing. We'd have to bring her up to speed.

So, I said, "Oh, yeah – it's a great car for that. Listen, when we leave here, come out with me for a minute. I want to show you a special feature on it."

"Yeah, okay – cool", she said. "Can't wait to see it. 'K – I gotta get this order in. Catch you guys." And off she went to the kitchen.

When we'd finished and the twenties had fluttered onto the table, I caught Suze's eye and motioned with my head to have her meet me outside.

The three of us – Parker, knowing what was going on and deigning to take the back seat – got into the car to get out of the rain and I launched right into what we'd learned.

"Wow, that's fucked up. They wanna screw with kids?", she said, once I'd finished. "But you are planning on tomorrow night, right?" I nodded. "Can I come?"

"Sure", I said, having looked back at Parker and gotten a nod. "Same drill as last time, same time and all, okay?"

"Yep."

We vacated the car, Suze went back inside and walking to his truck, Parker said to me, "Let's get that poop mucked and the waters filled and head down to Crockett's."

"Ten-four."

We headed out.

———————————————

Down in Hyde Park, Frank Branson had gone into his office to do some paperwork. He was separating receipts into piles – which paid receipts belonged to which job – when Sheila walked in.

"Hey, hon", he said, looking up over his reading glasses. "What's up?"

She looked a little upset and sat down in the chair in front of his desk.

"Frank, I'm still a little worried that that – *thing* – might make good on its promise and come back here."

"Oh, hell, kid – I wouldn't worry about it. Like I said, I think it was just some left-wing prank. Some asshole found out about the damned parade and tried to scare us off. The parade's over and I don't think we'll hear from him again."

"Frank, this is my home – our home. And it was violated. You and I were both violated. And I don't trust those people – not even one little bit. I wouldn't put anything past them."

"Well, I don't think – "

"I don't care, Frank", she interrupted. "I'm frightened. Yes – scared. Scared that we could be invaded again."

He looked at her and saw that she was pretty upset. She meant it. He thought for a few seconds, then said, "Look – if it'll make you feel any better, I'll speak to Gallagher about it and see if we can't get a couple of guys to – I dunno – stake out the house for a few nights. Sit in their cars or trucks and just keep an eye on the place. If that thing shows up again, they'll handle it."

"Handle it – how?"

He shrugged and said, "Hell, I don't know. Maybe the guy shows up – him and his horse. And maybe our guys spot 'em. And, somehow, chase 'em off. I'll bet a couple of gunshots into the air would do it, like, pronto."

"Oh, Frank – you think you could do that? Get some of your guys?"

"Yeah, maybe. Like I said, I gotta talk to Gallagher about it, but I'm sure we can round up a couple, anyway. Oh – how long do you think we should have guys here? I can see a night or two, but this can't be any long-term thing. Nobody'd go along with that."

Sheila gave it a little thought. "I don't know – maybe 'til later in the week. We're going over to the airport on Friday night, aren't we?"

"Yeah. And Saturday, too, maybe."

"Well, I'd think that if that thing was coming back here, it'd probably be sometime this week, wouldn't you?"

"Yeah, I suppose. Sure. Plus, if we do our thing at the airport, that'll put us almost into next week. The guy's gotta give it up by then."

"And you really think you can do this – round up some guys", she said and it was more of a statement than a question.

He nodded. "I do. I'll call Gallagher and get the wheels in motion."

She stood up, leaned across the desk and they kissed.

"Oh, thank you, sweetheart. That would just make me feel so much better."

"Consider it done", said Frank, smiling.

As soon as Sheila left the office, he picked up his phone.

Oops, he thought. I gotta be smarter than this. And he reached into a desk drawer and pulled out one of his burners. He'd already used it to call Gallagher, once, so his number was in it. He called.

"Hey", said Gallagher. "You're using the burner, huh? Smart man. Don't tell me you're calling to give me a job, are you?"

Frank chuckled and said, "Well, not really. Not a paying one, anyway. But, don't worry – I got several coming up that I can use you on. No, this is a little something else."

He explained Sheila's feelings and how she was worried about that guy showing up again and so on. And he told Gallagher his idea and asked him if he thought he could round up a couple of the guys from The Group. Gallagher was more or less the personnel director, if there was such a thing. At least he knew more of them than Branson did.

"Really?", asked Gallagher, with a fair degree of skepticism.

"Yeah, really, dude. If you'd'a been here and you'd'a seen that thing and all, you'd be thinking the same damned thing. The last thing I want is for that to happen again."

"Well, alright. But tell Sheila I'm doing it for her and not you. You oughta be able to take care of yourself."

"I can, man. You know that", said Frank. "And, yeah – this is for Sheila. And I know it'll mean a lot to her."

"Happy wife, happy life – or so they say", said Gallagher.

"You know it."

"Alright, let me make a few calls. Could be tonight by the time I get back to you – after guys get home from work. You don't think he'd show up tonight, anyway, do you? Raining like a fuck out there, right now."

"Oh, hell. I can't imagine he would. Not with still a good chance of rain. But it's supposed to be fairly decent, tomorrow. So, you might wanna tell whoever you talk to that tomorrow night and Thursday night oughta do it. And then, probably only 'til – what? – eleven, both nights?"

"Yeah, sure."

"And, hey – listen. If it's decent, tomorrow, like they say it will be, I should go give quotes on a job or two. Wanna ride along? Probably be something in it for you, too."

"Sure, why not? I'm goin' kinda nuts just sittin' around playin' with myself."

"Okay, then. You'll call me later and let me know what you find out?"

"Yep. Like I said – probably this evening."

And they disconnected.

Good, thought Frank.

He got up to go find Sheila and give her the good news.

____

By late morning, Parker and I had left Crockett's, armed with a whole shitload of Indian corn and a little basket to put it in. The basket even had a nice colored ribbon wrapped around it. It'd look nice.

We also had a couple of pies sitting on the back seat, next to the stuff Parker had gotten.

There was an apple lattice – somehow, apples were always available, no matter what time of year it was - and pecan-slash-maple walnut, which looked and sounded exceedingly good.

"Rain's lettin' up", said Parker as we turned out of the parking lot and onto Clinton Hollow Road. "Skies a little lighter, too."

"Maybe the weather guys were right. Maybe it is gonna move out pretty soon", I said.

"Mmm."

We drove in silence for a couple of minutes, then he said, "Hey, I think that piece is done – the one I've been working on."

"Yeah?"

"Uh-huh. And I think it's time for you to see it. Maybe when we get back, I'll go into the garage and put a cloth over it and stand it up. You know, for, like, an unveiling." I glanced over at him and he looked just a little embarrassed by saying that, but I also knew he was proud of what he'd done and wanted to make a big deal out of giving it to me.

"I think that'd be a terrific idea."

"Yeah. It'll probably only take me a couple of minutes to get it all set up."

"Cool. So, when we get back, why don't I take the pies into the house – we'll leave the corn and basket and I'll bring 'em with me in the morning - and you hit me with a text when you're ready and I'll come down."

"Yep. Good." And he smiled.

CHAPTER 42

After I'd gotten the pies safely placed on the kitchen counter and was headed back down to the garage, I noticed that the rain had let up. It was now somewhere between a drizzle and a shower. Good.

On my short trek to the garage, I noticed several standing puddles in various spots in the driveway and the barnyard. Funny how you never notice low spots in the terrain until a long driving rain reveals them.

Parker had the big door closed, so I shouted to him from outside. "Yo! I'm here! You ready?"

"Yep – just give me a minute." A few seconds later: "Okay – you can come in, now."

I opened the side door and walked in, saying, "Looks like the rain's letting up."

I looked to my right and saw something on an easel, with a canvas tarp over it.

"Come on over", he said.

I did and then he asked, "Ready?"

"Yup", I nodded.

And he reached down and took hold of the bottom of the tarp and slowly and carefully lifted it off.

And I was astounded.

Sitting right there, in front of me, were two black horses' heads, from the neck up, mounted on what appeared to be a brushed aluminum horizontal oval.

Zeus and Ceres.

Oh. My. God.

I stood there, speechless.

How he'd done it, I have no idea, but he'd captured both of them – especially their personalities – perfectly. There was no doubt that if you put the two kids next to that piece that anyone on this planet would say, "Oh, wow – it's those two horses".

"I – I – I don't know quite what to say, man. That is…..exquisite." It was fashioned from cut and carefully pounded metals and was just a hair on the abstract side and it was kind of three-dimensional. And it was just *so* good. Each horse's head was about eighteen inches tall and they were both looking to their left on, like, a forty-five-degree angle.

I reached over and touched it. Yep – it was real, alright.

"This is unbelievable, dude….just unbelievable. I'm stunned. *Stunned*. How'd you do it?"

He shrugged and said, "Well, I took a couple of pictures of them, one day, while they were standing at their gate, watching you walking toward them. I found the best shot and had it blown up and printed to almost that size. Then, I went to work. Got some metals that I thought'd work – the black one was easier than I thought it'd be to find. It was anodized black, actually. And then, I went to work."

"Dude – come here", I said, opening up my arms.

And, neither of us really being huggers, we kind of came together and more or less slapped each other on the shoulders. The thought was there, though.

"Where should we put it?", I asked him.

"Well, it's up to you, but I was kinda thinkin' that it would look nice over the barn door. There's plenty of room up there and it'd fit right nicely."

I walked over to the garage door and, because it was hardly raining, now, opened it.

And I looked over to my right – toward the barn - and, yep – Parker was right.

"That's exactly where it should go", I said. "Exactly. It's like telling everybody that it's their home."

"Uh-huh. That was the idea."

"Look,", I said, "it's supposed to be pretty decent, tomorrow. Think we should put it up, then?"

"Yeah, why not? Actually, we might not even need a ladder. I think we can go up in the loft and hang it by leaning out that window up there", he said, pointing at the white-trimmed window that was up there below the peak of the roof.

"Well, maybe one of us can do that while the other one goes up the ladder – just to make it a little easier."

He nodded. "Yeah, maybe. Whatever – it shouldn't be all that hard."

"Aw, man – that's gonna look so good, up there", I said, nodding in that direction.

"Wait, hold on", I said, still looking at the barn. "If we put it way up there, it'll be a little out of the way." I pointed and continued, "What if we put it there – just to the left of the door, like at eye level or something. Then, no matter who comes around, they'll see it right away."

Parker stared over at the barn and said, "Y'know – maybe you're right. In my head, I'd always thought it should be up there in that spot but, you're right. It probably would be better there. Easier to see." He paused a second or two, then said, "See, m'boy? You got a little artiste in you. Good call."

"Yeah - and it'll be easy to do, too."

"Yup."

"Okay", I said. "This calls for pie."

"Think so?"

"Oh, absolutely. Let's get into the apple and save the pecan thing for tomorrow night."

"Well, then – lead on, MacDuff."

I went back over to the piece, still amazed by it. I rubbed both of the kids' faces and said, "Perfect."

"Leave it right there", said Parker. "We'll just close the door and it'll be fine where it is."

We did that and walked up to the house.

By now, there was barely a fine mist in the air.

"Weather's clearing", said Parker.

———————————————————

Sheila Branson's phone rang.

It was Mark Fisher.

"Hi, Mark", she said.

"Hello, Sheila. I was just calling to check on you to see how you made out on Sunday."

She kind of chuckled and said, "Well, it didn't work out the way we wanted it to, did it?"

"No, not at all. And I'm so sorry for causing such a mess. I had no idea – "

"Oh, it wasn't you, Mark", she interrupted. "You were just addressing some concerns that a lot of us have and a couple of left-wing assholes tried to stomp all over your First Amendment rights. It's so typical of them – they always try to silence anyone who's pointing out some of the real problems that we face, today."

"Well, it's unfortunate that that little girl got hurt. I understand that she's fine, now, though."

"Again, Mark – if those people had just let you speak, instead of trying to silence you, it never would've happened. That was on them, Mark, not you."

"Well, I still feel somewhat responsible."

"You shouldn't."

"Well, thank you, Sheila. That makes me feel a little better. Hey – the reason I was calling, other than that, was to tell you that I've learned that one of our eighth-grade teachers has assigned the class to read 'To Kill a Mockingbird'. And, that they will be having a class discussion about each chapter every day."

"Oh,", said Sheila, "that is *not* a book those children should be reading, let alone discussing in class each day. It's full of sex and rape and a ton of curse words. Plus, it paints a horrible picture of upstanding white people."

"I know, right? That's exactly what I've been thinking."

"Well, what are you going to do about it?"

"That's why I'm calling you. I think we should get together and devise some sort of plan with the Moms for Liberty. If it's just me complaining about it at one of our board meetings, it'll probably get pooh-poohed by the rest of them. But, if we can get a decent-sized group of mothers - and, maybe, dads – together, maybe we can put an end to it."

Sheila thought about that for a minute. Sure, she thought. There should be some way......

"Okay, Mark. I'll tell you what. Why don't you and I get together and throw around a few ideas and come up with one that we think might work. Then, I can take it to my group and present it. But we have to be pretty buttoned up when I do. A few of them have gotten a little utzy since that thing at the parade. We have to get it right."

"I agree. Okay, when do you want to get together? Don't forget, I run my business during the day and, lately, we've been so busy that I've been getting to the office around seven and I'm going all day long. So, evenings would be better."

"That's fine, Mark. But we should do it, soon – the sooner, the better. Can you come over here?"

"Sure – I don't see why not. I only live a few miles north of you. But it can't be too early. We have to have dinner and get the kids situated. I could be at your place, um, around eight-fifteen, eight-thirty. Would that work for you?"

"I don't see why not. How about tomorrow evening?"

"Works for me", said Fisher. "No time like the present. Plus, we want to put the kibosh on that book thing as soon as we can."

"Good. Then it's a date. Oh, Frank will be here, too. And he might want to sit in."

"Oh, absolutely. The more minds, the better. Okay – just give me your address, so I can plug it into my GPS."

"Twenty-seven Kilmer Road, Hyde Park."

"Got it. Okay, then, Sheila. I'll see you tomorrow night. And, I'll bring a copy of the book so we can go through some of it, if we want."

"Good idea."

"Well, thank you, Sheila. I knew you'd understand and I'm glad you're willing to help."

"It's what we do, Mark. Every little bit helps, right?"

"That it does. Okay, then – see you tomorrow evening."

"Good, Mark. 'Bye, now."

And they disconnected.

Meanwhile, back at the ranch, Parker and I had put a pretty good-sized dent in the apple pie. Somehow, probably subconsciously, we left almost exactly half of it for another time. We were sitting at the kitchen table, having washed it down with some fresh coffee that my Mister Coffee had provided.

"Must be the time of year or something, but it seems like they put a little extra cinnamon in it, this time, doesn't it?", he asked.

"Yeah – it's better this way."

"No doubt."

My phone rang. Ron.

"Dude? Wassup?", I asked him.

"Hey – just another little heads-up. Your Mrs. Branson just got a call from – I think – that guy from the school board. Mark Something-Or-Other."

"Fisher", I said. "Mark Fisher."

"Yeah, okay. So, he wanted to yap about some eighth-grade class reading 'To Kill a Mockingbird' which, from what I gather, is kind of a no-no among the wingnuts."

"Yeah, that's what we've heard."

"Anyway, it seems that Fisher wants to, somehow, put a stop to it – the reading of it in that class."

Parker rolled his eyes and shook his head.

"So, he called Sheila", I said.

"Right. And he's asking her and her band of merry moms to get involved."

"How would they do that?", asked Parker.

"I don't know and, I guess, they don't either, at this point. And that's why I'm calling. They made an appointment for Fisher to go over to the Branson abode tomorrow night and they'll toss around some ideas."

"Tomorrow night?", I asked. "That's when we – "

"I know", Ron interrupted. "And that's why I'm calling you. You're supposed to do your thing tomorrow night, right?"

"Yeah. That's the plan." And I looked over at Parker and we exchanged glances.

"What time is Fisher supposed to be there?", he asked Ron.

"He said between eight-fifteen and eight-thirty."

"Well, shit", I said. "We're scheduled to do our thing right around nine p.m. sharp. That could bollix up the works – Fisher being there. And he might be, too. Hell, he's gotta be there for a half-hour or so, at least, right?"

"Wait", said Parker. "Let's think about this for a minute…..So what if Fisher's there? I mean, he's an asshole, too. Wouldn't hurt to scare the shit outta him, too, would it?"

"Well,", I said, "the stuff in the sack is all directed at the Bransons."

"Yeah, so? Maybe Fisher sees that stuff and maybe he doesn't. Doesn't really matter, does it? Him just seeing and encountering the ninja horseman would probably be enough for him to fill his trou. And, as far as I'm concerned, that guy can use a good pant load after that little di-do at the parade."

The three of us thought about that for a minute.

Me – I kind of had to agree with Parker. About Fisher, that is. But….

"What if he's coming out of the house right as Zeus and I show up?"

"So, he gets scared in the driveway and not in the house", said Parker, shrugging. "You know he's not gonna do anything, little weasel like that. Besides, the odds that he'll come out just as you show up are pretty slim, I'd think."

After another few seconds of silence, Ron said, "I kinda like it. Might be a two-birds-with-one-stone kinda thing. The Bransons and that guy who's raising a ruckus with the school board. Maybe it'd cause him to cool his jets, too – especially if he's in the house when you show up and he gets a little gander at that paperwork you'll be delivering."

Ron was right – it would be a two-birds-with-one-stone thing – if the timing worked out right. And, even if it didn't, and Fisher splits before we show up, we've still got the Bransons. And Fisher drives home, none the wiser.

"Okay", I said. "Yeah, okay – I guess it'll work, whether he's still there or not. If he is, great. If he isn't, that's great, too."

"I think so", said Parker. "And it shouldn't change our plans any, either. I mean, we'll make our ingress just like we did the last time. And the only few seconds we have to worry about is if he's walking to his car just as we cruise past the corner. Wait – we'll put an eyeball on the place just before we get to that intersection and, if he's getting into his car or backing out or whatever, we'll just wait 'til he moves out. Otherwise, we stick with Plan A."

"Well, you guys work it out", said Ron, "but I gotta go. I'm running late for a meeting. Catch you guys on the flip side."

And we disconnected.

My phone rang again, almost instantly. Suze.

"Suze", I said, looking at Parker and putting it on speaker. "What's up?"

"Well, I'm missing you guys - and the kids. And I was wondering if I could stop by on my way home from work."

"Well, funny you should ask", I said. "Look – the answer's yes. And we want to fill you in on a couple of new wrinkles for the Branson-slash-ninja horseman visit."

"It's still on for tomorrow night, isn't it?", she asked.

"Oh, yeah. But we want to make sure we have all of our ducks in a row, so we should go over all of that when you get here. Plus, there's a new little wrinkle that could actually turn out to be a plus."

"Okay."

"What time do you think you'll get here?"

"Well, I get off at two, so I suppose a little before two-thirty?"

"Perfect. We'll see you then."

"Okay, ciao, guys."

Parker got up and walked over to the kitchen window.

"Look", he said. "Blue sky. Not a lot of it, but there's some."

I got up to look, too. And, yep, there was a nice-sized patch of blue.

"Yep - and it's big enough to patch a Dutchman's britches", I said.

"Huh?"

"It's an old saying that my Aunt Winnie used to use when a storm passed and patches of blue started showing up."

"Okay, sure. Got it. And, look – it's stopped raining." He pointed at a puddle in the now-dormant garden and the surface of it was smooth as glass.

"Hey,", I said, "you don't suppose now would be a good time to go hang that piece on the barn, do you?"

He nodded slowly, then said, "Why not? Ain't nobody can see it sittin' in the garage. Yeah – let's go do that. That way, Suze'll see it when she gets here. Tell us what she thinks of it."

"She'll love it, dude. No doubt."

"Okay. And I don't know if you noticed it or not, but I put four eyelets on the thing – one at the top, one at the bottom and one on both sides. That way, we can use wood screws and washers to hold it in place."

"Good thinking."

"Well, how the hell else were we gonna hang it? Had to have something. Tell you what – I'll rustle up the screws, the washers and the electric screwdriver – the one with batteries. And we'll just go down and put 'er up."

"Yay."

And, as we made our way out the door and across the porch, I said, "I just can't wait to see it hanging there, m'man. It's gonna look outstanding."

"That was the point", he said, giving me a half-smile.

CHAPTER 43

Suze pulled into the lane at three-twenty-five.

A little while earlier, Parker and I had put up the piece he'd made. As we were standing back, admiring it, I said to him, "Y'know – we oughta call it something other than 'the piece'. That sounds – I dunno – a little goofy. Doesn't do it justice."

He looked at me a little askance. "Personally, I don't give a shit what you call it."

"I know, but I think it deserves something a little more – well, serious – than that."

He shrugged.

I thought.

And then I said, "Hey, you know what? This farm doesn't have a name, does it?"

"Nope. Never did. We always just referred to it as Bill's farm. Now, I guess, it's J.D.'s farm."

"Maybe we should name it – the farm. And that", I said, pointing at the artwork, "can be our logo."

"You want a name? And a logo?"

"Why not? Hell, we've got Buttonwood Farm, right up there, almost around the corner, and they have a logo. They've got a name and a logo. I think we should, too."

"Yeah, but they're a racehorse breeding farm – a big-time place."

"Yeah, well, so are we - a big-time place. At least to us, anyway. And we've got two of the best horses in the world right here - right there", I said, pointing at Zeus and Ceres, who'd come out of the barn and were watching us from their field.

"Well, yeah. There's that", he said.

"Okay, look - and go with me on this…..Zeus is a star in the constellation Capricorn, okay?"

Parker nodded.

"And Ceres – and I did a little homework on this – Ceres is the largest object in the asteroid belt between Mars and Jupiter. Actually, a few years back, scientists classified it a 'dwarf planet'."

"Okay."

"So, we have Zeus and Ceres here. And there they are", pointing at the piece on the barn wall.

He shrugged, but I could tell that I'd piqued his curiosity a bit.

"So, both of those objects are in the night sky, right? What if we called this place 'Night Sky Farm'?"

"Night Sky Farm", he said, obviously rolling it around in his mind.

"Yeah - and it's all because of Zeus and Ceres. So, that thing you made could be our logo. Zeus and Ceres - important things in the night sky."

"Whoa", he said.

"Whaddya think?", I asked him.

He looked over at the kids, then he looked at the thing on the wall.

"Not bad", he said. "It kinda makes sense, too, I guess."

"Sure, it does. It makes all the sense in the world. Night Sky Farm.

He nodded slowly, then said, "Yep. I think I like it – Night Sky Farm. Yeah – cool. Night Sky Farm. Why not?" And he raised his hand and I high-fived him.

"Kid", he said, "Maybe you're not as dumb as you look."

"Bite me."

"Oh, hey – now I'll have to make sign, with the name. We'll put it right under that piece."

"You mean our logo?"

"Yeah, our logo. Plus, it'll give me something to do. I hate it when I finish a piece and don't have anything new to work on. This'll solve that."

"There you go."

Anyway, when Suze had driven in, we walked her down to the barn to see the new logo on the wall.

"Oh, I *love* this!", she said, touching it all over. "It looks just like them. Omigod, yes! This is *so* cool! You did this, Parker?"

"Uh-huh."

"Wow – I had no idea. I mean, that thing on the restaurant wall is super, but this is beyond that. You're a real *artiste*, my man. And I mean that in the best way. Again – all I can say is 'wow'."

"It's the new logo for Night Sky Farm", I said.

"Night Sky Farm? What's that?"

"It's the new name of this place. We just came up with it a few minutes ago. Like it?"

She cogitated on that for a sec, then said, "Well, yeah – I like it a lot. But how'd you come up with that name?"

I explained it to her, just as I'd explained it to Parker, and she said. "Wow – that rocks. And it sure does justice to Ceres and Zeus. Puts 'em right front and center. Good job, you guys" and she high-fived both of us. High-fiving seemed to be going around, this afternoon.

"Parker's gonna make a new name plate or something to go right under the logo", I said. "How long'll that take, you think?", I asked him.

"I dunno – a week, maybe? Shouldn't take too long. I might already have the materials – I'll have to check."

After another couple of minutes and shooting the shit, I suggested we repair to the kitchen.

As we were walking up toward the house, my phone rang. It was Ron, again.

"Dude", I said, "Suze is here and the three of us are walking up to the house. Let me put you on speaker – we oughta be there in a few seconds."

Suze and Ron said hi to each other and bullshat about something insignificant. Then, we were in the house and sitting at the table.

"Okay, what's up?", I asked him.

"I got a call a little while ago from Schmidt."

"Yeah, and?"

"And he told me that your boy Branson's kinda freaked out – well, his wife is, really – she's kinda freaked out about the possibility of the ninja horseman showing up again. She didn't use that phrase, but that's what she meant."

"Well, maybe she should be", I said. "After all, they went ahead with that parade thing, even though we told 'em not to."

"Yeah, I know. But, according to Schmidt, Branson's trying to round up a few guys to kind of guard their house for the next couple of nights. Actually, I guess he asked Gallagher to do it for him."

"Oh, fuck", Parker and I said in unison.

"Yeah, that's what I thought you'd say. But we might be okay."

"Okay? How? If Branson's got guys guarding the place, how the hell can we do our thing?"

"One of the guys Gallagher called to guard the place was Schmidt."

"Schmidt?"

"Yeah, and look – Schmidt told Gallagher that he'd probably do it, but he'd have to get back to him with a final yes. He gave him some bullshit story about having to get out of some overtime at work or something before he'd know for sure. And that's when he called me to tell me."

"Does Schmidt know about the ninja horseman? He doesn't, does he?"

"Nope. And that's another reason I'm calling you. I want to tell Schmidt to go ahead and take the – um, assignment. Then I told him that some friends of mine – the guys he met at the Center – had a plan. And that I was gonna call you guys and tell you about this whole dealio and for him to hang loose until I call him back. Which I'm gonna do, as soon as I hang up with you guys."

"Oh-kay", I said.

"Look, I think we have to bring Schmidt in on this", said Ron. "The ninja horseman thing. He has no idea that it was you who went to Branson's the other night. Hell, I don't even know if Schmidt knows that anything happened. But I think if we bring him in on this, maybe he can help us on the ground. As in, maybe he can figure out a way to distract his fellow guards or something for a few minutes."

"How?"

"Well, he'll have to figure that out. Or, you guys will – you guys and Schmidt."

"What you're saying is that you want us to go outside of our little tightly-knit gang of five or six compadres and bring Schmidt in on it, too?"

"Precisely, my liege. And, don't forget – Schmidt's an FBI guy. He knows that, sometimes, we don't do things completely by the book. And, believe me, Schmidt's not a by-the-book guy, either. He's as crazy as you guys are. He'll be cool. Trust me."

I looked at Parker, then at Suze.

Parker said, "If you're cool with him, I guess we gotta be. Because I sure as hell don't want this thing to go all FUBAR on us, tomorrow night."

"Fubar?", asked Suze.

"Fucked up beyond all recognition", said Parker.

"Oh."

"Okay, if you say so", I said to Parker. Then, to Ron, "So, Ron – what's the plan, here?"

"Like I said, I'm gonna call Schmidt back and tell him to go ahead and tell Gallagher that he'll do it. Then, I'm gonna have him call you. And you guys make time to get together and talk about it. Tell him what the ninja horseman is and all that. And what you're planning to do – you know, your approach to the house and the info you're going to lay on the Bransons in your burlap sack – all of that."

"You're still gonna send out that email before we get there, aren't you?"

"Hell, yeah. We'll just have to figure an exact time for me to do it. Probably a half-hour or so before you make your grand entrance."

"Okay, well, we'll figure all that out tomorrow. In the meantime, I guess we'll wait to hear from Schmidt, right?"

"Yep. And I'd imagine that he'll be calling you within the next few minutes."

"Alright. But I gotta say, I'm not sure I'm liking any of this", I said.

"Look – dude….if we – you – can pull this off, this'll probably blow two potentially dangerous right-wing douchebag groups right outta the water. At least for a while. You know, cut off the head and the snake dies and all that. We just have to do it right. And I think that, with Schmidt on board, that can happen. He'll have your back."

"Okay, I hear you. And, what? You want us to get back to you after we've heard from Schmidt?"

"Well, not 'til you guys have gotten together and figured something out. Then, yeah, natch."

"It could be as late as tomorrow morning, depending on when we can get together with Schmidt. We're available any time, but it'll kind of be up to him."

"This is the most important thing on his plate, right now. And I'll guaran-goddam-tee you that he'll want to get together with you sometime today or tonight."

"Okay, got it."

And we all said our see-ya-laters and disconnected.

"Jesus", I said.

Parker was staring out the window and Suze's head was swiveling back and forth between him and me.

"Look", he said. "I've got no problem with bringing Schmidt in on the ninja horseman thing. After all, he'll be gone on another assignment pretty soon. What we need to talk about with him is how many guys are gonna be at Branson's and where they'll be."

I nodded.

"And then, Schmidt'll have to figure out a way to neutralize them for – what – five minutes or so? Maybe a little more. And he'll have to keep them out of view of the house. Once you're gone from there, they can do whatever they want. But it's important that they don't see the truck and the rig. We don't want 'em following us. That would suck."

"Maybe I can help with that", said Suze.

"How?", I asked.

"Well, maybe you guys could drop me off right before that corner and I could just walk up the street – you know, in the other direction, past Branson's. That might draw their attention. Maybe they'd follow me or something."

"Oh, hell, no", Parker and I said, more or less at the same time.

"We are *not* using you as bait", I said.

"Fuck, J.D. – I wouldn't be bait, I'd just be a distraction. And if they came after me – which they wouldn't do – I mean, why would they go after a chick just walking up the street? But if they did follow me, I can outrun any of those Meal Team Six guys. Plus, I could go all Krav Maga on 'em if I had to. Nah, don't sweat that."

"Well, I do sweat that, kid."

My phone rang. And it was a number I didn't know.

"Hello."

"Yeah, this J.D.?"

"Yes."

"Schmidt."

"Okay. Look – I'm putting you on speaker. I've got Parker with me – he's the other guy you met that day. And another one of our associates – Suze. She's in on this, too."

"Alright."

I did that and everybody more or less said, "Hey".

And, over the next couple of minutes, Schmidt basically told us what Ron had outlined, as far as Branson wanting guys to guard the place and Gallagher being the guy setting it up.

"How many will you be?", asked Parker.

"Gallagher said three – me and two other guys. And we'll be there both nights – tomorrow and Thursday. Branson's got some other hair-brained thing he's planning to do on Friday, so he and the wife won't be home, and he doesn't want us, then. Hell, I don't even know why he wants his house guarded in the first place, other than I guess something happened the other night."

"Okay – I'll get to that, later", I said. "Where will you guys be? Out in front, or what?"

"I don't know that, just yet. I Google Earthed Branson's place and from the overhead shot, it looks like there's a little tree line just to the east of his place – like, half-an-acre or so of woods-type thing between his house and the one on his left, facing the street."

"Yeah, that's right", said Parker.

"But first, before we go any further, Ron told me you guys have something pretty fucking weird up your sleeves. And I wanna hear what happened the other night, too, because I guess you guys were in on it. I wanna hear about that – all of it. Then, maybe we can figure out a plan."

"Can you come over here? To my farm? I want you to see something", I asked him, thinking about introducing him to Zeus, so he'd understand a little better. Maybe I'd show him my gear or maybe not. But I thought a face-to-face would also be good.

"Yeah, I was gonna suggest we get together. Where you at?"

I told him and he said, "I'm not too far from there, right now. I could probably be there in a half-hour or so. That work?"

"Yep. We'll be here. Just pull down the lane when you get here and park anywhere."

"Got it. See you in a few." And he hung up.

"Well, I guess we're about to get a new member of the Horsemen", I said. "At first, remember - we were the Four Horsemen? With Gretchen and Suze and, now, Schmidt, our little band of merry men – or merry people", nodding at Suze, "is growing."

"That's alright", said Parker. "I think we're gonna need all the help we can get."

While we waited for Schmidt to show up, Suze went down to hang out with her girl, Ceres, for a little while. Well, and I'm sure Zeus got himself in on the action, too.

Parker and I stayed in the kitchen and I got up and put on another pot of coffee.

"How much are you gonna tell Schmidt?", Parker asked me.

"About the ninja horseman? I guess we'll tell him everything, right? Thought I don't think I'll pull out all of my gear – just tell him about it. And, I think it'd be a good idea to let him know that Branson isn't our first rodeo – that we've done this a number of times in the past. So he doesn't think we're just pulling this out of our asses, y'know?"

"Yeah. And we've gotta impress on him how important it is for those guards to not know what's going on while you do your thing. That could fuck up the works. Like I said, he has to distract 'em for several minutes."

"They'll hear the bang and, probably, the commotion", I said.

"Yeah - and that's why you're gonna have to book it on outta there as quick as you can. Don't be hanging around. Throw the sack with the rock and as soon as that fucking door opens, fling the other one. Don't do any of that Zeus-up-in-the-air thing.

The Bransons have seen that. What we need 'em to see is the hammer – the notes in the sack. And then, as soon as you fling it at him, you goose Zeus, but good, and hightail it right around the corner of that tree line and into the trailer. We'll be outta there while everybody's still runnin' around with their dicks in their hands."

I smiled.

"Interesting visual", I said.

CHAPTER 44

When Schmidt got to the farm – Night Sky Farm, thankyouverymuch – we rounded up Suze and the three of us walked over to meet him at his pick-up.

After re-acquainting himself with Parker and me and being introduced to Suze, Schmidt looked around and said, "Nice place. You know, I grew up around farms. Used to work on a couple when I was in high school. Been a while."

He looked down toward the field and spotted the kids standing there.

"Jesus, those are big horses", he said.

"Ah – the kids", I said. "Come on – we'll introduce you to them. Their names are Zeus and Ceres. Zeus is the little bit bigger one, the one on the left. They're full brother and sister. And actually, you should meet them because Zeus is a big part of what we do, a big part of our plan. Well, Ceres, too, but Zeus is the main guy."

"I heard a whisper or two about some monster horse showing up at Branson's, but I kinda thought it was a rumor or something."

"Nope. Come on."

And the four of us walked down to the gate and the kids were on their best behavior. I was pleased to see that Schmidt introduced himself to them by approaching them with the back of his hand and letting them sniff him.

"My grandad had a couple of old horses", he said. "I used to groom them by the hour when I was a kid." He smiled and rubbed both of their faces. "Hi, you guys. So nice to meet you."

I liked Schmidt right away.

"Now that you've met the kids, want some coffee? I just made some. Let's go up to the kitchen, okay? And I'll explain how we use these guys."

"Yeah, sure", he said, still enthralled with the kids.

"But, first", I said, reaching over to the treat can and pulling a few out. I made sure there was an even number so neither kid would get shorted. "Here – give a few to each of them."

He did and I could tell that he really enjoyed it, too.

"Okay, let's go", he said.

Once we'd gotten settled at the table, with coffee all around, Schmidt said, "Okay – tell me what it is you guys do."

And, for the next several minutes, I regaled him with 'The Legend of Eighmyville Hollow' – aka, the ninja horseman and how it all works: The get-ups for me and Zeus, the little red lights, the sack I throw at the door and the one we use to deliver our message. Even the part about Zeus going up on his hind legs a couple of times before we split. Parker jumped in and told him our ingress and egress method – the trailer, how we do a recon mission or two ahead of time and all that.

"Scares the living shit out of our mark", I said, wrapping it up. "And, we do our homework on him – or her or them – ahead of time and that's part of our message: that we're onto their evil ways and are about to fuck up their lives unless they do what they're instructed to do. And even if they do what we've instructed them to do, sometimes, we fuck up their lives, anyway, as retribution for their actions."

"See", I continued, "a number of these people that we've done this to haven't necessarily broken laws in such a way as to actually get nailed by the authorities, but they've gotten away with cheating people who didn't need to get cheated. It's our little form of justice."

"So, you're sort of like Robin Hood meets the Headless Horseman, more or less", he said.

Parker and I both laughed and I said, "That's exactly it."

"The Headless Horseman was from around here, wasn't he?"

"Yep – just a few miles down the road. And we thought it would be cool if we brought him into the twenty-first century."

Schmidt shook his head, thinking about all that he'd just heard.

"Ron was right – you guys are fuckin' nuts" and he laughed out loud.

Then, I said, "Oh, let me tell you about our 'hammer' – or, in this case – 'hammers'." And I went on to explain that the messages we deliver, at that point, pretty much herald the downfall of our marks.

I explained about Branson and his Army stuff. And about Sheila and her abortion. And, that we were going to deliver those write-ups to the Bransons, tomorrow night, showing them that their little secrets are no longer secrets – because they didn't follow out instructions. Plus – via Ron - we were going to email those same messages to the members of both of their groups.

"Fuck", said Schmidt, when I'd finished. "Branson got drunk and got caught playing hide the salami with a fellow soldier?" He laughed. "Yeah – his guys oughta be real happy, hearing that. And, the wife? Mizz Anti-Abortion? I'm sure her group'll be pleased to find that out, too."

"Okay, that's our thing", I said. "And we're hoping that'll blow the lid off both groups."

"It sure might help and it sure won't hurt", said Schmidt.

"Okay, now – let's make a plan", I said.

I walked over to a drawer and pulled out a piece of paper and a pen. Sitting back down, I handed them to Parker. "Let's kind of draw the schematic and maybe work out a plan."

Parker drew out an overhead of the Bransons' place, along with Matuk Drive and where it intersects Kilmer. He scribbled in some trees and showed Schmidt where we parked the rig.

"I'm thinkin', though,", he said, "that maybe, we should come in the other way, instead of driving past Branson's place, this time. If he's got guys out there watching, they might see us drive past. Maybe we'll drive up Matuk – from this direction - and turn the rig around before we drop off J.D. and Zeus. I'll just back it up to our spot and they can get in and out like we did the last time."

"What if they see your lights?", Schmidt asked.

"We black out the tail and brake lights with tape just before we get there. And I douse the headlights beforehand, too. They won't see 'em."

Schmidt nodded. "Gotcha."

He pointed at the drawing - over on the east side of Branson's place - and said, "This here's another stand of trees. And, from what I saw the other day when I drove past on my own little recon mission, it's pretty thick along in there. I'd like to get those guys over on the other side of those trees when you do your thing. That way, Branson's house will pretty much be out of sight to them."

"Where will they park?", I asked.

Schmidt shrugged and said, "I'd imagine they'll park in front of the place. Or in the driveway. I think they'll want to demonstrate a show of force or something. You know – a few vehicles in front of the house should scare anybody away."

"I'd think that they'll be out of their cars or trucks and probably be standing around, shootin' the shit, right? At least for most of the time - or some of the time", said Parker.

"Yeah, depending on how cold it is", said Schmidt. "Maybe they'll get into one of the vehicles to warm up but, you know……Actually, if I know most of these guys, I'd imagine they'll have a flask or two between 'em to keep 'em warm. Might even be a little party atmosphere, after a while."

"Oh, great", said Parker.

"Alright", I said. "Here's the big question, no matter where they are or what they're doing: Are these guys gonna be armed?"

Schmidt looked at me and said, "I told Gallagher that I wouldn't do it if guns are involved. I lied to him and told him I have a felony and a couple of Class A misdemeanors on my record and I'm still seeing a P.O. and if anything bad with guns goes down - and I get caught anywhere near it – I'm headed back to stir. And he assured me that none of the guys would have firearms on 'em."

"Do you believe him?", asked Parker.

"I dunno. I guess. I mean, Gallagher's a fairly decent guy, way down deep. And I'm pretty sure that he'll pass that word to whoever he drafts into this, but you never know with some of these guys. They might promise one thing and do another, y'know?"

"Fuck", I said.

"But don't worry", said Schmidt. "Remember, I'll be with 'em and if I see somebody break out heat, I'll get on him, right away."

"That could be dangerous, couldn't it?", asked Suze.

"Probably not", said Schmidt. "These guys are militia-type wannabes and I'm pretty well trained in this stuff. I'd just have to be close enough to him to do something about it. And I'll make sure that we're pretty close together. Might blow my cover, though."

We all sat there for a minute, digesting that little part of the conversation.

"Okay, let's set that aside, for now", said Parker. "Schmidt – that's your bailiwick. What we've gotta figure is how to make sure you guys aren't right in front of the house or within easy eyesight when J.D. and Zeus make their move.”

“You’ll be coming up this part of the lawn, right?”, Schmidt asked me, pointing at that spot on the drawing.

“Yep – from around the corner of that tree line and straight across the lawn, right to the front of the house.”

“Well, that could be problematic – keeping the guys’ eyes off the front of the house, no matter where we are – even over by those trees. What about the back of the house? Is there an entryway – a door or sliding doors or something?”

“I thought there was”, I said, “but I’m not a hundred percent sure.” I looked at Parker. He gave a tilt of his head and a shrug. He couldn’t remember exactly, either.

“Wait – I’ve got an idea. Hold on.” And I got up and rushed upstairs to grab my laptop.

When I got back and got ‘er fired up, I went to Google and typed in Branson’s address. Even though houses aren’t for sale, oftentimes, a house will be described, along with an estimated value and the history of its sales.

“Found it – look”, I said, turning the machine. We all gathered around it and saw a couple of photos of the house, along with the pertinent details about it: the square footage, number of bedrooms – all of that. It was on Zillow.

“There”, said Parker. “There’s the back of it. And, yeah – it’s got a sliding glass door to the patio. Ground level, too.”

“Any chance you could use that door?”, asked Schmidt.

“Well, hell, yeah”, I said. “I mean, it would be an easier ingress. But what if the glass breaks? Those rocks are pretty damned hard and for me to fling the sack hard enough for the Bransons to hear it.….”, I trailed off.

“Look – it says there in that description that they’re insulated”, said Suze, pointing. “Does that mean they’re strong?”

“That means that they’re a double thickness, with a layer of air in between”, said Parker. “Pretty much have to have insulated glass around here – it gets too cold for it to be a single pane. But they still might break.”

We all stared at the computer, thinking.

“Hey”, said Schmidt, looking at me. “You got an old garbage can lid around here? Like the one on top of your horse treat can?"

"Well, yeah, sure."

"I see where you're going", said Parker.

"Right. Why not – instead of tossing a bag of rocks at the door – you fling a garbage can lid at it? It'll make a helluva racket and, chances are, it won't break the glass, especially if you aim for the piece of aluminum between the two."

I thought about that.

"Hmm…..why not, right? I can just hold it by the handle and let it fly, like a pitcher. And, you're right – it should be real loud, especially if I do it right."

"You will", said Schmidt. "Plus, even if we're out there by the driveway, we won't see you, anyway – the house'll be in the way."

"Yeah, but you guys'll hear it, too", said Parker. "And, by the time Branson gets down there, y'all will be running toward the back of the house, I'd imagine. And J.D. would be sitting there with his thumb up his ass, waiting on Branson."

"Hold on – how about this?", I said. "How 'bout I throw the lid – make a shit-ton of racket – then just throw down the sack with the 'hammer', right in front of the door, so he has to see it? And, if you guys are coming around the house - and, Schmidt, make sure you come around the east side, the garage side - and you see us, I'll just have Zeus run toward you and do the up-on-the-hind-legs thing. That'll stop y'all right in your tracks."

"Good enough, so far", said Parker, "but they'll see you turn tail and run toward the rig. They might chase you and that'd be a real clusterfuck."

Suze laughed.

"What?", I asked her, on behalf of the other two guys.

"Smoke bomb", she said.

Me: "Smoke bomb?"

"Yeah – they sell 'em at Walmart. I know, because I've bought one there, before. Back in Ohio, a friend of mine was doing a nighttime photo shoot and wanted a smoky effect. And he had me stop at Walmart – he told me they sell 'em there. And I got one and we used it. Worked great. And the good thing is, they've got a wire-pull ignition on 'em. All you do is pull the little wire and - POOF! - you've got smoke. They even come in different colors."

"That's a great idea", said Parker and Schmidt nodded. "We can stop at Walmart, tomorrow, and pick one up. Then, J.D., once you've thrown the lid and made a racket, you'll throw down the sack with the hammer in it, then, pull the little fucking cord on the smoke bomb and toss it toward that side of the house. Then, you guys run like hell back to the trailer."

"Why didn't I think of that?", said Schmidt. "Sort of like a flash-bang, but without the – um, violence. By the way, the public can't buy flash bangs, but the Feebs use 'em a lot. Yeah – a fucking smoke bomb. Great idea, kid!"

Suze looked proud of herself, as well as she should've.

"Okay, that's it, then", I said. "I'll do what you said, Parker, and as soon as I've tossed down the sack, I'll fling the smoke bomb in that direction."

"Wait", said Parker. "Better yet - why don't you wait 'til those guys see you? Like you said, just seeing you'll stop 'em in their tracks – you'll scare the shit out of 'em. Then, once they've seen you, *then* do the smoke bomb thing. That way you can disappear – like you were never even there. It'll freak the shit out of those bozos."

We all smiled or chuckled or whatever at the thought of that – this demon from hell on a monster horse from hell – red eyes staring down from both of them – then, all of a sudden, smoke envelopes the area and once those guys have fought their way through the smoke, nothing was to be seen. Like it never even happened.

"Yeah – plus we'll probably run into Branson at his patio doors and check out what's what with him", said Schmidt. "I'll make sure that happens. Give you a little extra time."

I sat back. "I think we've got a plan, you guys. It's a little different than what we're used to, but I definitely think we can pull it off."

"Will the smoke bomb freak Zeus out?", asked Suze.

"Good question", I said. "I don't think so, because I'll turn him, like, ninety degrees, when I throw it and by the time it hits the ground, we'll be facing the other way and we'll be off and running. Do they make a noise when they go off?", I asked Suze.

"Nope", she said. "Just start belchin' smoke."

"Good. What color smoke should we get?", I asked, with a certain amount of humor in the question. "Pink?"

"No, red", said Parker. "Blood fucking red."

And the three of us agreed.

"Okay, you guys", said Schmidt. "Like I said, this is - and you guys are – completely fucking nuts. This has to be the craziest goddamned caper I've ever been on. If it works, it's one for the books."

"It'll work", said Parker.

"Y'know", I said, "while we're all here, maybe it'd be a good idea to call Ron. We said we'd call him once we had our plan down."

The general consensus was, "Yeah, okay."

We filled him in on what we'd just discussed, including going to the back of the house, the sliding glass doors, the garbage can lid and the smoke bomb idea that Suze had come up with. Although he agreed with the red smoke, Ron was kind of partial to pink, too. He thought it made a statement about that group.

"We'll see", I said. "Maybe we'll get sky-blue pink."

"That'll work", said Parker.

"These guys are fucking nuts", Schmidt laughed. "And, obviously, you are, too, Mister Agent-In-Charge. Y'all are a fun group to work with."

"These guys get shit done, too", said Ron.

"Yeah – with a whole lotta your help", said Parker.

"Alright,", I said, "enough with the mutual admiration society stuff, we're about done here, right? Oh – Ron – we're planning on hitting Branson's at nine on the dot. Why don't you send out those emails about eight forty-five or eight-fifty. I doubt any of their members will be reading their emails during that ten- or fifteen-minute window. I mean, I doubt Branson or his wife will get a call, right then, before we show up and do our thing."

"Roger", said Ron. "And, hell, even if they do, it'll throw them into a swivet and they'll already be freaked out when you hit 'em. That wouldn't be the worst thing in the world. But, yeah, whatever – I'll send 'em out just before B-Hour."

"B-Hour?", asked Schmidt, as the three of us looked just a mite confused.

"Branson Hour, dammit. I thought you guys were on the ball."

"Ah, Jesus", said Parker. "That's lame as fuck."

"Says you", Ron retorted.

Looking around the table at the others' faces, I said, "Ron – I think we have general agreement, here, that that was highly lame."

"Oh, fuck y'all", he laughed. "Alright, I'll leave you to reconsider the genius of B-Hour. I gotta go. Let's all catch up, tomorrow, before the thing. And, Schmidt – you call me tomorrow, too, with anything else you see or hear."

"You bet."

After we'd hung up, Schmidt said he had to go, as did Suze.

"Call me if you need me for anything, tomorrow", said Schmidt. "And, look – can you text me when you're about five minutes out, tomorrow night? I want to know you're coming and that everything's cool."

"Sure", I said. "Suze – that'll be your job", and she nodded.

"Won't your guys hear the text come in?", asked Parker.

"Yeah, maybe. Who knows? But, either way, I won't take my phone out of my pocket and I won't text you back. It'll just be one little sound. I'll deal with it – don't worry."

We all got up and Schmidt and Suze left, with her saying that she'd see us in the morning.

"I think we're good", I said to Parker, once we were alone.

"Yeah – I like it. I actually like it a lot. Especially the smoke bomb thing. That oughta get you outta there, free and clear."

"Yep."

"Okay, I'm gonna head out, too. I need to get a good night's sleep – we both do. Plus, I might screw around a little with some designs for that new logo."

As he opened the door to leave, we fist-bumped, and he was off.

And I was feeling pretty good about tomorrow night.

CHAPTER 45

The next morning, the first words I heard when I arrived at my usual seat at the daily Geezers' meeting came from Joe: "How in the living hell could she do that? Drive that far down the embankment and end up in the damned creek?"

"I don't know", said Marquardt, looking down at the newspaper, "but, somehow, she did."

"I know that stretch of road and it's pretty hard to run off it, right along in there", said Joe. 'Suppose she did it on purpose? I mean, she'd not only have to drive off the road, but she'd have to steer around a whole bunch of trees on the way down. And you say she went clear into the creek?"

"That's what it says here", Bob replied.

It seems that, the morning prior, a Saugerties woman had driven off the northbound side of Glasco Turnpike – where the road is fairly straight, according to the report - and had gone a couple of hundred yards down a wooded embankment and finally came to a stop in Plattekill Creek.

Bob showed us the photograph in the paper of the woman standing in knee-deep water, next to her Subaru Outback. According to the report, the cops checked her out and she was fine, physically. They planned on investigating the incident further, to figure out how it might've happened.

"Seems to me,", said Parker, "that if she was high or smashed on booze, she might've nailed at least one tree on the way down. Maybe she was on a suicide mission and thought the creek was a lot deeper than it is."

"As it is, she does look fairly ridiculous standing there in the creek, next to her car", I said.

"You have a Subaru, don't you, J.D.?", asked Hal.

"Yeah, but it doesn't have a tendency to roll down embankments into creeks."

"Is that the car that Suze is driving, now?", asked Mike, nodding in her direction as she walked past us with a tray full of food.

"Yeah – I'm lending it to her 'til she can save up enough to get one of her own. And", I said, pointing at the photograph, "I'll bet that baby fired right up when she went to start it again. Those things can't be stopped."

Gretchen came up to the table, armed with her coffee pot, tapped Parker on the shoulder and said, "Hey, Bill – that basket of corn looks pretty good over there, doesn't it?"

We all looked over at the table next to the wall and Parker said, "Looks better than nothin', I guess."

"Well,", she said, "I'll have you know that I ordered a cornucopia from Amazon yesterday. Should be here in a couple of days. Then, I'll probably get a few gourds and so on at Topps and add it to the corn and it'll look real pretty for Thanksgiving."

We all nodded like we cared, then she said, "You guys ready?"

Just as we'd finished ordering and Gretchen was leaving for the kitchen, Suze walked up.

"I heard you guys talking about the Subaru when I walked past a couple of minutes ago. J.D. – just so you know, you'll be getting your car back soon."

 "Really? You found some wheels?"

"Yeah – if you remember, I was gonna go back to Ohio to get my old one, but I thought, fuck it – oops, sorry guys – screw it, that thing wasn't worth the money to do all that. So, I went up to Ruge Dodge/Chrysler on my way home, yesterday afternoon, and made a deal on a pretty nice used car."

"Good for you", said Mike. "What are you getting?"

"It's a '15 Toyota Camry. I guess some high school principal had traded it in on a new truck, a few months ago. The salesman said that it'd come in with some pretty rusty quarter panels, but they'd had another one on the lot that wasn't worth selling, but had decent panels on it, so they took the panels off that one and put them on the one I'm getting. It's in pretty nice shape, now, really."

Parker and I looked at each other, neither of us quite believing what we were hearing.

The 'high school principal' she was referring to was PJ Conway, the guy who'd tried to screw Parker's granddaughter out of being admitted to Brown University. He'd used some ill-gotten gains to buy the new truck and he traded in the Camry for it when he bought it.

Without going into any more detail, here, suffice it to say that the ninja horseman had

had everything to do with Mr. PJ Conway leaving his post and he and his wife leaving town, never to be heard from again, at least around these parts.

I couldn't help but laugh.

"What's so funny?", asked Suze.

"Ah, nothing", I said. "Sometimes, I just think funny things."

"Hey – isn't that from 'Arthur' – the Dudley Moore flick?", asked Hal. "That line, I mean, about sometimes, thinking funny things."

"Yeah, I guess it is", I said. "How'd you come up with that, so fast?"

"I just watched it the other night. I wanted to see it before I put it on the Movie Night schedule. It's a really cute movie."

"Hey", said Joe, "remember the Gielgud character's best line? 'Would you like me to wash your – "

"Never mind", I interrupted him. Suze was standing there.

"What?", she asked.

"You're too young", I said.

"Bite me, Spencer", she said. "Alright – we'll talk about getting your car back to you a little later. I'm supposed to pick up my new ride this afternoon. Catch you guys." And she gave us a little finger wave and headed off to another table.

She stopped and said, "Hey, J.D. – can I see you for a sec?"

"Sure", I said, getting up and walking over to her.

"What time you want me there, tonight? We're still on, right?"

"Yep. And we'll probably head out around eight-fifteen, so you might want to get there a little while earlier."

"Okay – why don't I come by around seven-thirty. That way, I can hang out with the kids and do anything else you need me to do."

"Deal", I said, giving her a fist-bump and heading back to the table.

Frank Branson picked up the phone to call Gallagher.

"Wassup, bro?", Gallagher answered.

"I gotta give a quote on a job up in Milan, this morning. Something about putting a pot-bellied stove into some man-cave or she-shed or something. Might be a fairly decent job and I can probably use you. Wanna go with me?"

"Yeah, sure – why not? Oh - and I can fill you in on the guys I've got coming to your place, tonight."

"You got somebody?"

"Yeah, three guys – three guys I know you can trust. Al, Mark and Schmidt."

"Ah, the originals."

"Yep. But I kinda wanna go over the logistics so I can fill 'em in before they get there."

"We can do it on the way up to Milan. Where should we meet?"

"I dunno. I guess the lumber yard is as good a place as any, right?"

"Yep. Okay, I'll pick you up around nine. I told 'em I'd be there around nine-thirty."

"Got it. See you there."

When Branson hung up, he went to look for Sheila, who was sitting at her desk.

"Hey, hon – guess what?", he said, rounding the corner into her office.

"What?", she asked, looking over her reading glasses.

"I just talked to Gallagher and he told me that he's rounded up three guys for tonight. You know, to hang out and guard the place. And, they're three guys I trust, too."

"Oh, honey", she said, removing her glasses, with a smile. "That makes me so relieved. Thank you."

"Sure, baby. And I don't want you to worry. I don't think that guy's coming back here, I really don't."

"Well, maybe", she said. "It's just that I'll feel a whole lot better knowing that we have people watching the place. Tomorrow night, too, right?"

"Oh, yeah", said Branson, not really knowing that, but assuming that Gallagher would come through again – maybe with the same three guys. "But probably only tonight and tomorrow. Don't forget – on Friday, we're going over to Orange County Airport."

"That's what I'm doing, right now", she said. "Writing an email to my Moms to see if any of them would be interested in joining us. You don't know what time, yet, do you?"

"Nah, haven't thought about it. I will though, and Gallagher and I'll talk about it when I pick him up. I'm taking him with me up to Milan for that quote. Picking him up at nine-thirty. What time is it, now?"

"Um", she said, looking at her computer, "eight-forty."

"Okay, I've got a few minutes. Think I'll go in and catch a few minutes of 'Fox and Friends'. From what I hear, they're gonna have an interview with DeSantis."

"Think he'll run against Trump?", she asked.

He shrugged and said, "I dunno, maybe. I know the two of them have been fussin' at each other, lately."

"If Trump runs, he'll crush DeSantis", said Sheila. "DeSantis is a Trump wanna-be. He can't hold a candle to him. I mean, I really like the guy and all, but Trump is the *man*."

"Well, DeSantis might be getting out there, just in case Trump's all tied up in court or something."

"I think it's just horrible how those Antifa-loving socialists are trying every trick in the book to bring him down. And, after years of all that shit, they still don't have anything on him. Maybe it's time they figured out that he's on the up-and-up – that he's really a great leader and, if the truth actually came out, they'd know that he won, too."

Frank nodded and asked, "What if Trump named DeSantis as his running mate?"

"Never happen, Frank. I don't think Trump trusts him any more than he does Pelosi - even though I think they're both really important for the country, right now. But, each in his own way."

"You could be right", said Frank. "Okay – I'm gonna go catch the tube for a few. I'll check in before I leave."

"Love you", she said.

"Love you more."

After we'd polished off our breakfasts, Bob had adjourned the meeting and our Jacksons had fluttered onto the table, Gretchen called me over to the little table by the wall, the one with the Indian corn. Parker moseyed over, too.

"Listen, you guys. Suze told me that you're going to do that thing of yours, again, tonight. Is that right?"

"Uh-huh", I said. "And she's coming with us, just like last time."

"Well, that's what she said. And I want you two to promise me – *promise* me – that you'll keep her safe. These people you're dealing with are not nice people."

"They're nowhere near as bad as Wolfe", I said, referring to a past caper that involved her.

"Yeah, well, maybe not – but they're still potentially dangerous", she said. "At least Wolfe was a smart man. These people? I'm not so sure. I mean, militias and so on? That's some dangerous stuff."

"Yeah, I know", I said. "But you have our word that we'll keep Suze out of any kind of trouble. Her job is to sit in the truck. That's all. That's it. She won't be anywhere near the action. That's just me and Zeus."

"I'll second what J.D. just said", said Parker. "She'll be with me the whole time and I won't let her out of my sight."

"Promise?", she asked, looking from one of us to the other.

"Scout's honor", I said, raising my hand in the three-fingered Boy Scout salute. Seeing that, Parker did, too.

"Okay. Just let me know as soon as you get back to the farm."

"We will. Oh - and by the way - we came up with a name for the farm", I said.

"You did? What is it?"

"Night Sky Farm. It kind of comes from Zeus and Ceres – two objects in the night sky."

"Night Sky Farm", she said, rolling it around. "Night Sky Farm – I like it." And she smiled.

"Okay – you're busy and we've gotta split", I said. "We'll call you tonight. It'll probably be a little after ten. Will you be awake?"

"Just call. If you wake me up, fine. I just want to know that everything's okay."

As Parker and I were walking to our trucks, he asked me, "We've got pie back at the place, don't we?"

"Oh, hell, yeah. Hazelnut walnut, remember?"

"Oh, right. Whipped cream?"

"There's still some left over from the last time."

"Cool. Catch you in a few", he said, and we got into our vehicles and headed out.

When we got back to the farm, we reconnoitered in the kitchen.

"Want some coffee?", I asked him.

"Nah – I'm coffee'd out."

"Pie's there on the counter", I said. "I'd better check on the whipped cream." And I opened the fridge and saw that we had at least half a container left. "We're good", I announced.

"What are you gonna deliver to the Bransons, tonight?", he asked. "I mean, you gonna print out those emails that Ron'll send to their groups?"

"I don't know. There are two ways to look at it, I think. One, we hold them back – we don't deliver them - and just let nature take its course. And, by that I mean that I'd imagine the revolt will start once those people start reading about ol' Frank and Sheila's shenanigans. And the revolt'll come as a total surprise to them and they won't know what the hell's going on, y'know? That'll freak 'em right the fuck out."

Parker nodded sagely.

"The other side of that is if we do deliver them and they read them and *then* the calls and so on start, I wonder if that'll have more impact. They'll sit there, stewing in their own juices for a little while wondering what the hell happens next and then the bombs start dropping. What do you think?"

"I think we should print 'em out and deliver them. Along with a note from the ninja horseman saying that, because they didn't listen to him, now, they're gonna pay the price.”

I thought about that for a minute.

“Yeah – you’re probably right. Just the idea that we know about their pasts will hit ‘em where it hurts. And, then, they’ll wonder what the hell the consequences will be.”

“Yep.”

“That means that I have to print out a copy of the emails and write a little something from the ninja horseman. Okay – I can do that.”

“Cool.”

“As a matter of fact, why don’t I go do that, now? I’ll run up and write the note and show it to you before I do the calligraphy thing. Where are you going to be?”

“Well, I’ve gotta clean up the kids’ poop and put a little water into their tubs, then I guess I’ll go into the garage and start playing with that logo.”

And he went out the door and I headed up to my office.

I fired up the ‘puter and began to type.

Frank and Sheila Branson……

On my last visit, I warned you.

I warned you not to go ahead with your plans.

You ignored that warning – and a little girl was

injured as a result.

Totally unacceptable.

And, now, by your actions, you must pay the consequences.

There will be no mercy.

Your secrets are secrets no more.

~ *The Specter from the Darkness*

There. Pretty good. Short and sweet.

I texted Parker, "Where are you?"

"Barn."

I printed out what I'd written and, three minutes later, I hustled into the barn with the sheet of paper in my hand.

"Check it out", I said, handing it to him.

"I like it", he said, reading it over. "Especially the 'There will be no mercy' line. And the secrets thing." He handed it back to me.

"Okay, cool. I'll run back up and do the calligraphy thing and print out the two emails. Oh – what about a garbage can lid? Do we have an extra one around here?"

"Probably not one that isn't being used. Tell you what – you go do your thing and, as soon as you're finished, we'll run across the bridge to that Walmart over in Kingston. We gotta pick up a smoke bomb, anyway, so let's get a new cheap-ass garbage can, too."

"Deal", I said and headed back to the house.

It only took me about half-an-hour to do what I had to do and I laid the ninja horseman's note and the two copies of the emails on my bed.

"Ready", I texted Parker.

"I'll drive", he texted back.

CHAPTER 46

The Walmart Supercenter was only about a quarter-mile on the other side the Kingston-Rhinecliff Bridge on Route 199. Big place, too.

"I hate Walmart", I said.

"Why?", asked Parker.

"Ah, mainly because it's so indicative of the country, today. It's eaten up all of the small mom-and-pop stores and they're all big boxes with zero personality and the company pays their employees squat and - I dunno – I just don't like it."

"Well, Amazon's eating their lunch, now, and you don't bitch about that – about it closing down the mom-and-pops."

"That's because they're already gone."

"Yeah, but you use Amazon all the time. They do the same thing – pay their employees shit and work 'em like dogs."

"Well, I guess I'm just a walking example of inconsistencies – pull in here."

Parker pulled into the parking lot and once we got into the store, we found the garbage can section fairly readily. We picked out the cheapest ten-gallon aluminum job we could find. The lid was about the right size, which was all we really cared about.

The smoke bombs were another story.

We found some guy in a blue vest and asked him. He didn't really know, but pointed us in what he thought was the right direction. After walking halfway across the store, we found another blue vest. He told us that they were probably on aisle thirty-seven or thirty-eight, though he could be wrong. He was, because the things on aisle thirty-eight were flares, like you put on the road if there's been an accident.

Eventually, we found the smoke bombs on aisle forty-one. Actually, they were called smoke grenades and most of the packaging referred to the fun they provide on Halloween. As such, there wasn't much of a selection left.

"Let's see", I said. "Yeah – they have red. But, look – they've got several other colors, too. You sure you want red?"

"That'd be my choice", he said, shrugging.

"Okay – yeah, sure – red it is." I picked up a box and saw that it had just what Suze said it'd have – a pull ring that triggered it.

"Why don't we get two of 'em?", said Parker. "I think we oughta test one when we get home. Just to make sure it works and see how it works. You know, how much smoke it throws off and shit."

"Good idea."

"Yeah – we'll go out into the field and let one off."

I grabbed another one and we headed off to pay for our stuff.

There were, maybe, thirty cashier's lanes lined up at the front of the store, but only two were working. Figures, I thought. One lane had four people in front of us, the other, three.

We finally paid for our stuff and, on the way out, a nice gentleman in one of those blue vests smiled at us and said, "Have a nice day, gentlemen. And thank you for shopping at Walmart." That was the best part of the experience. We thanked him for thanking us.

Now, back to the farm and the smoke bomb test.

____

Eric Gallagher was standing in the same spot he'd been the last time Branson had picked him up.

"You say this guy wants a man-cave?", he asked as they pulled out onto the road to Milan.

"Yeah, either that or a she-shed. I dunno, the guy said he wants a little place out back that he and the wife can use to write. I guess both of them are writers or columnists or something. And each of them needs an 'environment that's conducive to writing', is how he put it."

"Conducive to writing." Gallagher shook his head. "How big's it gonna be?"

"I have no idea. I guess we're meeting the two of them and we'll kind of toss around some ideas."

"Sounds like it's gonna be expensive", said Gallagher.

"That's what I'm thinking", rejoined Branson. "Hey, listen – you say you're all set for tonight, right?"

"Yep. I got Al and Mark and Schmidt showing up. I reached out to them first because they know you better than some of the guys."

"Good. And I like those guys, too. What time are they gonna be there?"

"I told 'em to show up around seven-thirty, quarter to eight. That work?"

"Yeah, it's fine. And I don't think they'll need to be there any later than ten. Nothin's gonna happen after that. The last time, it was around nine."

"You really think that guy's gonna show up again?"

"Well, no, I don't. But Sheila's still all freaked out about it and I'm basically doing it for her."

"Happy wife, happy life."

"You got it." He waited a few seconds, then said, "I think the guys oughta park on the street in front of the house. You know, make it look like a bunch of people are at the house. That way, if that asshole does show up, he'll think we've got a houseful of people and that might scare him off."

"I got a question for you, dude. What if the guy *does* show up again. What are the guys supposed to do? I mean, we can't just up and shoot him."

"Ah, Jesus, no. That'd bring the law down on us in a heartbeat. I mean, I think it's okay to shoot somebody if he's actually in your house, but just out on the lawn? I think that's a grey area I don't wanna have to deal with. Plus, if one of the guys does it, he isn't the homeowner and that part of the law wouldn't even apply to him. And that'd be bad, real bad."

"Yeah, but a baseball bat or two wouldn't be completely out of line, would it?"

Branson looked over at him and said, "Not if you don't kill the guy. Then, even if he gets hurt, we could all say that he attacked, first, and our guys were only defending themselves. You know, a broken arm or a broken leg? Tough shit – stay off my lawn!"

And they both laughed.

"Okay, then – I think we're set", said Gallagher. "Same thing tomorrow night, right?"

"Yeah, I think so. Don't forget – on Friday, we're going over to Orange County Airport."

"How are you gonna alert the guys? Phone tree again?"

"Nah, I think I'll send 'em all an email. I wanna spell it all out. You know, the whole shipping of a bunch of fucking border-crossing teenagers who'll undoubtedly add to our crime problem. And how this idiot administration is bending over backwards to ship 'em to nice, white, middle-class towns like ours. Fucking assholes."

"When are you gonna write and send it? Friday's comin' up pretty quick."

"Ah, probably first thing in the morning. Early. That oughta be time enough, right?"

Gallagher shrugged and said, "I guess so. Sure."

Branson made a turn and said, "We're pretty close to where we wanna be, now. I think it's only a mile or so up Milan Hollow Road."

"Not far from that other job we worked, right?"

"Yeah, not far. Keep your eyes open for Hidden Hollow Trail – should be up here on the left."

____

On our way back to the farm, a thought hit me.

"Y'know – rather than firing off that smoke bomb in the field, maybe we should do it in the general vicinity of the kids, especially Zeus. See how they react to it. I don't want him throwing a hissy fit when he sees it tonight."

"Yeah, okay. Let's do it kind of out in front of their gate."

"I'd like to fling that garbage can lid at something, too, just to see how loud it is. Well, and to make sure I have my delivery down."

"We can do that."

When we got back, we carried the bag with the smoke bombs over near the kids' gate and, of course, their curiosity as to what was happening brought them right over to it.

"Okay, you guys", I said. "We're gonna let off a smoke bomb, here. We just want to see how you react to it because, Zeus, we're going to do the same thing a little later tonight. Y'all okay with that?"

"I love how you always talk to them", said Parker, with a smile.

"Yeah. I figure that there's a possibility, however remote, that they actually understand what I'm saying. Either way, there's an energy that they feel and - ah, hell – I don't know. It makes me feel better, anyway."

"Alright, let's give this a try", he said, pulling one of the smoke 'grenades' out of the bag. "You wanna do it?"

"Well, yeah – so I can sorta practice how it works."

I took it from him and said, "All I gotta do is pull this and throw it, right?", knowing full well that that's how it worked, but I was a little bit nervous about it.

"Yup."

"Okay – here goes." And I pulled the little ring with a quick snap of the wrist and tossed the thing a few feet in front of us.

And, suddenly, a whole shitload of red smoke appeared. "Works", I said.

"Yup."

I glanced over at the kids as soon as the bomb hit the ground and the smoke began billowing from it. They both jumped and snorted a little and their heads bobbed up and down as they backed off a few feet. Thankfully, they were upwind of the breeze and the smoke didn't blow toward them. A few seconds later, with the smoke still coming out of the grenade-slash-bomb, they settled down and just looked at it curiously. As in, "What the hell is that? It doesn't seem scary, but what the hell is it?"

"Good, you guys", I said. "Just a little smoke. Nothing to worry about."

"It really gives off a lot of it", said Parker. "A real nice cloud. You toss that bad boy down in front of whoever's comin' around the corner of the house and it'll stop 'em in their tracks. Guaranteed."

Parker and I walked over and gave the kids a couple of treats. The smoke was still billowing, but maybe not as profusely as it had been a couple of minutes ago.

"How long will that thing keep going, I wonder?", I said.

"I dunno, another couple of minutes, probably. Just leave it and we'll toss the empty canister later."

"Okay, cool. Now, let's take that lid up to the house and I'll fling it against a wall or something. See how loud it is and get my pitching arm motion down."

Parker had put the can next to the barn and he went over and grabbed the lid.

We walked up to the driveway side of the house and I picked a spot on the wall, far enough away from any windows so we wouldn't have a disaster on our hands. I didn't really care about Branson's door, but I sure did care about mine.

I took the lid from Parker and held it by the handle. Reached back with it, imagining myself as the Braves' Kenley Jansen, and let 'er fly.

"BLAM!" And, yeah – it was loud.

"Whaddya think?", I asked Parker.

He shrugged and said, "Sounds pretty loud to me. It sure oughta get his attention."

"Okay, fine. I just wanted to make sure." And I went over and picked it up. "Think I'll leave it on the porch table."

"Cool."

"Okay, what now? I mean, are we all set for tonight?"

"Yep, as far as I can tell. Maybe I'll get the rig hooked up to the truck, now – it's easier in the daylight. Then, I'll get 'er pointed in the right direction so all we'll have to do is load up and split. After that, I guess I'll head home. Maybe take me a little nap."

"What time'll you get back here?", I asked.

"I figure around seven-thirty."

"Alright, good. I'm gonna head up to the house and get all the ninja horseman shit ready. Then, hell, I guess I'll try and catch a wee snooze, too. Hey – you make any progress on that logo, yet?"

"Ah, not really. I drew out a couple of things, but I'm not really happy with 'em. I'll work on it again, tomorrow. Maybe I'll fuck around with it a little when I get home, too. I dunno."

"You want any help with that rig?"

"Nah. Piece of cake – a one-man job, really. You go on – I'll catch you later."

About ten minutes later, I heard Parker give the double-toot on his horn and knew he was out of here.

I went upstairs and got everything laid out on the bed, next to the documents that we'd be delivering later. Everything was in order and all the garments were still nice and clean. I tested the lights on Zeus' fly mask and my balaclava and they worked, too. I put my boots next to the bed.

There. Ready.

Now, all I had to do was hang out for the next few hours, which wasn't something I was really looking forward to. On the afternoons before one of the ninja horseman's missions, I was filled with nervous energy.

If I still ran, like I did for several years a decade or so ago, this would be the perfect opportunity to do so. Maybe I'd take that up again, I thought. But not today. Soon, maybe – maybe in the spring – but not today.

I decided to watch the tube for a few minutes.

Knowing that there were no sports on at this time of day, I flipped to CNN.

And, of course, there was the ubiquitous panel of talking heads, blathering on about the election that was coming up in a few days. The mid-terms.

Now, I'd already voted by mail. I have to say that New York has as simple and easy a mail-in process as California. I'd even stuck my little 'I Voted' sticker on the fridge. Yay, me.

I was half paying attention to the monotony of the panel, but they seemed to be a little freaked by the possibility of some of the candidates not accepting the election results. I mean, how fucked up is that?

No nation on earth has election integrity even approaching what we have here. After the last election, that was proven in spades. And in court. All the way up to the Supreme Court.

Yet, that douchebag grifter who'd been President was such a sore loser, he kept going off at the mouth about how the election was rigged and fake and stolen and blah, blah, blah. Which, of course, a whole lot of people who thought he was the bee's knees bought with both fists.

And, as a result, people died. In the Capitol Building of the United States of America. And they'd gone hunting the Vice President through the building, fully intent on hanging the guy. And the Speaker of the House? They'd been after her, too.

Un-fucking-believable.

And, now, some of these half-witted jamokes were making noise about not accepting the upcoming results?

For the most part, they were nothing but mouth. Not an original idea between them. Not a single platform plank. Well, other than to promise to do things that were downright unfathomable in a working democracy.

How could this even be happening?

I switched to ESPN. I'd rather watch two guys debating whether or not the University of Illinois Fighting Illini could, somehow, make it to the national championship than the 'sky-is-falling', ratings-generating postulations from people who were getting paid, simply to give their opinions.

The thing is, I thought, there are no longer two or three television news outlets that serve as a central point of convergence for all viewers. The networks' nightly news broadcasts were trying mightily to do that, but their ratings were in the tank. Nobody watches them anymore.

And the cable outlets?

Either hard right or hard left. One or the other.

As a result, there's no real 'public address system' that will – or wants to – bring people together with just the facts. Oh, yeah, all outlets – most of them, anyway – do give viewers a certain amount of facts. The problem is, they choose the facts to fit their narratives. And they're spouting their noise into their own echo chambers.

It's a vicious cycle, cheered on, one-hundred percent, by the big multi-national conglomerates that own them. To those companies, it's all about the Benjamins. And ratings bring the Benjies. Screw what's right. Give 'em what makes us bank.

Inexcusable.

I finally turned off the TV, bored by all of the droning on about this or that.

I laid down on the couch, thinking that, when there's no real news or no real sports to broadcast, the world - and the cable outlets – would be better off with old reruns of 'The Rocky and Bullwinkle Show' or 'Popeye' or 'Gunsmoke' or 'M*A*S*H' or something.

I guess I must have dozed off thinking about Mr. Peabody and Sherman and the Wayback Machine.

CHAPTER 47

When I woke up it was pretty dark.

Four-thirty.

Okay, fine.

I got up and decided to take a shower.

That done, I went down to the kitchen, whipped up a grilled cheese and tomato sandwich and paired it with a fine vintage Diet Sprite. Oh, and a pickle.

Then, I put on my jacket and wandered down to see the kids, passing the truck and trailer that Parker had pulled into the driveway. I was beginning to feel my nerves.

Being with the kids made me feel a little better – well, until I told them that we'd be taking another ride, pretty soon – just like the last time. They didn't seem to care – but I did. I noticed that they'd stayed pretty clean so I wouldn't have to groom Zeus.

After telling them that I'd see them in a little while, I wandered back to the house.

To be perfectly honest, I can't remember what I did for the next little while. My mind was going a mile a minute and I couldn't really concentrate on anything. I must've done something, along in there, but I couldn't tell you what it was.

Finally, I heard Parker's toot-toot and looked at the clock: seven thirty-five.

I yelled to him as he got out of his truck and he came up to the house, into the kitchen.

"You ready?", he asked.

"Yeah, all I've gotta do is get the gear on and put the stuff in the sacks."

"Sack, singular. You're gonna use the trash can lid, remember?"

"Oh, right. It's upstairs on the bed. I think I'll run up and get the documents and the sack and the rock and the lid. We'll put the stuff in the sack down here."

"Don't forget the smoke bomb", he said, as I headed upstairs.

When I got back, I laid everything on the table.

"Okay – let's put the rock in the sack, first, then Ron's printouts, then place the ninja horseman's note on top of it, so it's the first thing he sees."

"Will you be able to carry all this shit?", he asked.

"Yeah, sure. I'll keep the sack between my legs, like I always do, and I'll stick the bomb under my thigh. I'll just carry the trash can lid. Zeus knows how to neck-rein, too, so I can steer him with one hand. Yeah, I got it."

"Put the glove on to make sure your finger'll fit in that little ring", he said, pointing at the smoke bomb.

I did and, yep, I could do that. Actually, the gloves were like a second skin.

We heard a car drive in.

Suze.

Parker yelled for her to come in.

"Hey, guys", she said, looking at all the stuff on the table. "Looks like you're just about ready."

"Look at you, all ninja-like", I said to her. She, too, was dressed all in black – pants, sweater and shoes. She even had a black stocking cap on her head and was wearing black gloves.

"Well, I don't wanna stand out like a sore thumb, just in case anybody looks my way."

"Probably a good idea. But, don't forget – you stay with Parker at the rig. I promised Gretchen that we'd keep you safe."

"Yes, dad."

We made a little small talk for a couple more minutes, then it was time to get a move on.

"Suze and I'll run down and get the tack onto the sawhorse and get the flakes of hay ready. You go on up and get your shit on", said Parker. He looked at the clock on the wall. "We should blow this pop stand in less than half-an-hour."

"I'll take the sack and the smoke bomb and the lid down", said Suze, "and lay 'em right next to your tack, J.D."

I went up and got into my duds: the black jeans, boots and black turtleneck. Then, I put on the black balaclava, pulling the mesh down over my face and testing the lights again before pushing it back up onto my head. Then, on went the gloves and the witcher's cloak. I kind of shrugged everything around a little, just to make sure nothing was pulling anywhere and that I was comfortable.

Okay, I thought, grabbing Zeus' fly mask off the bed, here we go.

And, just like always, I went into Mom and Bill's room to check myself out in the full-length mirror.

The only light was that which was seeping in from my bedroom across the hall. Other than that, the room was really, really dark.

I pulled my balaclava down, switched on the lights and pulled the hood up over my head. Then I walked over to the mirror.

And, because it was so dark, when I looked at the mirror, all I could really see was a black amorphous shape that had moved a little. But that black shape had two red dots where its eyes would probably be. It was almost like two tiny red orbs floating in the darkness. Usually, my reflection in the mirror gave me goosebumps – hell, it'd give anybody goosebumps. But just seeing those two floating red dots was a whole 'nother sensation. As otherworldly as the ninja horseman was, those two dots seeming to float in space were – well, just fucking nuts.

Okay – good to go.

On my way downstairs, I pushed the hood back, the mask up onto my head and laid Zeus' mask over my arm.

I walked down the driveway toward the sawhorse. I saw the saddle, the pad and Zeus bridle/reins combination, as Parker and Suze were walking up from the barn.

"Lookin' good, son", Parker said to me.

"Yeah – you get that mask down and that hood up and there ain't anybody's not gonna fill their trou when they see you", said Suze.

"Yeah, well – we 'bout ready?", I asked.

"Yep", said Parker. "We got two flakes in the back seat and I checked on the tape – we've still got plenty of it."

"Okay, let's get the kids", I said. "Suze, you can get Ceres, but hand her to Parker when you get to the trailer so he can get her inside. I'll go get Zeus."

And, just like always, Ceres hopped right up into the trailer. "I already put a little hay in each of their nets", said Parker. Ceres happily found it.

I got Zeus all tacked up, then put his fly mask on over his bridle. Then, I ran the wire to his lights up between his ears and affixed it to his mane with a little braid. It was secure.

"Alright, son", I said to him. "Ready to go scare some more assholes?"

Parker led him into the trailer and he, too, found his hay net. I closed the doors after Parker jumped down.

"Suze, you're in charge of the hay. As soon as we get there and get Zeus out, you'll stick a flake into each of the kids' hay nets, okay? They've only got a bite or two in there, right now."

"Got it", she said.

"Okay, let's mount up", said Parker.

I got into the passenger's seat, putting the sack between my legs and the trash can lid leaning against my shins. The smoke bomb was between my thighs. I noticed that that wasn't comfortable, so I set the sack and the bomb on the floor in front of me.

As I was doing that, Parker said, "Don't accidentally pull that ring, boy. Otherwise……"

I had to laugh at that.

"Okay, here we go", said Parker, dropping the gearshift into drive and turning on the headlights.

We pulled out onto the road.

My phone rang. Ron.

"Yeah? We're on our way, so be quick, okay?", I said, hitting the speaker.

"Roger. I just got a quick call from Schmidt and he's there with two other guys. He says they're hanging out in the street in front of the house. And, a new twist – he said a fourth guy might show up, too, but that's still up in the air."

"Fuck", I said.

"Yeah, well, Schmidt says he has it under control, so we'll have to believe him, I guess."

"Okay, yeah. Hey – have you sent out those emails?"

"I'm doing The Group's……right…….now. Okay, gone. Now, let me go to my other machine……okay……the Moms for Liberty's note is going right……now. Okay, done."

"Excellent."

"Yeah, they oughta have 'em in a few seconds. Wonder if anybody'll see 'em tonight?"

"Who knows?", I said. "But somebody'll see 'em at some point and I'd imagine that might cause an avalanche. At least I think it will. I hope it will."

"Yep. Okay – I'll let you guys go, for now. Call me when you leave there, okay?"

"You got it."

"And good luck. Knock 'em dead, kid."

"Yep."

I disconnected and said to Parker and Suze, "Well, it's happening."

Down in Hyde Park, Schmidt and Al and Mark and a guy named Drake were standing at the foot of Branson's driveway, when Branson came out the door to the garage.

"Hey, guys", he said, as he approached them. "Thanks a lot for coming, tonight. I mean it."

The guys all said something akin to "No problem."

"Look", said Branson, "I don't think anything'll happen. I really don't. But Sheila's still pretty freaked out and, just by you guys hanging around for a while, she feels a whole lot better."

"What if that thing – that guy – does show up?", asked Al. "Gallagher said we can wail on him, but no noisemakers, if you know what I mean." He nodded in the direction of Drake, the fourth addition to the team, his eyes resting on Drake's hip.

Pretty much all of Branson's guys knew Drake and Gallagher had called him, too, but he'd thought he'd have to work and wouldn't be able to show up. He'd called Gallagher an hour ago and told him that he'd learned he wasn't needed tonight, so he'd be glad to help guard Branson's, too.

Drake had a gun on his hip.

When Branson looked down at it, Drake said, "Hey – I've got a license for this. I'm perfectly legal."

"Yeah", said Branson, "but I don't want you using it. No how. No way. Gunshots'd bring the cops, for sure, and I don't want that. Plus, you can't just go shooting people, even if they are on my lawn."

"I could sure as hell scare him if I fired off a couple over his head."

"No. I said that'd bring the cops. And I don't want cops. Is that clear?"

Drake looked a little miffed, but said, "Yeah. Okay."

"Good. Now, can I get you guys anything? I've got a half-a-bottle of scotch in the house. Want me to bring it out?"

"Well, hell, yeah!", was the general consensus.

"Just don't go getting drunk on me", said Branson.

Mark piped up with, "You think half-a-bottle of scotch – between four guys – would be enough to get us loaded? Think again, bucko." And that brought chuckles all around.

"Okay, I'll go get it. Oh - and I think Sheila's got some paper cups in the cupboard. I'll bring those, too."

And off he went.

"I still think a couple over the head would be enough to put a stop to anything", said Drake, as Frank entered the house.

"You heard him, man. And he's the boss", said Schmidt. "So, I wouldn't, if I were you. Look – I gotta take a leak, so I'm going over behind those trees. Be right back."

"Hope everything comes out okay", said Al.

"Oh, Al – by the way – you wanna come over and give me a hand with this? Or did the doctor tell you not to lift heavy things?", asked Schmidt, tossing one right back.

"I hope you piss on your leg", Al retorted.

When he got behind the trees, Schmidt pulled out his phone and texted me: "Four guys, not three. One has a pistol. Was told not to use it. We're out front. Be safe."

My phone dinged with the incoming text and I read it out loud.

"Fuck", said Parker. "Might be a good thing that I've got my shotgun behind the seat."

"Oh, great", I said. "That's what we need – a friggin' gun battle. And, if you'll recall, the time you fired off those shots when we did that thing at Wolfe's place, Zeus 'bout freaked."

"I ain't gonna use it – don't worry", said Parker.

"Good", I said.

"Unless I absolutely have to."

If I was nervous before this, my nervousness scale just went up several degrees.

"How much longer?", asked Suze.

I could see Parker look over at me and he said in a whiny voice, "When are we gonna get there, dad?" Then, in his normal voice, said, "About ten minutes, maybe a little less."

Suze kicked the back of his seat. "Asshole", she said.

We were now on Crum Elbow Road, cruising along nicely.

A minute or so later, Parker said, "After we turn onto Matuk, I'm gonna follow it around to the right – not go straight, like we did before. That way, we'll be coming toward Kilmer from the other direction. Once we get to a big left curve, I'm gonna pull over and we'll put the tape on the lights."

"Got it", I said.

———————————————

Branson had come out of the house with the scotch and paper cups and he poured a little into each guy's cup, including one for himself. That done, he raised his cup and said, "Gentlemen – here's to you."

And they all drank up.

"Okay, I'm heading back into the house. Just keep your eyes open, though, like I said,

I doubt you'll see anything."

"You got it", said Al.

"Oh", said Branson, thinking of something. "I figure you guys oughta be outta here by ten, at the latest. I'll come out when I think it's time. But it won't be any later than ten."

The guys nodded and Branson walked back into the house.

"Hit me", said Mark, holding up his cup, and Al poured a finger into each cup again.

____

"Okay", said Parker, as we rounded a big curve to our left, "I'm pulling over here." And he doused the lights and turned off the cabin light.

The three of us, each armed with a roll of black tape, got out of the truck. I went to the back of the trailer, Suze to the back of the truck and Parker to the front of it, to tape over the running lights.

Thirty seconds later, we reconvened in the truck.

"You ready?", he asked me.

"Yup." It was all I could say, right then. And, for about the fourth time since we'd left the farm, I reached down to make sure everything I'd need was at my feet.

"You got the alfalfa, right, Suze?", I asked.

"No – I threw it out when we got out and covered the lights", she said. "Of course, I've got the alfalfa."

"Alright", said Parker. "I'm gonna pull into that driveway up there on the right. Then I'll back 'er around and get it up on the grass. Same place as last time."

Carefully, he pulled into the driveway and, fortunately, there was no yard light burning. It was dark. Then, he backed out and somehow, he got the thing up on the grass, right next to the tree line. I heard a couple of hooves stepping around, coming from the trailer. The kids were trying to keep their balance.

Unbeknownst to us, Schmidt had slowly edged his little group toward the side of the driveway furthest from where he knew the ingress point would be. Now, the guys couldn't see around the house. More scotch was poured.

"Okay, let's hit it", said Parker and we all alit from the truck.

I grabbed the stuff from the floor, Suze grabbed the hay flakes and Parker went around to the back of the trailer and opened the doors.

He climbed up into it and took ahold of Zeus' lead rope. "Okay, son", he whispered. "It's showtime." And he backed Zeus out onto the ground.

I pulled down my balaclava and pulled the hood up over my head, then walked over to Zeus' left side. Parker cupped his hands and I stepped into them and he boosted me up onto Zeus' back. I turned on his lights, then I turned mine on.

"Hand me the stuff", I whispered.

And Suze handed up the sack. I put it between my legs.

"Now the smoke thing." And she handed that to me and I stuck it up under my crotch. Then, she handed me the garbage can lid, which I held in my right hand. I had Zeus' reins in my left hand. I scootched around in the saddle a little, just to make sure I could move comfortably.

I nodded and knew that the two of them could see my lights in the dark.

Parker tapped me on the shin. "Go get 'em, kid", he whispered.

And I nodded again and turned Zeus around.

We walked to the edge of the tree line.

I took a deep breath, whispered, "Here we go, son." I patted him on the neck with my left hand.

And then I softly dug my heels into his flanks.

CHAPTER 48

We stuck right to the edge of the tree line, unlike the last time, when we went diagonally across the lawn toward the Bransons' front door. It was nice and dark along in here so I knew that we probably couldn't be seen. I'd turned our lights off for the walk toward the house.

We walked carefully and quietly along the trees until we got almost even with the back patio and the glass doors that were our target. I turned on both sets of lights again.

I could hear men's voices coming from the front of the house and there was laughter interspersed with the words that I really couldn't make out. Good, I thought – as long as I heard those voices, out front, I knew that they were oblivious to our presence.

There was a little light in the room on the other side of the sliding doors and it appeared to be a den of some sorts. There was a little bar with three stools, a couch, a couple of chairs and a wall-mounted television.

I focused on the aluminum piece that separated the doors, the spot where the movable door met the unmovable one. Like all those types of doors, the aluminum piece looked about two inches in diameter. I really wanted to hit that spot, not only because it should make a lot of noise, but I had no desire to break one of the big glass doors, either.

I had an idea.

I walked Zeus slowly across the empty patio and he only made a little noise with his hooves – not enough to be heard from inside or from the other side of the house. I turned him so we were parallel to the doors, not an arm's length away from it.

I switched the trash can lid to my left hand and pounded – hard – on the glass door four times. Boom! Boom! Boom! Boom!

Then, I quickly got us away from the door and faced it again.

Then, now having the lid in my right hand, I hard-balled it – the flat side – right at the spot.

CLANG! Followed by clangity-clangity-clang, as the lid rattled on the concrete floor. All of that was loud as shit, too, especially in the silence of the night.

I grabbed the sack and flung it right in front of the door that slid open.

Done!, I thought.

But, then, I heard yelling coming from the front of the building. And, yeah – I even heard a "Let's go!"

Fuck.

I quickly got Zeus up along the tree line, facing the end of the house that I thought the guys would come from.

And, just like we thought would happen, three guys tore around the corner, looking around for whatever had made that noise.

Suddenly, one of them saw our lights and yelled, *"There he is!"* and I saw him point in our direction.

I goosed Zeus and we hustled toward them, freezing them in their tracks. Yay, I thought.

Okay, let's try this……and I had Zeus go up onto his hind legs while I pulled the smoke bomb out from under my crotch.

I could see the terrified look on the guys' faces and thought I recognized Schmidt, standing in the middle.

After three or four seconds up in the air, Zeus came down and I timed it perfectly. As soon as he was on all fours, I pulled the pin on the bomb and let it fly, just as one of the guys yelled, "Get him!"

As the three of them started running toward us, the whole area between us filled with red smoke. I heard coughing and more surprised yelling.

I glanced to my right and saw Branson, standing there on the other side of the glass door, a look of confusion on his face. And, as I turned Zeus to get the hell out of there, out of the corner of my eye, I saw him slide the door open and rush outside.

However, he hadn't spotted the sack on the ground and tripped right over it and took a header.

One last look over my shoulder at my pursuers revealed arms swinging wildly. I knew they were trying to get through the smoke, but its cloud must've been a good fifteen, twenty feet wide and they were getting all bollixed up in finding the right direction to go.

I nailed Zeus in the flanks and we took off down the tree line for the corner of it.

Suddenly, *CRACK!"* and Zeus gave a mighty buck, scared as he was at the sound.

Not expecting anything like that, my feet weren't planted in the stirrups the way they would have been if I'd had even one second of warning and I felt myself losing my balance and, suddenly, with a second buck, I was gone.

I hit the ground like a ton of bricks, not having any time to help myself break my fall, except a little bit with my left hand. I felt a sudden, shooting pain in my wrist and I couldn't catch my breath. I lay there, stunned, for what seemed like forever, but must've only been a couple of seconds. I tried to breathe, but couldn't.

I turned my head and saw a figure running toward me with his right arm outstretched.

What?!? Oh, no. Oh, no. Oh, *NO! NOT A GUN!*

Still not being able to breathe – I instinctively knew that I'd had the wind knocked out of me – I couldn't really move, only wallow around on the ground.

The guy came close – like, maybe, ten feet from me - and I finally saw the gun glint in his outstretched hand.

"You motherfucker!", he yelled, slowing down a little. I stared at the barrel, which was pointed right at me.

You've heard people say that their life passed before their eyes at moments like that?

Yeah, well, that didn't happen, but I thought for sure he was going to shoot me. I had no other thoughts.

Suddenly, the guy disappeared. Gone. No, wait – he was on the ground!

The gun came flying toward me as I saw a shadow kicking him in the stomach and crotch and leaning over and pounding his face – once, twice, three times – hard!

"Can you get up?", the shadow whispered to me. All I could see when I looked up at it were two eyes in a black face mask.

"Uh…."

"Get up, J.D. Hurry!"

The shadow came toward me and grabbed me roughly under the arm. The left arm.

The one with the throbbing pain. *"Let's go!"*

We'd made it ten or fifteen feet toward the corner of the tree line when I whispered, "Suze?"

"Yeah, now hurry up, dammit!"

As we got to the corner, I spotted Parker jumping down out of the trailer and closing the door. Looking over my right shoulder, one last time, I saw two guys emerge from the smoke and start running our way.

"You okay?", he asked in a stage whisper.

"Where's Zeus?", I shot back. "And, quick - they're coming!"

"He's in the trailer. Now, come on – get in! Those guys'll be here any second."

The two guys rounded the corner.

Too late.

"There they are!", one of them shouted and they ran toward us.

"Here – take this", said Parker, tossing a branch to me. He must've picked it up off the ground.

I caught it in one hand, just as a guy was bearing down on me. I raised it like a lance and he ran right into it, the end of the branch nailing him right in the chest. *"OW!"*, I heard him yell and he doubled over. I swung the branch and broke it over his head. He went to his knees.

Next to me, I could see Parker fully engaged with another guy, fists flying everywhere, but I could see that Parker was getting the worst of it. Suddenly, that guy went down, too – like a ton of bricks. I saw a shadow – Suze – bolt over from the tree line and she'd chopped the guy in the back of the neck. Then, she kicked him full in the face two or three times. In the darkness, the blood running from his nose looked black.

Schmidt came running around the corner and quickly took in the situation.

He rushed up, grabbed my guy's collar and hauled him to his feet. "Come on!", he shouted.

Then, almost dragging the guy, he went over to the other fallen comrade, who was now up on his hands and knees. "Can you walk?", Schmidt asked him.

"Uhh…"

"Come on – get up!", he said, reaching under the guy's arm and pulling him up.

He looked in my direction, with both guys in tow, and pointed with his chin. "Get outta here", he said. "Now!"

Parker and Suze and I bolted for the truck and, just as I got in, I saw Schmidt pulling the other two around the corner of the tree line.

Because the truck was already running, Parker dropped it into gear, goosed the gas and we moved quickly. So quickly, that I heard the kids stomping around in the trailer, trying to keep their balance. It was fucking loud, too.

"What's up with those guys?", asked Parker, with his eyes on the road.

"Schmidt just took them around the corner", I said, looking in my rearview mirror.

Ten seconds later, we were five hundred feet up the street and still moving quickly. Parker was bent over the steering wheel, trying his best to see where he was going in the dark.

Finally, we made it to the big curve and I asked, "We gonna stop and pull the tape?"

"Yeah, but we'd better do it faster than we ever thought possible. If those guys get their heads together and get back to their cars and come after us, they'll be no more than thirty seconds behind us. Ready?"

"Yep", both Suze and I said in unison.

"Go!", he said, as he slammed the gearshift into park. I heard the kids jumping around again. I felt bad for them.

"It's okay, kids", I said, as I went past them to the back of the trailer. "We'll be home in just a few minutes."

Fifteen seconds later, we were all back in the truck and Parker hit the gas.

"Lights?", I asked him.

"Not yet. Not 'til we get to Crum Elbow."

Now, my wrist really started throbbing. "I hurt my wrist when I fell", I said, holding it up.

"Think it's broken?", asked Suze.

I swiveled it around and bent it backwards and forwards a couple of times. "It moves okay", I said.

"Probably just a sprain", she said. "We'll get some ice on it when we get back."

"How's Zeus?", I asked Parker. "That fucking gunshot really sent him over the edge. He okay?"

"Yeah, he came tearing around the corner of the trees, but I flagged him down – you know, waved my arms - and he slowed down enough for me to grab his reins. I patted him a couple of times and he snorted and so on, but he let me lead him right into the trailer. I think he felt safer there."

"Oh, thank God", I said, breathing a sigh of relief.

"You got the wind knocked outta you, back there", said Suze, now leaning forward between Parker and me. "That was close."

"I had no idea what the hell was going on", I said. "I really thought that guy was gonna shoot me – I really, really did. And then – all of a sudden – he just disappeared. What the hell happened? How did you show up?"

"Well, I talked Uncle Parker, here, into letting me go hide in the shrubs along this side of the house, just in case one of the guys came that way."

"I knew that she knows Krav Maga", said Parker. "I figured she could sneak up on a guy if that happened and just fuckin' wail on him."

"Jesus, you did, too", I said, looking over at Suze, who now had her stocking cap pulled up onto her forehead. "You hurt that guy."

"Fuck him", said Suze, defiantly. "He was gonna shoot you. Shoot an unarmed man. The motherfucker's lucky I didn't kill him. He oughta be okay. I mean, he was still conscious when we split. That's probably a good thing."

Parker said, "Okay – I'm turning onto Crum Elbow and I haven't seen any headlights behind us. I'm turnin' on the lights." And he did.

"I think we're cool", he said.

Back at Branson's, all hell was breaking loose.

When he'd come out of the house and tripped over the sack, Branson had cracked his kneecap pretty hard. He didn't think it was broken, but it hurt like fuck and he had a hard time standing up on it.

When Al and Mark and Schmidt had fought their way through the red cloud enough to see anything, Schmidt spotted him, struggling to get up. He rushed over to him as the other two ran across the lawn.

"Frank – you okay?", he asked, as he attempted to help him up.

"Ah, I really banged my knee, tripping on something coming out of – wait – what did I trip on?", he asked, turning to look.

"That sack, I guess", said Schmidt.

"Oh, fuck", said Branson.

"What?"

"Hand it to me, willya?"

Schmidt reached down to grab the sack and gave it to Frank.

"I don't know what the fuck that was, Frank, but Al and Mark are after him, now."

"You go on and help 'em", said Branson. "Hurry!"

And Schmidt ran off.

Just then, Sheila appeared in the doorway.

"Frank!", she yelled. "Frank! Are you okay?"

"Yeah – just tripped over this thing and cracked my goddamned knee on the floor."

"Are you alright?", she asked, rushing over to him. "Is it your leg?"

"Knee. It hurts like hell, but I moved it around, so I don't think it's broken. Hold onto me."

"Oh, Frank", she said, as he put his arm around her shoulders.

"Okay", he said. "Still hurts, but I think I can walk. Let's go inside."

And, with Sheila's help, he limped his way to the couch and sat down. He'd had the sack in his hand and dropped it on the floor at his feet.

"Oh, my *God*, Frank!", said Sheila. "I-I-I *hate* this! How could this even happen with – what? – four guys guarding the house? What the *fuck*?"

"I have no idea, honey. I really, really don't."

She pointed down at the sack and looked at him, her eyes full of fright.

"Ah, Jesus", he said. "Better hand it to me."

She did and he opened it and reached inside, coming out with a single sheet of paper. Sheila sat down next to him so she could read it, too.

And they saw…….

Frank and Sheila Branson……

On my last visit, I warned you.

I warned you not to go ahead with your plans.

You ignored that warning – and a little girl was

injured as a result.

Totally unacceptable.

And, now, by your actions, you must pay the consequences.

There will be no mercy.

Your secrets are secrets no more.

~ *The Specter from the Darkness*

"What the hell's this supposed to mean?", asked Frank. "What secrets?"

Sheila said nothing, just sat there, petrified.

"Look – there's something else in here", he said, pulling out another two sheets of paper.

He unfolded one and they read…….

Frank Branson Is NOT What He Seems. Read On……

Frank Branson is not who you want as a leader. As a matter of fact, you should not even want him in your group. He has a couple of incriminating secrets in his background that you should know about.

When he was in the military and stationed at Camp Humphreys, outside of Seoul, South Korea, he was found guilty of being drunk on duty, driving while intoxicated, illegally discharging a firearm, and caught in a 'compromising position and not in the proper manner of uniform' with another male soldier.

He was found guilty of violating Article 112 of the Uniform Code of Military Justice; Article 15 (drunk driving); and Article 134 ("prohibited conduct that is of a nature to bring discredit upon the armed forces or is prejudicial to good order and discipline").

He was given a general discharge from the Army and lost his rights to the GI Bill.

That is not the mark of a leader.

Furthermore, less than a year after returning home, he paid for an abortion for his then-girlfriend, now his wife.

Again, he:

- Got drunk on duty and got caught

- Drove drunk, while on duty, and got caught

- Carelessly discharged his firearm, while on duty, and got caught

- Fooled around, half-naked, with another male soldier, while on duty, and got caught

- Got kicked out of the military

- Paid for an abortion

If I were you, I would ask him about it.

And, although he may deny it, there are records to prove it. All of it.

Then, ask yourself, "Is this a person that I would trust or want as a leader?"

Be smart.

Sincerely,

~ The Specter from the Darkness

"Holy Jesus Christ", he breathed. His eyes went back to the top of the paper and he read it again.

"What is this, Frank?", Sheila asked. "This isn't real, is it?"

"Uhh…."

"Uh, what, Frank? Did this really happen? Tell me it's a joke, Frank."

He didn't say anything.

"Frank – you told me that you'd been in the military in Korea and that you'd been separated from it. But you never mentioned anything like this. Tell me this is just bullshit."

"It's a long story, honey……"

"Oh, God, Frank. Oh, dear God."

And the silence in the room became deafening.

Then, Sheila closed her eyes, took a deep breath, and said, "Okay, Frank. Maybe this all happened and maybe it didn't. It was decades ago – a lifetime ago - and you're a wonderful man and a wonderful husband. So, let's just consider it water under the bridge. Come here."

And she hugged him.

CHAPTER 49

They heard a phone ring from up in the living room.

"I'd better get that. It might be for me", said Frank, attempting to push himself up off the sofa.

"No, honey, it's my phone – I can tell by the ring. You sit right there. I'll run up and get it." And she hurried up the half-flight of stairs.

He yelled up to her, "Bring mine, too."

While she was gone, Frank reached into the sack and pulled out the other sheet of paper and opened it.

He read……

Anti-Abortionist Sheila Branson Had an Abortion

Sheila Branson is a total hypocrite.

As a member of the local chapter of Moms for Liberty, there is something that you should know.

Although Sheila is adamantly and vociferously pro-life and anti-abortion – even to the point of leading regular protests at Planned Parenthood facilities - I'll guarantee you that she never told you that….SHE HAD AN ABORTION.

On August 6, 1994, a young woman named Sheila Stark (now Sheila Branson) had an abortion performed at Auburn Community Hospital in Auburn, NY. She was twenty-two years old at the time.

Has she ever told you that?

If you question this fact, just know that the records exist, in black and white.

Ask her about it.

And ask yourself, is she the leader you really want?

Sincerely,

~ The Specter from the Darkness

Holy shit!, he thought. That guy knows about Sheila, too. Oh, fuck. Oh, fuck. Oh, *fuck*.

Coming back down the stairs, she said, "That was Mark Fisher calling again – I'd completely forgotten about that. I rushed him right off the phone but he said - what is it, Frank?"

"Come here, honey. Sit down."

"What?", she asked.

"You'd better read this." And he held up the piece of paper.

She took it and, as she was sitting down, she looked at it.

"Oh, no!", she screamed. And her eyes went wide as she read the entire page. *"Oh, no!"*

She turned to Frank with an expression of horror on her face.

His phone rang. He looked down at it and saw that it was Gallagher.

He grabbed his wife's hand and squeezed it as he answered.

"Yeah?"

"What the *fuck*, Frank?!?"

"Huh? What?"

"I just got a fucking email - and so did a bunch of the other guys – two of 'em have already called me."

"An email?"

"Yeah, Frank - a goddamned email! And you know what it says?"

Frank felt his bowels attempt to loosen.

"What?", he asked, quietly.

"It says that you were thrown out of the Army for being a complete and total fuck-up!" Gallagher was almost screaming, by now. "And, what? You and another guy got drunk and were playing hide the fucking salami?!? What the *fuck*, Frank?!?"

"I-I-I don't know what you're talking about, Eric", Frank mumbled.

Branson looked over at his wife who was in another state of near-panic.

"Frank,", said Gallagher, "this is bad. This is really fucking bad. You've got a lot of explaining to do – to me and all of the other guys. I dunno, Frank. I just don't know….."

"Look, Eric – can I call you back? Sheila's having a problem, right now."

"In the morning, Frank. Call me in the morning. My phone's blowing up, right now – I've gotten three texts since you and I've been talking. Call me in the morning. And you goddamned well better have an answer for this, Frank. And that's all I'm gonna say." And he disconnected.

Sheila was sobbing and rocking back and forth.

"Honey", he said to her. "Honey."

"I'm done, Frank. Done. Done! *Done!* I heard what Gallagher said – he was shouting. And it looks like this" – she reached for the paper and waved it around – "has been emailed to your entire group. And, if that's the case, I'm sure this" - and she picked up her sheet – "has been sent to mine, too."

"Well, maybe – ", he started.

"Maybe nothing, Frank! We're done. You and I are both done! There's no fucking way that either of us can talk our way out of this. No how, no way. Oh, I'm just sick……"

Sheila's phone rang again. She looked down at it in horror, but her curiosity took over.

She recognized the name of the caller.

"Hi, Sharon."

"Sheila, I just received a *very* upsetting email." Sheila felt her stomach turn over.

"Oh", she said.

"Yes, Sheila - and I'll come right to the point. It says that you had an abortion. Is it true?"

"I, uh –", and her mouth froze. She couldn't speak.

"Your silence is deafening, Sheila. Do I - and maybe others – have to call this…this….Auburn Community Hospital to see if there was a patient named Sheila Stark back in – what? – nineteen-ninety-four?"

Sheila disconnected. She didn't know what else to say or do.

"They know, Frank. They fucking *know*! All of them! Just like your guys know! We – both of us – are really and truly fucked, Frank."

They just stared at each other.

And, then, Frank's guys showed up at the sliding glass door.

Glancing at them, with Schmidt and Mark holding up Drake between them and Al trying to staunch the blood running from his nose, he said, "Oh, Jesus *CHRIST!*"

———————————————————————

Meanwhile, we'd gotten back to the farm and had gotten the kids unloaded, Zeus' tack all put away and had gathered in the kitchen. I'd taken off my cloak, balaclava and gloves and laid them on the counter as Parker and Suze sat down.

Joining them, I said, "We've gotta call Ron."

"Before we break out the pie?", asked Parker.

"Yeah – it'll just take a minute. You can get it, though, and grab the whipped cream out of the fridge. And don't forget forks."

"You got ice in the freezer?", Suze asked, standing up again. "We oughta get something on that wrist."

"Uh, yeah", I said, picking up my phone.

I hit Ron's number and the speaker.

"Well?", he said.

"We did it but, Jesus – it was rough, son."

"Tell me about it."

And I did. All of it. The whole nine. Right up until the time we got home.

"Holy shit, mano! Are you okay?"

"Yeah, except I think I sprained my wrist. Suze is putting some ice on it. And, I gotta tell you, I think she saved my life, back there. That sonofabitch was gonna shoot me."

"Holy Christ." He waited a couple of seconds, then said, "On behalf of all that's holy, Suze – thanks for saving my best friend's life", said Ron. "And I mean it."

"Ah, it was nothin'", she said. "That asshole never even saw me coming. And I just Krav Maga'd the shit out of him."

"And that other guy, too – the one I was fighting", said Parker.

"Yeah, well – none of 'em could fight worth a shit", she said. "I was just getting warmed up."

"I'd say she's a pretty decent addition to the group, wouldn't you guys?", asked Ron.

"The best", I said. "She sure saved our bacon." I smiled at her. "Hey, Ron – have you heard from Schmidt?"

"I got a text from him a few minutes ago. It said, 'Busy now. Mission accomplished. Will call later'. I guess he's still at Branson's place. Let me ask you – do you think his cover was blown?"

We all looked at each other and Parker piped up: "Nah, I don't think so. He did pull those two guys outta there, but they were pretty well beat up and they probably think he was just trying to get 'em away so they didn't get hurt any worse."

"Yeah", I said, "Up 'til then, there was no way he wasn't one of them. And I think Parker's probably right."

"Well,", said Ron, "he's a big boy and he'd know that if his cover'd been blown, he'd'a high-tailed it outta there, somehow. I guess I'll wait to hear from him."

I said, "I'd love to be a fly on the wall at the Bransons', right about now. If anybody's read those emails, I'll bet they're getting a few calls."

"They are", said Ron. "I can tell, here on my magic box, that both of their phones have been in use over the past little while. I can't listen in, right now, but my little lights are going on and off - and that means their phones are in use."

"I can only imagine", I said. I looked at Suze and Parker and asked, "How bad do you suppose those guys were hurt?"

"I think I might've broken the jaw of the guy who attacked you", said Suze. "I kicked him pretty hard. But, like I said, the motherfucker deserved it. The other guy – the one by the trailer? Broken nose, for sure."

"And I might've cracked a rib or two on the guy who came at me. Hey, by the way Parker – where'd you get that stick?"

"I almost tripped over the goddamned thing as I was walking toward the corner of those trees, trying to watch you guys around the corner. And, then, when I was taking Zeus into the trailer, I almost tripped over it again. So, yeah – I knew where it was and it all just sorta worked out."

"I don't think the end I got the guy with was sharp enough to really break the skin – especially through that jacket he was wearing. But it sure hurt. He stopped on a friggin' dime."

Ron laughed and said, "Listen to you guys – a bunch of gangsta street fighters!"

We all chuckled and, then, I said, "Okay, look, Ron - we're gonna let you go. We've got hazelnut pecan pie with our names on it, staring up at us. And, unless there's anything else, we're 'bout to devour it."

"You got whipped cream?", he asked.

"Is Branson dead in the water?", I laughed.

"Ha! Close enough! Alright – unless something else pops, tonight, let's catch up in the morning. I'll get some more intel from Schmidt, a little later – I hope - and I'll fill you in on it in the morning."

"Tell him how much we appreciated his help, tonight", I said, and Parker and Suze both chimed in with their agreement. "And tell him to call me or something when he gets a chance."

"Will do. Again – good job, tonight, you guys. You just might've put the kibosh on a couple of asshole groups out by you."

We disconnected and Parker said, "Pie."

Suze picked up the whipped cream and let 'er rip.

____

At Branson's, Schmidt said, "This guy's gotta get to a hospital. No doubt his jaw's broken."

Drake looked miserable. And dazed. Schmidt continued, "I think I oughta drop him off there. His truck can sit out front for a day or so, can't it?"

Branson kind of nodded, clearly still in shock.

Al mumbled, "I think my nose is broken."

Frank and Sheila just sat there, numb to all of this. Both of their heads were swimming with their own problems.

"What the hell did you get us into, Frank?", asked Mark. "That sonofabitch 'bout broke my ribs. Who the fuck was that?"

Frank just sat there.

Schmidt jumped in again. "Al – if your nose is broken, the best thing to do is go home and get some ice on it, tonight. Then, in the morning, go see a doc or go to the emergency room. They'll set it and you'll be fine. Happened to me a few years ago."

"I-I-I'm sorry", said Branson. It was all he could say.

"Okay – I gotta get this guy to the hospital. We're gonna split", said Schmidt, turning Drake toward the door.

'Frank,", said Mark, "all I can say is this was a disaster. A fucking disaster."

"Come on, Drake. Can you walk?", asked Schmidt. Drake nodded slowly. "Ah hink ho", he said.

And the four of them more or less limped out the sliding door, closing it behind them.

Frank sat there with his head down and his elbows on his knees.

Sheila grabbed Frank's phone off the couch and turned both his and hers off.

"I can't take anymore, tonight, Frank. I just can't." Then, with her hand shaking, she reached for a tissue out of the box that sat on the end table.

Frank just sat there.

Meanwhile, back at the ranch, Parker said, "This is one of the best we've had." He stuffed another forkful of pie into his mouth.

"Yeah – that chocolate seems to really add to the pecan flavor", I said.

"I should call Gretchen", said Suze, licking her lips.

"Oh, right – I forgot about that", I said. "Here – I got it." And I hit speed dial. Then I handed my phone to her.

"Hi, Gretchen", Suze said, brightly, when Gretchen answered.

"Oh – it went great", she said, looking at both of us and raising her eyebrows. "No problem at all. Mission accomplished.......oh, they're fine, too.....here, wait – I'll put it on speaker....."

"Hey, Gretchen", I said, and Parker mumbled his greetings, his mouth full.

"So – it went okay, huh?", she asked.

"Yep – just like clockwork", I said. "We got in, delivered our message, and got right back out, again. Just like always."

"Well, that's a relief", she said. "I've been on pins and needles all night long. Whew. Now I can breathe."

"Yeah, you can", I said. "And you'd better get to sleep. You gotta get up early."

"Yeah, well – now, maybe I can sleep. Suze – you can come in a few minutes late in the morning. It's late for you, too, and you're not even home, yet."

"Well, we'll see", said Suze. "Maybe, but I think I'll be just fine. Hell, I used to party all night, then grab a shower and work for the next eight hours. I think I can do this, too."

"It's up to you, but I don't want you to overdo it", said Gretchen.

"I won't."

"Okay, listen, Gretchen", I said. "We wanna wrap this up, here, and you've gotta get to bed. We'll fill you in on all the details in the morning."

"Okay, sounds good. Sleep tight, you guys. And thanks for the call." And we disconnected.

"Are you gonna do that?", Suze asked me.

"Do what?"

"Fill her in on all the gory details."

"Hell, no. We'll make it sound like it was a simple in-and-out. No need to give her agita."

"Yeah", said Parker. "I'm not sure she'd be too thrilled about hearing that you disarmed a guy and cracked his jaw."

We all chuckled at that, then a thought hit me.

"Oh, the gun. Wonder what happened to the gun."

Suze smiled, reached behind her back and pulled out the gun and laid it on the table.

"Umm….", she said.

"Holy shit! You took the guy's gun?", I asked.

"Finder's keepers", she said, still smiling.

"Oh, no", said Parker. "You don't want that thing. You ever get caught with that, you've got no license for it. Plus, you don't know its history. Who knows what it might've been used for. No, kid – we gotta get rid of it. Here – I'll take it and get rid of it on the way home." He took the gun off the table and began fiddling with it.

"What're you doing?", I asked.

"What's it look like I'm doing? I'm taking it apart – breaking it all down. Then, as I'm driving home, I'll toss the parts out the window, one at a time, a quarter mile or so apart. The thing will simply disappear forever. You got a paper bag?"

"Yeah, sure." And I stood up and walked over and took one out of a cupboard. "Here."

When he'd finished disassembling the weapon, he put all the pieces into the bag.

"Alright, look. It's late. Suze, we gotta go", he said, standing up. "We could all use a few hours of shut-eye. You ready?"

"Yep, guess so." And she pushed back her chair.

Once we were all over by the kitchen door, Suze said, "Okay – group hug."

And, though I wasn't really a hugger, I had to admit that that felt pretty darned good.

CHAPTER 50

After Parker and Suze left, I made one last trip down to check on the kids, but not before wrapping my wrist in an old Ace bandage that I'd found in a hall closet.

It hurt, alright, but it was more of a dull, throbbing pain than a sharp one. I'd also used a trick my old dentist had given me for a toothache, one time: two naproxen, aka Aleve, and two acetaminophen, aka Tylenol. They were beginning to work.

It was cold and dark walking down the lane but, hey, it was November.

I found the kids in the barn, turned the lights on and went over to meet them at their fence.

"How are you guys?", I asked.

Both seemed none the worse for wear and I said to Zeus, "Dude – I'm so sorry you got scared, back there. Scared me, too. And me hitting the deck was my fault, not yours." I rubbed his face. Then, Ceres wanted in on the face-rubbing action, too, so I rubbed with both hands.

"Alright", I said, "I gotta go to bed, but first……." And I reached down into the 'inside' treat can and pulled out a few for each, alternating between them. Once they'd had what I deemed was their fill, I bade them each a good night, turned out the lights and headed back to the house.

Walking up the lane, I thought how very fortunate I was to know them and live with them. Hell, they're the only family I've got, I thought. Well, them and Parker – sort of. And I kind of marveled at how my life had changed over just the past few months. From a somewhat high-powered media executive in LA to just a schmo living his best life on a farm in the Hudson Valley. Check that – living on Night Sky Farm in the Hudson Valley.

Damn, I felt like I'd hit the lottery.

Walking up the steps to the back porch, I looked over to my left and, in the darkness, saw Mom's garden, which had now gone to sleep for the winter. I couldn't wait 'til next spring, when we'd make sure it became an explosion of flowers, again.

As I finally crawled into bed, I allowed myself to rewind what we'd done, tonight. And I had to admit that – for those few seconds, lying on the ground with that guy pointing the gun at me – I'd never been as scared in my life. Thank God for Suze and her Krav

Maga.

As I began to doze, I wondered what was happening down at the Branson place. But I was pretty goddamned sure that their house wasn't as quiet and peaceful as my bedroom was, right then.

Z-z-z-z-z-z........

____

The next morning, I took off the bandage to check the wrist. It was a little swollen, but not bad. It could've been a helluva lot worse, that's for sure. I re-wrapped it and did the NSAID trick again while doing my morning toilette.

When I got to The Coffee Spot, the discussion around the table centered on the fact that some pizzerias in the area were going to be offering Thanksgiving pizzas. I sat down as Marquardt was reading from this morning's Hudson Valley News.

"It says here that, due to the high cost of turkey and all the fixin's, this year, some people might not be able to afford the traditional Thanksgiving dinner, so a few places are gonna whip up some pizzas with turkey and dressing and so on as toppings. It says that some might even be putting cranberries on 'em."

"Cranberries?", asked Hal, rather incredulously.

"I think that's bullshit", said Joe. "Who the hell wants turkey and dressing on a goddamned pizza? That's friggin' sacrilege."

"Hey – don't knock it 'til you've tried it", said Mike. "You never know."

"I think it sounds interesting", I said. "I mean, it's not your traditional Italian-type thing, but it might be alright."

"Ah, that's 'cause you're from LA", said Parker. "People out there eat all kinds of shit. You know, bean sprouts and raw fish and that."

"Hey – what happened to your wrist?", Hal asked me.

I held up my arm and said, "Ah – I fell offa Zeus. We were riding around, doing a couple of fancy moves, when my saddle slipped and I took a header. All my fault – I should've double-tightened his girth. It's just a sprain, though, and it isn't really bad at all."

"See? That's why I don't ride horses", said Joe. "I'm a man of creature comforts and a screwed-up wrist is not in what I consider my comfort zone."

Just then, Gretchen walked up.

"Gentlemen", she said, pouring coffee into my mug and topping off the other guys'.

"Hey, Gretchen", said Bob. "We're just reading, here, that a few pizza places in the area are gonna whip up some, what they call, 'Thanksgiving pizzas', with turkey and dressing and cranberries and so on for toppings."

"Yuck", she said, making a face. "Way to screw up two great things at once, in my opinion."

"Hey", said Mike, "is Artie going to put together a Thanksgiving meal here?"

"Yeah – he's talking about it and I think he will. But, you know, we won't be open very late. Maybe it's going to be more of a lunchtime thing. We all want to get out of here early."

"I'm surprised you're even open on Thanksgiving", I said.

"Well, we always have been. Irv said that there's a whole lot of regulars who come in every day and, if we aren't open, what are they going to do? So, yeah – we'll be open. I think we'll close up by two, though. Oh - and just FYI – I've told everybody here that I'll pay them double-time to work that day. Plus, they'll get one more day off, whenever they want."

"That's sweet of you, Gretchen", said Mike. "Is that new?"

"Well, yeah. I never got double-time when Irv had the place. And, the extra day off? He didn't do that, either."

"You rock, Gretchen", said Marquardt, raising his mug in a toast. "Good. Very good."

She smiled and gave a little 'thank you' curtsy, then said, "Alright – what'll it be, boys?"

We all ordered and she went into the kitchen. I can't remember what we talked about, but we were off the Thanksgiving pizza thing.

A minute or so later, Suze walked up and we all said our 'hiyas' and shot a modicum of shit for a few seconds. Then, she said to me, "J.D. – can I talk to you for a sec?"

I said, "Sure", and I got up.

"Ooh – secrets", said Joe.

Suze looked over her shoulder at him and said, "Yeah, Joe – we're talking about what I'm gonna get you for Christmas."

"I like the sound of that", he said.

"If you knew what I was thinking, you wouldn't", she shot back.

"Ooh", was the general consensus from the balance of the Geezers.

Suze walked over toward the little table with the cornucopia on it.

"Listen", she said, turning to me. "There's three guys at one of my booths. I don't know 'em. Never seen 'em. But, every time I go over toward them, I've heard the words, 'Branson' or 'Frank'. Then, when I get there, they shut up."

"What? Really?"

"Yeah. Weird, isn't it?"

"I wonder what it's all about", I said, glancing in that direction, though they were around the corner and I couldn't see them from where I stood.

"You don't suppose that they're part of his group?", she asked.

"I dunno. Could be, I guess." I thought for a couple of seconds, then said, "Actually, I think there's probably a pretty good chance that they are, especially if his name keeps coming up. Do me a favor – see if you can hear any more, but play dumb – don't let on that the name means anything to you."

"Playing dumb is one of my specialties", she said, with a smile.

"I didn't mean that."

"I know. Don't get your shorts in an uproar. How's the wrist?"

"Not bad. Really, it feels better than I thought it would."

"Good. Just take it easy with it for a couple of days." And she tapped me on the arm and went toward the kitchen and I headed back to the table.

At the booth in question, Eric Gallagher was sitting with two guys from The Group – Hank and Billy, two guys that were also friends of Gallagher's and were guys he pretty much trusted.

When they'd sat down and Suze had poured their coffees, Gallagher said, "Thanks for meeting me, here, this morning, you guys. I figured that this place was about equidistant for the three of us."

They nodded and made, "Yeah, sure" noises.

"Look – you guys got that email, too, right?", he asked.

They both shook their heads in a combination of wonderment and disgust. "Yeah", they said.

"It's fucked up, isn't it?"

"I can't believe that Frank was such an unadulterated fuck-up", said Hank. "Gettin' thrown out of the army? You've got to fuck up royally for that to happen. And dickin' around with another guy? Are you shitting me, right now?

"You think it's true?", Billy asked Gallagher.

He nodded and said, "Look – I talked to Frank, last night, right after I got it. And I asked him, point-blank, if it was true."

"What'd he say?"

"He didn't say anything. Well, he said he didn't know what I was talking about and rushed me off the phone in a hurry – something about his wife. He asked me if he could call me back and I told him we'd talk this morning. Actually, my phone was blowing up all over the goddamned place with texts and messages and, really, just by his reaction – he didn't deny it, right off the bat – you know, all pissed and shit - I think it's gotta be true."

"Any way we can check? You know, with the army?", asked Billy.

"Hell, I doubt it", Hank chimed in. "That stuff's pretty closely held. I think you've gotta be the guy, himself, or the spouse or something to get that kind of info out of 'em."

"I don't think it makes any difference", said Gallagher.

"I can't believe Branson. The sonofabitch comes off like Mister Tough Guy and, all the while – "

About then, Suze walked up and the conversation came to an abrupt halt. She asked if they were ready to order.

"Couple'a minutes", said Gallagher, smiling and opening his menu, and she nodded and left again.

"Look – you guys", said Gallagher. "I don't know about you, but I'm not altogether certain that we're on the right track, know what I mean? I mean, the one thing we've done, so far – the parade – was a total clusterfuck, all the way. We all ended up looking like a bunch of goofball jamokes."

"Yeah, we did", said Hank. "That whole thing was FUBAR."

"And, now this?" said Gallagher. "I don't know, man." And he shook his head and took a swallow of coffee.

"You think we've gotta get rid of Frank as the leader?", asked Billy.

Gallagher looked at each of them, individually, and said, "Leader? Leader of what? A bunch of bozos, like us, that have really no idea what we're doing? I mean, you think we can really change things by prancing around like a bunch of militia-types and doing the occasional spray painting or breaking fucking windows? Come on, man. That's bullshit and you know it."

"Yeah", said Hank, "but, really, we're just getting started. Tell you what – why don't you be the leader? You seem to know what you're doing. Better'n Frank, anyway."

Suze walked up again. "Ready?"

And the three of them ordered and she headed for the kitchen.

"Fuck, leader. I don't wanna be the (finger quotes) leader. Tell you the truth, I think the whole thing's a crock. I mean, who the hell do we think we are that can change things, especially around here?"

Both men stared at him.

"Look – I've thought a lot about this, last night and this morning, and, to my way of thinking, I'd just as soon let the whole thing die. At least, for now. We've got no traction and we've got no objectives and we've got no plan. We just seem to be playing at being Oathkeepers or Proud Boys wannabes or something."

Billy sat up a little straighter in his seat, as if to say something, but Hank jumped in first. "You might be right, Eric. So far, we've had – what? – one meeting and one fucked up mission. And, now, this thing with Branson. So far, I'd say we're oh-fer."

"Yeah, but – ", Billy started.

"Yeah, but nothing", Gallagher interrupted him. "Hank's right. We haven't accomplished a goddamned thing. And I don't know about you guys, but I ain't got the time or energy to fuck around that way. As far as I'm concerned, I'm out."

Suze walked up with their plates.

"Thank you", they all said.

"Anything else?", she asked.

"A little hot sauce, if you will", said Billy.

"Comin' right up", she said and, a few seconds later, sat it on the table. "Enjoy."

What Gallagher hadn't told Hank and Billy was that he'd heard from both Al and Mark, late last night, and, between them, they'd done their best to fill him in on what had gone down at Branson's. And, the upshot of it was that Al had a broken nose, Mark's ribs hurt like hell and they were both lucky that Schmidt had shown up when he did and had gotten them the hell out of there. Plus, Drake was in the hospital with a broken jaw. And there was this big cloud of red smoke that they'd had to fight through.

He'd tried to pump Mark and Al about the details – like how many guys had accompanied the guy on the horse – but they came up short trying to answer that. As far as Mark was concerned, there was only something dressed all in black with red fucking eyes who came riding up on a what seemed to be a horse, but it had red eyes, too, and it was fucking huge. And, that later, that – that thing - had stabbed him with something.

Al thought he was fighting another guy but had gotten blindsided by something, though he hadn't seen it. And, Drake? They hadn't seen anything of him – he must've gone around the other side of the house - and maybe the thing on the horse had been the one to beat the shit out of him, too.

And, this time, Gallagher had heard enough to finally believe that a guy – or something – on a horse had really been there. But red smoke? What the fuck?

It was fucking nuts, he thought.

When he'd asked them where the hell Branson had been during all of this, the best they could answer is that he'd taken a header coming out of his house and hurt his leg or something. He was sitting on the couch with the wife when it all ended.

Anyway, thought Gallagher, Hank and Billy didn't need to know all that – wasn't their business.

A couple of minutes later, Suze approached their table. "How's everything, you guys?"

"Great, thanks", said Gallagher, speaking for the three of them.

Back at our table, I wished that I could telepathically tell Parker about the three guys sitting over there in the booth, because he'd raised his eyebrows, quizzically, when I'd sat back down.

I'd just given a single nod with my head and tilted it, as if to tell him about something over in another part of the place.

We were all finished, having pushed our plates toward the center of the table, then Gretchen walked up with her coffee pot. As she was pouring, she said, "Okay – here's the skinny on Thanksgiving….Artie said that he is going to do a dinner, but only a limited number of them. We're not going to make a big deal out of it. We won't promote it or anything. So, over the next day or so, we'll ask the regulars if they're interested in it – just so Artie gets a general idea of how much to buy and cook. Any of you guys interested?"

Naturally, Bob and Al and Joe and Mike said they wouldn't be – they were having their own feasts at home.

Parker said that he'd originally planned on going down to his daughter's and her family's, but she'd called him and said that they'd been invited to her husband's parents' place. So, no dice, there. So, maybe.

I, of course, was on my own and thought that, sure, I'd come.

"I'll be here", I said. "After all, this is my home away from home."

"I might as well, too", said Parker. "Is Artie gonna have pumpkin pie?", he asked Gretchen.

"Well, I haven't asked him, but I'm sure he will."

"Good", I said. "We'll be here – what? – around noon?"

"Yep, sounds good", said Parker.

"I might even take a few minutes to join you guys, myself", said Gretchen. "And, depending on how busy we are, maybe I'll ask Suze, too."

"That'd be terrific", I said, and that whole last part of the conversation brought a round of Geezer knuckle-knocks.

Over at Gallagher's booth, they'd asked Suze for the check and Gallagher paid with a debit card. In ringing it up, Suze took note of his name.

"Thank you, gentlemen. Enjoy your day", she said, pleasantly, returning his receipt to him.

"So – you're really thinking of pulling out, huh?", Hank asked Gallagher, as they slid out of the booth.

"Yep – at least for the time being. I'm actually gonna go down and tell Frank, in person, right now."

"Well, without you around, I don't know if I wanna do this anymore, either", said Hank, as they made their way through the door. "Especially after this deal last night."

"Yeah – me, too, I guess", said Billy. "But it's a damned shame."

And they were gone.

CHAPTER 51

After Marquardt had called for an end to today's meeting, voted upon, unanimously, by the ol' Geezer knuckle-knock, we all dispersed.

Well, except for Parker and me, who met up outside the front door. I told him what Suze had told me about the three guys who'd been sitting at one of her booths and the fact that she'd heard 'Branson' and 'Frank' mentioned a couple of times.

"No shit", he said. "Really?"

"Yeah – that's what she said. Hold on." I saw Suze through the front door and motioned her out.

She came out saying, "I've just got a second, guys – I have an order that's almost ready."

"Did you hear those guys saying anything more?", I asked her.

"No, but they were in deep conversation and they didn't look like a happy bunch."

"But you distinctly heard Branson's name, right?", I asked.

"Yeah – exactly like I told you. Why?"

"We're just wondering what it was all about, is all. I wonder who they were."

"Wait", she said, a light bulb going off. "That one guy paid with a debit card. We've got our copy inside. If you'll wait a sec, I'll find it and bring it out. It'll have his name on it."

"Outstanding", I said.

We stepped down off the little porch-like thing and hung out over next to Parker's truck.

"If we can get the guy's name", said Parker, "I'll bet that, if we run it by Ron, maybe he can shed some light on him."

"Exactly."

A minute or so later, Suze came hurrying out. She pulled the receipt from her apron pocket and said, "Eric Gallagher – see?"

And, yep, that's exactly what it said.

"Eric Gallagher, huh? Didn't Ron mention his name a couple of times?", asked Parker.

"I think so", I said. "But we've gotta call him and find out. Look – thanks, Suze. Great work. Now, you get back inside and we'll check in with you later and let you know what we find out."

"Deal", she said. "Toodles." And she hustled back inside.

"Let's get back to the farm and make the call", I said to Parker and we both headed to our trucks.

———————————————

Fifteen minutes later, Eric Gallagher pulled into Branson's driveway. He knew it was early in the day and he figured that Frank would still be home, even if he had a job, today. Plus, he wanted to get this over with.

He hadn't called ahead of time because he didn't want Frank coming up with some sort of excuse for not seeing him. He walked up to the front door and rang the bell. Nothing. He waited a few seconds and rang it again.

Just after the second ring, the door opened to reveal a red-eyed Sheila. Her face was puffy and she was still in a bathrobe, no makeup or nothing. Gallagher wondered if he'd woken her up.

"Eric", she said, surprised. "What are you doing here?"

"'Mornin', Sheila. I have to talk to Frank."

"Now?"

"Uh, yeah – now."

"Well, hold on. He's in the living room with his knee up. He hurt it last night. I'll tell him you're here. Oh – come on in, but wait here for a minute." And she went off toward the living room.

About thirty seconds later – why was it taking so long?, he thought – Sheila called from the living room, "Come on in, Eric."

When he walked into the room, he saw Branson, sitting in a chair with his leg up on an ottoman. His hair wasn't combed and he looked miserable.

"Want some coffee, Eric?", Sheila asked him.

"Uh – no thanks, Sheila. I'll just be a couple of minutes."

She nodded and left the room, still with the same hang-dog expression she'd had since she opened the door.

"Hi, Eric", said Branson.

"Frank."

"Have a seat", said Branson, nodding in the direction of the couch.

He sat and said, "Frank, I'm gonna come right out and say this. I'm done. I'm done with The Group. And a lot of the other guys are, too."

Branson just stared at him. Finally, he said, "Huh?"

"Oh, come on, Frank. We all got that email, last night. And you know exactly what I'm talking about. And, after reading it, my phone just blew the fuck up. I got calls and texts 'til midnight, Frank. And there was no way that I could or would make excuses for you. Nah, Frank – you're done, man. And I'm done, too."

"But I can explain", said Branson, half-heartedly.

"Don't bother, Frank. The details were just too goddamned clear for somebody to just make that up. It happened, Frank, didn't it? Didn't it happen?"

"Well, it was a long time ago –"

"I don't give a fuck when it was, Frank. It happened. And, just by it happening, it cancels out any leadership you may have had with us. And I'll tell you another thing – I'm done with the whole thing. Not just with you, but with the whole (finger quotes) Group thing. Fer chrissakes, Frank – look what's happened – we completely fucked up that parade deal and, last night, three of our guys got hurt bad – all because of you. It's been nothing but a losing proposition from the get-go. Nah, Frank – I'm done with it all. It might be a case of 'good idea – bad execution', but that's enough for me and most of the guys."

"I – I don't know what to say, Eric."

"Don't say anything, Frank. There's nothing to say." And he stood up. "Look – I'm sorry, Frank. I'm sorry it worked out this way. And I know you're not asking me, but I think we should all just forget about changing the goddamned world, right now. That shit's above our pay grade. I think we oughta just go on with our lives and do our work and make our livings."

"Well, - ", said Frank.

"No hard feelings, man", Gallagher interrupted him. "You're still my friend. It's just that this didn't work out. Shit happens. But, I'm still here for ya, man – both as a friend and as a co-worker. Honest – I mean that." He stood up and held out his hand.

Frank looked at it for a couple of seconds, then reached up and shook it.

"Alright, Eric – I understand." He paused. "At least I'm trying to. And, I guess, thank you for being straight with me. I appreciate it and you've given me a few things to think about." He paused again. "Maybe you're right – I dunno. Will you still work with me if I call you with a job?"

"Hell, yeah, man. Like I said, water under the bridge. Let's just go on like before. A couple'a working stiffs."

Frank nodded and tried to smile.

"How's the leg?", Gallagher asked him.

"Ah, my knee's pretty fucked up, but I don't think anything's broken. Just a real bad bruise, prob'ly."

"Well, you rest it for a few days and we'll talk, okay?"

"Yeah – we'll talk."

Gallagher gave him a thumbs-up and walked to the door, yelling, "Thanks, Sheila! See ya!", and he left.

A few seconds later, Sheila came back into the room.

"I was listening from around the corner", she said.

"He's probably right", said Frank, discouraged.

"Oh, Frank. I think we're both in the same boat. I don't think the Moms will break up, but I'm done. I just know it."

Her phone rang and, when she looked down at it, saw that it was Mark Fisher calling.

Sheila blew out her lips and said, "I'd better take this. It can't be good, though."

"Hi, Mark", she said.

"Sheila, I have to tell you about an email I just received from one of your members."

"I know the email, Mark."

"Is it true, Sheila? That's all I want to know."

She had given up fighting. "Yes, Mark. I'm afraid it is."

"Oh. I see. That's what I was afraid of. And, I've been thinking, Sheila – if that email gets out - and you and I both know it will, somehow – then my anti-abortion stance on the school board will be put into jeopardy by my association with your group. It'll make me look like a hypocrite. And I can't have that. I'm having enough trouble as it is, trying to push my agenda and that would be the death knell for it. And for me."

"I understand, Mark", Sheila said.

"Now,", he continued, "I don't know what's going on with your group or what your plans will be, but I'm asking you – please – not for you or them to show up at any meetings or get involved with the schools, at all, until this whole thing blows over. Maybe soon, but certainly not now.'

"I'm afraid you'll have to talk to the next leader, Mark. There's no way I can continue with the Moms for Liberty – not after this. I'm resigning, effective immediately. And you're the first to know."

"Oh, Sheila", he said, with honest concern. "I'm so sorry it's come to this. I truly am."

"Well, thank you, Mark. And, believe me – so am I. We were on such a good track, but…", and her voice trailed off.

"I understand, Sheila, and I wish you the best of luck. Really."

She felt herself beginning to cry again, so she just said, "Goodbye, Mark." And she disconnected.

"Oh, honey", said Frank, looking at her.

But she'd looked down at her phone and said, "I only turned this on, again, just before Mark's call. And, look – I have eight voicemail messages and at least a dozen texts." She dropped the arm holding her phone and her shoulders drooped right along with it.

"I can't believe this, Frank. I just can't."

And they stared at each other.

She broke the silence, saying, "I'm going into my office, now, and write a resignation email that I'll send to all of the members."

"What're you going to write?", he asked her.

She shrugged and said, "Something simple. Something along the lines of 'In light of the email you received last night - and there is no proof that it's true - and all of the resulting communications from so many of you, I feel that it is only right for me to step down from my position, effective immediately'. And that's it. One and done."

"You're not gonna fight it?"

"Fight it? Frank – did you fight Gallagher? Are you gonna fight back? Fuck, no. No, Frank, there's no fighting this. But how anybody got ahold of this information – on both of us! – is simply beyond me. It's that – that *thing* – that came and invaded us, that's what it was. It was like something out of a nightmare - and it brought that nightmare right down on our heads."

And she started crying again and walked out of the room and down the hall toward her office.

Frank looked out the window, lost in thought.

Then, he picked up his phone and began writing his resignation email to The Group. If Sheila could do it, he had to, too.

Back at the farm, Parker and I had had to deal with a leaky faucet in the barn. When we'd gotten back, we saw a small lake on the floor and had to fix it right away. It wasn't a big problem – a washer had blown and, I guess, the thing had dripped a steady stream all night. There wasn't so much water that we had to bail it out – it would eventually just soak into the dirt floor - but it'd be muddy for a few days. No biggie – we'd just walk around it.

The kids found it quite entertaining. Part of the little lake extended into their house and they were having fun splashing their big hooves in it. What horses find fun and what humans find fun are often somewhat at odds with each other. "Just don't roll in the mud, you guys", I told them, knowing full well that that was a fifty-fifty proposition at best.

Once we'd finished in the barn, we walked up to the house and, sitting at the kitchen table, called Ron.

"Wassup, my bros?", he said by way of answering. "You tell me and then I've got something for you."

"Yeah, okay – look, have you heard of a guy named Eric Gallagher? Part of Branson's crew, we think", I said.

"Well, yeah – a little. Looks like he's Branson's second-in-command. I've seen a bunch of calls and texts between their phones over the past few weeks, why?"

"Because he was at The Coffee Spot with a couple of guys, this morning."

"Huh. How d'you like that? Maybe that has something to do with an email that Branson just sent out. Which, of course, through the wonders of modern chemistry, I was able to read. As a matter of fact, that's what I wanted to tell you."

"What's it say?", Parker asked.

"Well, he just sent out a pretty mass email – obviously to his entire crew – that said that he and Eric had just had a meeting and, in it, he'd stepped down from running the show. And, as a matter of fact, they'd decided that, maybe, now isn't the right time for The Group to go on. That, based on their recent experiences, maybe things weren't on the right track. Either way, he's stepping down and they should all decide, on their own, whether to go on or not. But that Eric had indicated that he was finished, too."

"Holy shit!", I said. "We did it!" And Parker and I high-fived.

"Yessiree-bob, I think you did, m'man", said Ron. "At least that group. And those were the ones that we were really concerned about. Those militia-type wannabes – you just never know what'll happen with those guys. Hold on....."

"What?", I asked.

A few seconds passed.

"You're not gonna believe this, but ol' Sheila just sent out a mass emailing, too. My other box just dinged and there it is, in black and white. Or, not really black and white, but you know."

"Read it to us", said Parker.

"Okay. 'My Dear Friends', it says. 'In light of the email you received last night - and there is no proof that it's true - and all of the resulting communications from so many of you, I feel that it is only right for me to step down from my position with the Moms for Liberty, effective immediately. Thank you for all of your support and I wish only the best for you.' Signed, Sheila."

"Wow", I said. "This is almost too good to believe." And Parker held up his hand and I high-fived him again.

"We did it, my brother", he said, with a big smile on his kisser. "Again."

Ron said, "You'll notice that she wrote 'there is no proof that it's true'. Asshole. She knows it's true and they know it's true and we know it's true, but she had to get that in there, didn't she? It's just like those people – always trying to play the victim. As if it's the fault of an email and not her fault for scamming her group for however long she's been a part of it."

"Well, I doubt anybody's gonna look into it", said Parker. "Like you said, her members know."

"Ron's right, though", I said. "All of those ultra-right-wingers – right from Trump on down – are always playing the victim. Like it's always somebody else's fault that they're – what? – trod upon? That their rights are being infringed upon by others who have their boots on their necks or something. Or have different beliefs than theirs. Or are just 'other'."

"Yeah", said Ron, "like it was George Floyd who caused that asshole, Chauvin, to put his knee on his neck and kill him."

"Exactly", I said "But, anyway, we can't do anything about things like that. But what we can do is what we just did – like we've done before: find dickwads that are taking advantage of people for their own greedy purposes or their own self-aggrandizement and give 'em a little homegrown justice."

"Amen", said Ron and Parker nodded.

"Okay,", said Ron, "on a totally different subject – well, more or less – I'm coming east in a couple of months and I wanna meet up with you guys. You know, see the farm and meet your horses and the like. And, hell, Parker – meet you face-to-face. You be up for that?"

"Of course! But why? I mean, why are you coming east?"

"Ah, my bosses want me to kind of run this new guy who's coming on board – he's a hacker, like me – through the ringer and see if he can do for the White Plains office what I do out here. All below the radar, mind you."

“You mean that one of the biggest FBI offices in the country doesn’t have a guy that does what you do?”, I asked.

“Well, yeah, they – we – did, but he took a gig with Google for more than double the money that the Feebs were paying him. Can’t blame him, really.”

“Would you ever do that? Take a job with a Google or something?”, Parker asked him.

Ron laughed and said, “No way, mano. You ask J.D. what I think of the corporate world. Been there, done that and got screwed for my trouble. Nah – I kinda like what I’m doing, here, and I’m pretty much my own boss, day-to-day. And I really don’t give a shit about money. It’s about something different than that.”

“Okay, so”, I said. “You’re coming east. Outstanding. When, again?”

“Don’t rightly know. Probably two or three months. That’s what they’re telling me, anyway. I guess this new guy set up his own cyber security business and, like a lot of us, decided that running a business isn’t for him. So, he’s shopping it around and thinks he has a couple of interested buyers, but it’ll take a little while to unwind himself from it, once the deal goes through.”

“You’ll get to see what winter’s like”, I said.

“Oh, fuck, I hope not”, he said. “I’m kinda hopin’ that it’ll be March or April before I get there. Hell, I don’t have any winter clothes.”

“Spring is a nice time to be here”, said Parker.

“Well, from your lips to God’s ears that that guy doesn’t start ‘til then. But, either way, I’m’a coming your way, so be ready.”

“We’ll have pie!”, said Parker, brightening.

“You damned well better. It’s all I fucking hear about with you two. Alright, look – I gotta split. Uncle Sam needs me. I’ll talk to you guys later, yes?”

“Yeah, we’ll keep you posted on what we hear about the Bransons and their shit and you do likewise, okay?”, I said.

“You got it. And, again – the ninja horseman and his compadres strike again! Great job, boys.”

And we disconnected.

"How do you like that?", I said to Parker. "Ron's coming here."

"I'm really looking forward to putting a face to the voice", he said.

I chuckled and said, "Yeah – me, too. Look – even when we were back at the newspaper company, he and I only saw each other, face-to-face, a few times. We were in totally different departments and, well, we just didn't see much of each other."

Parker nodded thoughtfully, then hit his palms on the table and said, "Okay – enough sittin' around and shootin' the shit. I'm going down to the garage and fuck around with that logo." He stood up and headed for the door. "What're you gonna do?"

"I have no idea. Just sit here for a little while, I think."

And, as I did, I smiled.